Undercover Bride

Undercover Bride

UNDERCOVER LADIES | BOOK TWO

MARGARET BROWNLEY

SHILOH RUN PRESS

An Imprint of Barbour Publishing, Inc.

Cover design: Müllerhaus Publishing Arts, Inc., www.Mullerhaus.net

Published by Shiloh Run Press, an imprint of Barbour Publishing, Inc.,
P.O. Box 719, Uhrichsville, Ohio 44683, www.shilohrunpress.com

*Our mission is to publish and distribute inspirational products offering
exceptional value and biblical encouragement to the masses.*

ecpa Member of the
Evangelical Christian
Publishers Association

Printed in the United States of America.

Where there is no counsel, the people fall;
but in the multitude of counselors there is safety.
PROVERBS 11:14

Chapter 1

Arizona Territory, 1882

Maggie Taylor spotted the thief the moment she stepped off the Southern Pacific train and onto the open-air platform.

As a Pinkerton operative, she'd dealt with her share of pickpockets through the years, but this one put the profession to shame. He made no attempt at discretion; he simply bumped into a male passenger and walked away with the man's gold watch.

Normally Maggie wouldn't hesitate to pursue the culprit, but today she had bigger fish to fry. Chasing after a third-rate thief could jeopardize months of hard work and careful preparation, and she couldn't take the chance.

That is, until he targeted a young mother with three small children. Maggie changed her mind. He had to be stopped.

Threading her way through the crowd, she reached the woman ahead of the thief and picked up the drawstring handbag she'd carelessly left next to a carpetbag.

"Your purse, ma'am. There are thieves around. Better keep an eye on it."

The harried mother took the bag from her. She looked no older than nineteen or twenty. "Thank you," she murmured, as if thieves were the least of her problems.

Satisfied that the pickpocket's latest attempt at larceny had been thwarted, Maggie pushed him from her mind and swung her gaze over the crowd. Never before had a new assignment filled her with such anxiety. But then again, never had she attempted such a daring venture.

Would she recognize the suspect on sight?

According to Pinkerton files, Garrett Thomas stood six feet tall, was forty-five years of age, and had dark hair and blue eyes. His one outstanding feature was a scar along the side of his face—a war wound. He was also extremely clever. Some said even lucky. A suspected thief and murderer, Thomas had endured the Battle of Gettysburg and a year in the Andersonville rebel prison—an impressive record of survival by anyone's standards.

Though he was suspected of committing a daring train robbery, his most notable achievement was evading Pinkerton's best detectives for nearly two years. *We'll see how long your luck holds out this time, Mr. Thomas.* Eventually even a cat runs out of lives.

After checking that her feathered hat was angled just right, she pushed a strand of auburn hair behind her ear and smoothed the bun at her nape. Her wardrobe had been chosen with utmost care, and her demeanor meticulously polished.

The goal was to look fashionable but not ostentatious: to act domesticated without appearing dull. At all times she had to be charming, well spoken, and industrious. In matters of politics, religion, and finances she must take care not to express a contrary view as she was often inclined to do. In other words, she had to look and act like a woman that any man would be proud, indeed anxious, to wed.

Given her somewhat opinionated and independent spirit, curtailing her impulsive nature would be her greatest challenge. She couldn't afford to do or say anything without careful consideration of the consequences. Not this time.

Not only did she have to make a fine impression but one that would throw no suspicion her way. "Dazzle Thomas with your charm and good looks," Mr. Pinkerton had said. "He won't suspect a thing."

In her current state, she'd be lucky to dazzle a horsefly. She was hot and she was hungry and more than anything, travel weary.

Despite the desert heat, she donned her kid gloves and smoothed the wrinkles from her blue velvet-trimmed suit. Steam hissed across the platform, and passengers sidestepped the heated blast.

A barefooted boy of nine or ten raised a folded newspaper in the air and yelled something about a fire. "Readallaboutit!"

A man bumped into her and almost knocked her off her feet. Regaining her balance, she pivoted just in time to see the same thief she'd spotted earlier snatch the paperboy's money bag and dart into the crowd. The nerve! It wasn't bad enough trying to steal from a young mother, but a child?

The youth's face turned red. "That man took my pouch!" His eyes brimmed with tears, though he tried not to let them fall. "Now I gotta pay the money back."

Maggie hesitated. If only the boy didn't look so needy. His tattered shirt was a size too small, and his threadbare trousers fell six inches short of his dirty bare feet. "Stay here!" she said and took off after the robber.

The thief moved at a fast clip, but the crowded platform and a limp kept him from altogether running. His long dark coat was more suitable for cold weather, and it made him stand out among a crowd dressed mainly in calico dresses and boiled white shirts.

Something was definitely wrong with his left leg. He dragged it along, toes pointing away from his body. She'd almost caught up to him when a dark-skinned porter pushed a cart of baggage in her path, momentarily blocking her way.

By the time the cart moved, the pickpocket had vanished. She ran to the end of the platform and immediately spotted him lumbering along the railroad tracks. Had he been physically able to run she might have given up the chase, but he looked like an easy mark.

Jumping to the ground, she raised her skirt above her ankles and took off after him. *Here I go again, tossing common sense to the wind.* But she couldn't seem to help herself. Not where children were concerned.

Running on the gravel in high-button shoes and a straight skirt wasn't easy, but she quickly gained on the man. She just hoped he didn't force her to pull out her pistol.

No more than a couple of yards separated them when the heel of her boot caught on a wooden railroad tie. All at once her feet flew from beneath her. Arms and legs windmilling, she fell facedown on the ground.

The wind knocked out of her, she fought to gather her wits. Now look what she'd done. Grimacing, she ever so slowly pushed to her feet and squinted against the blazing sun. On the left side of the tracks a bleak desert stretched for as far as the eye could see. Since the thief was nowhere in sight, he'd probably ducked through the adobe brickyard that paralleled the tracks on the right.

What kind of town was this anyway that a man could steal from a young boy in plain sight and get away with it?

Gritting her teeth, she stared down at her stylish blue traveling suit now covered in dust.

She brushed herself off with quick angry swipes and straightened her feather hat. When would she ever learn? One impetuous moment could jeopardize six months of careful planning.

The sound of crunching gravel made her whirl about. A tall, broad-shouldered man stood but a few feet away staring at her with eyes the color of a deep blue sea.

"Is everything all right, ma'am?"

Her mouth fell open, and her hand flew to her parted lips. The red scar slicing down the side of his handsome square face told her he could be no other than the suspect Garrett Thomas, the man she had traveled all this distance to wed.

❧

Maggie's mind scrambled. Normally able to think on her feet, she had a hard time coming up with a plausible explanation for standing on the railroad tracks. *God, don't let me mess up this job.* Not like she did the

Madison case, which had landed her in jail. This time she would get her man if it killed her. Reminding herself to "dazzle," she lifted her chin with a brilliant smile.

"I'm quite all right, thank you." Taller than she'd expected, he towered over her five-foot-seven-inch height by more than six inches. He was clean shaven with high cheekbones and a straight nose. His brown hair, neatly trimmed to just above his collar, was combed from a side part.

"Mr. Thomas, right?" she said, extending a gloved hand. At least the Pinkerton report got the color of his eyes right, though listing the color as merely blue hardly did them justice.

He stared at her for a brief moment before his hand swallowed hers in a firm grip. His wide shoulders filled his boiled shirt and low-cut vest with no room to spare. A large-brim hat shaded his face.

"And you must be Miss Taylor."

"Yes." She smiled and lowered her lashes as she imagined a woman meeting her fiancé for the first time might do. Under Allan Pinkerton's guidance, she had answered this man's advertisement for a mail-order bride and corresponded with him for nearly six months.

Much to her dismay, he didn't look particularly dazzled. Instead he frowned. "What are you doing here on the railroad tracks?"

"I was hoping to. . .convince a thief to return his haul." Sticking as close to the truth as possible was the key to creating a realistic illusion. She'd worked long and hard to arrange this meeting and would play her role to the hilt.

As if suddenly aware that he still held her hand, he released it. "And how, exactly, did you intend to do that?" His eyes shone with amusement. "Convince him, I mean."

With a strategically pointed gun, if necessary. Of course she couldn't say that aloud. "With charm and goodwill," she said instead.

He hung his thumbs from his vest pockets and grinned. "I don't know how it is in your hometown, ma'am, but here in Arizona, charm and goodwill won't get you the time of day."

So much for the principal's *dazzle* theory. "What will?" she asked, feigning a look of innocence.

"A firearm and a good left hook."

She would have felt a whole lot better had he said it with a smile like the one she'd seen before, but he looked serious. *Dead* serious. Nevertheless, she maintained her composure. "I didn't know that Arizona was so. . .civilized."

This time he did smile, which only emphasized his nicely shaped mouth. "Oh, we're civilized all right. We haven't had a shootout since last Wednesday." He crooked his arm and inclined his head. "Shall we? My rig's over there."

She slipped her arm through his and forced herself to breathe. It hardly seemed fair for a suspected killer to be so attractive, but she wasn't about to be fooled by his charm or good looks.

She willed the knot in her stomach to go away as they approached his horse and wagon. Her bout of nerves was annoying and totally uncalled for. He had no reason to suspect she was anyone other than who she pretended to be: an innocent farm girl and mail-order bride.

All she had to do was act like the perfect little fiancée until she found the proof to put him away and she'd be home free. It sounded easy enough during the planning stages, but now that she'd met him in person, something told her that nothing about this man would be simple.

Chapter 2

Garrett Thomas was surprised to see his Aunt Hetty on his doorstep later that day. Yesterday she was on her deathbed declaring, "This really is the end." And here she was no more than twenty-four hours later, dressed in her Sunday-go-to-meeting best and looking spry as a young hen.

Normally he would be delighted to see her up and about, but he knew from experience that any time his aunt donned feathers and silk midweek, it was never a good sign. Either this really was her last day on earth or she was about to put her nose where it didn't belong. The appearance of Reverend Holly could mean either one of his suppositions was correct.

"Don't tell me you're planning your funeral again," Garrett said wryly, bracing himself for her usual long and tiresome list of physical complaints, or what he called her "organ recital." Her last recitation started at the big toe and worked up from there to the cranium.

But she surprised him. No palpitating heart complaints today. No sciatic grievances. Nor any rheumatism updates. Instead, his aunt pushed past him in a cloud of rustling brown silk and lavender perfume.

"No, but now that you mention it, I do wish to make some changes." She pulled off her kid gloves as she spoke and gave them an emphatic shake. "I'll not have that awful Grace Lytton sing at my funeral." Aunt Hetty was a small, birdlike woman whose sharp tongue had, at one time or other, alienated everyone in town.

The minister splayed his hands and shrugged before following her inside the house with an apologetic air. He was a short, barrel-chested man with a goatee. Red suspenders held up his trousers, and his shirt-sleeves were rolled up to the elbows. His one concession to formality was his ever-present bow tie with the pointed ends.

His aunt planted herself on the divan as if intending to take root, and the minster took the nearby upholstered chair.

Before Garrett had a chance to find out what was really going on, his five-year-old daughter, Elise, ran into the parlor, her face bright with delight.

"Aunty!" she squealed.

Aunt Hetty wrapped her arms around the child's small frame, but other than a quick glance at Elise, her attention remained on Garrett. "Be careful of my back, precious, and watch my bad knee. Oh, and we must do something with your hair. We can't have you looking like a waif for your father's wedding."

Garrett stared at his aunt. So that's what this visit was about. He should have known.

"What's a waif?" Elise asked.

Garrett kept his irritation in check, as much for his daughter's sake as for the man of God. He didn't have much use for the church, but the reverend deserved respect, as did any guest in his household.

"I'll tell you later. Now run along like a good girl." She patted Elise on the backside. "I wish to speak to your father."

And Garrett wished to speak to her.

Aunt Hetty meant well, but he and he alone would decide if and when he married. Miss Taylor's letters had looked promising; she wrote with intelligence, warmth, and wit. But after meeting her in person, he had grave concerns about her lack of judgment. Chasing after a thief, of all things... She could have gotten herself killed. In the name of Sam Hill, what had she been thinking? And what other character flaws did she possess?

He waited until Elise had left the room. "As I explained the other day, Miss Taylor and I wish to wait until we've had time to get to know each other." Selecting a new wife was not a task to be taken lightly, especially when his two children were involved.

"Wait too long and I might not be around to enjoy your wedding. You know how my back has been acting up and—"

"A bad back is not generally a cause of death," Garrett argued.

Aunt Hetty stared down her pointed nose. "That's not all that's wrong with me and you know it."

The minister, apparently sensing she was about to run through another shopping list of ailments, interrupted. "Speaking of weddings, when do we get to meet the bride-to-be?"

"Good question." Aunt Hetty leaned forward, both brown-spotted hands atop her cane. "We stopped at the hotel and the clerk told us there was some sort of mix-up."

"There was a mix-up all right." The room he'd reserved for Maggie a month ago had been given to someone else. "No rooms are available."

"Hmm. How odd." Aunt Hetty gave him a questioning look. "So where *is* she staying?"

"Right now she's staying here."

Her eyebrows shot up. "Then there's no time to waste. I won't have you living in sin around my grandniece and grandnephew."

The reverend mopped his damp forehead with a handkerchief but refrained from comment.

Aunt Hetty sniffed. "It's a good thing I dragged myself out of a sickbed to come over here. I probably shortened my life by—"

"You shouldn't have done that," Garrett said.

"Nonsense. I promised your dear mother that I would take care of you."

"And no one could have done a better job than you." His widowed mother died when he was six, and his aunt devoted herself to his upbringing at great sacrifice. That's what made it so difficult to stand his ground now.

"Surely you see the advantage of getting to know my bride first before we tie the knot. Let the children get to know her."

"Hogwash! There'll be plenty of chances for the children to get to know her after you've made an honest woman of her."

The reverend tucked his handkerchief in his pocket. "It seems to me that the bride should have something to say about this."

Garrett inclined his head toward the bedroom where Miss Taylor had been closeted since they'd arrived home. "She's resting from her journey."

"Did you tell her about Toby?" his aunt asked.

Garrett inhaled. His eight-year-old son had become a sore subject between them. He wasn't a bad kid, just curious and adventuresome and far too active for his aunt to handle.

"There's nothing to tell."

"Tell me what?"

All eyes turned toward the young woman standing at the entrance-way. Suddenly Garrett had trouble finding his voice. Miss Taylor's good looks hadn't escaped his notice, of course, but nothing prepared him for the way she appeared at that moment—all rested and dewy-eyed. If her big blue eyes and wide smile weren't enough to make a man notice, her auburn hair and delicate features certainly were. He had the sudden need to protect her, not only from his aunt's critical eye but also from all the ugliness of his past.

Aunt Hetty gave an impatient nod. "Well, aren't you going to introduce us?"

"Yes, of course." Surprised to catch himself staring, he motioned Maggie to his side. She barely came up to his shoulders, and her every move released a delicate fragrance that reminded him of spring. Her easy smile seemed at odds with the alert way she carried herself. She had a dainty nose, a wide, curving mouth, resolute chin, and a graceful, long neck. Her slight but shapely form hardly seemed strong enough to contain her indomitable demeanor. A woman of contradictions.

Why would such a pretty and intelligent woman consider being a mail-order bride? *His* mail-order bride.

"Aunt Hetty, Reverend Holly, it's my pleasure to introduce Miss Maggie Taylor."

Chapter 3

Maggie smiled as Thomas introduced her. She'd dealt with her share of hard-nosed criminals through the years, but it was hard not to be intimidated by the old woman's sharp-eyed gaze. The Pinkerton file described Garrett's aunt as a no-nonsense type and marked her as being perhaps the most difficult to fool. Maggie had hoped to settle in before coming face-to-face with her, but since that was no longer possible, she would simply have to make the best of it.

She greeted the older woman with an extended hand. "Pleased to meet you."

His aunt had a surprisingly firm grip. After a quick shake, the older woman withdrew her hand. "Never thought you'd marry a Southerner," she said, surprising Maggie.

She was born in the South, but her family moved north when she was four. That made her a Yankee through and through. No one other than Thomas's aunt had detected anything in her manner or speech tracing back to her early roots.

Reminding herself to dazzle, Maggie kept a smile plastered on her face. Nothing was wrong with the old lady's hearing. And the way Thomas's aunt stared at her, as if seeing right through her, there was nothing wrong with the woman's eyesight, either.

"What difference does it make, Hetty?" the reverend asked, breaking the brittle silence. "The war's been over for a good many years."

Garrett nodded. "Yes, it has been."

"But the effects linger on," his aunt said, her gaze boring into her nephew's scar. He frowned. Taking the hint, she shifted her attention to Maggie. "How old are you?"

"Aunt Hetty!"

Maggie turned to Garrett. "It's all right. I have nothing to hide." *Much.* "I'm twenty-six." She could have said she was younger and probably gotten away with it, but it was wiser to stick with the truth whenever possible. Less to remember that way. Less chance of getting caught in a lie or fabrication.

Aunt Hetty slanted her head sideways. "That's rather old for a bride, wouldn't you say? Why have you waited so long to marry?"

"My family needed me at home," Maggie replied. Her real name was Maggie Cartwright, and she had no family. Not anymore.

Assuming a new identity was never easy. One of the jobs of an undercover agent was to prepare in advance for every possible question or situation. She couldn't just pose as a mail-order bride; she had to *be* a mail-order bride.

Aunt Hetty's eyes narrowed. "And I take it your family no longer needs you now?"

In her letters to Thomas she'd written at length about her loving family and the Indiana farm where she grew up—fiction, all of it.

"No, but this little family does," Maggie replied with a quick glance at Thomas. Had she said the right thing? Or had she been too presumptuous? It was hard to tell by his stoic expression.

"Hmm." The older woman's face showed reluctant acceptance. "Shall we get on with it, then? Where's Toby?"

Maggie's stomach knotted. "Get on with what?"

"Why, your wedding, of course," his aunt replied.

Maggie felt Garrett stiffen by her side. Obviously he was even less happy to hear this than she was. "I told you we intend to wait," he snapped.

Maggie glanced at Garrett's rigid profile. Waiting was one of the stipulations made clear in her letter to him, but his vehemence worried her. Did he suspect something? Had he changed his mind? Not that she would blame him, of course. After that fiasco at the train station, she wouldn't be surprised if he called the whole thing off.

Aunt Hetty's brow creased. "Have you any idea how it would look, a man and woman living together without benefit of God's blessing?" His aunt gave a determined shake of her head. "If Miss Taylor stays here, you'll both be the talk of the town."

"I don't care what people say, and I care even less for God's blessing." Belatedly Thomas added, "Sorry, Reverend."

His aunt refused to be deterred. "If you don't care about your reputation, then think about the children's. Miss Taylor can stay with me. In fact, I insist upon it."

"Oh no!" Maggie's outburst raised even the preacher's eyebrows. She cleared her throat and started again, this time in a more ladylike tone of voice. "What I mean to say is, I don't want you to go to any. . . bother on my account."

Aunt Hetty discounted her concern with a wave of her hand. "No bother at all."

"What about your health, Hetty?" Reverend Holly asked. "Your heart might not be able to stand the strain of having a guest."

Aunt Hetty sniffed. "A little strain is a small price to pay for saving my nephew's reputation."

Garrett opened his mouth to say something, but Maggie laid her hand on his arm and smiled up at him. His aunt had expressed concern for the children. Maggie hoped that was the key to getting the old lady to back down.

"We want the young ones to get to know me first before I become their stepmother. I'm sure you'll agree that would be in their best interests. Staying here might be"—*akin to sitting on a keg of lit dynamite*—"a blessing in disguise."

A shadow of indecision flitted across the older woman's face, and she glanced at the reverend as if seeking his counsel. "I. . .I don't know."

"Sounds reasonable to me," Reverend Holly said. "As long as you and Garrett here conduct yourselves in a"—he cleared his voice and stroked his goatee—"godly manner."

Since the minister was staring at her hand still on Garrett's arm, Maggie quickly pulled it away. "Rest assured that we would never do anything to shame the family or harm the children," she said with schoolmarm primness.

"Then it's settled." Reverend Holly slapped his hands on his thighs and stood.

"Not so fast," Aunt Hetty said, intent upon having the last word. "It's not settled until we set a date." She hesitated as if doing a mental check of her calendar. "June's a lovely time for a wedding, don't you think? And it's such a healthy month. Doc Coldwell told me he treated fewer patients that month than any other time of year. What about. . . the fifteenth?"

A quick calculation told Maggie that was little more than a month away. Five weeks at the most. She glanced at Thomas, hoping he would object, but he remained silent.

"That doesn't give us much time," she said. She hoped that was all the time needed to do the job she was sent to do, but things always took longer than planned. "The children—"

"That's a long time in a child's life," Aunt Hetty said in a voice that indicated the matter settled, at least in her own mind. "And if we wait much longer, I might not be around."

"Are you moving away?" Maggie asked.

The older woman gave her a fish-eyed stare. "I'm dying," she said in a straightforward tone that one might use to express a matter of less concern.

Maggie drew back, hand on her chest. "I–I'm sorry," she stammered. She glanced at Thomas, but he offered no help. If anything, he looked oddly unconcerned about his aunt's health.

Aunt Hetty put on her gloves and stood. "Maybe this works out for the best. Now we can plan a *proper* wedding."

Chapter 4

When Thomas's aunt left with the minister, Maggie let out a sigh of relief.

With her piercing looks and pointed questions, Aunt Hetty would have made a fine detective. Never had Maggie felt more like an insect beneath a microscope. It was a good thing his aunt didn't know her real reason for being there. That was one foe she'd rather not tackle.

After the two children finished waving good-bye, Thomas shut the door, and she could have sworn she heard him mutter something beneath his breath.

"I apologize for my aunt," he said.

It seemed like an odd thing to say about a woman whose days were numbered. "She's just concerned about you. I only hope the wedding isn't too much for her."

"Don't worry about Aunt Hetty." His eyes were so clear, so blue, so intense as he studied her, she feared he could see right through her disguise and know she was a fraud. "She'll outlive us all. But she just can't seem to leave well enough alone."

She frowned, not sure she'd heard right. "Are you saying your aunt *isn't* dying?"

His mouth quirked upward. "Let's just say she suffers from an embarrassing lack of ailments to go with her pains."

Laughter bubbled out of her unexpectedly; she couldn't help herself. So seldom did she get to laugh in her profession. Criminals were not known for their sense of humor.

His eyes warmed to her laughter, but his attention was soon drawn to his young daughter tugging on his arm. Elise's hair was more gold than blond, and her eyes a lovely pale blue. She probably took after her mother in appearance.

In contrast, eight-year-old Toby was the spitting image of his father. His eyes were the same deep shade of blue, and brown hair fell across his forehead from a single part. He looked like a normal active boy, but Thomas's aunt had indicated otherwise. So what had Thomas not told her?

"Let's go outside and give Miss Taylor some privacy," Thomas said. He opened the door and brushed the children through with a sweep of his arm. "If you need me—"

She smiled. "I'll know where to find you." The blood that rushed to her face surprised her. Either she was a better actress than she thought or the desert heat was adversely affecting her.

With a quick smile and slight nod, he turned and followed the children outside.

Grateful for the reprieve, she drew in her breath and wiped her damp hands on her skirt. The hardest part was over—or at least she hoped it was. Now all she had to do was find the seventy thousand dollars stolen during the Whistle-Stop train robbery and leave.

Backing away from the door, her skirt brushed against a chessboard, and several pieces fell over. Not knowing how to play, she had no idea where the pieces belonged. She stood the ivory chessmen upright across the board and hoped for the best.

She walked to the children's room she now shared with Elise. Toby would bunk across the hall in his father's room. It was a simple adobe house with two bedrooms, a parlor, and a kitchen. It also had a separate small room furnished with a cast-iron horse trough. Bars of soap and folded towels told her this was a bathing room, a luxury she hadn't counted on.

Surprised and overjoyed to find such a convenience, she gazed longingly at the tub. What she would give for a hot bath. Later... Closing the door, she moved away.

It appeared that the hall, bedrooms, and bathing room had been added to the original house. Outside there was a privy, barn, well, small corral, and vegetable garden.

Searching a house this size would take no more than a few short hours, and her spirits lifted. With a little luck, she'd find enough incriminating evidence on Garrett Thomas to quickly complete her task. If all went as planned, she could be on her way back to the States in a day or two—a week at the most.

The house was comfortable but needed work. The gingham curtains were faded, the furniture dull, and the carpets looked like they could use a good beating. The house had once been cared for but now looked as forlorn as a child's outgrown toy.

She finished unpacking her few belongings and glanced around the tiny room. Laughter coaxed her to the window. Thomas and the children were playing a lively game of hide-and-seek. A frisky white dog chased after them, its yippy barks mingling with their happy whoops.

From the window she had a clear view of the desert and the distant mountains. The sun rode low in the sky, casting purple shadows across the stark landscape. Tall, stately cacti seemed to beckon with upraised arms, and she was tempted to answer the call.

The closest neighbor was a good mile away, and she felt completely alone and isolated. An unfamiliar bout of nerves surged through her. It was as if the hot desert air had burned away her usual confidence.

In an effort to reassure herself, she checked the derringer holstered to her thigh. Reaching for it was just a matter of sticking her hand into the false pocket of her skirt. Tomorrow she would travel to town and meet with her colleague.

The Pinkerton principal thought the job too dangerous to send a woman alone and had dispatched another operative to work with her. For that she was grateful.

Most of her assignments had been in large cities like St. Louis, New Orleans, and Boston. This job was unlike any she'd ever known.

If something should go wrong. . . If Thomas came to suspect her real identity. . .

Shuddering, she said a silent prayer. Placing her worries squarely in God's hands forced her negative thoughts away.

Thomas ran past the window, and her eyes tracked his long, lean frame around the yard. He bore little resemblance to the stoic man who had driven her home from the station. A playful smile softened his granitelike features, and not even the red scar took away from his good looks. A slight desert breeze rippled through his hair. The strand falling across his forehead gave him a boyish look that was hard to resist.

Elise fell, and he was by her side in an instant, checking her over for injuries and soothing her with hugs.

He appeared to be a doting father, and that was a complication Maggie hadn't expected. It wasn't all that unusual for criminals to be good family men, of course. Some, like the head of the McMurphy gang, were downright neighborly and invited friends and family in for gala parties. But the Pinkerton file on Thomas pegged him as possibly psychopathic, and so far nothing about him seemed to fit that description.

She dropped the curtain in place with a sigh and moved away from the window. However much she felt sorry for the children, she had a job to do.

She glanced around the small but tidy room. Two beds occupied opposite walls, separated by a single bureau.

The Pinkerton principal would no doubt object to her staying at Thomas's house rather than the hotel as planned. The mail-order-bride ruse was dangerous enough without the added risk of staying at the suspect's house. But she was far more likely to meet with success here than in town. Especially now, for thanks to his aunt, she had only a few short weeks in which to conduct her investigation. Aunt Hetty had accepted the decision to postpone the wedding, but Maggie doubted she would again.

A wall shelf contained a McGuffey's Reader piled on top of books on civil government and penmanship. A metal locomotive the length of a bread box rested on a second shelf. It was a remarkably accurate model down to the last detail.

The room smelled like peppermint candy, reminding her that she hadn't eaten since breakfast. Walking out into the hall, she paused outside the closed door directly opposite the children's room. She could hardly wait to search it, but now wasn't the time. Thomas could enter the house at any moment.

Stomach growling she walked to the kitchen. It was well equipped with an icebox, cookstove, water pump, and coffee grinder. A butcher-block table seated four, and a large window over the sink gave a panorama view of the fast-setting sun over purple mountains.

Thomas had indicated earlier that there was fresh chicken for supper, along with garden vegetables. She'd heard it said that the way to a man's heart was through his stomach. But it wasn't Thomas's heart she was interested in as much as his secrets, and there was nothing like a good meal to loosen the tongue.

One by one she opened cupboards and drawers to get the lay of the land.

Never had she seen so much tinware. Cooking utensils, metal plates, and cups crammed practically every shelf. Some even hung from hooks on the wall. Garrett Thomas was a tinker by profession, and the GT stamped on the bottom of each pot and pan confirmed it.

It was this very stamp that had led to Thomas in the first place. A man fitting his description had emptied the safe of an eastbound train. The train had stopped at the Holbrook station for water and fuel. Passengers, engineer, and trainmen had disembarked for a thirty-minute supper break, leaving only the guard aboard.

Without warning, the train suddenly backed out of the station. Though the engineer and his crew gave chase, the train was soon a distance away. The guard was forced to open the safe, and by the time the crew reached the train, they found the man dead and the thieves long gone, along with seventy thousand dollars. It was the largest heist of its kind.

Train robberies were still relatively rare. Outlaws preferred robbing stagecoaches to trains. Maggie suspected that would change when more track was laid. That's why Pinkerton put his best people on this case. If this particular robbery went unsolved, it would send the wrong message to any would-be thieves.

It had been a daring robbery, and after a preliminary investigation, the railroad hired the Pinkerton detective agency. Allan's son, William, had walked the tracks where two men had been seen prior to the holdup. It was during this initial investigation that he found a money clip marked with the initials GT right next to the tracks.

This led to a two-year investigation that had stymied Pinkerton's best detectives. A witness described one of the men seen boarding the stopped train as having a scarred face. That, along with the money clip, pointed to Thomas, but they still lacked tangible proof. Scarred faces were a dime a dozen in the West, and anyone could have dropped the money clip.

The investigation went nowhere until six months ago when suddenly five one-hundred-dollar bills showed up in Furnace Creek during a school fund-raiser. That was more money than anyone living in a small Arizona town was likely to afford. The fact that the money happened to show up at the school where Garrett Thomas's children attended was too much of a coincidence to ignore.

Oddly enough, the money appeared around the same time Thomas had placed an ad in a popular mail-order-bride catalog, providing investigators with a daring plan.

It was now Maggie's job to find enough evidence against him to satisfy a court of law.

Pushing her thoughts aside, she found a woman's apron in one of the drawers and tied it to her waist.

Her detective work left neither time nor the inclination to improve her culinary skills. Since a mail-order bride would be expected to be well versed in the art of homemaking, Pinkerton arranged for training. Her teacher was a widow named Mrs. Cranston who insisted that oil heated to just the right temperature was the mainstay of life.

"Even manna from heaven tasted like oil," she'd declared.

Maggie stared at the chicken laid out on the counter waiting to be plucked. She sure did hope Mrs. Cranston was right.

Chapter 5

An hour and a half later, the four of them gathered around the butcher-block table that took up half the kitchen. Thomas sat at the head and Maggie took the chair opposite him at the foot. The children sitting on either side cast curious glances at her.

Toby had a strange-looking bowl-shaped hat on his head with coiled pieces of wire sticking out in every direction.

"That's an interesting hat you're wearing," Maggie said.

"That's his thinking cap," Elise explained.

"Oh, I see." Maggie spooned peas onto Elise's plate. "I dare say, we could all use a thinking cap on occasion."

Nothing on the table could pass as manna, but the chicken had been fried to a crisp golden brown and the peas cooked to perfection. The potatoes and gravy were almost but not entirely lump-free; hopefully no one would notice.

Thomas and the children dived into their food without benefit of grace. Had Thomas known her inexperience as a cook, he might have been more inclined to ask for the Lord's blessing.

Maggie said a silent prayer, and when she opened her eyes she found both children staring at her.

"Are you going to take care of us?" Elise asked.

Maggie glanced at the far end of the table. Thomas was smothering his food in salt with the same intent as one might use to put out a fire.

"Yes, I am," she said and smiled.

She just hoped her domestic responsibilities didn't interfere with her investigation. Fortunately, both children attended school, so her days should be free.

Elise considered Maggie's answer with a worried frown. "Are you going to be mean like my teacher?"

"I'm only mean to children who don't do their chores or school-work," she said.

Thomas set the salt dish down. "Well, it seems that Miss Taylor and I are in accord."

"What's accord?" Elise asked.

"It means that they like each other," Toby said, the metal wires on his head waving back and forth.

Maggie dabbed her mouth with a napkin. "Actually, *accord* means that your father and I are in agreement."

Elise's head turned from one to the other. "So does it mean that you don't like each other?"

"We like each other just fine." She lifted her lashes to find Thomas watching her, and heat rushed to her face.

She quickly looked away. She needed to keep her wits but for some reason couldn't seem to even control her breathing. Maybe she was just tired. The trip to Arizona had been long. After a good night's sleep she was bound to feel like her usual confident self again.

Satisfied that she had solved the mystery of her uncharacteristic behavior, she reached for the neglected plate of corn bread. "Would anyone care for some?" she said a bit too brightly.

Toby glanced at his father. The wires on his thinking cap quivered. "We're n–not allowed to—"

"Eat the bread," Thomas said, interrupting his son's protest.

Toby's bottom lip stuck out. "You said that corn bread—"

"I said eat it." Thomas looked up. "Or go to your room."

Toby regarded the bread with grave suspicion but, prompted by his father's stern look, reached for the smallest square. He dropped it on his plate and stared at it with downcast eyes.

Maggie sent a glance of inquiry to Thomas. "Is there a problem with the bread?"

"Don't worry about it. You had no way of knowing."

"Knowing what?" she persisted.

"We can't eat corn bread," Elise said, her eyes round as saucers. "It's poison."

"Poison?" Maggie set the plate of bread down and took a piece for herself. Biting into it, she said, "See? It's perfectly safe." *A bit dry, perhaps, but tasty.*

Both children stared in round-eyed horror as if they expected her to topple over at any moment. No one else touched the bread, and they finished their meal in silence.

Later, as she cleared the table, she discovered Toby's corn bread tucked inside his napkin.

∞∞

Thomas surprised her after supper by helping clear the table. A widower for two years, he obviously knew his way around the kitchen.

While they waited for the water to heat, he leaned his tall form against the doorframe, arms crossed, watching her. His presence seemed to fill the room, and she was extremely conscious of his every move.

"That was a mighty fine meal," he said, his voice warm with approval. "I didn't expect you to take over the household chores on your first day here."

"I don't mind." She turned to the iron cookstove just as a funnel of steam rose from the kettle spout.

"Let me get that for you," he said.

Before she could turn down his offer, he stepped to her side. His elbow brushed against her arm as he easily lifted the kettle off the cast-iron stove and poured the hot water into two basins in the sink. One was for washing, the other for rinsing. Returning the kettle to the stove, he lifted a pail of cold water and poured it into each basin to lower the temperature.

"Thank you," she said. Oddly aware of his strength, she reached for the stick tied with strips of linen. She swiped the swab against a bar of hard soap and swished it in the hot water until foamy suds bubbled up.

He grabbed a clean flour-sack towel from a hook. "I'll dry," he said with quiet authority.

She washed a plate, rinsed it off, and handed it to him. His fingers brushed against hers, and she quickly drew her hand away and plunged it into the warm water.

They worked for several minutes without speaking. Questions she wanted to ask about his past would have to wait until she'd earned his trust, but she felt safe querying about the children.

"I'm confused as to why your children think corn bread is poison."

The question hung between them a moment before he answered. "I spent a year in the Andersonville prison camp, and all they fed us was corn bread. I'm afraid Elise and Toby have picked up my aversion to it."

He'd never mentioned his wartime experiences in his many letters to her, and she couldn't let on that she already knew about his confinement. Instead, she afforded him a sympathetic look.

"I'm so sorry."

Raw pain glittered in the depth of his eyes. "I don't like to talk about it."

Surprised by a surge of sympathy, she set to work scrubbing a plate clean. She didn't want to feel anything for him. Certainly not empathy.

Still, she knew from painful experience that the mere act of putting some things into words was akin to ripping open a wound. That's why she never talked about her outlaw father.

At the tender age of twelve, she'd watched him hang from the gallows, and the shame never left her. Tracking down criminals was her way of making up to society for her father's heinous crimes, and right now, Garrett Thomas was on the top of her list.

"I would hope that my corn bread tastes better than what they served in prison," she said, breaking the awkward silence.

"You're an excellent cook," he said.

Hoping he didn't think she had been fishing for compliments, she glanced at him sideways. "Is that why you dumped an entire salt dish on your food?"

"A bad habit, I'm afraid. Acquired after the war. Salt was a rare commodity then and nonexistent in Andersonville." He shrugged. "It's since been my salvation. I can't stand my own cooking without it."

She laughed. She didn't mean to; it just bubbled out of her. A grin inched across his face, and a moment of rapport sprang between them. It was the very thing she had hoped to accomplish. Still, that one unguarded moment worried her. She'd been trained to control her emotions, but at the moment was having a hard time managing even her thoughts.

Turning her attention to the dishwater, she practically scrubbed the painted design off a dinner plate. When she agreed to take on this job, she thought her biggest challenge would be hiding her loathing for him. The opposite appeared to be the case, and that was a problem. Liking a suspected killer was not an option—no matter how blue his eyes or devastating his smile.

"Is there anything else I should know?" she asked, staying focused on the task at hand. "Anything I should avoid besides corn bread?"

"That about covers it. Just don't let Toby talk you into going to the moon."

"I'm sorry?"

"I'm afraid the boy's imagination runs away with him at times. He's now working on a contraption to take him to the moon."

"Oh, I see." Since he had introduced the topic of his son, she felt confident in pursuing it. "I got the feeling from your aunt that there's. . . something I should know about him."

He took his time answering. "He's got an inquiring mind," he said at last. "I'm afraid he was too much for Aunt Hetty to handle. The housekeepers, too, which is why I couldn't keep one."

His inability to keep a housekeeper explained the shabby condition of the house but hardly explained the difficulty with Toby. Since that seemed to be all he was willing to concede, she let the matter drop.

"Would you object to my teaching the children to say grace before meals?" If things worked out the way she hoped, she would soon have proof enough to send him to the gallows. Without their earthly pa, Toby and Elise would need their heavenly Father more than ever.

"If you feel you must." He hesitated. "You should know I have no regard for religion." This time his voice had a steel-like edge. She'd gathered as much but remained silent. If a suspect wanted to talk, you let him talk.

"I hope you can live with that," he said. Without another word he tossed down his towel and left the room.

Chapter 6

What kind of work was required of a tinker after hours? Maggie couldn't begin to guess, but that was the excuse Thomas gave for locking himself in his room for the remainder of the evening.

In a way she was grateful. Tonight she was feeling oddly vulnerable and in no condition to deal with him. She couldn't afford to make a mistake. Not this time.

After overseeing that both children had washed their faces and brushed their teeth, she settled down on the divan in the parlor, a child on each side of her. Elise read a story from McGuffey's. She struggled with every word, and the going was slow. Toby's reading skills were better, but he was far more interested in working on a sketch.

"What are you drawing?" Maggie asked.

He held his paper up so she could see. "A catapult to take me to the moon."

"The moon is a long way away," Maggie said.

"That's why the catapult has to be big." His eyes grew round. "As big as a mountain."

"I would imagine so." It was hard to believe that this was the very same boy who gave his father's aunt such a bad time. "Why do you want to go to the moon?"

"So I can see everything that's happening on Earth."

The thought made her smile. "Just like God."

Elise looked up from her book. "Is God on the moon?"

Maggie leaned over and tapped Elise's cute button nose with her finger. "God is everywhere."

After the children finished reading to her, she stood and yawned. "Okay, pumpkins, time for bed."

Elise giggled. "We're not pumpkins."

"You're not? Well, you could have fooled me. Come along now. It's late."

Actually, it was only a little after eight, but she looked forward to trying out that bathtub, after which she planned on hitting the sack. It had been a long and nerve-racking day.

Moments later she tucked Elise in bed. "Do you want me to hear your prayers?"

Elise shook her head.

Flat on his stomach on the floor, Toby looked under the bed and pulled out his slingshot. "You only have to pray if you've been bad or want something," he said.

"Actually, I think God would be disappointed if those are the only times we talked to Him," Maggie said. "He wants us to talk to Him when we're happy, lonely, or sad." How odd. Aunt Hetty had insisted that her marriage to Thomas be performed by a minister but neglected to teach the children the simple basics of communicating with God.

Elise looked confused. "You mean we can talk to Him even if we haven't been bad?"

Maggie brushed a strand of hair away from Elise's face. "Most definitely."

Elise pondered this for a moment. "But I only know what to say when I'm bad."

"Is that so? Hmm. Come and kneel next to me." Elise scrambled out of bed and dropped to her knees by Maggie's side.

"Fold your hands like this." Maggie steepled her hands together.

Elise followed her example. "Why do we have to kneel when we pray?"

"It's so God knows we're talking to Him and not to someone else," Toby said, scrambling to his feet, slingshot in hand.

Maggie resisted the urge to explain how kneeling showed humility and put God above all else. Better to let Toby think he had the world figured out. He would learn soon enough that he didn't; no one did.

"What should I say?" Elise whispered.

"You can thank God for giving you good food and a nice soft bed to sleep in. You can also ask Him to help you with your reading. You can pray for your brother and for your mother in heaven. You can pray for your teacher and your father, too." God knows, he needed all the prayers he could get. They all did.

"Just say what I say. God bless. . ." Maggie said a simple prayer, and Elise repeated after her. "Amen."

Elise's eyes flew open. "You forgot to pray for yourself."

Maggie smiled. "You can do it for me."

Elise clasped her hands together and squeezed her eyes shut. "God bless Miss Taylor, and don't let her die. Amen."

"What makes you think I might die?"

"You ate corn bread," Elise said, her voice hushed. "People always die when they eat corn bread."

❧

The following morning, Maggie walked into the kitchen to find that the children had already eaten breakfast and dressed for school.

Garrett greeted her with a smile and handed her a cup of coffee. "Morning."

"Morning," she said, taking the cup from him. "I'm sorry, I don't usually sleep in."

"You must have needed the extra rest after your trip." He set a plate of scrambled eggs and bacon on the table. "Here you go." He pulled out a chair for her.

"I didn't expect you to fix my breakfast." She wasn't used to being waited on, especially by a man.

"Hold your thanks till you've tasted it." He waited for her to be seated before lifting his voice. "Toby, Elise. Come and say good-bye to Miss Taylor."

Elise raced into the kitchen and grabbed a schoolbook from the table. "Good-bye, Miss Taylor."

Toby called from the other room. "Bye."

Thomas hesitated at the doorway. "If you need anything laundered, leave it for Lila. She comes tomorrow."

That was a relief. Washing clothes was one chore she'd sooner not tackle. "Thank you."

"Anything else you might need?" he asked.

"I'd like to go into town later. Would it be all right if I use the buckboard out back?"

"It's yours," he said. "Would you like me to hitch it for you?"

"I think I can handle it."

He nodded. "I'll pick the children up from school."

"All right." Had he expected her to pick them up? Having so little knowledge of domestic affairs, she hadn't even considered that carting them back and forth to school might be her responsibility.

Elise called to him, and with a final good-bye he followed his children through the parlor. The front door slammed shut, and moments later the rumbling sound of wagon wheels drifted through the open window and finally faded away.

Then all was blissfully quiet.

❧

Maggie quickly washed the breakfast dishes and scrubbed the sink. Should Thomas arrive home unexpectedly to find dirty dishes and an untidy house, he might wonder what she had done with her time. Not wanting to blow her cover, she was as diligent with the household chores as she was in her detective work.

Anxious to get started on her investigation, she decided to search Thomas's bedroom first. Finding the stolen money hidden there seemed like a remote possibility; the most she hoped to find was a bankbook or key to a safe-deposit box.

Whipping off her apron, she tossed it on a chair and hurried down the hall to his room. The door was locked. Surprised, she drew her hand away from the brass knob. Why would Thomas lock the door to his room unless he had something to hide? Maybe there was a key somewhere.

A quick search of the house soon relieved her of that hope. Since she couldn't search his room, she decided the next best thing was to drive into town and make contact with her Pinkerton partner. He'd arrived in town ahead of her.

Yesterday, while Thomas argued with the hotel desk clerk about the room he'd reserved for her, she'd wandered about the lobby hoping to make visual contact with her partner. Unfortunately, he was nowhere to be seen. She hoped to have better luck today.

Chapter 7

It was after ten by the time she'd harnessed the black horse in the barn to the buckboard and drove into town. Already it was hot, and the air shimmered from the heated ground. She was grateful for having the good sense to forgo her more stylish outfits for a lace-bibbed calico frock.

The main business area of Furnace Creek occupied two streets. A livery stable and blacksmith shop anchored the town on the north, the railroad station the south. An assortment of businesses, including a bank, hotel, icehouse, and general store, were strung from one end of town to the other like wash on a clothesline. The adobe buildings were fitted with false wooden fronts and faded signs that creaked in the slightest breeze.

She glanced at the sheriff's office housed in a freestanding building. Usually, the first order of business for a Pinkerton detective was to introduce him- or herself to local lawmen. But Sheriff Summerhay had a run-in with Pinkerton detectives a few years back and now refused to work with them. It was better to stay out of his hair until she and her partner had uncovered tangible proof of Thomas's guilt.

Horses tethered to hitching posts swung their tails to ward off flies, and wagons rumbled by filled with produce, dairy products, and other provisions.

She parked the buckboard across from the two-story hotel and set the brake. She was anxious to find her partner, but she had to do it discreetly. No one must see them together.

A familiar voice assaulted her ears. "Readallaboutit." It was the same paperboy seen at the train station.

He was a sorrowful sight. Unless she was mistaken, his were the same clothes worn the day before. Same patches, more wrinkles. He showed no sign of recognizing her.

She stepped onto the boardwalk next to him. "Why aren't you in school?"

He stared at her through a curtain of dirty, stringy hair. "Don't get paid for goin' to no school."

She frowned. "What's your name?"

"Linc," he said. "Short for Lincoln."

"Lincoln what?"

"Jones."

His parents must have once had high hopes for the boy to name him after a president. "Your ma and pa dead?" she asked. It was the only explanation she could think of to explain the boy's neglected appearance.

His eyes gleamed with suspicion. "How'd ya know that?"

She shrugged and reached into her drawstring handbag. "How much money did that thief take from you yesterday?"

He glanced at her bag, and a calculated look crossed his face. "Ten dollars."

She raised an eyebrow. He'd have to sell a hundred newspapers to earn that much, and his bag wouldn't hold many more than a dozen or two.

She narrowed her eyes to show she meant business. "The truth."

He adjusted his canvas bag. "How'd ya know that's not the truth?"

"Your nose turned blue," she said.

His hand flew to his nose and his face turned red. "Two dollars," he said.

She drew a bill from her purse and stuffed it in his hand. "The lie gets you only one."

Thomas's Fine Tinware was shoehorned in between Ben's Saddles and Jake's Gunsmith shop. She waited for the sprinkler wagon to pass before crossing the street, the heels of her high-button shoes sinking into the muddied ground. She opened the door to the jingle of bells and wiped her feet on the doormat before entering.

Angry voices greeted her. An argument raged in the back room of the shop.

"I told you I know nothing about it," Thomas yelled. "Now get outta here."

A man emerged and stormed through the shop. He didn't so much as acknowledge her. She barely got a glimpse of his angry red face when he brushed past her and out the door.

She whirled to find Thomas watching her. "I'm sorry. I came at a bad time."

"No, no, not at all." He looked genuinely happy to see her, and once again she was forced to conquer her unwelcomed response to his smile. "I'm glad you came."

She pointed a finger over her shoulder. "An unhappy customer?"

He shook his head. "I wish it was that simple. That was Charlie Cotton, my former brother-in-law."

She managed to hide her surprise behind an expressionless face. Nothing in the Pinkerton files suggested Garrett's dead wife had a brother; things just got a whole lot more interesting. "Why was he so angry?"

"He thinks I have something of his."

Before he could explain further, the shop door opened and a portly man walked in. "Got my order ready?" he called. He was dressed in a gray suit, vest, and bow tie.

Thomas touched her arm, and a brief shiver rippled through her. "Don't go away," he whispered. He then walked behind the counter and addressed his customer. "Right here."

The shopper acknowledged Maggie with a nod and doffed his hat. "I don't believe we've met." The gleam in his eyes revealed more than just a passing interest. "You must be new in town."

"She came all the way from Indiana," Garrett said.

"Is that so? Name's Benjamin Mooney, president of the Bank of Arizona."

She knew who he was. He had no way of knowing it, of course, but the Pinkerton National Detective Agency had initially investigated him along with all bank employees. The money stolen during the Whistle-Stop robbery was a bank transfer, and the chance of it being an inside job could not be ignored.

"Pleased to meet you, Mr. Mooney," she said, holding out her gloved hand. "I'm Maggie Taylor."

He took her hand and held it like a piece of delicate china. "Indiana, eh? That's a ways away, all right. I'm from Mizz-zur-rah myself."

"Are you now?" she said, smiling. Missouri was the train holdup capital of the country, and she'd spent a lot of time there in recent months. Of course, she would never say as much.

His carefully waxed mustache curled upward, as did the corners of his mouth. "Perhaps you would allow me the pleasure of giving you a tour of our little town."

"That would be very kind of you," she said.

"But totally unnecessary." Thomas stepped between them, forcing the banker to release her hand. "Miss Taylor is my guest," he said in a tone that left no room for argument.

Mooney looked from one to the other. "I see."

Maggie wasn't sure what the banker thought he saw, but he quickly backed away.

"Your package is ready," Thomas said, and Mooney followed him to the counter.

While the two men conducted their business, she wandered around the well-stocked shop. Never had she seen so many household goods in one place. Tin dishes, pots, pans, and candleholders were piled high on counters and shelves in no particular order.

Every imaginable kind of lantern hung from hooks. Tin cabinet panels and ceiling tiles were stacked against the back wall. One section of the store was devoted to toys. Tin soldiers, toy animals, and small wagons surrounded a train engine similar to the one in the children's room.

The banker finished his business and stopped to chat with her on the way out. "If Thomas here doesn't treat you right, you know where to find me." With that he left, package in hand.

She glanced at Thomas but couldn't tell much from his bland expression.

She drew his attention to the toy engine. The man suspected of being one of two Whistle-Stop bandits was evidently interested in trains, though there was nothing in his background that suggested he knew how to operate one. That meant his partner in crime probably manned the engine while Thomas emptied the safe and shot the guard. As bad as the crime was, it seemed even more horrendous now that she'd met him and knew him as a warm and loving father.

"You made that?" she asked, studying the model.

He walked around the counter and joined her. "I did. I started by making toys for Toby and Elise. Much to my surprise I discovered a market for them."

"Ever wish you could drive a train?" she asked, watching his face.

"Not me," he said and laughed.

She ran her fingers over the engine and marveled at the details.

"It's beautiful. I do believe you have a gift from God." She groaned inwardly. Knowing how he felt about religion she really did need to watch what she said.

"A gift?" He studied her. "You're the first one to accuse me of that."

"Why, Mr. Thomas. You make a gift sound like a bad thing."

"Calling me Mr. Thomas is a bad thing. I'd prefer that you call me Garrett."

"Very well." His insistence on informality had to be a good sign.

For the first time since coming to Furnace Creek, she relaxed—or at least as much as she dared. "Garrett it is, but to be fair, you must call me Maggie."

He smiled. "It's a deal." He inclined his head. "So tell me, Maggie. What brings you to town?"

"Nothing special. Just wanted to look around. Meet some of the residents."

"I'm sorry I don't have time to accompany you."

"That's all right." The last thing she wanted was to have him tag along while she was working.

"If you need anything—groceries or personal items—just tell the shopkeepers to add it to my account."

"Thank you." Considering he had no way of knowing whether she was a spendthrift or thrifty, it was a surprising offer. Shouldn't a small-town tinker be more careful with his money, especially one who lived as modestly as he did? Of course, if he really was the Whistle-Stop bandit, then he'd have no reason to worry about what she spent.

"Do you know Linc?" she asked, changing the subject.

"The paperboy? Only that his parents were killed a few years back during the Indian uprising. The boy is living with his grandmother. Why?"

"He should be in school."

"A lot of children should be in school. Unfortunately, for some families, that's not possible. Some live too far out of town. Some simply dropped out following the fire."

She didn't let on that she knew about the fire or the fund-raiser that led the investigation to his doorstep.

"There was a fire?" she asked.

He nodded. "The schoolhouse burned to the ground. It's been rebuilt, this time from brick and adobe."

"But why doesn't Linc attend?"

"His grandmother needs him. His income supports the two of them."

She now felt guilty for withholding the dollar. On the other hand, it wouldn't do the boy any good to get away with a blatant lie.

"Couldn't the church do something to help?" she asked.

His mouth dipped in a frown. "Been my experience that what happens in church, stays there."

His harsh tone rendered her speechless. She thought the kindly minister who helped her through those difficult years of her youth was representative of all churchmen, but maybe not.

"My apologies." He grimaced. "I have no right to saddle you with my personal views." He moved to the counter and reached into the cash box. "Do you know how much Linc lost yesterday in the robbery?"

"That won't be necessary. I reimbursed him this morning."

He looked surprised. "That was a kind thing you did."

"I guess you could say I have a soft spot for children." She wasn't just saying that to impress him. Had she not been a private detective she might have become a schoolteacher.

"You're all Toby and Elise could talk about when I drove them to school this morning." He chuckled. "It's Miss Taylor this and Miss Taylor that."

"They're very sweet, your children," she said. Recalling her own growing-up years as a daughter of an outlaw, she pitied them. It was always an outlaw's family that suffered most.

"If Toby gives you any trouble, let me know."

Toby again. "He strikes me as a very bright boy," she said. "And most imaginative."

Just then the door flew open and a tall, thin man stepped into the shop carrying a crate. "Only half our order arrived," he called and seeing her, stopped. "Sorry."

Garrett beckoned with his hand. "Come on over and I'll introduce you."

The man lowered the crate to the floor and ambled toward her. Dressed in dark denim pants and a checkered shirt, he wore a strange fabric hat gathered on top like a woman's nightcap. The hat was tied beneath his chin with rawhide laces.

"I want you to meet my fiancée, Miss Taylor," Garrett said. "Maggie, this is Panhandle."

"Pleased to meet you," she said politely. "Mr.—"

"Panhandle, ma'am," he drawled. "Just plain Panhandle. Great name for a tinker, don't you think?"

She smiled. "I guess it is."

Panhandle gave her a yellow-toothed grin.

"You can start cutting tin for the Stewart order," Garrett said.

Panhandle backed away. "Will do, boss."

By the time he picked up the crate and vanished in back, the store was full of customers. Some stopped by to pick up orders, others just to browse.

Pretending to study a skillet, Maggie watched from the sidelines. Garrett seemed to know his customers well and even asked about their families.

He appeared to work hard and was successful at what he did. He also lived a modest life. So what had he done with the money stolen from the train?

❧

Garrett worked behind the counter as he watched his fiancée exchange pleasantries with his customers. He didn't mean to stare, but her smile was a magnet drawing his attention to her pretty pink mouth without any effort on his part.

With a start he realized he wasn't the only one who seemed mesmerized by her. Not only had she caught the eye of his apprentice, but all seven male customers in his shop. Each man made it his business to walk up to her and introduce himself. Never had Garrett seen so many red-faced stammering fools in his life.

Not that he could blame them. A looker like her was bound to bring out the wolves. No doubt she could have her pick of men without scars or a soldier's heart. Men with no children to care for. Men without blood on their hands.

The thought gave him pause. What right did he have for judging her so harshly? All she did was chase after a beggar in an effort to retrieve the paperboy's money. While he. . .

He pushed the painful memories away with a shake of his head. A woman like her could have her pick of anyone she wanted. If he had the brains of a grasshopper, he'd marry her before she figured out what a bad choice she'd made.

Chapter 8

Maggie left Garrett's shop with more questions than answers. Why was Garrett arguing with his brother-in-law? *"He thinks I have something of his."*

His share of the holdup money, perhaps?

What was his name? Cotton, that was it. And why did that name sound familiar?

Picking up her pace, she headed for the hotel. Her first order of business was to make contact with her Pinkerton partner.

A red and yellow box wagon pulled by a dapple gray mare was parked in front of the land office. Dr. Kettleman's Miraculous Cure-Alls was written in big bold letters on the paneled siding.

A man stood next to the wagon dressed in a top hat and green checkered coat with a matching bow tie. "May I interest you in a bottle of snake oil, ma'am?"

"No thank you," She walked past him and stopped.

"Step right up, ladies and gentlemen, and I will detect what ails you and offer you a miraculous cure."

She should have known. Smiling, she turned and took a closer look at the salesman. This time she had no trouble seeing past the phony mustache and bold-colored suit.

His real name was Chuck Greenwood, and he, too, was a Pinkerton operative. Privately, she called him Rikker and he called her Duffy. Rikker was the name of the orphanage cat that used to curl up at the bottom of her bed. She pretended he protected her while she slept.

Duffy was what Rikker called his favorite sister who died in childbirth.

Their pet monikers saved them from having to remember each other's assumed names, which changed with each new case.

A portly man with a pox-marked face and close-set eyes, this latest disguise suited him to a T. Not only did he look like a snake-oil doctor, he had his sales pitch down pat. She couldn't help but laugh—talk about hiding in plain sight.

Looking left and right and seeing no one around, she closed the distance between them. Rikker was more than just a coworker; he was also a good friend and mentor. Secretly, she considered him the earthly father she wished she'd had.

"What took you so long to find me?" he asked.

"Long? I've only been in town for a day." Rikker was as impatient as he was clever. Nothing he hated more than sitting around waiting even though that was a very large part of a detective's life.

"How much did it cost you to bribe the hotel clerk into putting up a no vacancy sign?" she asked.

"Not as much as it'll cost me when our boss finds out you're staying at Thomas's house."

"He doesn't have to know. At least not yet."

"I'd hate to be you when the old Scotsman finds out," Rikker said.

"Allan Pinkerton worries too much." Since his stroke, his sons managed the company, but he was still very much involved in the planning and execution of investigations.

"That makes two of us."

It wasn't just her safety that worried the principal. This case was a thorn in Pinkerton's side. They had been working on it for two years, and that didn't speak well for an agency that had sustained much criticism in recent years for what some thought were bullying tactics. Allan and his sons were anxious to get some good press for a change, and catching the Whistle-Stop bandits would certainly serve that purpose.

"I'd feel a whole lot better if you were staying at the hotel. If anything happens to you. . ."

His concern touched her. "Nothing's going to happen. At least not in front of the children."

"If our suspicions are right, we're not only dealing with a thief, but also a killer. And I'm not just talking about the railroad guard. For all we know, he also killed his wife."

The memory of Thomas playing tag came to mind. His tenderness toward his daughter when she fell had seemed real. It was hard to believe that such a doting father could be a cold-blooded killer. But then, criminals came in all disguises.

"Her death was an accident," she said. That was the official ruling, and she had no reason to suspect otherwise.

"I don't believe in accidents, and if you know what's good for you, you won't believe in them, either."

"That's what I like about you, Rikker. A person is always guilty until proven innocent."

"And I'm usually right."

Before she could reply, a matronly woman walked out of the mercantile carrying a basket in one hand and holding on to a small child with the other.

Rikker shoved a bottle of snake oil into Maggie's hand, and right on cue she pretended to read the label.

Lifting his voice for anyone within hearing distance, he started his spiel. "That magical bottle contains the purest and most refined healing oil this side of the Miss'sippi. One teaspoon of this elixir and your troubles will be a thing of the past."

The woman walked by them without stopping, and when she was out of earshot he lowered his voice. "Watch your step. If he tries anything. . .sexual-wise, I mean, I want you out of there."

Heat rushed to her face. "Since when have you ever worried about my virtue?"

"Since you insisted on moving into an outlaw's house."

"Don't worry. He might be a thief and murderer, but where women are concerned, he's a perfect gentleman." With the declaration came the memory of blue eyes and a crooked smile—a disconcerting thought she quickly banished from her mind.

"I'm sure his wife appreciated being killed by a gentleman," he said wryly.

"We don't know that Garrett killed her."

His eyebrows rose. "So now it's Garrett."

"He insists I call him by his Christian name."

"The word *Christian* and Thomas should never be mentioned in the same sentence." He glanced around. A man was unloading a wagon at the end of the block next to a windmill, but no one was close by. Still, taking no chances, he stabbed the label of elixir with his finger as if trying to sell it to her.

"So what have you uncovered so far?" he asked.

"Since I've only been here for less than twenty-four hours, not much. But I do know he has an overbearing aunt and two adorable children."

"That was in the report."

"Not the overbearing and adorable part," she said. "Also, he has a brother-in-law. I heard the two of them arguing earlier. That's the first I heard that his dead wife had a brother."

"Interesting. What were they arguing about?"

"He thinks Garrett has something of his. His name is Cotton."

"Ah, now we're getting somewhere. Mr. Cotton was confined to Andersonville the same time that Thomas was there. He was one of the men who tried to escape with Thomas. The other man was shot dead."

That's why his name sounded familiar. "Do you think that's where they first met? In prison?"

"Actually they met before the war while Thomas was attending medical school. He might have even introduced Thomas to his sister."

It made sense. "It sounds like they must have been good friends at one time." Nothing made two people closer than sharing an ordeal. "We know there were two men involved in the robbery." One man backed the train away from the station and one robbed the safe and shot the guard. "Do you think Cotton was the second man? That would explain the bad blood between them." It wasn't unusual for criminals to have a falling-out.

"Could be," he said. "Have you sent a report to headquarters?"

"Not yet. I'll send one tomorrow."

"Drop it off here, and I'll mail it for you. I've arranged to send regular shipments to the States so no one will think anything of it."

She nodded. "That will help." Though everything was cryptically written, mailing daily reports without rousing suspicion always proved to be a challenge. She leaned closer. "Your mustache is crooked."

"It's part of my charm," he said, but he straightened it. "Be careful. You know where to find me if you need me."

Two men stepped out of the nearby general store, and Rikker took the snake oil out of her hands. Holding the bottle up, he hawked, "Step right up, gentlemen. Step right up."

∞

Smiling in amusement, Maggie left Rikker and walked to Grover's Mercantile to purchase a cookbook just in case things took longer than she hoped. Everything she knew about cooking could fill a postage stamp.

Several women were gathered around a single bolt of calico. As Maggie neared they turned and stared at her as if she'd given off some sort of signal.

"You must be the mail-order bride everyone's talking about," one woman exclaimed, and the five women closed in around her like the drawstring of a purse.

"Yes, that's right. I'm Maggie Taylor."

The matron in charge said, "Nice to meet you. I'm Miriam Higginbottom." A barrel-shaped woman with steel-gray hair, she fixed Maggie with a pop-eyed stare through a lorgnette suspended from a gold chain around her neck.

She quickly introduced the other four women. She talked so fast it was difficult to grasp their names. Mrs. Higginbottom then issued invitations to join the church quilting bee and ladies reading club.

"Though you don't have to be able to read to join," Mrs. Higginbottom assured her.

"Tell her about the dance." This from the woman with tight, springy curls and a jutting posterior that had no need of a bustle.

"Oh, yes." Mrs. Higginbottom described the upcoming dance in great detail. "You and Mr. Thomas must come."

Maggie had never been to a dance and had no intention of attending one. She was here to work, not socialize. "I'll mention it to him," she said vaguely when she could get a word in edgewise, but by then Mrs. Higginbottom had already changed subjects.

"So when is the wedding?"

"Not till next month."

"Are you staying at the hotel?"

"I'm. . .eh. . .staying at the house," she said.

The five women stared at her, and for a moment no one spoke.

Maggie broke the strained silence. "There was no vacancy at the hotel, so I'm sharing a room with Elise."

"Of course you are," Mrs. Higginbottom exclaimed. "I mean. . .it makes perfect sense."

"Such a dear, dear man," one of the other women said, filling in the awkward silence. "What happened to his wife was dreadful."

"Just dreadful," the other four murmured.

"If you don't mind my asking," Mrs. Higginbottom began. "Why would such an attractive woman as yourself agree to marry a man sight unseen? Not that there's anything wrong with Mr. Thomas, mind you."

One of the other women—Mrs. Trotter—looked appalled. "Miriam."

Miriam Higginbottom didn't look the least bit apologetic. "I have the right to know," she said, and her friends accepted her contention without further discussion.

"Some men fare better sight unseen," Maggie said lightly.

This brought appreciative laughter from the others. Mrs. Higginbottom, in her usual take-charge way, continued. "I just hope that the boy doesn't give you a bad time. Such a handful. Hetty's lucky he didn't burn down the barn."

"He set her barn on fire?"

"No. Just the chicken coop. But that was bad enough. He made a hot-air balloon and was trying to send it to the moon or some such thing."

"Instead it landed on Hetty's chickens," Mrs. Trotter added. "Never saw so many feathers fly in my life."

"Yes, and he confiscated the clothesline from Louise Martin's backyard," Mrs. Higginbottom continued.

"On wash day." Mrs. Trotter rolled her eyes. "Said he was just borrowing it."

"Well, if he was my son, he would have gotten a good licking." Mrs. Higginbottom sniffed. "If you ask me, Garrett is too lenient with the boy."

She said more, a lot more, but very little of it was of any use, and some of it bordered on just plain gossip about people Maggie had no interest in. By the time she managed to purchase a cookbook and leave the shop, her ears were ringing.

Chapter 9

Maggie returned from town determined to do a methodical search. The house had no cellar, but it did have an attic. Doubting she'd find the key to Garrett's bedroom on the uppermost floor, she decided to tackle the attic last.

Other than to learn about Garrett's brother-in-law and locate Rikker, her expedition to town had revealed little, except to answer her questions about Toby. Next to the mischief her brothers used to get into, Toby's escapades sounded mild in comparison.

If she was lucky, the house search would reveal something more useful. But where to start?

Recalling how a map found in a dictionary helped solve the case of a museum's stolen artwork, she settled on the crammed bookshelf in the parlor, next to the ivory chess set.

Garrett had a wide taste in reading. *Moby Dick* was shelved in between *Uncle Tom's Cabin* and *Journey to the Center of the Earth*. Medical books shared space with philosophy, science, and history.

Stooping in front of the bookshelves, she flipped through each tome looking for letters, bank receipts, or hidden compartments. A book of poetry was inscribed *to G love from K*.

She had just started on the last shelf when a knock on the door startled her.

Quickly replacing a book, she stood and opened the door.

"Aunt. . . I mean. . ."

"That's all right. Call me Aunt Hetty. I insist." The older woman ambled into the house with her walking cane, stabbing the floor with its tip as if checking the foundation's integrity. "Land sakes, it's hot out there."

"Yes, I can't get over the weather. Is it always this hot?"

"You've not seen anything yet. Wait till July and August."

Fortunately, Maggie had no intention of sticking around that long. "Would you care for some lemonade?" she asked.

"That would be nice. Long as it's not too sweet or too sour." Aunt Hetty followed Maggie into the kitchen and collapsed onto a chair. Her face flushed from the heat, she pulled off her bonnet and used it to fan herself. Wisps of white hair had escaped her topknot.

"Misery loves company, but trust me, it's better to have a pain in one hip than two," she said, rubbing her sides.

Maggie reached in the icebox for the pitcher of lemonade. "You shouldn't be out on such a hot day," Maggie said.

"No, I shouldn't. Especially in my condition. But you know what they say? What can't be cured must be endured." She laid her cane on the chair next to her. "What a pity that the wedding was postponed. I just hope I last that long." Obviously she intended to hold Maggie responsible should she not.

Maggie placed the pitcher on a tray and reached into the overhead cupboard for two glasses. "Is there any reason to think that you won't?"

Aunt Hetty looked startled. "Of course there is." She then recited everything wrong with her and, Maggie suspected, a great deal more. She brushed her forehead with the back of her hand. "Of course, no one will believe how ill I am until I'm dead and buried."

"What does the doctor say?" Maggie asked, setting the tray on the table.

Aunt Hetty made a rude sound. "It seems that everyone has a cure for what ails me but my doctor." She lowered her voice. "Would you believe he had the nerve to accuse me of being perfectly healthy?"

"No!"

"I jest you not." She lifted her shoulders and sighed. "I suppose I should be happy that you postponed the wedding. Now we can prepare for more than just a simple ceremony. It will be my parting gift to you both."

Maggie had no time to plan a wedding, but she had to play along. "I certainly hope you stick around awhile. The children will miss you, I'm sure."

"That's why I'm delighted that Garrett is marrying again. Seeing him settled will help me die a happy woman." She rubbed the small of her back and groaned. "They say the Arizona heat is good for what ails you, but you wouldn't prove it by me."

Sensing that another list of physical complaints was imminent, Maggie quickly changed the subject. "I'm sorry I don't have any baked goods to offer you."

"That's quite all right. You're just settling in. I should have thought to bring something." She pulled a small writing tablet and pencil out of her purse.

Maggie took a seat opposite her and filled both glasses with lemonade. Today, Aunt Hetty wore a dark skirt and matching shirtwaist. She looked determined and efficient as she opened her notebook and, except for her flushed face, robust. Maggie hoped she looked as well when she was Aunty Hetty's age.

"I went ahead and booked the church." Aunt Hetty made a little check on the page to indicate the task was complete and moved to the second written line. "I also spoke with the dressmaker. She'll need to take your measurements."

Aunt Hetty had no way of knowing it, of course, but she had done Maggie a favor. Male operatives spent much of their time in saloons and barbershops where men gathered and talked. Female detectives had to find other ways to glean information. Since few secrets could be kept from one's dressmaker, Maggie found that the town seamstresses generally knew everyone's business, and most were happy to share it.

Aunt Hetty continued down her list—and what a list it was. Invitations, food, guests, music, decorations... Even in her *sickly* condition, she'd thought of everything.

Maggie hated to put so many people to work for a wedding that would never take place, but she couldn't help but marvel at the woman's efficiency.

"Garrett and I agreed to keep things. . .simple," she said carefully. His aunt meant well, and it made no sense to alienate her.

Aunt Hetty sat back. "But why? It is your first marriage, is it not? So why would you not want to do something special?"

Maggie slid a glass of lemonade across the table. "Under the circumstances, we thought it best. For the children's sake."

"What circumstances?" Aunt Hetty asked, looking baffled.

"Garrett is a widower and—"

Aunt Hetty discounted this with a wave of her hand. "His wife died two years ago, and it does him no good to wallow in the past. Time marches on and so should he."

Maggie took a sip of lemonade. Fortunately, Garrett's aunt talked without prompting, stopping now and again to complain about her back, hip, or knee. She glanced down at her list. "Where was I?"

"You said that his wife didn't like it here."

Aunt Hetty rolled her eyes. "Katherine hated it here, and that's the God-honest truth. She wanted to take the children back East to get a better education, but of course Garrett opposed."

Maggie thought of the paperboy, Linc, and could understand a mother worrying about her children's future.

"How did she and Garrett meet?"

"Actually, they knew each other before the war. Garrett met her while attending school in Philadelphia. My sister—his mother—died when he was six, and he was convinced that had she had proper medical care, she would have lived. So he decided to become a doctor. A real doctor, not just a shingle-on-the-door one like Doc Coldwell." She rolled her eyes. "The man doesn't know a disease from a mule's backside."

Fearing another anatomy lesson, Maggie quickly brought the conversation back to Garrett. "What happened?"

"The war happened, and of course young men his age were conscripted. I offered to give him money to avoid the draft, but Garrett wouldn't hear of it. I was ready to take out a bank loan if necessary or even sell my property." Avoiding the draft involved either paying three hundred dollars or hiring a substitute. "He refused my offer. Said it wasn't fair to the men who couldn't afford the commutation money." She paused before adding, "Then came the Battle of Gettysburg."

"Garrett said he spent time in a rebel prison. Was that when he was captured?"

"Yes, along with Katherine's brother." Aunt Hetty sipped her lemonade. "After the war, Garrett came home to recuperate. He was in pretty bad shape, and I nursed him back to health. Katherine knew him before the war and apparently thought him dead. But when she heard from her brother that he was still alive, she traveled out here to see him. What she found was not the man she knew before the war, but a man with a broken spirit. He'd even given up his dream of becoming a doctor."

Aunt Hetty worked her neck back and forth. "Not that I blame him, of course. He'd seen too much sickness, too many deaths." As an afterthought she added, "At first I think Katherine had reservations about marrying him."

"But she did anyway."

"She probably felt sorry for him, having to spend time in that horrid prison and all."

Maggie took a sip of lemonade. It was hard to believe that a smart, educated woman would marry a man out of pity. It was harder still to think that a man who refused to avoid the draft out of fairness would suddenly board a train, shoot a guard, and take off with seventy thousand dollars.

Maggie set her half-empty glass down. "How did Katherine die?" She already knew the answer—or at least what was in the coroner's report—but it might appear odd if she didn't show curiosity about his first wife.

Aunt Hetty pursed her lips before answering. "The fool woman went outside during a storm. She fell and hit her head."

There was something in the woman's voice that made Maggie wonder if there was more to the story. "What a terrible thing. It must have been very hard for Garrett and the children."

"Yes, it was. And totally unnecessary, if you ask me."

The off-hand comment provided an opening too good to let pass. "How do you mean?"

"The accident occurred in the middle of the night while her husband and children slept. Now I ask you, who in their right mind would wander outside on a stormy night?"

Who, indeed? Maintaining a casual air, Maggie sipped her lemonade, but there was nothing casual about her thoughts. The peculiar circumstances of Katherine Thomas's death had been in the Pinkerton report, but not the time at which it occurred. This new information led to all sorts of questions.

What had possessed her to leave the house on a stormy night? With that thought came another: Was her death really an accident as reported, or was Rikker correct in suspecting something more sinister? And what part, if any, did Garrett play in her death? The possible ramifications sent chills down her spine.

Aunt Hetty had little nice to say about Garrett's first wife and went on at great lengths to say it. She especially disapproved of the woman's extravagant taste in clothes.

"She was one of those. . .what do you call them? Modern women." She sniffled and reached into her drawstring purse for a lace handkerchief. "She had this fancy education and resented letting it go to waste."

Katherine wasn't the only woman who felt that way. Society was changing—especially in large cities. College-educated women now questioned traditional female roles, and even the church had gotten into the debate. To hear some clergy tell it, working women were leading society down a wanton path.

"She even thought women should have the vote." Aunt Hetty shook her head in disgust. "Can you imagine? As if we don't have enough things to worry about."

Maggie clamped her mouth shut. She was a big believer in a woman's right to vote, but she didn't dare voice a dissenting opinion. She needed Aunt Hetty on her side.

Instead, she listened quietly and politely and nodded in agreement whenever Aunt Hetty's rants called for it. But the more the woman carried on, the more Maggie wondered if perhaps Katherine Thomas's death was more than just an unfortunate accident.

"Now, let's see. Where were we?" Aunt Hetty said at last. "Oh yes, your wedding gown."

Chapter 10

Garrett was in good spirits that night at supper and soon had the children roaring with laughter with his antics and riddles.

"Two bodies have I," he said with a twinkle in his eye, "though both joined in one. The stiller I stand, the faster I run."

"I give up," Toby said after several wild guesses ranging from twins to bodies of water.

"An hourglass," Garrett replied.

"Ah, gee," Toby complained, folding his arms across his chest. "Nobody uses hourglasses anymore."

Garrett winked at her. "Okay, how about this one? My nose is long, my back is broad and round, and in cold weather of use I'm found. No load I carry, yet I puff and blow, as much as heavy loaded porters do."

"A big bad wolf," Elise guessed.

"Bellows," Toby said.

"You're right," Garrett said, nodding at his son. Elise's face dropped, and he added, "You're both right."

Maggie laughed. "And I was just about to say the wind. Does that make me right, too?"

"Of course," he said and smiled.

Oddly enough, she'd never enjoyed herself more. This was how she always pictured a real family in her mind. Sharing a meal together. Laughing. She couldn't remember laughing with her own family. They were too busy staying ahead of the law.

Pushing her thoughts aside, she was startled to find that she had almost forgotten her real purpose for being here—and it wasn't to have fun.

∽

Later as she and Garrett finished washing and drying the dishes, she tried to think of how to broach the subject of his locked bedroom.

"Your aunt stopped by today," she said, pulling off her apron.

"You should feel honored. That's the second time this week she left her deathbed, and all because of you."

"I suspect your aunt is just lonely," she said.

Loneliness was something with which she was all too familiar. Her job required her to be constantly on the move, forcing her to live the life of a gypsy. She had no real home, no family. She hadn't seen her brothers since the day her father was hung. Hadn't even looked for them, out of fear that one or more had followed in Papa's footsteps.

Garrett hung the dish towel on a rack to dry. "I suspect my aunt misses my uncle more than she lets on." He leaned against the counter, arms folded. "What brought her here today?"

"She's planning our wedding."

He raised a dark eyebrow. "Do you mind?"

Trying to be tactful, she hesitated. She needed to earn his trust, and criticizing his aunt would likely defeat her purpose.

"I don't mind going for a fitting, but your aunt plans on making a big fuss, and"—she bunched the apron into a ball—"I hoped for something simple." Preparing for a wedding that would never take place would take up too much time.

Garrett studied her. "Believe me, the last thing I want is a big church wedding, but Aunt Hetty means well."

"I know that."

"And I'm her only living relative." He hesitated. "After my parents died, she raised me. I owe her a lot, and I know that planning our wedding would give her a great deal of pleasure. But if you're really against having a big affair, I'll talk to her."

She felt trapped. If she insisted on having her own way she would look childish—maybe even selfish. But if she granted his request, she would be putting a lot of people to work for nothing. Still, she was paid to do a job, and her allegiance was to the company paying her wages. That meant doing whatever was necessary—even if it meant planning a fake wedding—to get the job done.

"Very well," she said. "We'll do it your aunt's way."

His crooked grin was as engaging as it was disturbing, and she struggled not to fall under his spell.

"Then it's settled," he said.

It was far from settled, but she nodded mutely and, encouraged by his smile, decided to raise the subject of his bedroom. "I measured some of the windows for new curtains." The sun had faded the gingham curtains almost white. "I hope you don't mind."

"This is your home now."

The word *home* sliced through her like a knife. She never really had a home. Not a real one. For the first twelve years of her life, her family had been on the run. They traveled from town to town, state to state. Sometimes they shacked up in a deserted cabin and once even lived in a cave.

After her father's death on the gallows, her mother couldn't keep the family together any longer. Maggie spent her teen years in a cold, drafty, and regimented orphan asylum, run by a head mistress determined to pound the three Rs into her charges' heads. She wasn't unkind, just strict and had no patience with anyone who slacked off. Fortunately, the woman also taught her how to sew, though she never attempted to make anything so complicated as a dress or shirtwaist.

"Do you have a sewing machine?" she asked.

He nodded. "Yes. In the attic. I'll fetch it down for you."

"Thank you."

"You aren't going to hang lace curtains, are you?" he asked.

"Certainly not," she said, with unfeigned indignation. "That's like hanging one's undergarments in the windows for all the world to see."

No sooner were the words out of her mouth than she grimaced. Now why did she have to mention something so personal in his presence?

His gaze slid down the length of her, and his mouth softened. "We wouldn't want to do that." Something intense flared in his eyes. "Hang undergarments in the windows, that is."

Face blazing, she cleared her throat. The air between them suddenly seemed thick with double meanings, but she refused to be deterred.

"I would like to measure the windows in your bedroom." Her voice wavered even as she struggled for control. "If. . .if that's all right."

"Yes, of course. It'll soon be your. . ." He corrected himself. "*Our* bedroom. Do you want to measure the windows now? I'll help you."

Since she had no intention of marrying him, it never occurred to her to think of his room as theirs. Having him help her measure for undergar. . .uh. . .curtains was the last thing she wanted.

"Th–that's all right," she stammered. "I need to see that the children have finished their schoolwork. Tomorrow will be soon enough." Tomorrow when everyone was gone, including him.

"I'll leave the door unlocked. Like I said, it will soon be our room."

He watched her closely as he spoke. The smooth, rich timbre of his voice was both soothing and disconcerting. She felt guilty for her deceit, and that was odd. Working undercover had never bothered her before. But neither had children been involved, and for some reason that made her feel worse.

Folding the now wrinkled apron, she managed to squeak out a thank you. She left the apron on the counter and backed toward the open doorway.

"I—I better go and check on Elise and Toby." They'd been playing outside and both could use a bath.

"Would you mind taking them to school in the morning? I have an early delivery to make."

Grateful for the change of subject, she nodded. "I'd be happy to."

His mouth curved. "Much obliged. I'll hitch the horse to the wagon before I leave."

"That. . .would be most helpful." She turned and fled down the hall. Gaining access to his room had been easier than she expected, and she breathed a sigh of relief.

Dashing into the children's room, she turned to find two pairs of eyes watching her.

Chapter 11

When Maggie awoke the following morning, Elise's bed was empty. She quickly attended to her ablutions, dressed, and wound her braided hair into a coronet at the back of her head. Thus braced, she stepped into the hall.

The door to Garrett's room stood ajar. She hesitated briefly but didn't dare search it until everyone had left for the day.

She followed the smell of coffee to the kitchen where she found Toby at the table by himself, an empty plate pushed aside.

"Good morning," she said, ruffling his hair. Today his thinking cap was missing, and he was busy sketching with a charcoal pencil.

"Where's your father and sister?"

"Pa left for work and Elise is out back in the tree house," he said without looking up from his sketch.

She poured herself a cup of coffee from the metal pot on the stove. "You have a tree house?"

"Uh-huh."

"How is it possible to have a tree house without a tree?" She'd yet to see a tree since coming to the Territory. If she ever spotted one in this arid land, she'd be tempted to hug it.

"You don't need a tree to build a tree house," he assured her.

"Is that so?" Both children lived in a make-believe world; no doubt that was how they dealt with their mother's death. She wouldn't have survived her own childhood without flights of imagination. She'd even made up an elaborate fantasy about her father and pretended he was a hero instead of an outlaw. That particular fantasy ended the day he hung from the gallows.

Shuddering at the memory, she inhaled the brew's rich aroma before taking a sip. It was just as she liked it: neither too strong nor too weak. "May I visit your tree house?"

Toby looked up from his drawing. "We only let special people inside."

The back door flew open and Elise ran into the kitchen, her round cheeks as shiny as two red apples. The little white dog padded in behind her.

Maggie knelt down to pet the animal. He was all wagging tail and licking tongue.

"Have you had breakfast?"

Elise nodded. She glanced at her brother as if sharing a secret. Or perhaps she thought she was in some sort of trouble. "And Whitewash and Patches had breakfast, too. I fed them while Toby milked the cow."

"Whitewash. Is that your dog's name?"

Elise nodded. "Uh-huh."

"And who is Patches?"

"Patches is our horse. Pa's horse is named Brownie."

"Let's see if I have them right. Whitewash, Patches, and Brownie. Any other names I should know?"

"The cow's name is Milk Can, but the chickens don't have names."

"What? No names? Well, we'll have to come up with some. Meanwhile, we need to fix your hair. We don't want to be late for school."

Elise raced to the bedroom, and Maggie followed. She reached for the silver-handled hairbrush on top of the bureau. Elise's hair was long, almost to her waist, and had a natural curl.

"Your brother was telling me about your tree house," she said as she worked the bristles through Elise's long locks.

"Shh. We don't want the boogeyman to hear."

Playing along, Maggie lowered her voice to a whisper. "Absolutely not." She glanced out the window, pretending to look for lurkers. "The coast is clear," she said and proceeded to brush Elise's thick hair. "So I think it's okay to talk. I always wanted a tree house."

Elise's watched her in the mirror. "You did?"

"Yes, indeed."

"Ouch!" Elise cried out, grabbing the side of her head.

"Sorry." Maggie worked the knot gently out of the child's tresses and quickly weaved the hair into two braids. She then tied both with a blue ribbon. "There, all done."

She held up a hand mirror so Elise could see the back of her head. She really was a pretty child, though far too serious for such a young age.

Elise looked pleased by her reflection. "Papa doesn't know how to make braids. He makes them all crooked."

Maggie tapped Elise's pert nose with her finger. It was hard to believe that a man who could bend metal into the most amazing shapes was stymied by a little girl's hair.

"Don't tell anyone, but I think that it's a job for a woman."

Elise giggled. The child seemed to thrive on secrets.

"Get your books. We don't want to be late." Maggie was anxious to take the children to school so she could have the house to herself. It was time to do some real detective work.

∽

Maggie dropped the children off and drove straight home. A mule-driven wagon was parked in front.

Curious, she walked around the back of the house and was greeted by Whitewash. She petted the dog. "Down, boy."

Sidestepping a mound of dirt where the dog had been digging, she moved to the porch. A small Chinese woman was bent over a metal tub scrubbing a pair of Toby's trousers on a washboard.

"You must be Lila. I'm Maggie Taylor."

Lila straightened and nodded. She wore a blue tunic with contrasting borders and loose sleeves. Her shiny black hair was parted in the middle and her bun anchored with what looked like knitting needles.

"Very pleased to meet you," she said in a singsong voice. It was hard to know how old she was, but Maggie guessed her early twenties.

"I'm pleased to meet you, too," Maggie said, her detective mind at work. Perhaps the woman could shed some light on Katherine's mysterious death. "How long have you worked for Mr. Thomas?"

Lila nodded her head again. "Thank you, good-bye."

Maggie tried again, enunciating each word with care. It soon became clear that the girl spoke very little English and had memorized only a few polite phrases.

"I'll let you get back to the wash," Maggie said.

"Very pleased to meet you."

With a smile and a nod, Maggie entered the house through the back door, anxious to get to work.

She made certain the front door was locked before attempting to search the bedroom. She didn't want anyone walking in unannounced. Several chessmen were scattered on the floor, and she stooped to pick them up.

Odd. The pieces weren't on the floor when she left to take Elise and Toby to school. She glanced toward the kitchen. Had Lila knocked them over? The dirty laundry had been placed in a basket and put on the porch next to the washtub. Far as she knew, the laundress had no reason to enter the house. Still, the chess pieces didn't fall by themselves. Someone had entered the house in her absence—if not Lila, then someone else.

But who? And why?

∞

Garrett's bedroom was larger than the children's. A double bed occupied one wall; a wardrobe, small desk, dry sink, and ladder-back chair another. The room lacked anything of a personal nature. No pictures on the wall. No daguerreotypes of his deceased wife and mother of his children.

Had Garrett removed reminders of his first marriage knowing she planned to enter the room? It was a possibility. It would also explain why the room had been locked. Maybe he didn't want her seeing signs of his first wife.

She stepped over the bedroll on the floor that made up Toby's bed and opened both wardrobe doors. The scent of bay rum hair tonic, moth balls, and old oak greeted her. On one side Garrett's clothes hung from wooden pegs. The second half contained four drawers, and these she opened one by one. The drawers stored socks, handkerchiefs, and neatly folded shirts but, again, nothing of interest.

She closed the wardrobe doors. Hands at her waist, she glanced around the room and then moved toward the desk. A chessboard dominated the desktop, and the arrangement of the pieces suggested a game in progress.

Careful not to disturb the board, she sat at the desk. The top drawers held stationery and writing supplies. Much to her surprise, she found her letters to him tied with a piece of rawhide and stacked in the back of a drawer. Fiction, all of them, the contents spun as cleverly as a spiderweb.

After putting a shadow on Garrett Thomas, Allan Pinkerton learned the suspect had placed an ad for a mail-order bride and approached Maggie with a daring plan.

At first Maggie thought the idea foolhardy. The chances of Garrett choosing her out of dozens and perhaps even hundreds of women looking for a husband seemed remote. But Allan was convinced that he knew enough about Garrett Thomas to make the plan work, and he was right.

Under Allan's tutorage, she answered the ad, and much to their delight, Garrett wrote back. So began a six-month correspondence. He wrote about the children, the weather, and the town, but little about himself. Her letters to him were equally impersonal. She didn't want to chance forgetting what she'd written and later say something that would contradict the letters.

Garrett finally asked her to come to the Arizona Territory so they could meet in person and allow his children to get to know her. He even sent her money for travel expenses. All expenses incurred from the investigation were paid by the railroad and bank, but Allan thought it might look odd if she didn't accept his monetary offer, and so she did.

Seeing how her letters had been so carefully saved filled her with guilt. Lying was a necessary part of her disguise, and she was only doing her job. Surely God made allowances for those working undercover for law and order.

The second drawer revealed something of much more interest: a leather notebook.

She pulled the notebook out. Turning to the first page, she quickly scanned the bold masculine handwriting that was all too familiar. Was this what he did at night after locking himself in his room? Write?

She sat back and began reading. At first she thought it was a novel, but it soon became clear that this was no made-up story. Garrett had written about the year spent at the Andersonville Rebel Prison. It was a story of survival, courage, and quiet desperation. He wrote about the lack of sanitary conditions and food. About disease and death. Escape and capture. Not only was Garrett a gifted tinker but also a gifted writer.

He wrote about successfully nursing a soldier—a boy, really—through an illness. Tears rolled down her cheeks as she read the rest:

> *The boy was shot by a guard for simply reaching beyond the swamp that ran through camp for fresh water. As long as I live I shall never forget this day or that boy who died too young.*

Her breath caught in her chest upon reading the next sentence.

> *I knew only the boy's first name—Toby.*

So Garrett had named his son after a boy soldier who died in that awful prison.

It was well after noon by the time she finished reading the manuscript, and his harrowing tale left her emotionally drained.

Garrett Thomas had no record of criminal activity prior to the war, and that was unusual. Almost every serious criminal she'd known had a history of unlawful activities, many starting in early childhood.

But after reading Thomas's diary, she could well understand how even the most virtuous of men could change. That's what war did to people. It changed habits and beliefs and turned good and evil upside down. The warrior mind-set could remain long after the battle cries faded away. After killing on the battlefield, robbing a train or even a bank might seem mild in comparison. Perhaps that explained why every war was followed by a crime wave. This was as true for the Napoleonic Wars as it was for the War between the States.

Many veterans returning from that awful war were said to have a Soldier's Heart—a poetic name that failed to describe the sometimes horrific changes that made these men strangers even to their own families.

Did Garrett have a Soldier's Heart? His war journal suggested he might. If that was true, had the emotional scars cut so deep as to blacken his soul?

Allan Pinkerton was so convinced of it he had even written as much in Garrett's file. Not only was the Scotsman a good detective, he was also an expert on the criminal mind. He blamed the war for producing criminals such as the James, Reno, and Farrington brothers.

He'd traced the prevalence of "holdup" thieves all the way back to the gold mining camps. Prospectors too lazy to work robbed the more successful miners. When the mines closed, these same thieves graduated to stages and eventually trains. He'd also traced cattle rustling back to early cowboys who grew tired of riding the range for low wages.

Garrett's journal and Allan's teachings were very much on her mind as she wrote a detailed report back to headquarters.

Chapter 12

After picking the children up from school, she drove to Mrs. Button's dressmaking shop on the corner of Main and Jefferson.

Mrs. Button was a pleasant, middle-aged woman with a body as round and plump as a pincushion. Dressed in a floral dress with a frilly white cap atop her white head, she greeted each child with a buttery smile and a handful of penny candy.

The small, cramped shop was as colorful as a patchwork quilt. Fabric and sewing notions were scattered across a table next to a treadle sewing machine. Gowns, skirts, and petticoats hung from wall pegs or were fitted on wooden forms in various stages of completion.

Mrs. Button released the children and peered at Maggie over her wire-framed spectacles. "You must be the lucky bride-to-be. Maggie, right?"

"Yes, that's right. I hope this is a good time."

"Couldn't be better." The dressmaker rubbed her hands together. "Hetty also ordered outfits for the children to wear at the wedding, so I'll need to measure them, too." She regarded each child in turn. "Who wants to go first?"

Elise raised her hand. "I do."

"Come on along then. Step on my magic stool."

Elise's face lit up at the word *magic*, and she giggled. Mrs. Button helped her onto the stool and circled her small waist with a cloth measuring tape. Elise watched with wide-eyed curiosity as the dressmaker wrote the measurements in a notebook.

Toby had no interest in new clothes and practically had to be pulled away physically from the marmalade cat perched in front of the sunny window. While standing on the stool, he squirmed and wiggled so much he fell off twice.

After duly recording all necessary measurements, including Maggie's, the seamstress showed them a wedding dress she had just completed for the butcher's daughter. The white silk gown had an intricately embroidered bodice, and the sleeves and neckline were edged with lace. A soft paneled train fell from a large satin bow set below the bustle in back.

Elise stared at the gown with shiny bright eyes. "Are you going to wear a dress like this, Miss Taylor?"

"Not quite as fancy," Maggie said. Even under different circumstances she couldn't imagine wearing anything so elaborate or confining. "And I don't wish to have a train."

Mrs. Button nodded. "This would be too much for your dainty figure, but I think we can find something that will wipe the worried look off your face."

"I'm not worried," Maggie said, irritated at herself for not staying in character and playing the part of a happy bride. In the past, she'd had no trouble playing the roles required by her job. "I'm just not used to making such a fuss over clothes." At least that part was true.

Once she had even managed to manufacture real tears while pretending to be a grieving widow. But a mail-order bride was the hardest role yet, especially now, after reading Garrett's story. How could she not feel sorry for what he'd experienced?

Still, an innocent man had died during the Whistle-Stop holdup, and his family deserved to see justice. Nothing Garret Thomas had gone through justified the taking of a life.

Elise's giggles snapped her out of her reverie. "Can I have a caboose on my dress?"

Mrs. Button laughed. "We're not talking about *that* kind of train. It's what we call a long piece of fabric attached to the back, like this."

She held out the fabric panel. "You're too young for a train, but you can have all the ruffles you want."

Satisfied with the answer, Elise skipped across the room to join her brother at the window.

Mrs. Button pulled a bolt of white satin from a shelf. "So when is the big day?"

"June fifteenth," Maggie replied.

"Oh my. That doesn't give me much time, does it?"

"We could change the wedding to a later date, if you like," Maggie said. *Like maybe a year from next Tuesday.* But even a week or two would give her more time to conduct her investigation. She was beginning to think it might take longer than planned.

Mrs. Button immediately discounted the idea with a wave of her hand. "I wouldn't think of asking you to postpone your wedding." She lowered her voice. "Having a case of cold feet, are we?"

Maggie shook her head. "No, it's just. . .there's so much to do."

The dressmaker patted her on the arm much like a mother might comfort a child. "God always provides enough time to get the important things done. And Hetty will help all she can, even with her health problems. I know her nephew's wedding will make her very happy."

It was just the opening Maggie had hoped for. "Did you know his first wife?"

"Everyone knew Katherine." The seamstress shook her head until her neatly stacked chins wobbled. "It was a terrible thing. A woman that young and beautiful. . ."

"Aunt Hetty said it happened while the family was asleep."

Mrs. Button pushed her glasses up her nose. "That's the oddest thing. No one could figure out what she was doing outside on such a stormy night." She lowered her voice. "Don't pay any attention to what some are saying, because none of it is true."

Maggie ran her hand casually across a bolt of blue velvet. "What exactly is everyone saying?"

Mrs. Button glanced at the children still playing with the cat before answering. "Just before her death, Garrett and Katherine were heard arguing. Right there in his shop."

"Do you know what they argued about?" Maggie asked.

"No, but I've known him since he was a wee lad, and he wasn't the same after the war. He was much more serious, if you know what I mean. Hardly ever smiled."

No surprises there. After reading the horrors in Garrett's notebook, Maggie could well understand why. "He smiles now," she said. Time healed some wounds, but not all.

"Not like he used to as a young lad. As for Katherine, she never really fit in, if you know what I mean. She never liked it here. Said it was too hot and uncivilized."

"Is that what they argued about?"

"I'm not really sure what their last argument was about, but some think she was seeing someone else."

Maggie frowned. "You mean like another man?"

Mrs. Button nodded. "I never believed it, of course. On the other hand, it would explain what she was doing out in the middle of the night, wouldn't it?"

Maggie had considered every possible explanation she could think of for Katherine going out during a storm—but a romantic rendezvous? That one never entered her head. If the rumors were true, the question was, did Garrett know?

He did seem rather protective of her the day she visited his shop. Did that mean he had a jealous streak? Jealousy as a motive for murder dated back to Cain and Abel and caused half of all domestic crimes on Pinkerton files, so the idea wasn't all that far-fetched.

The bells on the door announced the arrival of another client; a young mother with an infant in her arms needed a dress tailored to fit her new shape.

"I won't take up any more of your time." Maggie thanked Mrs. Button and motioned to the children. "Come along."

No sooner had Maggie and the children left the shop when they encountered a barefooted man in ragged trousers and dirty shirt sitting on the boardwalk. He sat with his back against the building, his face half hidden by a salt-and-pepper beard. Long, unkempt hair fell from beneath a brown slouch cap.

"Can you afford a pittance, miss?"

She recognized the voice at once. Rikker!

The man never failed to amaze her. Successful disguises involved far more than just appearances. They required the right attitude and demeanor, and Rikker had perfected both to a fine art. She reached into her purse for a coin and leaned over to hand it to him.

"What happened to the quack doctor ruse?" she whispered.

"That's my morning job," he whispered back. "Your fiancé mails a letter every other day or so on the way to work. Find out who he's writing to." Louder, he said, "Thank you, ma'am, and may God bless you and your young'uns."

A man with a cane tossed a coin in Rikker's hat as he walked by. Rikker pocketed the money and winked. He was obviously enjoying himself. With a fond smile, she hustled the children away.

"How come you gave that man money?" Elise asked after settling on the front seat of the buckboard.

" 'Cause he's a beggar," Toby said, climbing in back.

Elise peered up at Maggie from beneath the brim of her sunbonnet. "What's a beggar?"

"A begger is a person who has fallen on hard times. And the reason I gave him money is because God wants us to help those in need."

Elise thought about this for a moment before asking, "Why doesn't God help them Himself?"

Maggie grabbed the reins and released the brake. "Because God doesn't want to keep the fun of helping others all to Himself."

Chapter 13

The following morning, Maggie stopped at Grover's Mercantile and purchased several yards of pretty floral calico. Since she'd made an issue about measuring windows, Garrett might think it strange if he didn't see new curtains in the works.

She then hurried home, intent on tackling the attic. Garrett's house was unusual for it was one of the few houses in the area with a second floor.

The attic had a single window for ventilation. The thick cover of fine sand told her that no one had been in the attic for months, maybe even years. The chances of finding the missing money up there seemed remote.

Still, she did a thorough search. All she found was a treadle sewing machine and a couple of old trunks filled with women's clothing. Katherine's, no doubt.

Maggie had never paid much attention to fashion, but it was hard not to be impressed with the quality of the gowns and hats. Most of the outfits were dated, favoring the straight sheaths and draped skirts of the seventies, but all were well tailored.

She was so intrigued with the colorful finery that she almost missed the envelope at the bottom of one of the trunks. It was addressed to Katherine's brother but wasn't stamped. It looked like the letter had never been mailed.

She broke the seal, pulled the single sheet out of the envelope, and unfolded it. Written in an ornate script, it read:

Dear Charlie,

The matter we discussed has given me grave concerns. Mama and Papa would turn over in their graves if they knew. I will not be a party to this. You have a week to take care of it, or I will.

The letter was signed simply *Katherine.*

Maggie folded the paper and slipped it back into the envelope. Take care of what? The letter was undated so there was no way of knowing when it was written.

She put the envelope back into the trunk and slammed the lid shut. Careful to smooth out any traces of foot or handprints, she returned to the first floor.

⌒⌒

Two days later, Garrett joined her in the kitchen while she prepared the children's breakfast. She hid her frustration at not finding any condemning evidence in the house beneath a bright smile.

"Morning," he said cheerfully. He ruffled his son's hair and tweaked his daughter's cheek before taking a seat at the table. Toby was laboring over a drawing and didn't look up.

"Morning," she said. Now, as always, his presence struck a chord in her that was hard to ignore. Why he affected her so, she had no idea. She only knew he did.

"I set the sewing machine up in the parlor for you," he said.

"Thank you," she said, filling his cup with coffee. Confound it! Now she would have to make those blasted curtains.

A stamped envelope stuck out of his vest pocket, but she couldn't read the address. She spilled the coffee, and he jumped back.

"I'm sorry." She quickly set the pot back on the stove and reached for a towel.

Their hands touched as he took the towel from her. The brief contact, along with his clean manly scent, sent warm shivers rippling through her, and her mind whirled in confusion.

"You okay?" he asked.

Chiding herself for being so careless, she blinked and forced a smile. Every movement, every word, every facial expression had to be carefully guarded so as not to give him cause for suspicion. Whatever hold he had over her must stop.

"I'm fine. Just clumsy." She wiped her hands on her apron. "You're not working today?"

He tossed the damp towel onto the counter and took his seat. "I open late on Saturdays."

"Oh." She couldn't believe it was already the weekend. Never had she known time to fly by so quickly.

He dropped two sugar cubes into his coffee and stirred. "What's that you're working on, son?"

Toby lifted his pencil off the paper. "It's a slingshot. It'll be two miles high and three miles wide."

"A slingshot, eh? Why so large?"

"It's gonna send a man to the moon."

"Can I go to the moon, Toby?" Elise asked.

"Nah, you're a girl," Toby said. "Girls can't do anything."

"If a boy can go to the moon, then so can a girl," Maggie said.

Elise spit her tongue out at her brother. "So there!"

The corners of Garrett's mouth quirked up. "We're going to have to watch our step, son. It's now two against two." He sipped his coffee before adding another lump of sugar. "So what are you three doing today?"

The moon forgotten, Elise brightened. "Let's go on a picnic, Miss Taylor. Pleeeeease."

Going on a picnic was the last thing Maggie wanted to do. As much as she enjoyed the children, caring for them meant less time spent investigating, and that was a downright nuisance.

Garrett watched her over the brim of his coffee cup. "A picnic sounds like a grand idea, don't you think?"

"Yes, doesn't it?" Maggie turned toward the stove and poured batter onto the hot skillet. "Too bad you can't join us."

"Maybe I can."

She glanced over her shoulder and met his gaze. For some reason, she suddenly had trouble breathing.

"I think Panhandle can manage the shop for an hour or two," he said. "Pick me up at noon."

Elise squealed with delight as she wrapped her arms around her father. The child never failed to bring a smile to his face, and today was no different.

Turning back to the stove, Maggie scooted the spatula under a flapjack and flipped it over. It was strange the way his relationship with his children made her own loss seem so poignant.

As a child she'd prayed her father would change his outlaw ways, but he never did. He didn't even acknowledge her on the day he hung from the gallows. As they lowered the rope around his neck she yelled, *"I love you."* She wanted so much to hear those same words from him, but they never came. Instead, he cursed her in that hateful way that he cursed everyone—even God.

Putting criminals away helped to alleviate her shame, but that was before she met Garrett Thomas. Now the thought of taking him away from the children who adored him nearly broke her heart.

Garrett sent Toby and Elise out of the room and joined her at the stove. "Smells good," he said.

Obviously he had something on his mind, and her mouth went dry. Had she misspoken or made him suspicious?

Forcing an outer calm, she asked, "Would you like me to mail that letter for you?" She'd searched but failed to find an address book anywhere in the house.

"No need," he said, patting his pocket. "I'll drop it at the post office on the way to the shop." He hesitated. "As you know, my former brother-in-law is back in town." He paused, and she relaxed. Her secret identity was still safe.

He cleared his throat before continuing. "He might try to see Toby and Elise, and it's imperative that he stays away from them."

Her eyes widened in alarm. "Are you saying he means them harm?"

"No, nothing like that. It's just. . .he blames me for Katherine's death, and I don't want him planting ideas in the children's heads."

She frowned. "Why does he blame you?"

"He doesn't believe her death was an accident," he said, his voice harsh.

"Why would he think such a thing?"

"Probably because it's true."

Surprised by his unexpected admission, she stared up at him. Most confessions came after a skillful interrogation by an investigator, but this one fell in her lap. Still, it was only a small breakthrough; it was her job to elicit the rest.

"What happened that night?" she asked. Her voice, the way she looked at him, her very stance was adapted to invite his trust.

Before he could answer, black smoke spiraled up from the stove.

"Oh no!" Removing the skillet from the flame she dumped it into the sink. The flapjacks were burned to a crisp. Worse, their conversation had been interrupted at a most inopportune time.

Garrett flung the windows open, and Maggie wielded a towel to clear the air until only a thin haze of blue smoke remained.

"I'm sorry," she said, hoping to reestablish their earlier rapport. She reached for the bowl of batter.

He stayed her hand with his own, and she felt her pulse thud. "Don't worry about it," he said, removing his hand. "I'll get something to eat in town."

She turned to ask him not to go, but he'd already left.

Slamming the bowl down, she glared at the soggy mess in the sink.

∞

Maggie drove the buckboard through town, reaching Garrett's shop twenty minutes before the prescribed time.

The children climbed out of the wagon, whispering among themselves.

"What are you two pumpkins up to?" Maggie asked.

Toby gestured to his sister. "Ask her."

"Ask me what?"

"Can we go to Mrs. Button's shop?" Elise glanced at her brother. "She always gives us penny candy."

"All right. But don't be long."

The two children ran along the boardwalk toward the dressmaker's shop.

Shaking her head fondly, she glanced up and down the street. Rikker was nowhere in sight, though his bright-colored medicine wagon was still parked near the hotel.

Toby and Elise returned smelling of peppermint just as Panhandle and Garrett walked out of the shop together.

Panhandle regarded Toby. Even though it was a warm day he still wore his funny cap, the rawhide ties hanging loose. "Hello, Aloysius Pepperpot," he said and turned to Elise. "And you, young lady, must be Penelope Peachpit."

Elise giggled. "I told you my name is Elise." Apparently this was a standing joke between them. "And that's Toby."

"Ah, Toby. How could I forget?" Panhandle said, looking straight at Maggie. "Nice to see you again, Miss Taylor."

"Nice seeing you, too," Maggie said. She slid over and, taking the hint, Garrett heaved himself up to the driver's seat.

"I shouldn't be any longer than a couple of hours," he said, taking hold of the reins.

"Take as long as you want." Panhandle backed away from the buckboard.

"Gid-up!" Garrett called, and the rig rolled forward.

Maggie eyed Garrett's profile, their interrupted conversation very much on her mind. What did he mean when he said Katherine's death wasn't an accident?

"How come Mr. Panhandle always wears that funny hat?" Elise asked from the backseat.

"He doesn't want anyone to know he's bald," Toby said.

"When I'm bald I'm not wearing a hat like that," Elise said.

"Girls don't get bald, silly," Toby said, his tone edged with brotherly exasperation.

"Are you going to be bald, Papa?" Elise asked.

"Maybe." Garrett said, his eyes warm with humor. "You know what they say? Hair today, gone tomorrow."

Maggie laughed. She couldn't help it. At that moment it was difficult to believe him guilty of anything but an all-too-intriguing smile—and some very bad jokes.

⚭

It didn't seem possible to find water in that dry desert land, but after an hour's drive Garrett pointed to a river that cut through an outcrop of red rock and wound its way between two ribbons of sand.

Overhead the sky was azure blue and the air crystal clear.

"That's the Gila River," Garrett said. "Flows all the way to the Colorado." He pulled on Patches's reins and set the brake. "Caught me a four-pound squawfish awhile back. Tasted almost as good as salmon."

He looked relaxed, and Maggie was hopeful that they could pick up their earlier conversation.

Toby and Elise jumped out of the wagon with whoops and hollers. Leaving their shoes and stockings scattered on the sand, they ran toward the water's edge.

"Watch for snakes," she called after them.

Garrett lifted the picnic basket from the back of the wagon, and she reached for the blanket.

"You're beginning to sound like their mother," he said.

Not sure how to take his comment, she quickly apologized. "I'm sorry. I don't want you to think I'm trying to take Katherine's place." Though she had to admit the thought of being a wife and mother held a surprising appeal. A foolish notion at best. She'd seen too many broken families to think that domestic bliss was possible, given her profession.

"I meant it as a compliment," he said. "The mother part I mean."

She drew in her breath. "Oh. I thought—"

"Papa! Hurry!"

He waved at Elise. "Coming." He waited for Maggie to spread the blanket on the sand in a spot of shade cast by a boulder. After setting the basket down, he pulled off his boots and rolled up his trouser legs. Growling like a bear, he dashed after the children.

Elise and Toby screamed at the top of their lungs with feigned terror and splashed him with water.

Maggie gathered the children's shoes and stockings and arranged them neatly next to Garrett's boots. Watching the three of them romp in the water, laughing together, filled her with mixed feelings. Never had she seen a man enjoy his children more than Garrett.

Their early morning conversation streamed through her head for perhaps the hundredth time. *He doesn't believe her death was an accident.*

If not an accident, what did his brother-in-law think it was?

Garrett was thoroughly soaked by the time he joined her. She tossed him a towel, and he wiped himself dry and plopped down on the blanket next to her.

"I'm famished."

"I'm sorry I burned your breakfast," she said, hoping he would take the hint and finish where he'd left off that morning before they were so rudely interrupted.

He wiped his face dry and draped the towel around his neck. His mussed hair gave him a boyish look that did nothing for her peace of mind.

"No need to apologize. It was my fault," he said.

She waited for him to continue. When he didn't, she reached for the picnic basket and pulled out slices of roast beef left over from last night's supper.

It probably wasn't wise to wheedle a confession from him there, in the middle of nowhere. Anything could happen, and the last thing she wanted was to pull out her gun, especially with the children present. Still, a detective had to make the best of every opportunity, no matter how small.

As if to fill the gap between them, she spread plates of cheese, bread, and wild strawberries across the blanket. She then poured lemonade into two tin cups.

He picked up a fork and stabbed a slice of roast beef.

The roast beef had been cooked exactly as he liked it, with just a hint of pink in the center. Thank God for Mrs. Crowen and her *American Lady's Cookery Book*.

The little ways Maggie had come to know him struck her as odd. Not since leaving the orphanage had she known another person's likes and dislikes to such an extent.

She knew Garrett preferred his eggs over easy, his bacon burned to a crisp, and his coffee hot and strong. His preferences came to mind so easily she was momentarily struck by surprise.

That's not all she knew. He liked two lumps of sugar in his coffee—and on some days even more—and salted his food as freely as a farmer scattered seed. He had trouble sleeping and often paced the floor between one and three in the morning. In little less than a week, his habits were almost second nature to her.

What she didn't know was how to reconcile this loving parent and talented craftsman with the outlaw written up in the Pinkerton report.

As if sensing her gaze on him, he looked up and frowned. "I guess you're wondering about this morning."

That was putting it mildly. "You can't drop a cannonball like that and expect me not to wonder."

"I apologize." He stabbed another piece of meat. "I don't know why Katherine left the house that night."

She studied his profile. "You said it was your fault."

A look of resignation crossed his face. "Earlier that day we'd argued. Katherine never liked Arizona. That night she told me she was going back to Philadelphia with or without me and taking the children with her. That would have meant giving up my business and starting over. It also meant leaving Aunt Hetty here without family to watch over her. I didn't want to do that, and I told Katherine as much. We argued, and she slept in the parlor."

His voice grew hoarse. "Had she been in our bed that night, things might have turned out different."

"You mean she might not have gone outside?"

His face was fraught with pain. "That's exactly what I mean."

"But why did she? Your aunt said there was a storm." Supposedly it wasn't a night for man or beast. It didn't seem likely that she'd leave the house in such weather to meet someone, even a lover.

"I don't know why. I've gone over that night a million times, and I still can't come up with an answer that makes sense."

He sounded sincere, and she believed him. He might be a thief and murderer, but he was also a grieving husband, and that's the man she reached out to comfort. She laid her hand on his arm, and he covered it with his own.

"I'm so sorry," she said softly. "I didn't mean to bring it all back."

"You have a right to know what happened that night." He squeezed her hand. "I wish I knew myself." His gaze traveled to the distant horizon as if looking back in time.

"There was another reason I didn't want to leave Arizona. A selfish reason. I spent a brutally cold winter in Andersonville, and hundreds of men froze to death." His jaw tightened, and she heard his intake of breath. "I never wanted to see another winter like that. Never again wanted to know that kind of cold." He gave her a sheepish look. "Like I said. Selfish."

"I don't think it's selfish at all." She shuddered at the thought of men freezing to death. No war could justify such inhumanity. "Did Katherine know how you felt about the cold?"

He shook his head. "She never liked me to talk about the war."

The silence that followed was broken by Elise's excited voice. "Miss Taylor. Over here!"

Maggie drew her hand away from his arm and waved. "I'll be right there," she called back. She turned to Garrett. "Anything else I should know?" she asked. *Like what you did with all that money?*

"Only that you better watch your step." Just like that the darkness left his face, and he grinned like a schoolboy. "Toby and Elise are about to get you wet."

hapter 14

Already it was hot that Sunday morning as she pulled the buckboard behind the long row of wagons parked near the Furnace Creek Community Church.

Despite his negative opinion of organized religion, Garrett didn't object to her taking the children to Sunday worship, but neither did he offer to join them.

Elise, as usual, was full of questions. "If God is everywhere, why do we have to come to church?"

"It's easier for God to keep track of us if we're all together," Toby said.

Maggie smiled. It seemed the boy had an answer for everything. "Worshipping with others also helps us grow stronger in our faith. Just like spending time together makes a family strong." That last thought caught her off-balance. Since when had she become an expert on families?

She set the brake and straightened her hat. "Come along, children."

Church bells began to ring and a raven flew out of the bell tower, squawking in protest. With a child on either side, she walked up the graveled path to the carved wooden doors. People greeted them warmly as they threaded their way down the center aisle to the empty pew in the middle row. Sun streamed through the stained glass windows, bathing the giant cross in front with bright rays of light.

The church was packed and only a few empty pews remained. Mrs. Higginbottom and her friends waved from across the aisle, and Maggie acknowledged them with a smile.

"There's Aunty," Elise said, pointing to a front pew occupied by Aunt Hetty and several other women.

"Shh. You can talk to her after the service."

No sooner had they settled into their seats than the choir director turned to the congregation. "Please stand and turn to page one fifty."

Maggie reached for the hymnal and flipped through until she found the right page. Standing, she held the book so the children could follow along. The organ ground out a few mournful chords, and the choir director turned to the choral group, arms raised. Right on cue, voices lifted in song.

"Rock of Ages, cleft for me. Let me hide myself in thee..."

For once Toby stood perfectly still. He seemed mesmerized by the choir and never took his eyes away from the altar. Today he looked more like his father than ever. For once his shirt was tucked into his waistband. His hair fell neatly from a side part, except for the cowlick that resisted all efforts to tame it.

Elise coughed, and Maggie reached into her drawstring purse for a piece of hard candy. Elise woke her up coughing last night, but she seemed perfectly all right this morning.

"Here, suck on this."

The last chords echoed away and the congregation was told to sit.

Reverend Holly took his place behind the pulpit. Today he was dressed in a black robe that afforded him a commanding presence that his short stature otherwise failed to provide.

"Let us pray."

The reverend didn't lack for words. On and on he went, asking for God's help with every possible affliction known to humankind—or at least known to Aunt Hetty.

Elise tugged on her arm and whispered something. "Shh," Maggie hushed. "Tell me later."

"Amen," the minister said at last, and a collective sigh rippled through the sanctuary.

The moment Maggie opened her eyes she noticed the empty pew next to Elise. "Where's your brother?" she whispered.

"I don't know." Elise looked up with a worried frown. "That's what I was trying to tell you."

Maggie gave her a loving pat on the leg. "Don't worry. I'm sure he'll return any minute." Despite her confident tone, she shot an anxious glance to the back of the church, craning her neck to see around the tall feathered hats blocking her view. The doors were closed and an usher stood on either side.

Toby had probably left to use the facilities. No reason for alarm. Still, she worried. Garrett trusted her with his children's care, and she felt responsible for their well-being.

Reverend Holly launched into his sermon, his voice rising and falling as easily as the tide. Minutes passed and still no sign of Toby. Where was he? During the five years she was an operative, she had tracked down some of the most difficult outlaws. And here she was having trouble keeping track of one young boy.

Elise grew increasingly restless, and Maggie couldn't blame her. The minister seemed to think that God's eternal words required an everlasting sermon. Anyone taking note of the number of nodding heads might surmise that the congregation was in total assent. The heavyset man seated next to her began to snore.

"God spoke to Moses, and He speaks to us," Reverend Holly said, switching to a quiet monotone voice more conducive to putting babies to sleep than inspiring a spiritual awakening. "Show us a sign, God. Show us a sign."

"Stay here," Maggie whispered in Elise's ear. But before she could leave her seat, a gasp swept through the church and a woman cried out.

Maggie glanced at the front of the church and her mouth dropped open. Unless she was seeing things, the cross on the wall behind the organ was swinging from side to side like a pendulum.

"A sign from God!" someone yelled.

The man next to her awoke with a start. "Lord, have mercy."

"Hallelujah!" shouted an older woman who jumped to her feet then fainted dead away.

Reverend Holly looked startled, but apparently thinking his message was the inspiration behind the congregation's sudden outbursts, decided to make the most of it. Lifting his voice, he raised his arms and looked like a raven about to take flight.

"Speak to us, O mighty God!" he cried, and the worshippers went wild.

Eyes rounded in fear, Elise grabbed hold of Maggie's arm and had a coughing fit.

"Don't be afraid." Maggie pulled her onto her lap to comfort. "Let's go and find you a drink of water."

She was just about to carry Elise up the aisle when she caught a movement behind the organ, just to the left of the cross. Blinking she sat forward. That couldn't be. . . Please don't let it be—

Toby!

With Elise in her arms, Maggie rose to her feet for a better look. It was hard to see much behind the waving arms and swaying bodies in front.

The cross was no longer moving, but the congregants continued to plead for mercy and forgiveness. Aunt Hetty tossed her cane away and flung her arms around one of the church elders—an older man with stooped shoulders and muttonchop whiskers.

The worshipper sitting next to Maggie recited his sins, making it necessary to cover Elise's tender young ears. Another man was pulling money out of his pocket and flinging it in the air.

Elise held her arms tight around Maggie's neck. "Are. . .are we gonna die and go to heaven?"

Maggie glanced at the pandemonium around her, looking for a way to escape. How would she ever explain Toby's behavior to Garrett?

"I'm afraid not, pumpkin. I'm afraid not."

Garrett looked up from the chessboard, his face a mask of disbelief. "Toby did what?"

Hands on her hips, Elise harnessed all the righteous mortification a five-year-old could muster. "He tried to steal the cross."

Garrett shot to his feet. Chess pieces flew to the floor, startling Whitewash and sending him scampering from the room. "Is this true?" he asked, facing his son. "Did you try to steal the church's cross?"

Feeling a maternal need to protect the boy, Maggie hastened to intervene. "He didn't mean any harm."

Ignoring her, Garrett stared at his son. "Answer me!" he thundered. Toby flinched.

"I only wanted to borrow it," Toby said. He looked close to tears, and Maggie felt bad for him. Fortunately, she managed to drag the children away from church before anyone discovered the "miracle" was a fraud.

Garrett drew back. "You wanted to *borrow* the cross?" He looked incredulous. "Why?"

"For my slingshot."

Garrett's eyebrows shot up. "What in the name of Sam Hill were you thinking? Don't you know that the cross is sacred? You can't just take it and do with it as you please." He raked his fingers through his hair. "What did Reverend Holly say?"

"He started shouting," Elise said. "And a lady died."

"She didn't die," Maggie hastened to explain. "She merely fainted." Suddenly, the affair struck her as funny, and laughter bubbled out of her like water from a well.

Garrett turned to her, his forehead creased. "May I ask what you find so amusing?"

"It's just that—" She covered her mouth and gazed at him over her fingertips. "I don't believe I've ever seen so much ardor and reverence in church."

He tilted his head. "Is that so?"

"Yes." She had to control her mirth before she could continue. "One man swore off alcohol for good, and another promised to give up gambling. And you won't believe this, but your aunt tossed her cane away."

His eyebrows rose. "Aunt Hetty did that?"

"Oh, Garrett. I wish you could have been there. When the congregation saw the moving cross they thought it was a sign from God." Despite the stern look on his face, she burst into another peal of laughter. "Reverend Holly called it a miracle."

Garrett rubbed the back of his neck, and a shadow of indecision flitted across his face. "Drat, Maggie. Now I don't know if I should praise the boy or punish him."

She afforded him a beseeching look. "He didn't mean any harm and might have done some good."

Hands behind his back, Garrett paced the room, stopping once to eye the scattered chess pieces. Finally, he faced his son. "I'll give you a pass this time, but if anything like this happens again, you won't get off so easy."

Relief crossed Toby's face as he backed across the room. "Thank you, Pa."

"Don't thank me. Thank Miss Taylor."

"Thank you, Miss Taylor," Toby called as he turned and ran from the room, Elise at his heels.

Maggie waited until the children were out of earshot. It was hard to judge by Garrett's stoic face what he was thinking. "You made a wise decision," she said, hands folded primly in front.

"We'll see." He picked the chess pieces off the floor and rearranged them on the board. "From now on I'll accompany you to church. That way I can keep an eye on Toby myself and save you the trouble."

Knowing how he felt about organized religion, the offer surprised her. It also delighted her. Attending church with their father was one more memory the children could hold on to after his arrest.

"As you wish."

He looked up with knitted eyebrows. "I agreed to attend Sunday worship, but that doesn't mean I've changed my mind about church. So you needn't look so pleased."

"I'm trying not to," she replied. "Look pleased, that is."

"Well, try harder."

Chapter 15

That Monday, she was about to leave for town to mail her report when suddenly the front door burst open and Garrett stormed into the house with Elise in his arms.

"The school sent someone to fetch me." He hurried past her and raced down the hall to the child's bedroom, calling over his shoulder, "She's burning up with fever."

Alarmed, Maggie ran to the kitchen and quickly pumped water into a basin. Grabbing a washcloth from the hall cupboard, she hurried to Elise's room. By the time she reached the bedroom Garrett had already pulled Elise's shoes and stockings off and had undressed her down to her petticoat.

Maggie set the bowl on the bedside table. Dipping the cloth into the basin she squeezed out the excess water and ever so gently dabbed Elise's heated face with the cool, wet cloth. It wasn't the fever that worried her as much as Elise's labored breathing.

She had seemed perfectly healthy that morning, except for a slight cough. It was hard to believe that a few short hours later she could be so desperately ill.

"We need the doctor."

"I sent Panhandle to fetch him," he said, pacing the floor like an expectant father. "He should be here soon."

She ran the wet cloth down Elise's arms and legs. "She'll be all right," she whispered. She had no way of knowing that for sure, but he looked so worried she had to say something to relieve his mind.

His gaze met hers for an instant before returning to his daughter's flushed face. "I hope to God you're right."

∽

It was almost an hour before Whitewash's frantic barks announced the doctor's arrival.

Maggie left Elise's room to let the doctor in. An older man with white shoulder-length hair and neatly trimmed beard, he carried a black leather bag.

"I'm Dr. Coldwell," he said by way of introduction.

"Thank you for coming, Doctor," she said. "This way." He pulled off his top hat and followed her.

Garrett greeted him with a handshake and stood aside so the doctor could examine Elise.

Dr. Coldwell set his bag and hat on a chair and leaned over the bed. He thumped on Elise's chest, cocking his head intently. "Pneumonia," he said grimly.

The very word struck terror in Maggie. Many at the orphanage had died from the illness, including her best friend, Alice.

"Boil water and get some steam in here," Coldwell said. "It'll help her breathe."

She glanced at Garrett's tight expression, and she ached inside—not for the man, but the father. She turned to the doctor. "Is she going to be all right?"

"We won't know that until the fever breaks. Right now all we can do is make her comfortable." He prescribed a flaxseed poultice and strong tea. "As much as you can get her to drink."

After the doctor left, Maggie hurried to the kitchen. She ground the flaxseed, added hot water, and stirred until it was a fine paste. She then carried the bowl into Elise's room. While Garrett applied the poultice to Elise's chest, Maggie returned to the kitchen to make tea and refill the basin with hot water.

Elise's labored breathing could be heard even before Maggie reached the room. Her respiratory difficulties now racked her small body and tinged her lips blue.

Garrett left to wash his hands and then returned to hold Elise upright while Maggie spooned tea down her throat.

Elise turned her head away. "Come on, pumpkin, just a little bit more," Maggie said. "This will make you feel better."

Working together, they finally got the rest of the tea down Elise's throat. Garrett sat on a chair next to his daughter's side, his face drawn. Maggie knelt on the floor next to him.

"She's going to be all right," she whispered. *God, please make it so.*

He raised his hands to cover his face. "We don't know that."

"That's what we must believe," she said. "Hope is the anchor God sends down whenever we need it, and that's what we have to hold on to."

He lowered his hands, and she thought she saw a flicker of optimism in his eyes. Or maybe it was just wishful thinking on her part.

Elise coughed, and her slight body shook the bed.

Garrett leaned over her. Talking softly, he stroked his daughter's head until she grew still again.

They took turns sponging Elise's face, rubbing her back, soothing her coughs, applying the poultice, and forcing liquids into her. Hardly a word passed between them; there was no need to speak. They worked in perfect harmony, each seeming to know what to do and when.

Maggie had just finished filling the bowl with boiling water when Garrett surprised her by talking about his time in prison.

"We lost a lot of men in Andersonville from pneumonia." His voice sounded distant, as if coming from a source buried deep within. "Hundreds."

"This isn't the same, Garrett. Those men lived in terrible conditions." She never knew how bad those rebel prisons were until reading his journal. "Elise is a healthy child."

"If anything happens to her—" His voice broke.

She laid a hand on his arm. She knew how he felt about church, but did he have similar feelings about God?

"Garrett, would you pray with me?"

He pulled back from the bed as if it had burst into flames. "Pray?"

She nodded. "It might help."

His jaw tightened. "I prayed over many sick soldiers in prison and never once saw a prayer answered."

She was all too familiar with unanswered prayers. She couldn't begin to count the times she'd asked God to save her father. Even after her father hung from the gallows, she continued to pray for his soul and had no way of knowing if even that prayer had been answered.

"I don't know why God answers some prayers and not others," she said softly. The minister who worked at the orphanage had told her that even when God didn't answer prayers, He worked through them to change lives. "All I know is that we have to keep praying."

She heard his intake of breath. "The entire time I was in the stockades not one Christian church showed us prisoners any mercy or care."

"It was war," she said. "You were the enemy."

"That didn't stop the Southern Masons from sending provisions to Northern Mason prisoners. Should, God forbid, there ever be another war, my advice to soldiers would be to forget the church and join the Masonic lodge."

"The church isn't perfect," she said. "It was never meant to be perfect, and yet, God works through it, just as He works through our imperfections."

She might not have survived those turbulent years with her family had God not worked through her obsessive need to save face.

Garrett said nothing, and they sat in waiting silence, deep in their own thoughts. She didn't want to think about the past, but once the door had been opened, there was no stopping the memories.

Her family fled to the United Province of Canada during the war, along with thousands of American draft dodgers. Running away from conflict was not much different than running away from the law, so the move hardly affected her. It wasn't until after returning to America and her father's death that the full impact of the War between the States become evident. By then she had joined the ranks of war-orphaned children.

She soon learned that wartime losses were socially acceptable; hangings were not, so she invented a new past. She told everyone she lost her family in the North–South conflict. It was the only way she knew to fit in with the hundreds of other orphans. The only way she knew how to preserve any sort of dignity.

Her pretense provided ample training for her job as an undercover detective. Making up a good cover story was the least of it. An operative had to live the deception, and the only way to do that was by repetition. State a lie enough times and soon even the most outrageous falsehoods seemed like the truth.

No longer wishing to dwell on the past, she leaned over and pressed her hand gently on Elise's forehead. She still felt hot to the touch. Maggie ran her knuckles along the child's flushed face.

"Our Father," she whispered, and the words fell from her lips as if of their own volition. "Who art in heaven." *Heal this precious child.* "Hallowed be Thy name." *Protect her and make her strong.* "Thy Kingdom come." *Help her to grow in her faith even when it seems like You have deserted her.* "Thy will be done." *Help her to follow Your plan for her.* "On earth as it is in heaven."

"Give us this day, our daily bread."

Her eyes flickered open at the sound of Garrett's voice. She waited for him to say the next line, but when he didn't, she said it for him. "Forgive us our failings as we forgive those who fail us." They finished the prayer in tandem, after which there was nothing left to do but wait.

But as they kept vigil, something happened in that room; something changed. The very air around them seemed to move more freely. At times, in the past, they had acted cautiously with each other. Wary, even. But not now. Their concern for Elise was the bond that united them in a way no pretense ever could.

Maggie studied his profile as he leaned over his sleeping daughter. He would have made a wonderful physician. She shouldn't be thinking such thoughts but couldn't seem to help herself.

"Why did you choose to become a tinker?" she asked. That was a long way from his original desire to pursue a medical career.

"Actually, I didn't," he said quickly, openly, without his usual circumspection. "The profession chose me." He paused for a moment before continuing. "There were no utensils, plates, or even cups in prison. Someone gave us rice, but we had nothing to cook it in." He reached into the basin of water for a washcloth and squeezed it out before continuing.

"I was able to make a pan from my canteen. From there, I learned how to make spoons from brass buttons and cups from wood. Eventually I traded what I made for extra rations. That helped keep me alive."

"It must have been hard," she whispered.

"Hard doesn't even begin to describe it."

He talked about the war, his imprisonment, and the difficulty of adjusting to civilian life. The scar on his face was the result of trying to break up a prison fight. It was as if his daughter's illness had uncorked memories that had long been bottled up inside.

"The town greeted me like a hero when I got home," he said. "But I sure didn't feel like one." He pressed the cloth on Elise's forehead, and Maggie heard his intake of breath. "She's so little."

"Yes, but she's strong," Maggie said.

"It's odd but some of the biggest and the strongest men in prison were the first to die. Scrawny men were the most likely to survive."

The same was true in the orphanage, though she hadn't really thought about it until then. It was as if those who'd led a hardscrabble life had somehow acquired an extra layer of protection against physical stresses.

"You survived, and you're strong."

"I guess you could say I was just lucky." He tossed the washcloth in the basin and rubbed his neck as if to work out the kinks. "Let's talk about you."

A knot tightened in her stomach. "Me?"

"I'm curious. Why would a woman as...attractive as you answer an advertisement for a mail-order bride?"

His compliment made her blush. "I could ask the same of you," she said, throwing the verbal ball back at him. "Why would you place such an advertisement? I'm sure you could have your pick of local women."

"A scarred widower with two children? Not likely."

She studied him and felt a worrisome shift of allegiance. Her job required her to uncover the truth no matter the circumstances. There was no better time to question a suspect than when his defenses were down. But she had no desire to play detective. Not today. Taking advantage of Garrett's vulnerable state would be like shooting an unarmed man, and that she could never do.

"You underestimate yourself," she said.

He discounted this with a shrug. "You still haven't answered my question," he said. "I imagine you could have had your pick of suitors."

She felt another rush of warmth to her cheeks. "An old maid like me?"

He laughed.

"What's so funny?"

"I was just thinking about the day I picked you up from the train station. I have to admit to having second thoughts. I worried that a woman who willingly put herself in danger might be too impulsive for my family's needs." After a moment he added, "I was wrong."

Her pulse quickened. "What...changed your mind?"

He glanced at her hand lovingly stroking Elise's forehead. "That."

Chapter 16

At four o'clock she left the house and drove the buckboard to the edge of town to pick Toby up from school. Worried about Elise and shaken by her confused feelings, she imagined herself falling into a bottomless pit with no means of escape.

Pulling up in front of the school, she forced her worrisome thoughts aside.

Toby greeted her with a frown, his slouch cap askew. It must have scared him to see his sister being carried out of the classroom, and she wished now she had thought to pick the boy up earlier.

"Is Elise gonna die?"

She didn't want to answer the question—not even to herself. "Dr. Coldwell told us Elise will be fine once the fever breaks."

He scrambled onto the seat next to her, his eyes narrowed. "What's wrong with her?"

"She has pneumonia." Since she wasn't sure if he knew what pneumonia was, she added, "Her lungs are sick. She needs our prayers."

Toby tightened his hands into fists and closed his eyes. "God, if You make my sister better, I'll let her go to the moon. Promise."

She waited for him to finish his prayer. "She'll like that," she said with a nod of approval. Releasing the brake, she flicked the reins. The buckboard trembled as the wheels began to roll.

Toby leaned forward as if urging Patches to hurry.

She glanced at his stern young face. If she didn't watch out, this kid would grow on her. The whole family would grow on her—if it hadn't already—and that was a problem she didn't know how to handle.

∽

For five days and four nights, Garrett and Maggie hardly left Elise's bedside except to take Toby to school and to open the door to church members dropping off casseroles, thanks to Aunt Hetty who had sounded the alarm.

Some offered to sit with Elise, but Garrett always turned them down, his manner brusque.

"They just want to help," Maggie said, gently, after one such episode.

"They only want to help when it suits them," he said and stalked away.

Another time she found him in the parlor staring at the dish that someone from the church had just left.

"That smells good," she said.

He shoved the casserole into her hands and returned to Elise's room.

During the course of the days and nights, they spent hours talking. Garrett spoke of his childhood, and the words flowed when he spoke about growing up with Aunt Hetty and Uncle Harry. It was harder for him to talk about the war, and long pauses accented his speech.

"The prison was designed to hold ten thousand men, but there were more than thirty thousand of us cramped together. That's another reason I didn't want to move to Philadelphia like Katherine wanted. I couldn't bear the thought of living in a crowded city. I like looking out the window and seeing nothing but land and mountains and sky."

Knowing what he went through, Maggie couldn't blame him. But neither could she blame Katherine for wanting a better education for her children.

"Your turn," he said.

Maggie didn't want to speak of her childhood for fear of giving too much away, but he persisted. "The day my father died was the worst day of my life," she said. That was the truth as far as it went. What she didn't say was how he died.

He studied her as if detecting something in her voice. "Were you close to him?"

"No," she said. "Not at all."

He looked at her with sympathy or maybe even compassion. "Sometimes those are the hardest deaths to deal with." Following a stretch of silence, he asked, "What about your mother?"

"We weren't close, either," she said a tad too quickly. She could never understand why a woman would stay with a man as mean-spirited as her father. Even more puzzling was how a woman could abandon her own children. At the age of seventeen she found out her mother had remarried. Though her new husband was well-to-do, her mother never bothered fetching her from the orphanage or tracking down her sons. In some ways, Maggie envied her mother's ability to wipe the slate of her past clean and start over. But it hurt Maggie to think she could so easily be forgotten. It hurt a lot.

"I'm sorry," he said.

A lump rose to her throat, and a heavy mass settled in her chest. Not because of his understanding or empathy, but because she couldn't tell him the rest.

∽

On the morning of the fifth day, Maggie awoke to find a thin sliver of dawn slicing through the curtains of Elise's room. She lifted her head from the foot of Elise's bed and rubbed her stiff neck.

Garrett was still in his chair, his head on the mattress next to hers. He was so close she could feel the warmth of his body, smell the sweet, spicy fragrance of his aftershave.

Though she had persuaded him to go to bed, he had returned sometime in the night to be by his daughter's side. Even in sleep his hand never left Elise's. The tense set of his jaw remained, as did his furrowed brow.

Elise's breathing no longer sounded labored. Feeling a surge of hope, Maggie tiptoed around Garrett's chair and laid her hand on the child's forehead. Tears of relief sprang to her eyes.

"Garrett," she whispered, shaking him.

He lifted his head from the bed and blinked away the haze of sleep. "Her fever broke."

He stared at her a moment then sprang to his feet and felt Elise's forehead for himself.

"She's going to be all right," Maggie assured him. "Praise the Lord!"

Garrett looked terrible. He hadn't shaved, and dark stubble shadowed his jaw and cheeks. His hair was mussed and his clothes wrinkled.

She was in no better condition. Her hair, usually so carefully coifed, fell down her back in tangled curls. But none of that mattered as they stood smiling at each other like a couple of children sharing a secret.

He reached for her hand. "Thank you," he whispered. And just that quickly he pulled her into his arms.

Emotions spent, she clung to him, and he buried his face in her hair. A sob rumbled through him. "Thank you," he said again. His heart pounded in her ear matching the fast rhythm of her own.

"For. . .for what?"

He lifted his head. "For being here. For being you. For caring. For giving me hope."

For a moment—a brief and surprising moment—she saw a woman reflected in his eyes that she didn't recognize. Garrett and his children brought out a part of her she hadn't known existed; a nurturing, loving, and warm part far removed from the cool and relentless detective she had prided herself on being all these years.

She pulled out of his arms, but only because she feared losing herself completely to the woman—the stranger—she hardly recognized as herself. That woman could never do what had to be done. She could never lie to him, betray him, or plot against him.

No, the woman reflected in his eyes didn't exist, but oh, how Maggie wished that she did.

Chapter 17

Elise's illness had put a hold on the investigation, and now Maggie had to make up for lost time.

She'd just completed a rather sketchy report to headquarters when she heard a knock. Thinking it was Aunt Hetty, she quickly slid the report under a chair cushion, smoothed the bun at the nape of her neck, and hurried to the door.

"Howdy, ma'am. Have you got any rags for me today?"

"Rikker!" Garrett was at work and Toby at school, but just in case Elise woke from her nap, Maggie stepped onto the porch. She left the door ajar so she could hear Elise should she cry out.

"What are you doing here?"

He moved his burlap sack from one shoulder to the next and threw the question back at her. "What are *you* doing? Haven't seen hide or hair of you for days. I wouldn't have even known you were alive had I not heard in town that Elise was sick."

She felt a surge of guilt. Her mind had been so occupied with concern for Elise, she'd hardly given her partner or the case more than a passing thought. That went against everything she'd been taught.

"Then you must know that Elise has been ill." The child still had a slight cough but otherwise had made a fast recovery, though she had yet to regain her appetite.

Rikker dropped his persona. "Your purpose here is not to play nursemaid."

"I know what my purpose is," she snapped.

He reared back. "Oh my. Testy, aren't we?" Eyes narrowed beneath his furrowed brow, he studied her like he would a suspect.

"You look terrible."

"Thank you. I needed to hear that." Even now that the crisis had passed, she'd hardly been able to sleep.

"What's really going on?"

She blew out her breath. Drat! He always could read her like an open book. She rubbed her face with her hands. "I don't think Garrett Thomas is our man." It was the first time she admitted her doubts out loud.

His eyebrows shot up. "What makes you say that?"

"It's just—" Rikker would expect her to think and act like a detective, but it was hard. So hard. She had come to know Garrett quite well these last few days as they watched over Elise. Could a man so kind, so gentle and loving, really be the coldhearted killer she was sent to investigate? Or were personal feelings getting in the way of good judgment?

"I haven't found anything to substantiate his guilt." For a man who stole that much money, Garrett lived a comfortable yet modest life.

"Need I remind you that a witness put him at the scene of the crime?"

"You know as well as I that witnesses aren't always reliable."

"This witness was quite credible. He described one of the men as having a scar, and his description fits Thomas to a T." He ran his finger the length of his face to indicate. "In any case, how do you explain the money clip left behind with the initials GT?"

"He's a tinker." The principal's orders were to follow the money clip, and that's what they'd done. "He's probably sold dozens of them. Anyone could have left it behind."

"And the five large bills that showed up at the school fund-raiser? How do you account for that?"

"I can't," she admitted. "It's just so odd. I mean, the money suddenly showing up like that."

"Did it ever occur to you that Thomas was testing the waters to see if the money was marked? It's not the first time something like that happened."

She'd considered that possibility at length. "Garrett's no fool. He must have known that five Lincolns would draw attention. Especially since banks are no longer issuing them." The last legal tender banknotes in hundred-dollar denominations were issued in 1880, the year of the robbery. "All the other donations had been smaller bills, fives and tens.

"Maybe he thought enough time had passed. Or perhaps he was just pressing his luck. In any case, we can't discount the clues." Holding up his hand, he ticked them off on his fingers one at a time. "Money clip, witness, and five banknotes."

She did a mental count of her own. Garrett was thoughtful, gentle, and kind, but such traits would hardly hold up in a court of law. "I've searched this house from stem to stern and found nothing."

Rikker blew out his breath. "Found nothing at his shop, either. Nor is there a safe box at the bank belonging to him." He shrugged in frustration. "I also checked the banks in Yuma and Phoenix. Nothing."

She arched a brow. "You've been busy."

"One of us has to keep the investigation going." He shifted his bag of rags. "It's got to be here at the house somewhere."

"Or maybe there isn't any money. Maybe Garrett is exactly what he seems, a hardworking man and loving father."

Rikker's gaze sharpened. "Has it ever occurred to you that the real reason he sent away for a mail-order bride is because he plans to leave town? Maybe he just wants someone to care for his children while he disappears and lives high on the hog somewhere else."

It was a shocking thought, but not all that far-fetched. Many outlaws had left the country to do exactly that. Some had to learn the hard way that no place on earth was out of Pinkerton's reach. Recently an operative had crossed the Atlantic in an attempt to catch a jewel thief, cornering him in Rome.

"I don't know—"

The door opened, and Elise stood in the entryway rubbing her eyes.

"Oh, there you are pumpkin." Maggie smoothed the hair away from Elise's face. She still looked pale with none of her usual sparkle. "Wait for me in the kitchen, and I'll fix you something to eat."

Elise vanished inside the house, and Rikker waited until she was out of earshot.

"I have a plan."

"You always have a plan," Maggie said. "What is it this time?"

"Thomas is growing careless. He's already spent five bills that we know of. It's possible he's spent more that we haven't caught."

"We don't know the money came from him," she said stubbornly.

"No, we don't, but I think I know how we can find out. If the school donation came from your fiancé's stash, then we might safely assume he has a weakness for a good cause."

She eyed him warily. "So what's your plan?"

"You, my dear, will tell him that the wedding is off. Your *family* is about to lose their farm and are in desperate need of money." He thought for a moment. "So what do you think? Brilliant, huh?"

Maggie rolled her eyes. "Your brilliance is second only to your modesty."

"You'll change your tune once you see how well this works. Tell Thomas you have to leave to help save the family farm. I'm willing to wager he'll give you money on the spot to wire home." He smiled. "What do you say to that?"

"It's a good plan," she said, reluctantly. It wasn't as elaborate as most of his plans, but the simple plans were always the ones that worked best. If only the idea of setting a trap for Garrett didn't make her feel so downright miserable.

Rikker was too busy congratulating himself on this latest scheme to notice her depressed state of mind. "Unless I miss my guess," he all but crowed, "Thomas Garrett isn't about to let his bride-to-be out of his sight. He'll give you the money to save the farm. Mark my words."

Later that night, Maggie tucked Elise in bed and listened to her prayers. Earlier Garrett had raced through the house with his daughter on his back. It did Maggie a world of good to hear Elise's childish giggles.

The doctor said she could return to school Monday, and that was a relief. Maybe things could go back to normal—or as normal as circumstances allowed.

She thought about Rikker's plan. It was a good one, easy, uncomplicated. She had nothing to lose if Garrett didn't fall for it and everything to gain if he did. So why was she so reluctant to put it into action?

"Sleep tight," she whispered. Dropping a kiss on Elise's forehead, she walked out of the room.

The door to Garrett's room stood wide open. Toby sat on the floor, building some sort of contraption from scraps of metal from his father's shop.

He was too engrossed in his project to notice her. She watched him for a moment, unseen. Being the daughter of an outlaw had been difficult, but how much harder might it be for a son? Sighing, she moved away from the bedroom door.

She found Garrett in the parlor bent over the chessboard. Elbows on his lap, his hands were folded beneath his chin. Earlier he and Toby had played a game. For such a young child, Toby was able to hold his own, and the game ended in a draw.

Garrett glanced up as she neared, an easy smile tugging at the corners of his mouth. "You play?"

" 'Fraid not," she said.

He considered her answer for a moment. "I learned to play chess while in the rebel prison. We drew a board in the dirt and used stones for chess pieces. Playing chess helped keep our minds sharp."

"Staring at stones did that?" she teased.

He chuckled. "Sounds crazy, I know. But there's actually a lot of mental work that goes into the game. It was also a great way to know my fellow prisoners. Know who to trust. Who was motivated. Honest. Know who was most likely to rob me."

She arched her eyebrows. "You can tell all that from a game of chess?"

"Pretty amazing, huh?" He moved a piece across the board. "The goal is to force your opponent to yield." He looked up. "I'd be happy to teach you, but only if you promise not to beat me at my own game."

"Since I always play to win, I'm afraid that's a promise I can't keep."

"Is that so?" His eyes clung to hers. "Actually, I like a woman who plays to win."

Had he known the game she was playing he might feel quite different.

"Take a seat," he said, pointing to the chair opposite him. "I want to get to know you one square at a time."

A warning voice whispered inside, but still she sat. "What do you hope to learn about me?" she asked, the thought as worrisome as it was intriguing.

His eyes twinkled. "What do you want me to learn?"

"That I'm a good loser."

His grin widened as he reached across the board for a red piece. "Did you know that chess was once a game of courtship?"

"Really? I thought it was a game of war."

"Some would say there's no difference between war and romance. Both require disarming the opponent and being aware of the dangers. I've even heard it said that love is a battlefield."

Her colleagues might well describe love that way. Maintaining a marriage or even a romance was almost impossible for a private investigator. Of necessity, secrets must be kept and an operative was always on the move.

"Do you agree?" she asked.

He shook his head. "I've been on a battlefield, and there's no comparison." He moved the remaining pieces into place. "Some people are lucky in love, but never in chess. That's because it's a game of skill."

"And yet you say that chess was once a game of love."

"We have two queens on the same board as thirty men. How can love not flourish?"

"I never thought of it that way," she said, charmed by the idea.

"Chess matches were once quite common between a woman and her suitor. The purpose of the game is to *mate*. Actually, the word *check-mate* comes from an Arabic word meaning 'to submit.'" The intense look he gave her sent a shiver of awareness down her spine. "The king is the weakest piece and the queen the most powerful."

She smiled. "Just as it should be."

He smiled, too. "It wasn't until the Middle Ages that the game changed. Rather than a social affair it became a competitive game. That's when most women lost interest."

His expression held both a challenge and a promise, and she quivered with anticipation.

"Chess is all about making the right moves," he continued. "Just like life." He put the last piece in place and sat back. "Ready?"

She studied the chessboard. Chess had been described as the game of life, but nothing in life was as black and white as that chessboard. "Checkmate," she said. It was the only chess term she knew.

Garrett laughed. "Not yet, my dear. Not yet."

His term of endearment surprised her. More than that, it warmed her. Despite her best efforts to remain alert and on guard, she found herself relaxing.

After he explained a few basic rules of play, they began. He described several possibilities for each move.

He corrected her gently when she slid a bishop sideways instead of diagonally. She playfully accused him of cheating whenever he captured one of her men.

He never lost patience and was quick to praise her on the rare occasion she did something right. "With a little practice, you'll be a champ," he said.

She doubted it. "So what have you learned about me so far?" she asked.

His mouth curved. "You're smart and quick to learn. You refuse to back down when faced with trouble. Your fighting spirit won't let you give up even when your plan goes awry. You simply change course and attack from another direction." He folded his hands beneath his chin. "How am I doing so far?"

She smiled. He just described the traits necessary for a detective. "Not bad," she said.

"So what have you learned about me?" he asked.

"Hmm, let me think." She tapped her chin with her finger. "You're clever, focused, and never make a move without careful thought." He was also handsome, charming, and fun to be with, but she thought it best not to mention such traits. "You're also highly motivated and goal-oriented. Oh yes, and patient."

Never could she remember enjoying herself more and was completely taken by surprise when the clock chimed the hour of eleven.

It was his turn to move, but after a moment he looked up and shook his head. "Stalemate," he said.

"What does that mean?" she asked.

"It means," he said, rearranging the pieces on the board, "that neither of us has to submit to the other." His gaze held hers, and she felt herself sink into the dark depths of his eyes. "At least not tonight."

Chapter 18

She woke the following morning with a smile on her face. The memory of the evening spent playing chess flashed through her mind. *"Actually, the word* checkmate *comes from an Arabic word meaning 'to submit.'"*

Never had she submitted or surrendered to a man. Her faith kept her virtue intact, and her job prevented her from becoming emotionally involved. Still, she had to admit the idea did capture her imagination. Her smile died abruptly, as did her thoughts. What was she thinking?

Palms on her head she groaned. She had completely forgotten about Rikker's plan.

Oh, God, what is happening to me? I've never had trouble doing my job before. Why now, Lord? Why now?

Chess was a game of skill, but so was the cat and mouse game she played. Remaining objective was essential. Impartiality was crucial to any investigation. Bias could prevent her from correctly weighing information and drawing accurate conclusions. A detective must never force the facts to fit a theory.

Jumping out of bed, she hurried through her morning ablutions. She then woke Elise and helped her dress in the clothes laid out for her the night before.

She found Garrett sitting at the kitchen table with his coffee and newspaper. "Morning." The magnetism of his smile almost made her forget her resolve.

Turning abruptly toward the stove, she murmured, "Morning." She poured herself a cup of coffee and sat opposite him. Elise and Toby were outside feeding the animals, so she had his full attention.

He folded the paper and laid it on the table. "I hope I didn't keep you up too late last night playing chess."

"Not at all." She kept her attention focused on the cup. Actually, the game was only half the problem. Recalling how she had shamefully returned his flirtatious glances, she felt her cheeks redden. Such nonsense must stop. She had a job to do, and like it or not, she intended to do it. Bracing herself with a sip of coffee, she set her cup down.

"I do have a problem, though." She moistened her lips. "I should have mentioned it before, but. . . I'm afraid we'll have to postpone our wedding."

His brow furrowed. "Why?" He reached across the table for her hand, but she quickly pulled away and pretended to fumble in her sleeve for a handkerchief.

His jaw tensed. "You aren't having second thoughts, are you? Have I done something to upset you?"

She dabbed at her eyes with her handkerchief. Oddly enough, the single tear that rolled down her cheek was not faked. "You haven't upset me—"

"Is it Arizona?" He tilted his head. "Don't you like it here?"

"I like it here just fine," she replied, surprised to find herself speaking the truth. Maybe it was the wide-open spaces or the desert warmth. Perhaps it was the adobe house—the closest thing to a home she'd ever known. She didn't want to think what else it could be.

"It's my f–family," she stammered. She'd written about her make-believe family in her letters to him, and she hoped he'd remember enough so she didn't have to go into detail. She dropped her hands to her lap and fought to hide her inner turmoil with an outer calm. "They're unable to pay the taxes on the farm and have asked for my help."

The lie felt like acid on her tongue, and it was all she could do to continue. "I can't do that from here. I'm afraid I must go home."

He rubbed his hand across his chin. "How much do they owe?"

She'd considered the amount of money to ask for at great length. Asking for too much might cause suspicion. But if she asked for too little, he might not have to draw from the stolen cache.

"Five hundred dollars."

He let out a low whistle. "That's quite a bit of money."

It was hardly the kind of response she would expect from a man who supposedly had so freely donated that very same amount to the school. She kept her features composed so as not to give away her thoughts, and nodded in agreement.

"Yes, it is a lot of money," she said. "I'm not sure how I can help, but I have to try."

He studied her for a moment before pushing back his chair. "Wait here." He stood and walked out of the kitchen.

Her stomach clenched, and she clasped her hands together in a silent prayer. Would this be the moment the case was finally solved? It's what she wanted, what she had worked for all these months. So where was the jubilation normally felt whenever she came close to solving a case? Where was the joy?

Instead she felt torn by conflicting emotions. *The children—oh, dear God, the children.* They would hate her, just as she had hated the United States marshal who had arrested her father. Years passed before she realized how misdirected her anger had been.

How can I do this to Toby and Elise? God, will You tell me that? But it wasn't just them. It was—oh, how she hated admitting it—Garrett himself.

Some criminals were pure evil, but not all. Some were good family members and were even active in church. But never had she met one with more basic goodness than Garrett.

Or maybe she was just too close to the family to see the truth. That was her greatest fear.

Hearing Garrett's footsteps advance down the hall toward the kitchen, she squeezed her eyes shut and prayed.

Chapter 19

Maggie hesitated at the entry to the hotel dining room and scanned the tables. The breakfast rush was over and only two diners remained, including Rikker, who sat at a corner table reading a newspaper. She gnashed her teeth. How like him to look perfectly relaxed while she was an emotional wreck.

She stormed toward him.

He looked up surprised, and no wonder; when two operatives worked a case it was imperative that they not be seen together, but this assignment wasn't like most.

She slammed her hand on the table.

He folded the paper and set it aside. "I trust things didn't go as planned." She moved her hand, and he stared at what she left behind. "What's that?"

She pulled out a chair and sat. "*That* is a check for five hundred dollars drawn on Garrett Thomas's business account."

Rikker's eyebrows shot up. "He gave you a check?" He thumped the table with a fist, rattling his cup and saucer. "Blast it! The man's as sly as a fox."

"Or he doesn't have the money." She was convinced of it.

"Just because he gave you a check doesn't mean he's not our man. You should have asked for more. Then he would have had to reach into his stash."

The waiter came over to the table. "Can I get you something, ma'am?"

"No, thank you," she said without looking at him. "I'm not staying."

The waiter left, and she leaned forward. "Why write a check for me but not for the school building fund? It makes no sense."

"Unless he suspects something."

A cold chill settled in the pit of her stomach. Had she given Garrett a reason not to trust her? Had she slipped up somewhere? Had all that talk about playing games been a veiled warning?

She sat back. "Do you think that's why he wrote a check? Because he suspects something?"

"You know him better than I do." He watched her over his cup as he sipped his coffee. "Would you have asked for the money had you thought him guilty?"

She frowned. "What kind of question is that?"

"A necessary one." He set his cup on the saucer. "You know the dangers of getting personally involved."

"I don't need a lecture."

"And I don't need a partner with her head in the clouds."

They glared across the table at each other, neither wanting to give an inch.

Finally he picked up the newspaper and tucked it under his arm. Tossing two coins on the table he stood. "All I can say is that you better watch your step. Or should I say heart?" With that he walked away.

❧

On the way home, Maggie spotted the paperboy Linc walking into a small adobe house at the end of town. She steered the buckboard to the side of the road and set the brake.

The house was run-down. Not only was the front window boarded up, but the weathered fence leaned to one side and the gate hung from a single hinge. Tumbleweeds vied for space in the small enclosed yard, along with a broken water pump, wagon wheel, and other trash.

The old woman who answered Maggie's knock was dressed in a tattered housecoat. Unfocused eyes stared from a thin, deeply lined face. Her hair fell to her shoulders in a matted white mass.

Maggie was just about to introduce herself as a friend of Linc's when the woman's face lit up. "Come in, come in," she said as if she'd been expecting her. She waited for Maggie to enter the house before closing the door. The one unbroken window provided some light, but not much. The air smelled of decay.

"Carolyn, how nice of you to visit. Where's the baby?"

It took a moment for Maggie's eyes to adjust to the dim light. "I'm not Carolyn. My name is—"

But the woman ignored her protests. "Don't look at the place," she said as she removed clothes and dishes from tables and chairs. She tossed the clothes into a corner and carried the dirty dishes into the kitchen, talking all the while. "It's seems like forever since I've seen you. Is the baby sleeping through the night yet?" she called from the kitchen. "I hope he doesn't take after his mother. You didn't sleep through the night until you were six months old."

"Like I said, I'm not—"

The woman returned to the room. "Would you care for some tea?"

"No, thank you," Maggie said. It was hot and she would have preferred something cool, but she didn't want to put her host to any trouble, especially in her confused state.

"I came to see Linc."

The woman gasped. "You think I have your baby?"

She looked so alarmed that Maggie reached out to pat her thin arm. "No, of course not. How silly of me."

Just then Linc walked into the room. He glanced at Maggie and quickly hid his hands behind his back, but not quick enough to hide the half-eaten apple, which no doubt he'd stolen.

His grandmother regarded him as if he were little more than an acquaintance. "Carolyn is my daughter," she said. "And she has a darling baby named Lincoln."

Linc didn't look the least bit surprised by his grandmother's confusion. "How come you're here?" he asked, his eyes gleaming with suspicion.

"I came to see you," Maggie replied.

"I ain't going to no school."

His grandmother's gaze darted around the room as if she was trying to make sense of her surroundings. "What are you talking about, boy? You can't go to school. It's time for my meal."

Linc backed toward the kitchen. "I'll fix you something to eat."

"Fix Carolyn something, too," his grandmother called after him.

"No, that's all right," Maggie said. "I'm not staying."

"Oh, but you must. I so seldom see you since you had the baby."

The woman wouldn't take no for an answer, and finally Maggie relented. "Very well. Why don't you sit down and rest, and I'll see if. . . he needs help."

"That would be very nice." The old woman slumped into a chair as if it took all her energy to do so.

Maggie stepped into the kitchen and was appalled by the filth. The counter, table, and even the stove were piled high with dirty dishes, and flies swarmed everywhere.

"How long has your grandmother been like this?" she asked.

Linc set two pieces of bread on the grimy table. "She's been old for a long time," he said. "Since before I was born."

"I'm not talking about her age. How long has she been so forgetful?"

He put some moldy-looking cheese onto the bread. "Sometimes she's not forgetful. Sometimes she even knows I'm Linc." He glared at her. "She's not crazy. She's not. And I'm not letting her go nowhere with you. So you can leave."

Maggie realized that the boy wasn't just defiant; he was scared. "I'm not here to take your grandmother away," she said gently.

Wariness replaced the suspicion in his eyes. "You're not gonna put her in an asylum?"

"No, of course not. Why would you think such a thing?"

"Some people want to."

"Who?"

"The woman from the Orphans Society."

"Oh, Linc." He was the age that many criminals first turned to illegal activities. Some began stealing as a matter of survival. Others knew no other way of life. Linc was at a crossroads, and if something wasn't done to help him, he might one day end up on Pinkerton's most-wanted list.

"Don't you have any other family who can help you?" If only life could be played like chess. If only it were possible to protect someone from temptation as one might protect a king.

"It's just me and Granny, and I ain't letting 'em take her away." With that he ran from the room.

No sooner had he departed when his grandmother walked into the kitchen shaking her head. "That boy will be the death of me yet."

Considering the moldy cheese, stale bread, and grimy table, the old lady was closer to the truth than she probably knew.

She looked at Maggie, and this time her eyes were clear and focused. "What did you say your name was, dearie?"

That night over supper, Maggie told Garrett about her visit to Linc's house. She was so incensed by what she'd found there, she pushed Rikker's warning to be careful to the back of her mind.

"I don't understand why someone hasn't stepped in and helped them. The church—"

As soon as she said it, she regretted her words. Garrett already thought poorly of organized religion. "There must be something that can be done."

"I had no idea that things were that bad," he said. He looked every bit as concerned as she felt.

Bad didn't begin to describe the poor conditions of the house. "Would you mind if I gave Linc some of Toby's outgrown clothes?" Toby was large for his age, and though his clothes might be a tad too small for Linc, they were better than anything the boy currently owned.

"That's a good idea. I'm sure Toby won't mind, will you, son?"

Toby shook his head. "Long as you don't give away my thinking cap."

"I can give Linc one of my dolls," Elise offered.

"Boys don't play with dolls," Toby said.

Maggie smiled at her. "No, but it's very kind of you to offer."

Garrett looked up from cutting his meat. "Purchase whatever else he and his grandmother need. Just bill everything to my account."

Maggie dabbed her mouth with her napkin. It was a kind and generous offer, but she couldn't think about that. She had to keep a clear mind, an unbiased mind. The truth was that she couldn't have planned this whole thing better had she tried.

If she ran Garrett's accounts up high enough, he would have to dip into the stolen money to pay them. No doubt Rikker would approve the plan. She only wished the idea of taking advantage of Garrett's generous nature didn't make her feel so utterly wretched.

❦

Maggie got to work the very next day. Her first stop was Grover's Mercantile where she purchased crates of tin goods, along with safety matches, lye soap, candles, and kerosene. She ran up such a large bill that the bespectacled clerk behind the counter added the numbers three times to make sure he hadn't made an error.

The next stop on her list was Adams's Boots and Leather shop to purchase a pair of black boots for Linc. She also bought yards of gingham fabric from Murphy's Dry Goods.

The shopkeeper had recommended a young Mexican housekeeper who agreed to clean Linc's house for a fee. She spent a full day just organizing the kitchen.

Convincing Linc to take a hot bath at the hotel bath house was the real challenge—that, and getting him to sit still in the barber chair.

After the barber cut Linc's hair, she stood him in front of a store window where he could see his reflection. "What do you think?"

"It don't look like me," he mumbled. "Granny won't recognize me." Considering the old lady's condition, it was a strange thing to say, but the boy looked dead serious.

"She'll recognize you," Maggie said, smoothing his hair to one side. "Just like always."

∞

Linc and his grandmother were very much on her mind that night as Maggie stood at the stove stirring the stew. She was especially worried about the boy. He was far too young to shoulder so much responsibility.

If something happened to his grandmother, he would probably end up in an orphanage, but few institutions did little more than turn out vagrant and unlawful people. The number of former orphans who turned up in the Pinkerton files was no accident.

The word *orphanage* was actually a misnomer; a surprising number of children had a parent or parents who couldn't or wouldn't take care of them. Much like her own mother refused to take care of her and her brothers.

Some orphanages did try and even taught their charges a trade. She had been lucky. Her orphanage was run by a Christian organization, and though the headmistress was strict, almost everyone who left turned out to be a responsible citizen. But homes like that were rare. Most directors ran highly regimented facilities that applied corporal punishment and shaved children's heads. They were also dangerous places, and the mortality rate was often the same as it was for urchins living on the streets.

Hurtled back to the present by the mouthwatering smell rising from the stew pot, she sniffed in appreciation. She'd found the recipe in her new cookbook. The liquid was thick and savory and not watery like the stew served at the orphanage.

After putting the ingredients together, she carefully hid the cookbook.

God was in the details, and the same was true of cloak and dagger operations. An Indiana farm girl would most certainly know how to make lamb stew and wouldn't need a recipe.

It surprised her how much she enjoyed cooking. Mealtime at the Thomas house was nothing like the silent orphanage meals where no one was allowed to talk except in whispers.

In contrast, the evening meal here was boisterous and full of laughter. She ached to think it would soon be coming to an end, and she would once again face an endless panorama of impersonal hotel rooms and poor eating establishments.

The telegram she'd received earlier from headquarters was curt and to the point: keep investigating.

The problem was, she was quickly running out of time. The wedding was little more than three weeks away. She felt conflicted, at odds, and so unlike herself.

She set the spoon down and walked over to the table where Elise sat doing schoolwork. She was learning about plurals and having trouble with words ending in *y*.

"Oops! You got *baby* wrong," Maggie said, peering over Elise's shoulder. "Remember, you have to change the *y* to *i* and add the letters *e* and *s*."

Elise erased what she'd written and tried again.

The front door slammed and Garrett's voice thundered through the house. "Maggie!"

Grimacing, Maggie turned to face the doorway as Garrett stormed into the kitchen. He waved a bunch of bills in her face.

"Twenty pounds of beans? Two dozen boxes of. . ." On and on he went, his voice rising with each item, along with his eyebrows.

"Three cans of kerosene, fifteen boxes of tea, and ten bars of lye soap." He looked up from the bill of goods. "Does Linc even know what to do with soap?"

She wiped her damp hands on her apron. "I'm afraid I may have gone overboard."

His eyebrows rose so high they practically disappeared into his hairline. "You didn't just go overboard, you sank the whole confounded ship!"

As if suddenly realizing that Elise was present, he lowered his voice. "When I said to purchase whatever Linc and his grandmother needed, I didn't mean for you to run us into the poor house!"

"I'm sorry—"

"Sorry!" He shook his head, sputtered, and left the room.

Maggie blew out her breath, surprised to find herself shaking. At least he didn't make her take her purchases back.

Elise looked up from her paper. "What's a poor house?"

Toby walked into the room and grabbed a slice of bread from the counter. "It's a place you go when you're not rich."

"Are we going to a poor house?"

"I'm not," Toby said. "I'm going to the moon."

Elise chewed on the end of her pencil. "Is Papa going to the poor house?"

"No," Maggie said. "Your papa's not going to the poor house." *Jail maybe, but not the poor house.*

"There," Elise said after a while. She held up her paper. "I made the plural of poor house."

Chapter 20

Supper wasn't the usual happy occasion. No jokes or riddles tonight, though Garrett did question the children about their day. Maggie could sense the barely contained anger coiled within him, but he did his best to maintain a civil tone for the children's sake. They both did.

As usual, Elise was more than happy to share what she'd learned that day. "Miss Taylor taught me how to make babies," she said.

A startled look crossed Garrett's face. "Did she now?" His narrowed eyes bored into Maggie as he pushed his empty plate away. "It would seem that Miss Taylor has had a busy day."

Before Maggie could explain, he rose from the table and retired to his room. She hated that he left such a void. Hated even more that she missed him when he was gone.

"Is Papa angry?" Elise asked, looking worried.

Maggie rose to clear the table. "Maybe a little. But not at you."

She glanced at Toby who was busy trying to balance a fork on his nose.

Later, after the dishes were done, Maggie walked into the parlor and found the children whispering among themselves.

"Who wants to read first?"

"I do," Elise said.

Elise's enthusiasm brought a smile to Maggie's face. Their nightly reading sessions had paid off and already Elise had shown improvement, though she still struggled with some vocabulary.

Maggie settled on the sofa next to Elise. "Tomorrow, can we stop in town after school for ice cream?"

"I guess we can do that," Maggie said.

Midway through the story, Whitewash started barking furiously outside.

"Toby, open the door for Whitewash, will you?"

Elise looked up from her book, her eyes wide. "Maybe it's the boogeyman," she whispered.

"Or maybe Whitewash just wants to come in," Maggie whispered back.

∞

The next day, Maggie headed for the dressmaker's shop to drop off the fabric she'd purchased from the dry goods store. After his initial outburst, Garrett had made no more mention of the bills, and things had returned to normal between them that morning at breakfast. Apparently he didn't hold grudges. Not like her father used to do. . .

She blew out her breath. But would Garrett pay his debts with stolen money? *Oh God, please no!*

Mrs. Button greeted her with a mouthful of pins.

"I was hoping you'd have time to make some nightgowns for Linc's grandmother," Maggie said.

The seamstress nodded and quickly finished pinning up the hem on a skirt.

"Will next week be soon enough?" Mrs. Button said, stabbing a pin back into the pincushion.

"That will be fine," Maggie said. She set the bolts of cotton on the table.

"While you're here, we can do a fitting for your wedding dress."

Maggie had neither the time nor inclination to try it on, but the dressmaker insisted.

"It won't take but a few minutes, and it will save you a trip later."

Refusing to take no for an answer, Mrs. Button rose and vanished into the back of the store. She reappeared a moment later carrying a white satin gown.

Maggie's mouth dropped open. She didn't know what she expected, but it wasn't this. It was a simple, yet elegant gown, and the fitted bodice was trimmed with white crystal beads and faux pearls. A slight bustle in back fell from a large satin bow, and the sleeves were puffed on top and tapered to the wrists.

She gasped. "It's beautiful."

Mrs. Button looked pleased. "Try it on and I'll measure the hem." She ushered Maggie into a curtained area that served as a dressing room.

After Maggie stepped out of her skirt and pulled off her shirtwaist, Mrs. Button helped her into the gown. The satin slid down the length of her body like a soothing cool breeze.

Every detail, from the delicate lace at the neckline to the fitted sleeves and flared ruffles at her wrists, was exquisite.

Mrs. Button laced up the back and fussed with the skirt until it was draped to her satisfaction. She then lifted a wedding veil off a hook and pinned it in place upon Maggie's head.

Overwhelmed with emotion, Maggie stared at herself in the mirror. She looked and felt like she was floating on a cloud. Never had she worn anything so elegant.

The satin fabric felt soft and smooth to her touch, and whispered with her every move. She imagined herself walking down the aisle and into the arms of the man she loved. Startled by the vision of blue eyes that suddenly came to mind, she quickly turned away from the mirror.

"Everything all right?" Mrs. Button asked with a worried frown.

"Yes, I just didn't expect the dress to look so—"

"Perfect on you?" The dressmaker gave a dimpled smile and pressed her hands together. "You make a beautiful bride." She separated the draperies hanging at the doorway for privacy and stepped out of the small confined area. "Come and I'll pin up the hem."

Maggie lifted the skirt and ducked through the opening.

"Stand on the stool," Mrs. Button said, indicating a four-legged one in the center of the room next to her worktable.

Maggie inched her skirt to just above her ankles and stepped onto the stool. Mrs. Button grabbed her cloth measuring tape and pincushion and dropped to her knees.

"It looks like we need to take up a good two inches," she mumbled around the pins in her mouth.

Still shaken by her thoughts, Maggie held herself rigid and tried not to think or feel. Silly schoolgirl dreams about love and marriage had no place in her life. Certainly she had no right to feel anything toward Garrett Thomas.

She curled her hands into balls by her side. Mustn't think about the blue eyes staring back at her. Or the crooked smile or...

She blinked twice, but the vision refused to go away. With a start she realized it wasn't her imagination. It really was Garrett Thomas standing outside Mrs. Button's window, gazing back at her.

Something intense flared in his eyes—not anger but admiration and something else she dared not name. He looked at her like she was the most beautiful and desirable woman in the world, and at that moment, she believed that what he saw was real.

∞

Maggie?

Garrett stepped closer to the window to peer inside. His pulse quickened, and it was all he could do to catch his breath. Beautiful didn't begin to describe the way she looked in her wedding gown, all soft and dewy-eyed. She looked like an angel.

It shocked him to realize he'd memorized every plane and angle of her face. Beneath the wedding veil her hair held golden highlights, but he also knew that the shifting light would turn it a radiant auburn at day's end. Just as the sapphire of her eyes as she watched him through the window would later pale to robin's-egg blue on nothing more than a whim.

Stunned by the overwhelming feelings that assailed him, he was momentarily riveted to the spot. He'd only known her for a few weeks, but already she'd worked her way into his heart. How was such a thing possible?

Her smiles commanded his dreams. Her laughter seemed to echo, even from the metal he pounded into shape in his workshop.

Nothing had gone as planned. He'd never intended to have feelings for another woman. Losing Katherine had been too painful. Her death devastated him. He'd vowed never again to put himself through that much pain and grief and sorrow.

A marriage based on mutual respect was safe and sane. A marriage based on love was not. That's why he'd picked out a wife through a mail-order-bride catalog. That seemed safe enough.

What were the chances of falling in love with a woman picked at random, sight unseen? None. Absolutely none. And that's how he had wanted it.

It took every bit of strength he possessed to finally pull away from the window. Even then, he had trouble walking away, though he knew he must. He needed time to think, to organize his thoughts. Dare he take a chance on love again? Did he even have a choice?

Chapter 21

Something had changed. Maggie sensed it the moment Garrett walked into the house later that day.

He made no mention of seeing her in her wedding gown. Nor did he say anything about the bills she ran up, but she noticed him watching her intently at times, noticed a softening in the eyes that regarded her, heard a disturbing gentleness of voice whenever he said her name.

After the children had been bathed and tucked in bed, he invited her to join him outside to look at the nighttime sky. His attentive manner told her he had something more than stars on his mind.

Rikker's voice echoed in her mind. *"You better watch your step."* But Garrett looked anything but dangerous tonight—at least not in the way that Rikker meant.

"It's a beautiful evening," he said as if he sensed her hesitation.

"Let me get a wrap," she said.

She hurried down the hall and tiptoed quietly into the children's room. The light was out, but she was able to locate her shawl.

Out of habit, she reached into her false pocket. Her holstered weapon was loaded and ready. Not that she thought she'd need it.

"Are you coming to bed?" Elise asked.

"Soon, pumpkin. Soon."

Wrapping the shawl around her shoulders, she left the room.

Garrett held the door open as she walked out to the front porch. He startled her by reaching for her hand.

He must have felt her stiffen because the light from the open door revealed his questioning look. "Are you all right?"

She nodded. If only his touch wasn't playing havoc with her senses. Her heart thudded, and suddenly she had trouble drawing air into her lungs.

He reached back to close the door. With a slight nod, he led her down the steps but didn't release her hand until they reached the front gate. Just then a shooting star arced across the northern sky.

His soothing voice washed over her like a gentle wave. "Some people believe that a shooting star foretells good fortune."

She shivered. Why did he have to mention the word *fortune*? "Some people also believe they bring bad luck."

"I like my version better," he said. The light from the house reflected in his eyes, and the slight desert breeze ruffled his hair. "Look, there's another one."

She looked up just in time to see the tail end of a meteor fade away. He was right; it was beautiful even without the moon. The stars sparkled like diamonds scattered across a silky black sky.

She couldn't get over the weather. She'd grabbed a wrap out of habit, but didn't really need it. It was like summer, but without the humidity of the East.

"That's Orion," he said. "And that's the Big Dipper." He pointed out several more constellations, some she'd never heard of.

"How do you know so much about the stars?" she asked.

"Not much to do in the stockades but look up." She waited for him to continue, but he changed the subject. "You said you liked it here in the Territory," he said. "A lot of people don't."

No doubt, he was thinking of Katherine. "I didn't think I would either, at first. I heard so many horror stories." Arizona had appeared bleak and desolate from the train window, but she had since come to appreciate the ever-shifting light across the desert sands and mountains. No artist could capture such splendor. "I was also a bit nervous about the Indian problem."

"I won't lie to you. There are still some small Apache bands causing trouble in parts of the Territory. But most of the Indians abide by the treaties and are peaceful."

"That's good to hear," she said. "Crazy as it sounds, I even like the weather."

He laughed. "You may change your mind come summer." He fell silent for a moment before asking, "And the children? You like them, too?"

"I love them both," she said with meaning. Somehow those two little pumpkins had stolen her heart, and there wasn't a blasted thing she could do about it. "Why all the questions?" she asked.

"I just want to make certain," he replied, his smooth baritone voice wrapping around her like a velvet ribbon.

She furrowed her brow. "Make certain about what?"

Even in the darkness she could see the flash of his teeth as he smiled. "You'll see. Let's go inside. I have something for you."

She couldn't help but be curious. "You've done enough for me already. The check for my family—"

"I was glad to help," he said.

"You didn't sound glad last night," she said.

"I take the blame for what happened," he said, sounding apologetic. "We've never discussed money or budgets. You had no way of knowing our limitations."

She stared at him in a mass of confusion. Budgets? He was talking budgets? A man who supposedly stole seventy thousand dollars?

Rikker had nearly convinced her she was wrong, that she had let personal feelings get in the way. But what if she was right? What if the agency that was usually so methodical had made a mistake? What if they had their sights set on the wrong man?

The thought froze in her brain, and she quickly banished it. The Pinkerton Detective Agency didn't make mistakes. Thinking him innocent was only wishful thinking on her part.

Momentarily lost in her reverie, she was startled when he took her by the hand again. "Come," he said softly.

They walked side by side along the gravel walkway to the porch. Once inside the house, he released her and reached into his pocket for a small square box.

She stared at the box, and her mouth went dry. "That's not—"

"I think it's time we made our betrothal official. So there's no confusion."

It was all she could do to find her voice. "I'm not sure what you mean. What confusion?"

He chuckled. "You haven't noticed the way other men look at you?"

She blushed and shook her head. "I—I don't know what to say."

He handed her the box and rubbed the back of his neck. "Hopefully you'll know what to say when you open it."

Fingering the small box, she lifted the lid. The gold ring etched with ornate scrolls took her breath away. "It's. . .it's beautiful." She looked up to find him watching her intently. "You made this?"

He nodded. "It was originally my mother's thimble. My grandmother brought it all the way from England."

Obviously the ring meant a lot to him, and she was at a loss for words.

He took the box from her and pulled out the shiny band. Stuffing the box back in his pocket, he held the ring between his thumb and forefinger.

"I think this is where I'm supposed to recite some poem or say something halfway intelligent. But the only poem that comes to mind at the moment is a silly nursery rhyme I used to recite to Elise about a couple of children tumbling down a hill with a pail of water. That hardly seems to suit the occasion."

She couldn't look away from him even if she'd wanted to; she couldn't even breathe.

He continued, "As for saying something intelligent. . . Miss Maggie Taylor, would you do me the honor of wearing this ring as a symbol of our betrothal?"

She moistened her lips. Things were going exactly as planned.

Accepting his ring was her job; it was part of the methodical plan Pinkerton had devised. If only the object wasn't a family heirloom. If only she didn't feel like a criminal for accepting it.

Still, she had prepared for this moment. Rehearsed it. After watching a woman accept a marriage proposal in a play, she'd practiced the exaggerated fluttering of hands and eyelashes in front of a mirror.

Now she couldn't bring herself to act so inanely coy.

When she said nothing, he arched an eyebrow. "I think the customary answer is yes."

"I'm sorry. I didn't expect—" She cut herself off. Nothing had changed. They were already betrothed—or at least that's what she'd led him to believe. Still, something about the ring made it all seem so impossibly real that she felt trapped.

"Well?" he asked.

"The ring is beautiful, and yes. . . . It would be my honor to wear it."

His grin widened as he took her left hand in his and slowly slipped the gold band onto the fourth finger. Next to her lily-white flesh, his sun-darkened hand was the color of fine leather. His fingers were long, tapered, strong—and surprisingly gentle. Her pulse pounded in her temple.

The ring slipped on easily. The embossed metal captured the light from the lamp, which turned it into a dazzling gold star.

"It's beautiful," she said, surprised at how much she wanted it to be hers to keep.

"Beautiful like my bride," he said.

As he spoke, she imagined herself in her white satin gown standing at the altar by his side. A lump rose in her throat. Marriage, family, a home—she'd always dreamed of such things, but never thought they could be hers.

A shudder rushed through her, and she shook the thought away. What was she thinking? None of this was real. It was all make-believe. A carefully devised plan—nothing more. It could never be anything more.

He released her hand. "I believe it's traditional for a man and woman to seal a moment like this with a kiss." He hesitated. "Would you mind?"

Her heart fluttered. She thought she could do this; she thought she could play the blushing bride; she thought she could remain professional and keep her wits about her. She thought wrong. Suddenly she was a mass of quivering jelly.

He inclined his head, apparently sensing her hesitation. "If you'd rather not, I understand."

"Oh no." She fought to depict an ease she didn't feel. "I mean. . .I'd like for you to kiss me." As much as she hated to admit it, she spoke the truth. *Just don't let my knees give out.*

"All right, then." He stepped forward and cupped his hands ever so gently around her face. She quivered at the tenderness of his touch.

"It won't hurt, I promise," he whispered.

She wasn't afraid of his kiss hurting her; she was afraid of liking it.

The moment his lips brushed hers she knew she had good reason to worry. Warm currents rushed through her, and somehow her arms found their way around his neck. The pressure of his mouth increased, melting away the last of her resistance.

The scent of bay rum hair tonic filled her head and a tingling sensation ran down her spine. Her mind went blank and her senses took over. Nothing seemed to exist but the breadth and depth of his mouth on hers.

He pulled back, and just like that, it was over. He hadn't forced her, hadn't pushed her, hadn't expected anything in return—only what she had been all too willing to give.

As far as kisses went, it was pretty straightforward. Yet it left her lips burning with need and her heart wanting that which she could never have.

He studied her with a knitted brow. "I'm sorry," he said, apparently misreading her expression or maybe her silence. "I should have waited to kiss you."

"N–no," she stammered. "I mean—"

A moment of awkwardness stretched between them. He rubbed his neck and cleared his throat. She looked away and moistened her still-burning mouth. She tried to think what the actors in that play had said after the couple kissed. Something about his having to leave before her husband returned home.

The thought made her smile, and he smiled, too, a look of relief on his face. It was a good thing he didn't know she was thinking about an unfaithful wife in a silly stage play.

Apparently her smile reassured him, or at least he seemed to relax. "There's a dance planned for Thursday night. If my aunt agrees to watch the children, I thought it would be a good place to announce our engagement."

She remembered hearing something about a dance. "Well, I—" The principal had sent her to Arizona Territory to earn Garrett's trust, and that's exactly what she had done. So why did it suddenly feel like something was happening over which she had no control?

She cleared her throat and tried again. "I'm not sure I have the proper clothes for a dance." Not that it mattered. If he paid the bills she ran up with stolen money it would all be over by Thursday.

His eyes traveled down the length of her blue printed dress, but she had the strangest feeling he was seeing her not as she was but rather how she had looked in her wedding gown.

"What you're wearing is fine. We're very informal around here."

"I guess it's settled then," she said.

His crooked grin tore through her defenses, and her pulse skittered. "Thursday night it is."

❧

Toby was curled up on the floor asleep when Garrett entered his room. He picked up the tools and pieces of metal surrounding his son's prone body with an amused shake of his head. He then drew the blanket over the boy's shoulders before lowering himself onto the edge of his bed.

He was too tense to sleep. Every cell in his body was on edge. He hadn't meant to push her. It wasn't like him to act in haste. Certainly he'd never planned to give Maggie the ring so soon. But after seeing her in her wedding gown, he realized how much he wanted to marry her. How much he wanted to make her his wife.

He also feared losing her.

He often caught her watching him—studying him—and he couldn't help but wonder what went through her mind. Did he fall short of her expectations? A man with a disfigured face and an even more deeply scarred soul?

He rubbed his hands together. Her lavender fragrance still taunted him as did the memory of her sweet, soft lips on his.

She hadn't objected to his kiss and had in fact kissed him back. Still, he felt. . .what? Reluctance on her part? Hesitancy? She certainly didn't hold back with the children. She hugged and kissed them freely. The tenderness on her face at times as she looked at them made him ache with envy.

Would she ever look at him like that? Would she ever laugh as openly with him as she did with Toby and Elise? Would he ever hear the words *I love you* fall from her pretty pink lips?

Somehow she had quickly and unexpectedly won his heart, but he hadn't won hers. Not yet. But he would. By jove, he would.

Chapter 22

The ring on her finger caught her eye the moment she woke the following morning. Sitting up in bed, she rubbed the band with her thumb. The memory of Garrett's kiss brought a rush of heat to her cheeks, and she touched her fingertips to her lips.

She'd handled herself as well as could be expected under the circumstance. Never before had she been required to *kiss* a suspect. Far as she knew, neither had the other operatives. The thought brought a rush of heat to her cheeks.

What was wrong with her? It wasn't as if she'd never been kissed. But none of the stolen kisses shared with men in the past compared to Garrett's.

Naturally she'd considered the possibility that he might wish to kiss the woman he planned to wed.

She thought she could handle it. She thought she could endure a kiss from him without undergoing any kind of emotion. But never before had a kiss affected her so. It was as if he had done more than simply kiss her; somehow he had branded her and reached into her very soul.

It was less than three weeks to the wedding, but she couldn't stay around that long. She had to get the proof she sought and quickly leave town.

Meanwhile, there could be no more kisses. Nothing like that must happen again. It was too disconcerting. How could she concentrate on doing her job when all she could think about was his full, sensuous mouth on hers?

If Garrett insisted on repeating the kiss, she would simply say she wished to wait until they were wed. The thought made her groan. For the love of Betsy, why hadn't she thought to say that last night?

She pulled her fingers away from her mouth, surprised to find the memory of his lips still lingered there.

If only he wasn't a suspected criminal...

If only her job wasn't to find out what he'd done with the stolen money...

She sighed and slipped out of bed. No sense wasting time wishing things were different. No sense at all.

∽

No sooner had Maggie finished washing the breakfast dishes than she heard a knock. Drying her hands, she rushed from the kitchen to open the door.

"Aunt Hetty. I...wasn't expecting you."

The woman hobbled past her. "I have some exciting news." She turned to face Maggie. "Oswald has agreed to sing at your wedding."

Maggie closed the door. "That's...great, but who is Oswald?"

"His full name is Oswald Dinwiddie. He's this nice man from church. A deacon. I didn't really know him that well until the day of the miracle. You know when the cross—" She moved her head from side to side to demonstrate. "He was kind enough to take me home after the service." Her face turned red. "He even stayed for supper."

Surprised to see Aunt Hetty blush, Maggie couldn't help but smile. "Ah, so now you have a gentleman friend," she teased.

Aunt Hetty blinked. "Why, yes, I guess I do." She giggled like a schoolgirl. "Would you believe Oswald's arthritis was cured by the miracle, too? Just like mine was. Of course, he still suffers from palpitations, rheumatism, and gout, but he's not complaining. You can't expect to be completely cured from a single miracle, now can you?"

"No, I guess you can't."

"There's a new doctor in town. His name is Dr. Kettleman, and I bought this new miracle cure from him."

Maggie blinked. "Don't tell me you bought from that quack. . .?" The words were out of her mouth before she could stop them.

Instead of taking offense, Aunt Hetty laughed. "Oh, you healthy people are all alike. You think every ailment a fake and every doctor a quack."

"Not all," Maggie said and then changed the subject. "You said this man—Mr. Dinwiddie—has agreed to sing?"

"He did, and he gave us three hymns to choose from. Personally, I think you should skip the first two. I don't think songs about suffering belong at a wedding."

"I'm sure there are those who disagree," Maggie said with a wry smile.

"Oh my! Is that a ring?" Aunt Hetty took Maggie's hand in hers.

"Garrett designed it from a thimble that belonged to his mother."

"Well, now." She turned Maggie's hand to better capture the light. "It sure does look better on your finger than it ever looked on my sister's."

Aunt Hetty let go of Maggie's hand. "Garrett asked me to watch the children while you attend Thursday's dance. It'll do you two the world of good to get out and socialize."

"I hope you don't mind. I know the children can be a handful, but it's a school night so they'll have to go to bed early."

"Land o' living, why would I mind? Long as Toby doesn't get into mischief, I'm sure we'll get along just fine." She pulled a notebook from her purse. "There're a couple of things we need to go over for the wedding."

Aunt Hetty hobbled toward the kitchen and lowered herself onto a chair. "My back is killing me." She spread the notebook open on the table.

"Perhaps you'd rather wait till you feel better."

"Nonsense. There isn't much time left till the wedding. We need to go over the guest list."

Maggie jumped at the opening Aunt Hetty had provided. "Speaking of the guest list, I wonder if we should invite Katherine's brother."

Aunt Hetty's eyes widened. "Good heavens! Whatever for?"

Maggie sat opposite her and folded her hands on the table. "He's still the children's uncle, and I thought perhaps Katherine might have wanted us to treat him as family."

"Katherine would have wanted no such thing. She was tired of bailing him out of trouble and thought him a bad influence on the children."

"Really?" People like Aunt Hetty, who weren't afraid to express their opinions or spread rumors and gossip, really were a detective's best friend. "What kind of trouble?"

"He was always getting into fights and couldn't keep a job to save his soul. I can't tell you how many nights he spent in jail for disturbing the peace. Katherine insisted he wasn't always like that but had changed during the war."

"I guess that's true of a lot of men."

Aunt Hetty nodded. "Thank goodness it's not true of Garrett. I mean, he changed but not in a bad way. Now about that guest list. . ."

⁂

The Finnegan dance hall was packed that Thursday night when Maggie and Garrett walked in.

Curious stares followed them as they threaded their way through the crowd, her arm in the crook of his.

She wore a simple blue print dress, the sleeves and neckline edged with lace. The shoulder to hem panels showed off her trim hips and small waist.

A quick glance around the room put any lingering doubts about her wardrobe to rest. Arizona wasn't Boston, New York, or even Chicago. Local women dressed mainly for comfort and practicality, not fashion. Poor Katherine must have felt like a fish out of water.

A fiddler played a lively tune, his bushy eyebrows moving up and down in time to the music, along with his foot. The lights were low and the dance in full swing. Men and women stood at both sides of the hall clapping for the couples whirling about the dance floor beneath the watchful eyes of matronly chaperons.

A knot of younger women exchanged whispers behind gloved hands and cast flirtatious glances at Garrett. Not that Maggie blamed them. Dressed in dark trousers, white shirt, vest, and bolo tie, Garrett looked especially attractive tonight. His hair combed neatly from a side part, he was one of the few clean-shaven men in the room, and his scar was hardly noticeable in the dim gas lights. Under normal circumstances, Maggie might have considered herself lucky to be escorted by such a tall and handsome man.

Garrett introduced her to several older couples. "I want you to meet Miss Maggie Taylor," he said, rattling off names.

Maggie shook hands and smiled. People seemed less reserved here than in the States and thought nothing of asking pertinent questions.

A blond woman looked her over with a critical air. "How did you come to know Garrett?"

"We corresponded," she said vaguely, not sure if Garrett wanted it known they'd met through a marriage broker.

The questions kept coming and she answered most with confidence, sticking to the background she'd invented, the story carefully composed. Yes, she liked Arizona Territory. Yes, the heat did take some getting used to. She was from Remington, Indiana. No, she wasn't homesick.

She'd never been to Remington, but one of the other operatives had. He had drawn her maps and drilled her relentlessly on every detail of the town until she felt she knew it inside and out.

As long as she avoided looking at Garrett, she was able to maintain her composure. She played her part with none of the uncertainties that had plagued her since arriving in town.

Mrs. Higginbottom tapped Garrett on the chest with her lorgnette. Her bright floral dress made her look like an oversized flower pot.

"Hetty said you've set a date for your wedding," she said.

"Yes, and you should all receive an invitation soon." He smiled down at Maggie with a look that tore through her defenses. She never really had a beau and wasn't certain how to act with one in public.

"Show them your ring," he said.

Maggie held up her hand, and the women all oohed and aahed.

"It's beautiful," Mrs. Higginbottom declared. Lifting the glasses to her eyes, she added, "We must announce your engagement tonight."

Maggie dropped her hand to her side. "We don't want any fuss."

"Of course you do," Mrs. Higginbottom said. "It's not every day that a girl becomes engaged."

Her husband stroked his mustache. "Did you ever wonder why we use the word *engagement* to describe both a promise of marriage and a war battle?" His comment brought chuckles from the other men and glares from their wives.

"Don't mind Paul," Mrs. Higginbottom said. "Do you wish to make the announcement now or later?"

"Later is fine," Garrett said. "Right now I would like to dance with my beautiful fiancée." He turned to Maggie with a smile and crooked his elbow. "Let's show them how it's done."

She slipped her arm through his, and a wave of anxiety rushed through her. She'd helped to chase down some of the country's most dangerous criminals, but never had she been as nervous as she was at the thought of dancing in Garrett's arms.

"I don't know how to dance," she said as they walked away from the group. Life in an orphanage left no room for parties or dances. So far, none of her other assignments had required it of her.

He ducked beneath the low-hanging paper streamers and led her onto the dance floor. "Nothing to it," he said. "Just do everything I do, backwards."

She laughed. "That easy, eh?"

He faced her, and her pulse beat erratically. Was it only her imagination that everyone in the room appeared to stand still at that moment as if holding a collective breath? Even the music seemed to hold a longer beat.

Placing his hand at her waist, he drew her close. His gaze locked with hers. "Ready?"

Nodding, she placed her left hand on his shoulder and moistened her lips. He closed the distance between them completely by taking her right hand in his. Nervously she followed his movements.

She felt the rhythm of the music pulse through him as they whirled about the room, his eyes never leaving her face. With a gentle pressure of his hand he drew her around the dance floor as smoothly as a butterfly flitted from blossom to blossom. For such a tall man, he was surprisingly light on his feet.

It took two turns of the room before she could relax enough to enjoy herself. By the third turn she was almost ready to believe she was a woman with no secrets, dancing with a man with nothing to hide.

The fiddler finished his frantic tune and switched to a slower-paced melody. Some couples left the floor, but Garrett's hand tightened around her waist—an invitation to stay.

He held her so close she feared his leg would brush against the gun hidden beneath her skirt. She would have a hard time explaining why she carried a firearm to a dance, especially since all the men had been required to leave their weapons at the door.

"Where did you learn to dance so well?" she asked in an effort to distract him.

"I'm not dancing. I'm just trying to avoid stepping on your toes."

She laughed. "You could have fooled me."

They made a couple more turns around the room, her movements matching his. She couldn't remember ever feeling so lighthearted.

She threw her head back like a child on a swing. "Wheee. Look at me, I'm dancing," she said, and his smile deepened into laughter.

Surprised at how quickly she'd learned to follow his lead, she didn't want the night to end.

Chapter 23

A man wearing peg-topped trousers and a flaming red shirt took his place next to the fiddler and called out. "Grab a partner, men. Grab a partner."

A flurry of activity followed as people lined up two by two and took to the dance floor.

"Choose your partner, form a ring," the caller chanted in tune to the music.

Garrett grasped her hands, and they shuffled around in a circle. His eyes shone with merriment as he flashed her a smile.

"How will you swap, and how will you trade? This pretty girl for that old maid?"

Maggie suddenly found herself partnered with someone else. She hardly recognized the debonair man dressed in a three-piece suit and bow tie.

She gasped. "Rikker!"

"Shh," he cautioned. Interlocking elbows, they made an awkward turn around the dance floor. Dancing with her coworker was like dancing with a centipede. He stepped on her foot, and she grimaced.

"What are you doing here?" she asked. His presence was an unwelcome reminder that she had failed so far to produce any evidence against Garrett.

"The same as you," he said as they circled each other back-to-back in a do-si-do. "Working. Or at least that's what I hope you're doing."

"You know it is." She didn't need him telling her that a detective was always on the job. That had been drilled into all operatives.

"Either you're a better actress than I gave you credit for or you were having the time of your life."

"There's nothing that says you can't enjoy your work," she retorted.

Rikker opened his mouth to respond, but the caller said to switch partners, and after several turns around the room she was back with Garrett.

"When you meet your partner, pat her on the head, if she don't like coffee, give her corn bread."

Garrett laughed at the mention of corn bread. Like an old married couple sharing a private joke, she laughed, too. All too soon she was sashaying with another partner—an older man with bowed legs.

Several partners later, Rikker grabbed her by the arm and whirled her about with the grace of a bull. "We have a problem."

She grimaced. "You always know how to spoil a gal's fun."

"Thomas made arrangements to pay the debts you ran up in installments. But don't worry. Something came up." After dropping that piece of tantalizing news, Rikker promenaded off with Mrs. Higginbottom.

She had to wait until she met up with Rikker again before she found out the rest.

"It looks like more of the stolen money showed up," he said. "A vagrant purchased tobacco with a stolen hundred-dollar bill. He's locked in jail."

That was an unexpected surprise. "Where did he get the money?"

"Claims he hasn't the foggiest, but I don't believe it. A man hands you a hundred-dollar greenback, you're not likely to forget where you got it."

She frowned. "So you think he's lying?"

"Maybe, maybe not. You know what poor interrogators these desert lawmen are. Most of them couldn't get a confession from a dying man if their life depended on it."

"Swing 'em east and swing 'em west, swing the girl that you like best."

And just like that, she was back with Garrett. The dance ended, and he led her over to a row of chairs. They were both hot and out of breath.

He pulled out his handkerchief and dabbed the beads of perspiration from his forehead. "I'll get us a cold drink."

She gave him a grateful smile. "I could sure use one," she said. "Thank you."

He walked away with purposeful strides, and she looked about the room for Rikker.

What he'd said about the local lawmen was true. The Pinkerton agency was way ahead of most local officials in crime-fighting abilities. Most jurisdictions didn't have the manpower, knowledge, or resources available to the Pinkerton Agency. This created bad blood between the detectives and Arizona lawmen. While most eastern sheriffs and constables were willing to work with the Pinkerton Agency, Arizona lawmen were not.

Rikker appeared seemingly out of nowhere, startling her out of her reverie, and took the seat next to her. He leaned over and pretended to tie his shoe.

"I wondered where you were." She glanced toward the refreshment table where Garrett stood in line. "Something about this whole thing doesn't make sense. Why would Garrett pay his creditors in installments and drop a hundred-dollar bill in someone's hat?"

"I don't think vagrants accept installments," Rikker said.

"You know what I mean." She sensed they had all the pieces of the puzzle if only they knew how to put them together. "It's been two years since the train robbery. Then nothing. It was as if the thieves and money vanished into thin air. So why now? Why has the money started showing up now?"

"Thomas is getting married. Wives don't come cheap."

"I wouldn't know," she said. Rikker had been married twice; one wife died in childbirth, and the other couldn't live with the weeks and sometimes even months he was away from home.

"So now what's the plan?" she asked. Nothing they tried had worked so far.

"I figure that the vagrant might appreciate a little company. An iron-bar hotel can be pretty lonely at times. Perhaps you can give me some pointers on how to get arrested."

During her last case, the suspect under surveillance had her arrested for being a public nuisance. She took pride in her shadowing ability, and still didn't have a clue as to how he had spotted her.

"So the plan is to give the sheriff just cause to arrest you, right?" It wasn't just a lucky guess; she knew how he worked. "You could always get drunk." Drinking on the case was forbidden by the agency, of course, but Rikker didn't need alcohol to play the part of a drunk. He was a natural.

He inclined his head toward the refreshment table. "The sheriff might be short a hat size or two, but I doubt he'd believe I got wasted on sarsaparilla."

"You could just come clean and tell the sheriff who you are."

"Knowing how he feels about Pinkerton operatives, that and a nickel won't get me a cup of coffee."

"If you weren't so clumsy, you could start a fight." Not only was Rikker uncoordinated on the dance floor, he couldn't punch his way out of a paper bag.

"Not a bad idea." He grinned. "What's a black eye among friends?"

"If poor dancing was a crime, you wouldn't have to start a fight," she said.

He chuckled. "Not to worry. I'll pick a fight with the smallest, skinniest man in the room."

"You better," she said, though it wasn't only this latest plan that bothered her. "I still don't understand why Garrett would take a chance on giving money to a vagrant."

"Maybe he just felt sorry for the man."

"But he had to know a large bill like that would attract attention." The fiddler started playing again, and she leaned toward her partner, her voice low. "It's almost as if he wants to get caught."

Rikker finished tying his shoe and sat upright. "Maybe he has a guilty conscience. He wouldn't be the first outlaw who did. Or maybe the more time that passes, the more confident he is of not getting caught. That's when criminals start making mistakes."

"There were two robbers. How do we know the money didn't come from the other one?"

"We don't. But all of the other parents attending the school fund-raiser checked out. Only Thomas remained a suspect."

She glanced at the refreshment table. Garrett was next in line. "I want to be there when you question your cell mate. Maybe he's not a vagrant. Maybe it's just an act. You know I'm better at picking out frauds than you are."

"And how would we explain your presence to the sheriff?"

She hated to admit it, but Rikker was right; showing up at the sheriff's office was bound to raise eyebrows unless she came up with a legitimate excuse.

She opened her mouth to say something, but Rikker stopped her with a shake of the hand. "Nice meeting you," he said loudly then switched to a softer voice. "Oops, better go. Your fiancé is coming back. See you tomorrow morning. Don't be late." With that, he stood and walked away.

She watched him disappear into the crowd. Don't be late? What did he mean by that?

She was still wondering about Rikker's puzzling statement when Garrett returned to her side and handed her a glass of sarsaparilla.

She smiled up at him. "Thank you."

"Sorry it took so long." The line between his brows deepened. "Was that man bothering you?"

"Man? Oh, you mean. . ." She shook her head. "He was just being friendly." She raised the glass to her lips. The cold beverage quickly quenched her thirst but did nothing to settle her thoughts. Every time she convinced herself of Garrett's innocence something happened to make her doubtful again.

He sipped his own drink more slowly, and when he was done he took her empty glass from her. "Ready to announce our engagement?"

She hid her disquieting thoughts behind a smile, but her lips felt stiff, almost wooden. "I think so."

He nodded. "I'll only be a minute."

She waited for him to return the empty glasses before glancing around the room. There was no sign of Rikker. Garrett stopped to talk to Mrs. Higginbottom behind the refreshment table, bringing a smile to her face.

Maggie's mind prickled with everything Rikker said. Why now? Why was the money suddenly showing up after all this time?

Garrett returned to her side with a silly grin. "Mrs. Higginbottom is ready to make the announcement," he said. He crooked his elbow. "Shall we?"

She nodded as she slipped her arm through his. Her calm demeanor belied her churning emotions, but she almost lost her composure when he brushed his lips against her ear.

Garrett walked her across the dance floor to the front of the room. He exchanged a few words with Mrs. Higginbottom, and she hurried over to the fiddler, her bustle swinging from side to side. The music stopped, and dance partners pulled away from each other as if suddenly forbidden to touch.

"Nervous?" Garrett asked in a hushed voice meant for her ears only.

"Not at all," she said. She wasn't nervous, but she was worried about Rikker. *Please, please, please, God, let Rikker's plan work.* The sooner they got the answers they sought, the sooner she could be done with this charade.

Mrs. Higginbottom joined them. "Look at you two. Don't you make a lovely couple?" She pressed her hands together. "After I make the announcement, everyone will want to see your ring."

"Yes, of course." Maggie rubbed her finger and finding it ringless stared down at her hand in horror. She looked up and saw Rikker a short distance away. He held up her ring just before turning away, and her mouth gaped open. Why did he take her ring? What was he thinking?

Mrs. Higginbottom lifted the speaking tube to her mouth, and her voice carried over the noise of the crowd. "Ladies and gentlemen, may I have your attention, please?" A hush fell across the room, and everyone turned to face the front.

While the woman spoke, Maggie began to panic. How would she explain her missing ring? She glanced up at Garrett, but his attention was focused on Mrs. Higginbottom.

"Tonight," Mrs. Higginbottom continued, her voice cracking, "we have a very special announcement to make, and—"The rest of her words were gobbled up by a loud crash.

All heads swiveled toward the back of the room and loud protests rose from the crowd. Two men were going at it tooth and nail.

One was Rikker; the other a short, wiry man wearing spectacles. Outranking his sparring partner in height and weight, Rikker appeared to have picked a fight with the right man. Maggie was soon relieved of that notion.

If only Mr. Wiry wasn't so quick on his feet or so accurate with his punches, Rikker might have had a chance. Much to Maggie's dismay, he appeared to be losing ground—fast.

Clutching his nose, Rikker picked up a chair with one hand and flung it at his opponent. Wiry ducked just in time, and the chair hit one of the matronly chaperons on the leg. That's all it took for spectators to jump into the fray. Fists flew in every direction, followed by grunts and groans as men doubled over or landed on their backs.

One man slid across the floor like an oversized lizard and crashed into the refreshment table. Dishes fell to the floor with a loud clatter. A woman screamed and people stampeded from the dance hall.

"Let's get out of here," Garrett shouted, grabbing Maggie's hand. She didn't want to leave. Her coworker might need help, but Garrett's firm grip left no room for argument.

A blast of cold air greeted them as they joined the throng rushing outside. He helped her onto the buckboard before running around Patches and scrambling into the driver's seat. Grabbing the reins he released the brake and clicked his tongue.

The brawl had spilled outside, and Garrett was forced to steer the wagon around a knot of men rolling on the ground.

Holding on for dear life as they raced out of town, Maggie glanced back, but there was no sign of Rikker.

Chapter 24

Maggie hardly slept that night. She twisted and turned until her bedding ended up in a heap on the floor. Not only was she worried about Rikker, but something else kept her awake—something over which she had no control. It filled her with guilt as well as pain.

She couldn't shake the memory of dancing with Garrett. Even staring wide-eyed at the dark ceiling couldn't keep her from reliving every moment spent in his arms.

She finally gave up trying to sleep and slipped out of bed. Not wanting to wake Elise, she quietly paced the floor.

The first light of dawn crept into her room, and she heard Garrett's door open. Sensing him pause outside her room, she held her breath. A moment passed. Two. He finally moved away, his footsteps echoing down the hall. She gasped for air, but nothing could be done for her pounding heart.

She rubbed her finger, surprised to find how much she missed the ring. Not that it meant anything, of course. It was just a prop—part of her disguise.

Still, questions remained. Rikker had taken her ring, but why? He never did anything without good reason. Pressing her hands against her temples she tried to concentrate, and finally the answer came. Of course!

She pounded her forehead with the palm of her hand. What took her so long to figure it out? With no time to lose, she quickly dressed.

Garrett had an early morning delivery and was already gone by the time she walked into the kitchen. Fortunately he'd made the coffee, and she gratefully poured herself a cup.

The coffee helped settle her nerves, and so did the children. It was hard not to laugh at their antics. While Aunt Hetty took care of them the night before, she had engaged them with a lesson on human anatomy and all the things that could go wrong.

"What's a fibula?" Elise asked.

"It's a person who tells a lie," Toby said.

Elise thought about this for a moment. "Did you know that Aunt Hetty's legs tell lies?"

Maggie laughed. "Actually, a fibula is a bone, pumpkin, and we all have fibulas in our legs. We wouldn't be able to walk without them."

After fixing breakfast and driving the children to school, she waited for them to enter the adobe schoolhouse. A movement in the distance caught her eye. Someone else was watching, too. A man on a brown and white horse was half hidden behind the school privy.

He was too far away to identify, but there was something vaguely familiar about him. Was he watching the schoolhouse? Or watching her?

Only one way to find out. Grabbing hold of Patches's reins, she gave them a good shake. No sooner had the wagon rolled forward than the man swung his horse around and took off in the opposite direction, leaving behind a cloud of dust.

Frowning, she watched him ride away, not knowing what to think. His presence at the school could have been entirely innocent, but by the time she reached town, she was fairly convinced otherwise. The presumption of innocence was all well and good in the courtroom, but experience taught her that everyone was guilty of something, and most of her suspicions had proven true in the past.

There was no sign of a brown and white horse in town, so she forced herself to focus on the task at hand. She parked the buckboard in front of the hotel, which was as far away from her destination as possible. She glanced down the street to where Garrett's horse and wagon was tethered in front of his shop. If by chance she bumped into him or his aunt, she would have a hard time explaining her business with the sheriff.

It was early and most of the shops were still closed. The street was deserted, except for the mule-drawn sprinkler wagon, allowing her to duck into the sheriff's office without being seen.

The sheriff looked up from his desk as she entered. A small sign stated his name as Sheriff L. C. Summerhay. He peered at her from beneath bushy black eyebrows that rose and fell like two caterpillars doing push-ups.

"Can I help you, ma'am?"

She glanced at Rikker behind bars. The poor man had two black eyes and a swollen lip. The sleeve of his shirt was torn and his bow tie missing. He probably could use a bit of sympathy, but that would have to wait.

His cell mate was hunched over on the bunk, head in his hands. Unable to get a look at his face she turned to the sheriff. Though the Arizona sun had baked his skin to a dark leather color and carved deep lines into his forehead and around his eyes, she guessed Summerhay was only in his late thirties.

"My name is Maggie Taylor," she said.

"I know who you are. You're Garrett's woman."

"Actually, I'm his fiancée," she replied. So this was the lawman who steadfastly refused to work with Pinkerton detectives. What would he say if he knew her true identity?

"What can I do for you?" he asked.

She pointed at Rikker. "That man has my engagement ring."

Summerhay's eyebrows did a couple more push-ups before he rose to his feet. "That true?" he called over to Rikker.

Rikker shrugged and tossed the ring on the floor just outside his cell. She walked over to retrieve it. The vagrant lifted his head, and she got a good look at his face. He didn't seem to recognize her, but she sure did recognize him. It was the pickpocket she'd encountered at the train station the day she arrived in town.

She slipped the ring onto the fourth finger of her left hand and turned. The sheriff watched her with narrowed eyes. "Do you wish to file a complaint?"

"Oh, no, nothing like that," she said, giving him her most brilliant smile. "I dropped the ring last night at the dance and that gentleman was kind enough to fetch it for me. But before he could return it, a fight broke out."

"It didn't just break out. He started it," the sheriff said, indicating Rikker.

"Ha!" She gave her head an indignant toss. "Whoever told you that, told you wrong. It was the other man who started the fight. A short man wearing glasses. I saw it with my own two eyes."

"Is that so?" The sheriff looked dubious as he took his seat.

"Yes, that's so. As for your other prisoner. . . He stole from a man and a boy at the train station. I saw him do it."

The sheriff rubbed his chin. "You're just all over the place, aren't you? Well, rest assured. Crankshaw won't be causing any more trouble for a while."

"His name sounds familiar," she said. "Would that be *Joseph* Crankshaw?" Since the pickpocket had purchased tobacco with stolen money, he was a suspect in the Whistle-Stop robbery, however unlikely.

"Harry," Summerhay said. "Harry Crankshaw."

She smiled. No need to spend the night in jail with the man to learn the basics about him. "My mistake." She made a mental note of Crankshaw's height, weight, and possible age, more out of habit than need. It was always hard to estimate a beggar's age. Most looked older than they actually were, especially the ones who had lived on the street for any length of time.

Rikker would surely include a full description of him in his report to headquarters, but she was trained to pay close attention to details.

"Will that be all?" the sheriff asked. He looked anxious to get back to the paperwork piled on his desk.

"There is one other matter," she said and looked the sheriff square in the face. "I would like to post bail for the man who was kind enough to return my ring."

The sheriff sat back in his chair and tapped his fingers on the desk. "Why would you do that?"

"It's the least I can do to show my appreciation."

Summerhay cast a glance at the jail cell. Rikker shrugged, though it seemed to pain him to do so, and the sheriff turned back to her.

"Bail is five dollars."

She arched an eyebrow. "That much?" Since the sheriff didn't look like he was in the mood to bargain, she reached into her purse, counted out the exact amount, and handed it to him. She could well imagine what the Pinkerton accountant would have to say about this additional expense. She and Rikker were already over budget.

The sheriff placed the money in a desk drawer. He then stood, reached for the keys hanging from a hook on the wall behind his desk, and unlocked the cell.

"You're in luck. This little lady just bailed you out."

"That's mighty kind of you, ma'am." Rikker pressed a bowler on his head and hobbled out of the cell, rubbing his chin. Whether he was really hurt or putting on an act was anyone's guess.

"I wonder if you'd be so kind as to keep this little transaction between us," she asked the sheriff. The last thing she needed was for Garrett to find out she was bailing prisoners out of jail.

Summerhay slammed the cell door shut. "Why is that?"

"You know what gossips some people are." She put on her best damsel in distress look. "Someone could jump to all the wrong conclusions, and with the wedding so close. . ."

"Don't you worry none, ma'am. No one will hear a thing from me." He replaced the keys on the hook and glanced at Rikker. "And you! Stay out of trouble, you hear?"

Maggie left the jailhouse first, and Rikker walked several steps behind her. "It took you long enough," he groused.

She stopped to look at a display of brooms and shovels in the hardware window and waited for him to pass. Apparently his limp wasn't an act.

"I got here as fast as I could. I had to take the children to school. Learn anything?"

His answer came moments later as he stood by a lamppost lighting a pipe. Her eyes focused straight ahead, she slowed her pace and pretended to look in the window of the barbershop.

"Claims he was at the train station panhandling," Rikker said. "A number of people tossed money into his hat. Said he paid no attention and didn't know who did the tossing."

She didn't believe that for a second. Pickpockets were experts at targeting potential victims. A stranger tossed a bill into a hat or cup, and the thief immediately knew where the contributor kept his money. He would also have a pretty good idea how much money was his for the taking. It seemed unlikely that Crankshaw hadn't taken careful note of his generous donor.

At the corner, they stood side by side waiting for a wagon to move out of the way. She opened her drawstring handbag and pretended to look for something.

"Certainly you don't believe him," she said.

"As a matter of fact I do," Rikker replied and stepped off the boardwalk ahead of her.

She thought about this as she followed Rikker across the street. In any crowd a pickpocket had a choice of ideal targets. A distracted mother; a man carelessly carrying his coat over his shoulder; an enamored couple or trusting youth were all easy pickings.

It didn't seem likely that he would target Garrett, a man with a military bearing and purposeful walk. Perhaps Crankshaw was watching someone else when Garrett dropped the banknote in his hat. It was a possibility, however slight.

"Did you find out who Garrett is corresponding with?" he asked as she passed him moments later.

He caught up to her in front of the mercantile store where she stopped to pet a black and white terrier tied up in front.

"Not yet." She'd considered asking Garrett outright but decided against it. If it was addressed to the second Whistle-Stop bandit, chances are he would only lie. "We'll have to intercept his letters at the post office."

A half block away he stopped to read a handbill in the window of the assay company. "You know we can't do that. Can't mess with the US mail."

No, they couldn't. The Pinkerton General Order Book was clear about that; operatives had to adhere to the letter of the law—no exceptions. Rather than tie a detective's hands, however, abiding by the law inspired the most creative crime-solving methods ever devised by humankind. She and Rikker would just have to come up with a lawful way of breaking into the post office and stealing the mail.

"There's something else," she said. "His brother-in-law's still in town, and there's bad blood between them. I'm more than certain I saw him at the school this morning."

"What was he doing there?"

"That's what I want you to find out. While you're doing that, I'll work on the letter angle."

"Make it fast," Rikker said. "The longer this case drags on, the less I like it."

"I don't know what you're complaining about. I'm the one under pressure. You're a free man."

An all too familiar voice from behind made her freeze momentarily before swinging around. Garrett stood only a few feet away, an inquiring look on his handsome square face. He had just stepped out of the bank. Behind him, Rikker quickly dodged into the confectioners.

"You were saying something about a free man?" he prompted.

She was momentarily stymied as to how to explain herself when a hand-drawn sign in the window gave her an idea. "Fre. . .mont," she stammered.

The sign was one of many posted in shop windows criticizing the governor for hardly ever setting foot in the Territory. Some citizens were demanding his resignation.

"Are you referring to *Governor* Fremont?"

She gave a determined nod. "He should either resume his duties or resign."

Garrett regarded her with a tilted head. "I quite agree."

She eyed him warily. The principal had warned her against expressing views on politics and other male-oriented subjects as she was prone to do.

"I fear you must think poorly of me for saying as much."

"Actually, I like a woman interested in public affairs." He arched a dark eyebrow. "Do you do that often? Talk to yourself I mean?"

"Only when I want to make sure someone's listening," she said.

His appreciative chuckle made her smile in response. She couldn't help it. She glanced over his shoulder, but there was no sign of Rikker.

He stood grinning at her, and it was startling to find she was grinning back. She couldn't seem to help herself. Though he was dressed in his work clothes and wore a wide-brimmed hat, he looked every bit as handsome today as he'd looked the night before.

"I really enjoyed the dance," she said to cover her embarrassment.

His eyes flared with warmth. "I did, too. Aunt Hetty was disappointed that we didn't properly announce our engagement. I'm afraid she's a bit old-fashioned in that regard."

"I'm sure that by now our betrothal is common knowledge," she said. Even the sheriff knew who she was.

"I'm sure you're right." As if catching himself staring, he looked away and rubbed the back of his neck before turning back to her. "I'd like to stay, but I have an appointment." He splayed his hand in an apologetic gesture.

"And I have errands to run."

He hesitated. "I apologize for last night." He hadn't said much on the way home from the dance, and by the time he returned from taking his aunt home, Maggie had retired.

"It wasn't your fault."

"I know, but I don't want you thinking ill of the town. Our dances aren't normally so rowdy."

"I like your dances just fine," she said.

He studied her for a moment as if judging her sincerity. Seeming to find his answer, he tipped his hat. "I better go. See you tonight."

He turned and walked away with his usual purposeful strides. Shading her eyes against the morning sun, she watched him.

So where was he going in such a hurry? She waited until he was a distance away before following him. Shadowing criminals was a big part of her job, but it was far easier to do in a large eastern city than in a small western town. During her training as an operative she had been given the task of shadowing one of the other detectives through the streets of Chicago. All went well until he suddenly halted and turned. She stopped, too—a dead giveaway, and she flunked her first test. Never again did she make that same mistake.

Garrett didn't stop. Instead, he turned down a side street, but by the time she reached the corner, he had vanished.

Only a few businesses occupied this part of town: an undertaker, the newspaper office, a lawyer. She eyed each business in turn before settling on the lawyer's office.

Not only did it appear that Garrett might want to get caught, but now he was seeing a lawyer. Rikker had suggested that Garrett might be planning to leave the country, but what if he was getting ready to turn himself in? Was that why he sent away for a mail-order bride? To care for his children after he'd been hauled off to jail?

Chapter 25

Maggie hadn't expected Garrett to remember his promise to accompany them to church on Sunday, especially after Elise's illness made them miss a week.

She was more than a little surprised when he announced that he had already hitched the wagon and if they didn't hurry they would be late.

He wore his usual work pants, vest, and shirt, for it was too hot in Arizona to dress up like folks did back East. Though women did their best to dress with reasonable regard for the Lord's house, none of the men wore suits or jackets.

Garrett didn't say much during the thirty-minute drive, except to warn Toby to behave himself.

Aunt Hetty greeted them in front of the church and could hardly contain her delight at seeing Garrett. "Oh my," she exclaimed. "First God moves the cross, and now this!"

Elise giggled and looked about to tattle on her brother. Alarmed, Maggie glanced at Garrett. As if reading her mind, he quickly pulled Elise to his side.

"Let's go in and get a seat," he said, but his way was blocked by a tall man with a goatee.

"Well, well, well. Look who decided to honor us with his presence."

Anger flared in Garrett's eyes, but before he could say anything, Aunt Hetty stepped in. "Maggie, this is Wayne Peterson. He and Garrett practically grew up together."

"How do you do," Maggie said.

Peterson gave a curt nod and moved away.

Garrett hustled both children toward the church. Before entering the carved oak doors, he met Maggie's worried frown and winked as if to relieve her concerns.

Heat rushed to her face, and she quickly turned her attention back to his aunt. Distracted by another church member, a matronly woman, Aunt Hetty hadn't seemed to notice the conspiratorial message Garrett sent—a message that seemed every bit as personal and intimate as a kiss.

The other woman moved away, and Aunt Hetty turned to Maggie. "What's so funny?"

"What?"

"Just wondering what brought such a pretty smile to your face."

Maggie quickly covered her mouth with her fingertips. She was smiling? "Just. . .something the children said earlier."

Certainly it had nothing to do with Garrett or his wink. At least she hoped it didn't. True, they tended to act like an old married couple at times. Oddly enough, they had even started finishing each other's sentences.

Either she was a better actress than she thought or something else was going on, and she didn't want to consider the implications.

Aunt Hetty gave her a funny look, and Maggie quickly changed the subject. "I take it there's bad blood between Mr. Peterson and Garrett."

"I'm afraid so. It goes back to their teens when they both took a fancy to the same girl. She chose Garrett. It didn't help that Garrett came back from the war a hero."

"That was a long time ago."

"Yes, it was. But some things don't ever go away. Take Garrett and the church—" Before she completed her thought, an older man walked up to her and greeted her with a peck on the cheek.

"Morning, Hetty."

Looking flustered, Aunt Hetty blushed like a schoolgirl. "Maggie, this is Oswald. He's the one I was telling you about. He kindly agreed to sing at your wedding."

"Pleased to meet you," Maggie said.

Oswald took her offered hand in both of his. "The pleasure is all mine."

"Oswald used to work for the railroad," Aunt Hetty said. "He was an engineer."

The offhanded information made Maggie give Dinwiddie her full attention. One of the Whistle-Stop robbers knew how to drive a train, so Oswald's profession was something to consider.

"You must tell me more," Maggie said.

"Not much to tell." If he was surprised by her interest, he didn't let on. "Had to quit when my back starting acting up. You won't believe the havoc engine vibrations can do to one's body."

While he explained in excruciating detail the discomforts of an engineer's life, including the dangers of shaking bones and rattling teeth, she made a mental note of his height and weight. He was in his early fifties—a plus in his favor. Most criminals were under thirty. Older men preferred what Allan Pinkerton called "gentlemen crimes," which included forgery, fraud, and other nonviolent transgressions. Still, it was possible that a former engineer would agree to drive a train while a younger partner committed the actual crime.

"And the burning coal bothered his lungs," Aunt Hetty was saying. "It's a wonder he still has a voice left. And don't forget to tell her about the noise." As an aside, she whispered, "He's almost deaf in one ear."

Maggie had already guessed as much. Not only did Aunt Hetty address him in a louder than normal voice, he inclined his right ear to the person speaking.

"Yes," he said, "and you won't believe what the constant change of temperature and drafts can do to a body, and. . ."

Fortunately, before he could finish describing the entire scope of physical dangers of riding the rails, one of the other church members called to him.

"You ladies will have to excuse me. It's my turn to usher today."

With a tip of his hat, he ambled away.

Aunt Hetty watched him go with wistful eyes. "Such a dear man."

"Yes. . .he seems very nice." Maggie hoped for Aunt Hetty's sake that he was exactly what he seemed. "What did you say his last name was?"

"Dinwiddie. Oswald Dinwiddie. I was so hoping that Garrett could meet him. Why do you suppose he was in such a hurry to grab a seat? The service doesn't start for another ten minutes."

"Perhaps he's just a bit anxious. His first time in church in how many years?"

"He hasn't been to church since his wedding day." Aunt Hetty sighed. "And then it was only under protest. He wouldn't even come for his children's baptisms." She lowered her voice. "How did you manage it? How did you convince him to come?"

Maggie wrapped her arm around Aunt Hetty's, and together they walked into the church. "Let's just say it was a miracle."

∽

Maggie dropped Toby and Elise off at school on Tuesday and drove into town. She and Rikker had planned to meet before the post office opened at nine.

Spotting his snake oil wagon across the street from the post office on the corner of Main and Grand, she parked. Careful to make sure no one was around, she walked to the wagon and handed Rikker her report to headquarters.

"Did he mail the letter?" she asked.

"About an hour ago. And I mailed mine." He tossed her envelope into the truck and dug into his vest pocket for his watch. "But you better hurry." He flipped the case open with his thumb. "You have only a few minutes left."

"Wish me luck." She crossed the street to the post office and waited by the night box. Less than ten minutes later the postmaster stepped outside the adobe post office, keys rattling.

Fortunately he was a middle-aged man; old enough to want to look good in a young woman's eye and young enough to consider bending a rule or two. Beneath a beaked cap, his peppery sideburns hugged a round red face.

After a quick assessment, Maggie greeted him with a worried frown. "I wonder if you could help me, sir."

The postmaster pushed back the beak of his cap. "What can I do for you, ma'am?"

He gave no indication of knowing she was Garrett's fiancée.

"I mailed a letter and changed my mind." She looked at him through lowered lashes. "I should never have written in. . .anger." She pulled a handkerchief out of her purse and dabbed the corner of her eye. Sniffling, she added, "I shouldn't bother you with my problems."

He looked flustered, and his face grew a shade redder. "That's quite all right, ma'am. Don't cry now, you hear?" He glanced around as if to check that no one was watching. He regarded Rikker's wagon across the street before turning back to her.

"Let's see what we can do."

Squatting down on his haunches, he opened the box with a twist of the key and pulled out the stack of letters. "Let me know which one is yours."

Thanks to Rikker, she had no problem identifying Garrett's letter. Rikker had dropped a yellow envelope into the mailbox, timing it precisely so that Garrett's letter was directly beneath his.

"It's that one there," she said.

"Ah, well there you are." The postmaster handed over Garrett's letter. Thankfully he didn't bother looking at the return address. "Mum's the word," he said.

She afforded him a brilliant smile. "I don't know how to thank you."

"Just remember, the next time you write a letter in haste, wait a day or two before mailing it. It'll save you a lot of trouble."

"Thank you. That's very good advice."

Tucking the letter into her purse, she hastened away in the opposite direction of Rikker's wagon. She would circle a block or two before doubling back.

~~~

Less than fifteen minutes later, she and Rikker stood behind the painted wagon and examined the envelope. While Rikker kept watch from behind the wagon, Maggie studied the address. It was addressed to a Paul Whittaker in Massachusetts.

"You do realize we're tampering with the US mail, right?" he grumbled. Rikker wasn't against breaking the law on occasion to get his man, but he considered such tactics beneath him. He much preferred the challenge of working around any legal obstacles that stood between him and justice. He would have made a fine lawyer.

"Naughty us," she said. She held the envelope up to the sun and smiled. "We're in luck. There's no need to tamper." The envelope was constructed of paper thin enough to see through in the bright light.

She couldn't read all of it. "It says 'Nxe5 Q' something." She frowned. "What's that supposed to mean?"

Rikker laughed. "It's a chess move."

"What?"

"Chess. You know king, queen, checkmate."

The mention of chess brought back a myriad of memories, and her mouth ran dry. *Did you know that chess was once a game of courtship?*

Fortunately Rikker didn't notice her momentary lapse. "Mr. Whittaker is evidently Thomas's corresponding chess partner."

"You mean people actually play chess through the mail?" She often saw Garrett studying the chessboard, but never had it occurred to her that he was playing an actual game with someone a distance away.

"All the time," he said. "Judging from the number of letters Thomas mails, I'd say he has several mail partners."

She thought about this. "He said he learned to play in prison. Do you think that's where he met these people?"

"Possibly." He reached into the wagon for a pencil and writing tablet and jotted down the address on the envelope. It would be up to Pinkerton headquarters to check if Whittaker had a criminal record or was in Arizona during the robbery.

"What have you found out about Dinwiddie?"

"Not a whole lot. He lives at a boardinghouse outside of town. Pays his rent on time and had to quit his job with the railroad because of his health. He is currently a trusted bank employee."

Her eyebrows shot up. "He works for the bank?" He talked about his job as a train engineer but never mentioned his current employment.

"Yes, and he's also a terrible faro player. Almost as bad as what's his name—Panhandle." Rikker had no patience for a man who couldn't hold his own with liquor or cards. "Dinwiddie blames losing on his sacroiliac. Though what that's got to do with the price of eggs is anyone's guess." When she made no comment, he tilted his head. "What are you thinking?"

"Katherine's brother Cotton returned to town shortly after the school fund-raiser. Not many people knew about the five large bills that showed up there."

"But a bank employee would know," he said, finishing her thought.

"A bank employee who just happened to be a former train engineer," she amended.

He pulled out his pipe and a package of tobacco. "So you think Thomas and Dinwiddie could be in cahoots?"

She frowned. That wasn't at all what she was thinking. "Or Dinwiddie and Cotton."

"Maybe Dinwiddie, Cotton, and *Thomas* were all involved in the Whistle-Stop robbery."

"There were only two robbers," she said.

"That we know of," Rikker said with quiet emphasis.

Early train robberies almost always required five or more men. In recent years, successful robberies had been committed with fewer men and, in a few cases, lone individuals.

"There's nothing to indicate that there were *three* men," she insisted.

"No, but we can't overlook the possibility." Thinking out loud, he continued. "Suppose the money disappeared following the robbery and no one admitted to having it."

She frowned. "Go on."

"Suppose the thief among thieves was Thomas. That would explain why no one saw hide or hair of the money for two years. Thomas wasn't worried about the authorities finding out he had the money. He was worried about his partner or partners finding out. So after holding on to it all that time, he decided to distribute a couple of bills to see what happened."

"There's one problem with your little theory," she said. "His donation to rebuild the school brought Cotton back to town. Why would Garrett take a chance on releasing more?"

Rikker shrugged. "I'm rather curious about that, myself. That's a question we'll have to ask him when the time is right." He looked at her askance. "You have to admit, my theory does explain Dinwiddie's sudden interest in Garrett's aunt. Maybe he thinks she knows where Thomas is hiding the money."

That's what she was afraid of—that, and the possibility Rikker's theory could have a semblance of truth.

Rikker tossed a nod at the hotel. "There's Cotton now."

Maggie rose on tiptoes to look over his shoulder. Cotton purchased a paper from Linc and walked into the hotel. She couldn't be certain, but it sure did look like the same man on the brown and white horse she had seen outside the schoolhouse.

"He's staying at the hotel. Room five," Rikker said. "Nothing incriminating in his room, but that doesn't mean anything."

"Have you also checked Dinwiddie's place?"

"Of course."

"And you found nothing?"

"Not a diddly." He took Garrett's envelope out of her hand and slid it into his coat pocket. "Cheer up, Duffy. Unless I miss my guess, Cotton is now sitting at a corner table in the hotel restaurant and is about to order his usual flapjacks and coffee. I also happen to know he enjoys the company of a pretty woman. I'll mail Thomas's letter"—he patted his pocket—"and you go and see what you can pull out of Mr. Cotton."

∞

Moments later, Maggie stood at the entrance of the hotel dining room. As usual, Rikker's information was accurate. Charlie Cotton sat at a corner table reading a newspaper.

Having made the decision to take the direct approach, she walked over to his table and pulled out a chair. "Do you mind?" she asked.

He looked up, but before giving him a chance to speak she sat. "Maggie Taylor," she said and offered her hand across the table.

He folded his newspaper and set it next to his plate. "I know who you are."

Since he ignored her hand, she drew it away and pulled off her gloves. "I thought we should get to know each other," she said.

He gave her a squinty-eyed stare. "Why?"

"I'm about to marry your brother-in-law."

"*Former* brother-in-law." He leaned on the table, and his eyes glittered. "You should know I blame him for my sister's death."

Recalling Katherine's letter, she studied him. What had he done to cause his sister such distress? "I'm sorry for your loss. It was a terrible thing that happened."

"Is that why you're here? To express condolences?"

"Partly. But I must admit I'm a bit curious. Your sister died two years ago. Why come back to Furnace Creek now?"

"Maybe I like it here."

Or maybe he was lying. He arrived in town exactly two weeks after the school fund-raising event. That seemed like an awfully big coincidence.

"Do you, by any chance, know Mr. Dinwiddie?"

"Who?"

"Oswald Dinwiddie. He's a friend of Aunt Hetty's."

"Never heard of him."

She decided to try another tactic. "I heard you and Garrett arguing that day in the shop." She paused and waited for him to offer an explanation—something—but he said nothing.

"Do you mind if I ask what you were arguing about?"

"Why don't you ask Thomas?"

"He's not much of a talker," she said, maintaining a conversational tone. "He doesn't like to talk about the past."

He narrowed his eyes. "Why do you care what we were arguing about?"

"I hate to see family members at odds with one another."

He leaned forward. "Any relationship Thomas and I had ended the day my sister died."

"Is that what she would want?" Maggie asked.

"You know nothing about my sister," he hissed.

"No, but you are her children's uncle." When he made no reply, she continued. "I saw you at school this morning. You're not thinking of causing your niece and nephew harm, are you?"

He sat back. "Course not. I miss them is all. Thomas won't let me see them."

He sounded sincere, but there was something unsettling about his dark, flat eyes. It was like looking into two black holes.

"I feel I must warn you that if you cause any harm to the man I love—" The word *love* escaped before she could think about what she was saying. She coughed to clear her voice.

"—harm Garrett or his children, and you'll have to deal with me."

He gave her a thin-lipped smile. "I'm trembling in my boots."

"You should be."

Standing, he tossed a single coin on the table and walked away. She watched him leave the hotel dining room with a sense of impending doom.

Chapter 26

Maggie was hardly aware of her surroundings as she left the hotel. Her conversation with Rikker kept running through her head. Was he right about a third man being involved in the Whistle-Stop holdup?

Cotton professed not to know Dinwiddie, and she believed him. If she was right, that was the only true word the man had spoken. So if Dinwiddie wasn't his partner, then who was?

She was so deep in thought she almost missed seeing Sheriff Summerhay drag Linc across the street by the ear.

Worried that the boy might have gotten into serious trouble, she picked up her pace and followed the two into the sheriff's office. Linc, looking pale and close to tears, was emptying out his pockets.

"What's going on?" she asked.

The sheriff looked none too pleased to see her. "Not that it's any business of yours, but the boy's a thief."

She turned to Linc. "Is that true?"

Linc dumped a handful of penny candy and coins onto the desk and shook his head.

The sheriff pulled something out of his pocket and waved it in front of the boy's face. "Then suppose you tell me where you got this?" It was a hundred-dollar bill. To Maggie he said, "Bought a bagful of candy with it."

Maggie stared at the note in disbelief. It was the second bill to show up in little more than a week. What was going on?

The sheriff tucked the bill in his pocket. "If you don't want to tell me now, you can sit in that cell over there till you do."

"Wait," Maggie said. "Let me talk to him."

Summerhay looked about to object but then changed his mind. "All right, but make it quick."

Maggie placed her hand on Linc's shoulder and looked him square in the eye. "I won't let anything happen to you, but you have to tell me the truth. Do you understand?" After getting a reluctant nod, she asked, "Where did you get the money?"

"I found it," he muttered.

"Found it where?"

"Right there in front of the barbershop."

She pulled her hand away. "By 'in front of the barbershop,' do you mean it was on the ground?"

Linc nodded. "I was inside selling my newspapers. When I walked outside, there it was. Like I said, right in front."

"Do you know how it got there?"

Linc shook his head. "Nope." She studied him, and he said, "Honest."

She turned to the sheriff. "He's telling the truth."

Summerhay made a face. "The boy doesn't know the truth from the backside of a mule." He turned to Linc. "Sittin' in jail for a while is bound to change your tune."

Maggie's temper flared. "He's responsible for his grandmother's care. Unless you wish to care for her yourself, I suggest you let him go."

He glared at her. "The boy's a thief."

"His name is Linc, and he told you how he got the money."

"And you believe him?"

"I do. So either you let him go, or you'll have to put us both in jail because I'm not leaving without him."

Okay, maybe giving the sheriff an ultimatum was not Maggie's most brilliant idea, but who would have guessed he would have the gall to throw her in jail? And what was taking Rikker so long to come to her rescue? He kept his ear to the ground. Surely he must have heard about her arrest by now.

So far she'd spent three hours pacing the tiny cell back and forth while Linc alternated between sleeping and complaining of hunger. Finally the door of the sheriff's office flew open. Much to her shock, Garrett, not Rikker, barreled inside, and he looked fit to be tied.

One glance at her behind bars and he whirled about to face Summerhay. "What is the meaning of this?"

The sheriff scowled from across the desk. "Your woman insists on putting her nose where it doesn't belong."

"What are the charges against her?"

"I told you. Being a busybody."

"If that was a crime, you'd have to arrest half the people in this town."

The sheriff sat back and folded his arms across his chest. "I don't like people questioning my judgment."

Garrett placed his palms on the desk and leaned over. "And I don't like you throwing your weight around. . .especially since you're up for reelection. Either release her or you'll have to deal with my lawyer."

Glowering, the sheriff rose and pulled the keys off the wall. Muttering beneath his breath, he unlocked the steel jail door.

Maggie motioned to Linc, and the boy walked out of the cell ahead of her. The sheriff started to protest, but one look at Garrett changed his mind.

Chapter 27

Suppose you tell me what that was all about," Garrett said once they reached the privacy of his shop. He'd turned the sign in the window to read CLOSED. Linc had already taken off, and it was just the two of them.

She quickly explained about the hundred-dollar bill. "I think Linc was telling the truth." She studied him. "So where do you suppose the money came from?"

He looked as mystified as she was. Of course that could be an act, but somehow she didn't think so.

"Search me," he said. He then surprised her by laughing.

"What's so funny?"

"You should have seen the indignant look on your face when I walked into the sheriff's office."

"It's not every day that one is thrown into jail," she said. It was the first time she'd been in jail for at least six months. "You looked pretty incensed yourself."

He studied her. "Is this what married life will be like?" he asked. "You getting into trouble and me coming to the rescue?" Glints of humor sparkled in his eyes.

"It could be the other way around."

"You think *I* need rescuing?" he asked.

"Do you?" she asked.

His hands slipped up her arms, and she felt an unwelcomed surge of want and need, and more than anything, excitement. "Not anymore," he whispered.

The brush of his lips against hers made her senses spin. Leaning into him, she absorbed his manly essence before pulling away.

"The ch–children," she stammered. "I—I don't want to be late picking them up." Before he could respond, she whirled about and dashed out the door.

∞

The next day, Maggie glanced at the calendar on the kitchen wall. Only two weeks left until June 15. How quickly time flew! Fourteen days. The clock was ticking.

Rikker's theory about three robbers was possible but didn't explain why suddenly the stolen money had begun to surface. Working at the bank Dinwiddie had to know that large bills would attract attention, so his involvement in spreading them around made no sense. Cotton wasn't even in town for the school fund-raiser, so that omitted him. That left Garrett.

Did he think that giving the money away anonymously offered protection? Was it possible that he just wanted to rid himself of the money and be done with it?

The thought nearly crushed her. No matter how much she wanted to believe in Garrett's innocence, things always pointed back to him.

Garrett's voice floated from the other room, startling her out of her reverie. "Toby, Elise, in the wagon, or you'll be late for school."

His footsteps echoed behind her. He laid something that looked like a legal document on the kitchen table. "Some papers for you to sign," he said.

She ran her hands down the front of her apron. "Papers?"

"I had my lawyer draw up a new deed with your name on it. Should anything happen to me..."

She stared at him, speechless. Was that what he was doing at the lawyer's office?

He chuckled. "Don't look so alarmed. Just a precaution. You never know what the future holds, and I want to make sure you and the children are taken care of."

"I. . ." She cleared her voice. "I don't feel comfortable signing anything until after we're married."

He frowned, and his eyes sharpened. "Yesterday. . .in the shop. I didn't alarm you, did I?"

She held herself still. Alarm her? No. What he did was confuse her. He kept peeling away her defenses, and that scared her. It made her feel vulnerable and want things that a hard-nosed detective could never have.

Hiding her rampaging emotions behind a calm demeanor, she shook her head. "It was late, and I was worried about the children," she said. The words—the lie—left a bad aftertaste. In a couple of short weeks this would all be over, and he would know the truth. Everyone would.

His gaze latched onto her lips as if he regretted the disrupted kiss as much as she did. "I'll leave the papers on the table. You can sign them when you're ready."

Grateful that he didn't press her, she forced a smile. "Thank you."

"I've got a delivery to make this morning. I'll drop the children off on the way."

He studied her a moment before turning. "Toby, Elise, hurry!"

A flurry of activity followed as the children grabbed schoolbooks, gave her quick hugs, and followed their father through the house and out the door.

All at once it was silent and the walls seemed to close in around her. Maggie picked the document up from the table. Rikker expressed concern about Garrett leaving town after ascertaining his children were in good hands. His willingness to put her name on the deed led her to believe that perhaps Rikker was right. Maybe that had been the plan all along.

⌾⌾⌾

Less than two hours later, Maggie pounded on the door of Rikker's hotel room with both fists. They'd agreed that she was not to visit him in his hotel room, but this was an emergency, and she had taken care to make sure that no one had spotted her.

The door opened and Rikker greeted her with a frown, his jaw covered in white foamy lather. He glanced up and down the empty hallway before pulling her inside. Shutting the door, he turned. "What are you doing here? Something happen?"

"I can't do this anymore." She paced a circle around the room, wringing her hands.

He reached for a towel. "Do what?"

She whirled around to face him. "This job. This—" She shook her head, and her voice wavered. "Don't you ever hate what you're doing? Hate the lies? The deceit?"

Rikker's face darkened. "I'll tell you what I hate. I hate crime. Last month I helped put a mass murderer away. Did I feel guilty for befriending his wife to get to the truth? Not one bit. It's our job. It's what we're trained to do."

He turned to the dry sink and scraped the lather off his chin with a straight razor. He met her eyes in the mirror. "What's the matter with you? I've never known you to act this way."

"No job has ever required so much from me." She clenched her hands into fists by her side. "No job ever involved children or—"

"Or what?" He wiped his face off with a towel and turned. "What happened to get you all riled?"

"This morning. . ." She swallowed hard and forced herself to continue. "This morning Garrett handed me papers to sign. The deed to his property. He's putting my name on everything. Don't you see how that makes me feel? It's not bad enough that he trusts me with his children. Now this."

"You knew it was a tough assignment when you took it."

She thought she did know, but she was wrong. Never had she imagined how hard it would be. "It's not just that." She sank into the only chair in the room. "I don't believe he's the man we're looking for."

Rikker shook his head. "We've gone all through this."

"I know."

"Everything points to him."

"I know." She closed her eyes. Big mistake, for a vision of a crooked smile came to mind. She looked up at Rikker. "You always told me to go by my gut feeling, and that's what I'm doing."

She knew he hated it when she tossed his own words back at him, but she didn't care.

Rikker flung the towel onto the dry sink "You're letting your personal feelings interfere with your job, and that's not like you."

"That's not what this is about."

"Isn't it?" His eyes blazed. "You're a professional. You have a job to do. Whatever feelings you have for Thomas or his children can't interfere."

"That's easy for you to say!" she snapped. "You don't have to live with them. You don't have to tuck the children in bed and hear their prayers. You don't have to see the love and trust in their eyes as they look at you." Nor did he have to lie in bed at night and listen to Garrett pace the floor, and fight the urge to go to him and give in to the desires of her heart.

Rikker's expression softened, and he blew out his breath. "I know this is hard, Duffy. But it will soon be over."

That's what she was afraid of. Because no matter what happened, she couldn't imagine a happy ending for anyone. Not for Garrett. Not for her.

Rikker pulled his suspender straps over his shoulders. "If we don't come up with something soon, we'll both have some explaining to do. You know Allan. He wants results, and he won't be happy to hear that his best agents came up empty-handed. Is that what you want?"

"What I want is out." Her mind suddenly made up, she added in a quieter, more contained, voice: "I'm leaving on tomorrow's train."

"Don't be a fool!" He snapped the last suspender into place. "You mess this job up and your career is over."

"That's the chance I'll have to take." She stood and reached for the doorknob. "Sorry, Rikker."

She hated leaving him in the lurch, but it couldn't be helped. Her only hope was that in time he would forgive her. Opening the door a crack, she peered into the hall. Seeing no one, she slipped out of the room and down the hall.

Chapter 28

A hot breeze blew across the desert when Maggie picked up the children from school later that afternoon. Sand and dust spiraled upward, turning the sky a murky brown.

"Can we stop for ice cream?" Elise asked.

"Not today, pumpkin. It's too windy," Maggie replied. The children liked nothing better than to stop in town for an after-school treat. Elise looked disappointed but didn't argue.

For once Toby's and Elise's chatter failed to raise her spirits. This would be the last day they spent together, and the thought nearly crushed her. She only hoped to get through the night. The worst part was leaving town without an explanation—of simply disappearing. But what could she say?

I'm sorry, but this was all a farce. I never intended to marry you.

She turned the wagon homeward with a heavy heart. Toby said something, and Elise's laughter barely cut into her troubled thoughts.

Concerned about Elise's still delicate lungs, she handed her a clean handkerchief. "Put this over your mouth and nose."

Toby, as usual, was in his own little world. "Did you know that even when you can't see the moon it's still there?"

"Why can't we see it?" Elise asked.

"Because the man in the moon turns out the light," Toby said.

Maggie smiled through her tears. She was going to miss the boy. Miss both children. She didn't even want to think about missing Garrett.

"Why are you crying?" Elise asked.

Maggie swiped away a tear. "It's the wind. It's making my eyes water."

Elise peered at her from over the top of the handkerchief. "Can we have a tea party when we get home?"

Maggie was just about to say no when she changed her mind. She wasn't leaving until tomorrow. No reason not to make a little girl happy today, especially after denying her request for ice cream.

"I think that's a very good idea."

Elise's eyes shone. "Can we have it in our tree house?"

Maggie drove the wagon alongside the house and set the brake. A tree house, boogeyman, and a man in the moon; there seemed to be no end to the children's imagination.

"Toby said that only special people get invited to your tree house."

"Papa said you're special," Elise said.

Maggie's breath caught. "Your. . .your papa said that?"

Elise nodded. "Can we have a tea party in the tree house? Pleeeeeeee-ase?"

"It's *may* we have a tea party."

"May we, can we?" Elise asked.

Maggie forced her brightest smile. She'd played dozens of roles as an undercover agent, but none were as difficult as the role she now played.

"A tea party it is!"

∞

Much to Maggie's surprise, there actually was a tree house. Not the kind she expected: this one was located in the barn's hayloft.

Whitewash greeted her in the yard with wagging tail, and she bent to pet him.

Straightening, she studied the open window above and stepped back. Whitewash had been up to his old tricks and her heels sank into the newly turned soil.

"You must train your dog to stop digging," she said.

Elise's face grew serious. "It's not Whitewash. It's the boogeyman."

"Whitewash, the boogeyman, whatever. These holes are a hazard." She stared up at the ladder clinging to the side of the barn. "You aren't going to make me climb that, are you?"

"It's the only way to get into our tree house," Elise assured her. "I'll show you."

Elise scampered up the ladder with the ease of a cat climbing a tree. Toby placed the picnic basket in the wooden hay lift next to the ladder. He then scrambled up after his sister.

Both children hung their heads out of the narrow window above and beckoned to her.

"You can do it!" Elise called.

Maggie wasn't so sure about that, but she wasn't about to disappoint the children on her last day in town. Tongue between her teeth, she grabbed hold of the ladder and placed a muddy sole onto the lower rung.

The ladder trembled beneath her weight and the wind played havoc with her skirt, but somehow she made it to the top.

With the children's help, she crawled through the loft opening and landed on a prickly bed of hay. Standing, she brushed off her skirt and looked around. So this was the tree house she'd heard so much about.

The loft was cut off from the barn's first floor by a wood partition. Elise pointed to a corner piled high with scraps of metal and an assortment of tools. "That's Toby's room," she said with sisterly disgust. "Over here is mine."

Her area was much neater and included a doll bed and small rocking horse. A child-sized table and two chairs stood on a rug beneath a hanging lantern.

"I like your house," Maggie said.

Toby flung his upper body over the window ledge. Crying out, she rushed to his side and grabbed him by the shirt. "Be careful."

He turned the hay lift handle. With a grinding of gears and a clank of metal, the picnic basket rose from the ground.

Together, they hauled the basket inside. "Cookies and lemonade," Maggie announced.

Elise frowned. "I thought we were going to have tea."

"It's a bit warm for that, don't you think?" Maggie pulled out the canteen. The wind had made the temperature rise, and it felt like summer.

Toby returned to his "room" and began fiddling with a strange-looking object.

"What is that?" she called.

"A horse," he said. "A wind-up horse that will take you anywhere you want to go."

Maggie smiled. "Now wouldn't that be something? A horse that you wouldn't have to feed."

"You wouldn't have to clean up after him, either," Toby added.

"Can you make a wind-up horse for me?" Elise asked.

Toby shook his head. "You're too little. You're not strong enough to turn the key."

Maggie handed Elise a cookie and whispered, "Don't worry. When you grow up, you'll be strong enough to do anything you want."

"I want to be big and strong like Papa," Elise said.

Maggie's heart wrenched at the thought, and her misery felt like an iron weight. Garrett was strong all right, and she could sure use his shoulders right now.

She rubbed the ring on her finger. The band would have to come off, of course. Not that it meant anything. It was nothing more than a prop, like in a stage play.

Still. . .it surprised her, how much she enjoyed wearing it. How special it made her feel, like she finally had a place in the world—a home, a family. A purpose.

The ring. Oh God, that was the least of it. She'd lied to him, forced herself into his home—into his children's lives—under false pretenses. And for what?

Not wanting to upset the children, she blinked away her tears. Fortunately, they were too occupied to notice her misery. Toby pounded on a piece of metal with his hammer, and Elise pretended to feed her rag doll.

Maggie tried sitting on one of the chairs, but when her knees came up to her chin, she dragged a bale of hay over to the table to use instead. After arranging the cookies on a plate, she placed the picnic basket on the floor and poured the lemonade into three tin cups.

"What's in the bag over there?" she asked, pointing to a worn leather satchel. It was the one thing in the playhouse that seemed strangely out of place.

Elise looked up from her doll. "It's a secret," she whispered, her eyes wide.

"Hmm, a secret, eh," Maggie said, playing along. "I'm very good at keeping secrets."

"Toby said we can only open it if it's important."

"I think tea parties are important," Maggie said. "Don't you?"

Elise gave her a dubious look. "Kind of. But it's not like when the school burned down."

"No, I guess not," Maggie agreed. Apparently the school fire had left an impression.

"Or when Linc needed new clothes," Toby called from his "room."

Elise nodded. "And don't forget the beggar with the crooked foot."

Maggie stared at her. "What. . .what did you say?"

Elise looked worried. "Did we do something wrong?"

"No, no, of course not." She could think of only one thing that the school, Linc, and the beggar had in common, and that was a Lincoln banknote. Was it possible? Could it be?

Willing her trembling limbs to still, she cleared her throat. "Will you let me see inside the bag?"

Elise glanced at her brother who shrugged. "I guess it's okay," he said. "Long as you don't tell nobody."

Elise hopped off her chair and tugged on the handle. It was heavy, and her brother had to help her drag it to the table. Toby then undid the clasp and opened it.

Maggie's body stiffened in shock, and it was all she could do to breathe. The satchel was packed with money.

∽

For several moments all she could do was stare. *God, no!* She'd wanted so much to believe in Garrett's innocence. The moment she had waited for—prayed for, worked for—now felt like a nightmare. The case that had stifled Pinkerton operatives for two years had now been solved. But at what cost? Dear God, at what cost?

Not wanting Elise to think she'd done something wrong, Maggie took hold of her small hand. No matter her feelings, no matter how much it hurt, she had a job to do. Interrogating a witness came easy to her, but never had she questioned one so young.

"Did you and Toby give money to help build the new school?" she asked, keeping her tone soft and voice gentle.

Elise nodded. "Our teacher said if they didn't build a new school she'd have to go back to Boston, and that made her sad."

Anxious to return to his mechanical horse and completely unaware that his life was about to take an alarming turn, Toby scooted back to his corner on hands and knees.

"What about the beggar?" Maggie asked, forcing a light tone. "Did you give him money, too?"

Again Elise nodded. "You said God wants us to help others."

"He does," Maggie assured her. "I guess that means you helped Linc."

"Uh-huh." Elise scratched her side. "Toby said we can only give money to people who need it. We can't spend it on ourselves."

Maggie released the small hand. "That's. . .that's good."

All the pieces fell into place, including the sudden and puzzling appearance of stolen money.

She reached for a packet of greenbacks, but Elise pushed her hand away. "You can't have any. It's not ours."

"It's not?" she asked, feigning surprise. "Well, then whose money is it?"

"It's Pa's," Toby called with a pound of his hammer. "The money belongs to Pa."

Elise fiddled with the clasp. "And he don't want anyone to know about it."

Chapter 29

Normally Maggie would have gone straight to the sheriff after discovering the stolen money, but nothing was normal about this case. Her first thought was for the children. After thinking it over, she hustled them back to the house and, keeping up a stream of mindless chatter so they wouldn't think anything was wrong, she tossed their clothes into a carpetbag and discreetly packed her own.

She threw the last of the carpetbags into the back of the rig and ordered the children to take their seats.

She climbed into the driver's seat. "Toby, hold on to Whitewash. Don't let him get away."

The children had such somber expressions she asked lightly, "What do elephants and trains have in common?"

"I give up," Elise said.

"They both carry trunks."

"Are we going on a train?" Toby asked.

"Not today," she said, releasing the brake and giving the reins a shake.

A half hour later, she pulled up in front of Aunt Hetty's house. The still-brown sky turned the setting sun to a dull bronze color. The windstorm had ended, leaving behind only an intermittent gust that fanned her fevered brow but did nothing to settle her nerves.

"Why do we have to stay here?" Elise asked.

"It will just be for a short while," Maggie said.

"But why can't we stay with you and Pa?"

"They want to be alone so they can kiss," Toby said from the backseat.

The boy's comment was followed by an echo from the past. *I believe it's traditional for a man and woman to seal a moment like this with a kiss.*

Giving her head a shake, she clamped down on her thoughts. No matter how much she wished things were different, she could no longer deny the evidence against him. Allan Pinkerton had been right all along. Garrett Thomas was a thief and very possibly a killer.

She yanked on the wagon brake, but putting a brake on the memory of being in Garrett's arms was harder. Harder still was forgetting the memory of dancing with him.

"I'm scared," Elise said.

Maggie's control began to slip. "Why are you scared?" She'd tried hard not to let on that anything was wrong but had apparently failed.

Elise's eyes filled with tears. "I don't know."

Maggie took the trembling child in her arms. She had every reason to be scared; they all did. "I want you to be a good girl for Aunt Hetty and to be brave."

Elise knuckled the tears away with both hands. "What does brave mean?"

Toby scrambled out of his seat and ran up the path to the door with Whitewash at his heels. "It means not telling anyone you're afraid."

Maggie retied the ribbon on Elise's braid. "Actually, it's okay to say you're afraid. It's even better to tell God. Remember how I taught you to talk to Him?"

Elise nodded, and Maggie kissed her on the forehead. "Come along. Last one to the door is a purple frog." Her ploy worked because Elise scrambled out of the wagon and ran ahead of Maggie, laughing.

Maggie sighed. What she wouldn't give for the resilience of a child and the ability to go from tears to laughter as easily as the wind changed directions.

Aunt Hetty came to the door in robe and slippers and looked surprised to see them. "I'm so glad you came." She checked that both children were healthy and not harboring any diseases before letting them inside.

"You can't be too careful with all this wind," she said. "What brings you here on a day like this?"

"I have business to take care of." Maggie tried to smooth down Toby's cowlick, but only so she didn't have to look the older woman in the eyes. "I wonder if you'd mind watching the children for a day or two." It would be for much longer. The children might even have to stay there permanently, but she didn't want to say that. Not yet.

Aunt Hetty's eyes bored into her. "Is everything all right?"

"Pa and Miss Taylor just want to kiss," Elise said.

"Oh." And after thinking about this for a moment, Aunt Hetty repeated herself, this time with more meaning. "*Oh!*" She lowered her voice. "You and Garrett promised to wait until *after* the wedding."

"It's not what you think," Maggie said, blushing. "We. . .uh. . .just want to talk." She hated lying to his aunt, but she didn't want to upset the children.

"I see," Aunt Hetty said, though it was obvious by her dubious expression that she knew something was afoot. "It's actually a good thing you came. Would you mind mailing your wedding invitations? I don't dare go outside." She waved her hand in front of her face. "All that dust from the wind."

Maggie glanced at the stack of envelopes on the table by the door, and her already low spirits fell another notch. It looked as if the whole town had made it onto the guest list.

"All you have to do is drop them off at the post office," Aunt Hetty added.

"Yes, all right." Maggie turned to the children. "Be good for Aunt Hetty, and don't give her any trouble. And Toby, stay away from matches." Resisting the urge to take both of them in her arms and hold them tight, she rushed to the door before tears threatened to give her away.

"Don't forget the invitations," Aunt Hetty called.

Maggie grabbed the stack of envelopes and raced outside.

〜

Garrett was anxious to close up shop and go home to his family. The thought made him smile.

Following Katherine's death, he never thought he'd be happy again. Never thought it possible. How lucky can a man get?

Maggie.

Just thinking her name made him want to jump with joy. He never believed that God had a plan for his life, but it sure was beginning to look that way.

In little more than two weeks they would be husband and wife. Two weeks would be the beginning of a whole new life. Wait till she saw what he planned for their honeymoon.

Counting the minutes until he saw her again, he focused on the task at hand. The sooner he finished this order, the sooner he could leave.

Fort Verde wanted three dozen tin drinking cups, and he had only one more left to make to complete the order. Apparently tracking Apaches was hard on utensils as it was the second such order this year.

His apprentice thought making cups a bore. Panhandle much preferred working on more intricate pieces. That's because he was never deprived of a cup or fork or spoon or plate. A cup—a crudely made cup chiseled out of rotting wood—helped restore human dignity. Nothing boring about it.

The year spent in Andersonville sure did teach him to appreciate the simple things in life, that's for sure.

Whistling to himself, he shaped the tin on a bar holder and grooved the seam on the Roys & Wilcox grooving machine. Next he turned the lip on the turning machine. He held the cup up to the light, and satisfied, he snipped off a piece of wire.

The wire made the lip stronger; it also prevented a user from cutting his or her mouth. Stepping over to the wiring machine, he set the tin tube on a roller.

The jingling bells announced a customer. Pulling away from his workbench, he walked out to the shop and halted in the doorway. The last person he expected to see this time of day was Maggie.

Chapter 30

The shop was empty when Maggie walked in. It was almost closing time.

Neither the sheriff nor Rikker wanted her to face Garrett alone, but she insisted. She owed him that much.

Stepping from his workshop in back, his face lit up at seeing her. Even now, his smile affected her. She tried staying cold and emotionless but failed miserably. Her lower lip quivered and a lump settled in her throat. Even now that she was certain of his guilt, her pulse leaped at the sight of him.

His smile faded a little, and a shadow of worry touched his forehead. "You're in town late," he said. "Everything okay? The children?"

She nodded. "They're with Aunt Hetty. I. . .I had some things to take care of."

"I see." He rubbed the back of his neck. "Maybe she won't mind keeping them for a while longer. We can have supper at the hotel. It will give us a chance to talk. I planned to show you this tonight, but since you're here. . ." He reached for a leaflet on the counter.

She stared at it a moment before taking it from him. "What is this?"

"Flagstaff."

She looked up, and his grin widened. "There isn't much there, but they have a halfway decent hotel, and it's only a couple of hours away from the most magnificent natural site you've ever seen. They used to call it the Big Canyon, but now they call it the Grand. I thought it would make a perfect place to spend our honeymoon."

The flyer slipped from her fingers and fluttered to the floor.

He glanced at the leaflet. "We don't have to go there if you don't want."

"It's not that."

"Then what?" A worried look crossed his face. He cupped her elbow. "Maggie? What's wrong? Tell me." He released her arm. "Your family? Have they lost the farm?"

She stared at him in confusion. What family? What farm? Her mind was in such a muddle it took her a moment to remember yet another lie she'd told. She shook her head. *Oh, God, help me. This is so hard.*

She yanked the ring off her finger and held it out to him. He made no effort to take it from her, but the eyes staring back were dark as night. "What's going on?"

"Take it!" she pleaded. "Take it."

His mouth in a straight line, he took the ring and stared at it a moment before lifting his eyes to hers. "Are you going to tell me what this is all about?"

"I'm not who you think I am." Her voice wavered, and forming the words felt like spitting out rocks. "My name isn't Maggie Taylor." She faltered but kept going. "It's Maggie Cartwright."

He shook his head in confusion. "I don't understand. Why are you telling me this?"

Before she could answer, the door flew open and Sheriff Summerhay walked in, followed by Rikker.

"I'll take it from here," Summerhay said, striding up to Garrett. He reached for the handcuffs hooked to his belt. "Garrett Thomas, I'm arresting you for robbery and the murder of one Joseph A. Beckett."

Color drained from Garrett's face. He looked like a man who'd just been shot. "What are you talking about? Robbery? Murder? I don't even know anyone named Beckett."

The sheriff scoffed. "Not much you don't. He's the guard killed during the Whistle-Stop robbery."

"The Whis—" A look of disbelief crossed Garrett's face. "Surely you don't think that I had anything to do with that." His earnest eyes sought hers. "Maggie? What's this about? How could you think—?"

She wanted to die. She'd insisted on being present at his arrest, but now she knew what a mistake that was. Rikker had tried to talk her out of it. She should have listened.

Summerhay answered for her. "Case you don't know it, the lady's a Pink." He chuckled. "Don't that beat all? A woman detective, of all things?" He shook his head as if he still couldn't believe it himself.

Garrett stared at her in astonishment. "Maggie?" His voice broke. "Is this true?"

She nodded and struggled to find her voice. "I was sent here to investigate the train robbery." She pulled her metal shield from the waistline of her skirt and held it up for him to see. She indicated Rikker. "This is my partner, Mr. Greenwood."

Garrett glanced at Rikker before turning back to her, incredulous. "I don't understand. None of this makes sense."

"The money you stole from the train. . . I found it." She practically choked on the words. She wanted to say more, but the sheriff ordered Garrett to put his hands behind his back.

"What money? What are you talking about? I've done nothing wrong."

Summerhay snapped the manacles around Garrett's wrists. "That's for a judge and jury to decide. Right now, my job is to put you in jail."

"You can't think I had anything to do with that robbery. Maggie, you know me. How could you think—?"

"I found the money in the children's playhouse." The money was intact except for the few bills Toby and Elise had given out. "How do you explain that?" Something snapped inside, and anger flared. "What were you planning? To leave town? Is that why you sent away for a mail-order bride? So you could leave the children behind?"

"Leave the children?" He spoke like a man in a daze. "How could you think such a thing?"

She faltered. "What. . .what do you expect me to think? The money—"

"I know nothing about any money!" The shock and disbelief left his face, leaving behind a look of hurt and betrayal. "I let you into my home. I trusted you. I—"

He shook his head. *I held you and kissed you and loved you.* That's not what he said, but it's what she heard—what she saw in his eyes, read on his face, heard in her heart.

The sheriff grabbed him by the arm and shoved him toward the door. "That's enough."

Garrett pulled back. "What about my children?" he demanded. "What's to become of them?"

"I'll see that they're cared for," she said, ignoring Rikker's disapproving look.

Garrett's cold and unforgiving stare chilled her to the bones. "I don't want you anywhere near them."

He searched her face, for what she didn't know. Seeming to have found his answer, he pulled his gaze away and walked out the door ahead of the sheriff.

∞

Garrett paced the tiny cell like a caged animal and pounded his fist into his palm. He still couldn't believe the turn of events. One moment he was on top of the world; the next—

It was a nightmare. Worse than even being locked up in Andersonville. At least then he had known who his enemies were. Knew why he'd been captured. Even during the senseless craziness of war, that much had been clear.

But this. . .this was beyond comprehension. And what in the name of Sam Hill was taking his lawyer so long to get here?

He battled for restraint. He needed to calm down. Crazy thinking wouldn't have gotten him through the war and wasn't about to get him through this. His children's future depended on his keeping his wits about him. There had to be a logical explanation. He just needed time to think and figure out what it was.

He slumped on the cot, elbows on his lap, and covered his face with both hands. He'd gone over his arrest a dozen times, and none of it made sense.

Maggie a Pinkerton detective? How was that possible? How could he have been so blinded by her smile and those big blue eyes of hers? How could he have been so fooled by her sweet, loving nature?

He could still hear her voice in his head—cold, hard, uncompromising. *"The money you stole from the train. . . I found it."*

A sharp pain started in his chest and radiated outward. What had he ever done to make her think him capable of such a heinous crime? He'd had his problems with the church, but never had he gone against God's commandments. Not since returning from that dreadful war.

Heaving his shoulders, he stood and wrapped his hands around the rough steel bars. *Oh, Lord, what's happening to me?*

The bitter taste of gall filled his mouth as he thought of Maggie's accusations. Robbery? Murder? How could she think such things of him? He'd danced with her, held her, kissed her. Would have done anything for her. Given her the moon if such a thing had been possible.

And all this time—God, all this time—she had been plotting against him.

Chapter 31

On the morning the trial was scheduled to start, Maggie left her hotel room early to meet Rikker downstairs in the dining room. The sheriff asked them both to stay in town to testify. It wasn't by any means an unusual request. She had testified at other trials but never with such dread.

Though evidence all pointed to Garrett's guilt, many in town had expressed shock and disbelief. No one could believe that Hetty's beloved nephew would do such a thing.

"It was that terrible war," some said. Though the war had been over for a good number of years, many still blamed it for everything bad that had happened since.

Rikker waved his hand as she entered the dining room, and she quickly headed for his table. He was already halfway through his breakfast. She envied his ability to eat and sleep no matter what happened.

She ordered coffee and scrambled eggs with bacon, though she didn't feel like eating.

She couldn't shake the feeling that something was not right. Too many unanswered questions remained for her peace of mind.

"Why do you suppose Garrett refuses to name his partner?" she asked. If Cotton was the second robber as they suspected, Garrett's silence was even more puzzling. Why protect a man for whom he had so little regard?

"I gave up trying to understand the criminal mind a long time ago," Rikker said between bites. He glanced across the table at her. "Oh no, the look."

"What are you talking about? What look?"

"Every theory of yours, no matter how harebrained, is always preceded by a certain look."

She rested her arms on the table and leaned forward. "If he's found guilty of theft, he'll go to Yuma." At half capacity Yuma Territorial Prison was still new enough to have a fairly good reputation. "Murder... he hangs."

"So what's your point?"

"I don't believe him capable of murder." His sadness as he talked about the war had been too real. "So why is he shouldering the blame?"

"It wasn't that long ago that you didn't believe him guilty of theft," Rikker said.

He had her over a barrel with that one. How could her instincts have been so wrong? "I just hate loose ends." After a moment she added, "And I know Cotton's involved."

"Shh," he said, slanting his head sideways.

She glanced over at a corner table where Cotton sat having breakfast alone. She leaned forward. "Oooooooh. I'm so tempted to go over there and—"

"Pray for strength, Duffy," Rikker said, buttering his bread.

"I would, except I'm afraid what I would do to the man if I was any stronger."

He sighed, and she could guess his thoughts. While waiting to testify, neither had stopped working. He shadowed Cotton while she tracked Dinwiddie's every move. They both came up empty-handed.

"Without Thomas's cooperation, we have nothing but speculation," he said.

"Anything from headquarters?"

"Only that Dinwiddie has no criminal record, but they still haven't been able to track Cotton's movement for the last two years."

The waiter came with her order, but she felt even less like eating than before.

Watching her push her food around her plate, Rikker shook his head. "It'll soon be over, Duffy," he said. "Then we can go home."

Home wasn't a place to Rikker; it was the next assignment. Once he got his man, he was ready to move on. Stuck in town for a week waiting to testify had been sheer torture for him.

Thankfully, he didn't nag her to eat as he usually did, and he even paid the check without comment. He tucked the receipt into his pocket to be turned in to Pinkerton headquarters later, and reached for his hat.

"Ready?"

No, she wasn't ready; she was shaking, and it felt like ice water flowed through her veins. Nevertheless she nodded, but it took every bit of energy she could muster just to rise to her feet.

As they walked out of the hotel, they were greeted by Linc's voice. Maggie recognized the trousers and shirt at once as belonging to Toby. Already, the toes of his new shoes were scuffed and his hair slightly mussed, but he no longer looked like a waif.

"Readallaboutit," he yelled. "It's the trial of the century."

Rikker stopped to purchase a paper, giving the boy a quarter. "Keep it," he said.

"Thank you, sir," Linc said, grinning. He dropped the coin into the canvas apron that he now carefully tied around his waist to prevent theft.

"How's your grandmother?" Maggie asked. The boy was still not in school, and that worried her.

"She's okay," Linc said. "She even knows who I am most days."

"That's wonderful," Maggie said.

Rikker tucked the newspaper beneath his arm, and they continued on their way. The trial was scheduled for nine o'clock.

Something made her glance back at Linc. She tugged on Rikker's arm. "Why do you suppose Cotton is so interested in Linc?"

Rikker turned and squinted against the bright morning sun. "Maybe he's just purchasing a paper like everyone else. Come on." He took her by the arm. "Don't want to be late."

❦

Furnace Creek's first courthouse was still under construction, so Garrett's trial was to be held on the first floor of a deserted two-story building painted a shocking pink.

The courtroom was already packed when they arrived. The flocked red wallpaper and scarlet draperies suggested the building had a less-than-virtuous past. Maggie could well imagine what image was hidden behind the carefully draped picture hanging over the mantel.

Judge Campbell sat up front behind a makeshift bench. He was a bald-headed man with muttonchop whiskers and what looked like a permanent scowl. Twelve jurors sat along one wall, while spectators vied for the few remaining seats.

As witnesses, Rikker and Maggie were directed to sit in the first row behind the prisoner.

Garrett turned to look at her as she took her seat, his eyes as remote as his expression. Hot blood rushed to her face. She didn't want to believe him capable of the charges against him. No matter how many times she sifted through the facts, her heart refused to believe what her head told her was true.

Face grim with cold fury, he held her gaze for a moment before turning away. Her hand found its way to her naked finger, and the weight of a boulder settled in her chest.

The courtroom was stifling, and a blue haze of cigar smoke hung in the air. If only someone would open the windows. She fanned herself with her gloves, but that offered little relief.

Rikker gave her a fatherly pat on the arm. "Hang on, Duffy," he whispered, as if guessing how very close she was to falling apart. "It'll soon be over."

The trial would end and the jury would make its decision, but she knew it would never be over. Not completely. Not for her. Not as long as the memories remained.

The last one to take his place in one of the witness seats was Linc.

She nudged Rikker's arm. "What's he doing here?" she whispered.

"Probably here to testify about the hundred-dollar bill he found."

The judge banged his gavel. "Order in the court."

A hush fell over the courtroom.

The judge eyed the prosecutor. "You may call your first witness."

The prosecutor's name was Leonard Theodore Fassbender, an impressive name for a man who barely stood five feet tall in his stocking feet. But what he lacked in stature he made up for with a strong and vibrant voice.

"I call Miss Cartwright to the stand."

Stomach clenched, Maggie rose, squeezed past Rikker, and walked to the front of the room on shaky legs. Placing her right hand on the Bible, she raised her left hand and swore to tell the truth, the whole truth, and nothing but the truth. She sat and held her hands together on her lap.

Fassbender measured her for a long moment before he began. "Would you please state your name and occupation for the court?"

"My name is Miss Maggie Cartwright." She paused to clear her voice. "I work for the Pinkerton National Detective Agency."

"In what capacity do you work for the agency?"

"I'm an operative."

"And could you please tell the court how you came to be acquainted with Mr. Thomas?"

Her hands tightened in her lap. "I answered his ad for a mail-order bride."

"Could you please tell the court why you did that?"

Maggie explained that it was her boss's idea. *God, please let this be over soon. I just want to die.*

"So you traveled here to meet with the defendant," Fassbender said. "Is that correct?"

She stole a glance at Garrett and was momentarily silenced by his stony-eyed expression.

"Is that correct, Miss Cartwright?" Fassbender repeated, this time louder.

She lowered her lashes. "Yes."

"For what purpose did you agree to become his fiancée?" he asked.

She looked up with great effort. "To find the money stolen from the Whistle-Stop train robbery."

Cheeks blazing, she kept her focus on the prosecutor. The lies, the betrayal—they were all part of her job. So why did she feel so ashamed? It was like watching her father hang all over again. Only this time it felt like she was the one who had done wrong.

"Are you telling this court that you never intended to marry the defendant?"

"That's correct." She spoke in a suffocated whisper.

"I ask again, Miss Cartwright, if you ever intended to marry Mr. Thomas. Please speak up so the jury can hear your answer."

She swallowed the lump in her voice. "That's correct. I. . .never intended to go through with the wedding."

Aunt Hetty gave an audible gasp, and a murmur rose from the spectators like a swarm of bees. The judge called for order.

Mr. Fassbender continued. "What led you to believe that Mr. Thomas had the money that was stolen from the train?"

The jurors hung on to her every word as she walked the court through Pinkerton's investigation and subsequent findings.

Determined to mine her testimony for all it was worth, Fassbender continued with the questions. He was good at what he did. Like a Shakespearean actor, he knew when to pause for effect and when to raise or lower his voice.

Finally, the prosecutor turned his attention to the day she found the money in the children's tree house. He wasn't satisfied until every last detail of that awful day had been hammered out of her. By the time she was excused, she barely had enough strength left to stumble back to her seat.

Chapter 32

The next witness to be called for the Territory was Linc. The boy looked scared to death as he took the witness stand. He didn't even know his right hand from his left, and the bailiff had to help him place the correct one on the Bible.

"State your name for the record."

"Linc Jones."

Not only did the boy look scared, he looked vulnerable and seemed to shrink beneath the prosecutor's steady gaze. Feeling a surge of protectiveness toward him, Maggie clenched her hands together and pressed her lips tight.

"Would you please tell the court how you happened to come across a hundred-dollar bill?"

"Yes, sir." He stared down at his hands. "I was selling my newspapers in the barbershop like I do every day. I stepped outside and found the money right there in front of the door."

Linc's story was consistent with what Toby and Elise had told her.

"And do you know how the money ended up in front of the barbershop?"

Linc glanced at Garrett and then at Katherine's brother sitting in the opposite side of the courtroom. "I—I do," he stammered.

Maggie sat forward and noticed Cotton do likewise. She frowned. Why would he show so much interest in Linc's testimony? It made no sense unless—

She coughed in an effort to capture Linc's attention, and when that failed to work she jumped to her feet. This time he looked straight at her. She rubbed her nose before taking her seat again. The boy's nose didn't turn blue, but his face blazed red enough to hide his freckles.

Rikker leaned sideways. "What was that about?" he muttered beneath his breath.

"I'll tell you later," she whispered.

The prosecutor repeated his question. "Would you kindly tell the court how the money happened to appear in front of the barbershop?"

Linc glanced at Maggie. "I—I don't know."

"What!?"

The prosecutor's outburst made Linc jump, and murmured voices filled the courtroom.

"Order!" the judge bellowed.

Fassbender followed his outburst with an apology to the judge. He straightened his bow tie, cleared his throat, and stepped up to the witness stand. "You are under oath to tell the truth," he said in a quieter, though no less emphatic, voice.

Linc glanced at Maggie, and again she rubbed her nose. "I am telling the truth, sir. I found the money and don't know who dropped it. Honest."

⁂

During the afternoon break, Maggie stepped outside to get some air. Rikker followed her from the courtroom but had since disappeared.

It was hot and the air still, but the smell of heated soil was a welcome change from the airless, smoke-filled courtroom.

Anxious to talk to Linc, she caught him by the arm as he emerged from the building.

"We need to talk," she said, pulling him aside.

Linc's face paled. "I didn't tell no lie, honest."

"No, but you were thinking about it."

Linc worried her. In the past, he'd had to steal and lie to survive. Thanks to Garrett's generosity, Linc and his grandmother now had plenty of food and clothing. But behavior begun from necessity could easily escalate into a lifetime habit of illegal activities.

"How much did Cotton pay you to lie?" It was a guess on her part, but the look on Linc's face told her she was right.

"He didn't pay me nothing."

"But he was going to." When he didn't deny it, she continued. "What did he want you to say?"

"Nothing. He didn't want me to say nothing." And with that, Linc took off running.

She watched him go with a sense of sadness. As soon as the trial was over she would leave town. So there really was nothing more she could do for Linc. Couldn't do much for Elise and Toby, either.

She turned with a sigh and was just about to reenter the courthouse when she was accosted by Aunt Hetty.

"You claim to be a Pinkerton detective." The old woman stabbed the ground with her cane and her eyes glittered. "Prove it."

Maggie pulled her tin shield out of her waistband and held it up.

Aunt Hetty discounted her badge with a shake of her head. "That tells me nothing."

"Then what will?" Maggie asked.

"Proving my nephew innocent!"

Sighing, Maggie repinned the shield to her waistband. "The evidence is stacked against him. The money—"

"Anyone could have put it there. It's not like the barn was under lock and key."

"But that would make no sense. Why would anyone hide the money in the tree house and forget about it?"

Aunt Hetty sniffed. "Why would Garrett? He would never do anything to bring harm to his children. And that includes exposing them to stolen money."

She couldn't blame Aunt Hetty for not wanting to believe Garrett guilty. She was having a hard time believing it herself. And what she said about the children was right on target. It made no sense that he would hide the stolen cache in the playhouse. He had to have known that the satchel would be irresistible to a curious mind like Toby's.

"I guess we just have to hope the truth comes out in the trial," she said vaguely, her thoughts still on the playhouse.

"You know as well as I that the jury has already made up their minds, and it has nothing to do with truth."

"Aunt Hetty—"

"Do you know what Garrett told me after he was released from that awful prison? He said the one good thing that came out of his stay at Andersonville was that it kept him off the battlefield. That's how much he hated the thought of killing. Do you honestly think him capable of killing that guard in cold blood?"

Maggie shook her head. "No, I don't think that—"

"How much do you charge?"

"What?"

"I want to hire you to prove Garrett's innocence. How much do you charge?"

"I can't take your money."

Aunt Hetty's eyes sharpened. "Can't or won't?"

"There's nothing I can do," Maggie said.

Aunt Hetty studied her. "Are you absolutely one hundred percent certain of Garrett's guilt?" She waited for an answer, and when none came, nodded. "That's what I thought."

Without another word, she ambled away.

∞

Garrett's defense began the following day. A tall, thin man with a sweeping mustache, attorney Robert King had done a great job in rounding up people willing to testify on Garrett's character.

Customers testified that he was a fair and reasonable businessman.

Panhandle took the stand without removing his ever-present pompadour cap. With every question put to him by the defense, he blinked like someone who just woke from a long slumber or stepped out of a cave.

"Yessir," he said. "Mr. Thomas is a good employer and pays my salary on time. And nope, he never overworked me. No, sir, never did."

Next to take the stand was Miss Nancy Riden, the children's teacher. She testified that Garrett was a caring parent who always saw that his children arrived for class on time and turned in their assignments.

A long line of witnesses followed, all testifying to Garrett's good character.

Just before noon, Aunt Hetty was called to the stand. She walked up the aisle with her cane and took her place in front of the court. "My nephew is innocent of all charges lodged against him," she announced.

The judge's scowl deepened. "You can't say anything until you've been sworn in."

"Then hurry up and do it," she ordered. "It's nearly time for my medicine."

The clerk hurried to her side with the Bible. "Raise your right hand..."

After Aunt Hetty had been sworn in, she immediately restated her earlier contention.

"You're here to answer questions, not give your personal opinion," the judge said.

"That's not my personal opinion," Aunt Hetty argued. "That's the gospel truth."

Aunt Hetty spent more time arguing with the judge than she spent answering questions. Apparently thinking she was doing his client more harm than good, Garrett's attorney quickly dismissed her.

⁓

That night, Maggie sat with Rikker in the hotel dining room. It was their custom to go over every bit of testimony at the end of each day.

"I give up," he said in answer to her question. "Why would Cotton pay Linc to lie on the witness stand?"

Maggie set her fork down and reached for the napkin on her lap. Her run-in with Aunt Hetty had bothered her more than she cared to admit, and she'd thought about it ever since. Was she a hundred percent certain of Garrett's guilt? Not by a long shot.

"You're not helping," she said.

"And you're letting your feelings color your judgment."

She dabbed her mouth. "If that's true, I'm only doing what you taught me to do."

"Me?"

"Do you remember when we were shadowing Jason Wells?" Wells was suspected of being the notorious Black Hooded bank robber. "Everything indicated he was about to rob the St. Louis Bank."

"I remember. We had all our men in place to nab him when he did, but you were certain it was a trick."

She nodded. Finding that map in his hotel room had seemed a tad too convenient. "When I came to you with my concerns, do you remember what you said?" He shrugged, and she continued. "You said, *follow your instincts.*'"

"Which was probably the last time you took my advice," he said.

That wasn't true, but she let the comment pass. "Because of your good counsel, we caught him trying to rob a bank in the next town."

He pushed his plate away. "All right, you made your point. What's on your mind? And it better not involve my wearing a dress."

She laughed. Rikker still hadn't recovered from having to disguise himself as a woman to infiltrate a group of female outlaws.

She leaned forward. "I need to see Garrett. I want to talk to him."

"Then talk to him."

"I can't. The sheriff won't allow visitors." Summerhay was up for reelection and wasn't happy that two Pinkerton detectives—one a woman and the other a man in his fifties—were credited with solving the Whistle-Stop train robbery.

"Only his lawyer can see him."

"So what do you plan to do? Disguise yourself as one of his legal mouthpieces?"

"Not exactly."

Rikker mopped the last of the gravy up with a piece of bread. "Please don't tell me you're going to break into the jailhouse."

"Not me. You."

He groaned. "That's what I was afraid of."

"It won't be that hard. And just think, you won't even have to wear a dress."

Chapter 33

It was almost midnight when Maggie and Rikker walked from the hotel to the sheriff's office. The saloons were in full swing on what the locals called Likker Row. The screech of fiddles kept up a steady whine in the distance, but the main part of town was quiet.

A silent prayer fell from her lips. Even if Rikker managed to break in, there was no guarantee that Garrett would have anything to do with her.

Directly overhead, the crescent moon seemed to mock them with its yellow smile. A *laughing moon* Elise called it, and the memory made Maggie ache. How she missed those little pumpkins.

"Shh." Rikker paused in front of the door of the sheriff's office and pressed his finger to his mouth. "I hear something."

Maggie heard it, too. It sounded like a whole army of horses, all heading their way.

"Hurry!"

Rikker reached into his pocket for a piece of wire. "I *am* hurrying."

The sound of hooves grew louder, and Maggie glanced up the street. The horsemen were now in view.

She tugged on Rikker's sleeve. "We better hide."

Together they dashed to the alley at the side of the building. Thinking the horsemen would continue down the street to Likker Row, Maggie was surprised when they stopped in front of the sheriff's office. She peered around the corner. The riders dismounted and tied their horses to the hitching post then stormed up the porch steps. There were five men in all.

"Looks like a lynch mob," Rikker whispered.

Icy fear twisted her heart, and she reached for her weapon. "What do we do? There're only two of us."

"On the outside chance they can count, we better keep that information to ourselves."

"They'll figure it out soon enough."

Rikker shrugged. "I've got a plan."

"It doesn't involve fire, does it?" Last year in Alabama, when she and Rikker were held captive by a couple of outlaws, he'd started a blaze in hopes of creating a diversion. It turned into a three-alarm fire, and they barely escaped with their lives.

"Don't worry. I'm all out of matches." Rikker pulled a knife from his boot. "Keep me covered." Bent low, he moved stealthily toward the horses.

Gun in hand, Maggie cast a quick glance around the corner. The men crowding around the door were arguing among themselves and didn't appear to notice Rikker cutting their mounts loose.

She recognized the brown and white horse and frowned. Unless she was mistaken, that was Cotton's horse.

She chanced another peek at the knot of men, but it was too dark to pick out any one individual. If she was right about Cotton, that opened up a whole lot of new questions. He missed no chance to blame Garrett for his sister's death, but why take the law into his own hands? The chance of jurors ruling in Garrett's favor were slim if not altogether zero. That meant Garrett would face the gallows without any help from Cotton or anyone else. So why bother with a lynch party? Or bribing Linc to lie? It made no sense.

Rikker straightened and slapped a brown gelding on the rump. He then took cover behind a barrel. The horse let out a loud whinny and galloped away. One of the men yelled, but this only spooked the animals more. With a flip of their tails, the rest of the horses raced away, their pounding hooves churning up dust.

The men jumped off the porch and ran down the street shouting and cursing and waving their arms.

Maggie slumped against the building with a sigh. She shuddered to think what might have happened to Garrett had she and Rikker not been there to stop them.

"Psst." Rikker motioned to her. "Hurry, before they come back!"

Maggie slipped her weapon into her leg holster and joined him in front of the sheriff's office.

Rikker greeted her with a chuckle. "Our friends did us a favor." He pushed the door open with the tip of a single finger and waved his arm in a gentlemanly manner. "After you."

∞

It was dark inside the sheriff's office and it took a moment for Maggie's eyes to adjust. "Garrett?"

A movement in back made her hesitate.

"Maggie?" A short silence followed before he spoke again, this time in a cold, hard voice. "What are you doing here?"

"Talk to him," Rikker said, nudging her forward with a hand to her back. "I'll stand guard."

She moved through the dark office until she reached the steel bars of Garrett's cell. A strong whiff of alcohol floated from the cell next to his, along with loud snores.

A scraping sound preceded the flare of a match, and Garrett bent to light a candle in a candlestick holder on the cell floor. The wick flickered into a steady flame, spreading a circle of light around them.

He frowned in cold fury. "What do you want?"

"We need to talk." She hoped her low, unsteady voice could be heard over the loud thumps of her fast-beating heart.

"I have nothing to say to you." His gaze bored into her like a dagger. "I want you gone."

After all that had happened, including her testimony in court, his anger was no more than she deserved, but it hurt. It hurt a lot.

"I'll go," she whispered. "But not till you hear what I have to say." She tightened her hold to steady herself. "I want to help."

"Help?" His cruel laugh slashed through her. "If it wasn't for you, I wouldn't be here."

"If it hadn't been me, it would have been someone else." Once a person was unfortunate enough to land in Pinkerton's orbit, there was no escaping him or his detectives. The agency never slept, and neither did it give up.

"I wish to God it had been someone else," he said. "Maybe then it wouldn't—" She heard his intake of breath.

She pulled away from the steel door and curled her hands into fists. If she had any chance of saving him, she must put her personal feelings aside. But it was hard—harder than anything she'd ever done.

"Let me help you. If you're innocent—"

"If?"

"It looks bad, Garrett." Her voice broke. "Real bad."

He stared at her, his eyes too dark to read. "Then why bother? You got what you came for. Your job is done."

She glanced over her shoulder. Rikker's large form outlined in the doorway renewed her courage. Turning back, she lowered her voice. "I care because—" *I love you.* Startled by the thought that so easily came to mind, she hesitated. She couldn't say that; shouldn't even be thinking it. Aloud she said, "The children—"

"The children?" he said with a note of sarcasm. "You weren't thinking of them when you wormed your way into my household under false pretenses!"

"I know you're angry—"

"Angry doesn't begin to describe how I feel. You wore my ring. You wrote me letters. You. . ." His voice shook with rage. "How can I believe anything you say?"

She swallowed, but the lump in her throat refused to budge. If only she could touch him, maybe he'd know she spoke the truth when she said she cared. But even as she longed for these things, something snapped inside.

"You want to know the truth?" This time she didn't care who she woke. "I'll tell you the truth. The day I found the money I planned on leaving town. I told Rikker I couldn't do it anymore. I could no longer lie to you."

"But you did lie!" he retorted. "Not only to me but to everyone."

She reached her hand through the bars touching him briefly on the arm. "Please, Garrett. Your children need you." When he made no response she continued. "You say you're innocent."

"I *am* innocent."

She withdrew her hand. "If that's true, let me help you. I'm good at what I do. And Rikker—Detective Greenwood—is the best. If you really are innocent, you'll let us help you."

"Help me how?" he asked sharply.

"I don't know how, but I'll find a way." And that meant having to think and act like a detective.

Training and experience had taught her the art of interrogation. Ninety percent of the time people will answer a direct question; not always truthfully, of course, but sometimes even a lie was revealing.

"First you have to tell me." It wasn't good enough to hear him declare his innocence; she needed it spelled out in clear and precise language. "Did you do the things they say?"

How could she in good conscience ask Rikker to put his career on the line if there was so much as a shadow of doubt that Garrett was guilty?

"Did you rob that train?"

"No!"

Encouraged by his quick, emphatic reply, she asked the next question. "Did you kill the guard?"

He thrust his hands through the bars and grabbed her around the waist. Barely able to control her gasp of surprise, she started to protest, but the words stuck in her throat. As if taking her silence for consent, he yanked her closer.

"Do you really think I did those things?"

His ragged, hot breath on her cheek made her tremble—not from fear, but from the overwhelming nearness of him. For a moment she didn't answer, but neither did she pull from his embrace.

"Do you?" he demanded with a gentle shake.

"No," she said. "I don't!"

His arms around her made it hard to breathe, let alone think, but she knew the moment the words left her mouth that she spoke the truth.

She longed to push away the lock of hair that fell across his forehead. Smooth away the frown. Touch his mouth with her fingers if not her lips. But something held her back. Perhaps it was pride. Maybe it was shame for the way she'd tricked him. Or simply fear of rejection.

His face blazed with sudden emotion, and with a groan, he let her go.

Her senses whirled and her mind went blank.

Rikker's voice cut through the silence. "Everything all right back there?"

Reality hit her with a thud. "Yes," she called over her shoulder and took a step away from the cell. She tried putting her thoughts in order as she had been trained to do.

"The train robbery occurred more than two years ago. In January. I have to ask, Garrett. Where were you on that day?"

"That's a long time ago. How can I remember?"

"It was a Sunday."

"The shop's closed on Sunday, so I guess I was home."

"Can you prove it?"

"I don't know. Katherine—" He hesitated. "She always took the children to church and—" He stopped and combed his fingers through his hair. "No, I can't prove it. I guess this is my punishment for refusing to attend church."

"God doesn't work that way," she said. Silence stretched between them for a moment before she asked the next question. "How do you think the money got into the tree house?"

"Don't you think I've asked myself that question a dozen times since my arrest?"

"This isn't helping. I need you to think!"

"Anyone could have put it there," he retorted.

"Shh," Rikker cautioned from the doorway. "You'll wake the dead."

She glanced at the cell next to Garrett's, but the loud snores confirmed that the drunk was still in a stupor.

"The children said the money was yours. Why would they say that?"

"They think everything at the house that's not theirs is mine."

That made sense, so she moved to the next question. "When's the last time you were in the tree house?"

"The last time?" He thought for a moment. "Not since Katherine died. That was her project. She told me she always wanted a tree house as a child. She and the children took over the hayloft. It wasn't my favorite place. All that small furniture. . . The last time I was there I banged my head on a rafter."

It was hard to envision him in such a confined area. Even she had trouble sitting on the child-sized chairs.

She hesitated a moment before asking the next question. "Do you think Katherine put the money there?"

"Katherine?" The surprise in his voice sounded genuine. "Why would you think such a thing? She's been gone for two years."

"The money's been there for at least that long." Toby had said he didn't know how or when the money got there; he only knew it had been there for a long time.

"But that meant that she—" He shook his head. "Katherine was an honest woman. A good Christian. She would never do such a thing." He paused. "But—"

She stiffened. "What? Tell me."

"Her brother insisted Katherine stored something for him. A satchel of personal papers. Deeds to some properties he owned. That's what we were arguing about that day in the shop. Even after all this time, he thinks I'm keeping it, whatever it is, from him. Maybe the satchel you found was his."

She felt a surge of hope. Could this be the breakthrough she'd been praying for? "But why would he wait two years before trying to retrieve it?"

"He didn't. He first approached me about it before the funeral. Even insisted on following me around the house while I did a search. Made me check the attic—everything.

"He left town shortly after the funeral, and that was the last I heard from him until—"

"After the school fund-raiser." The timing always bothered her. She glanced at Rikker, who continued to pace back and forth on the porch watching for trouble.

"Who else had access to the hayloft?"

"No one," he said. "I mean, anyone could have climbed the ladder." He frowned. "Do you suppose Katherine put it there?"

"I don't know. Maybe."

"But why hide it in the children's playhouse?"

"I don't know." Was that why Katherine went outside on that dark, rainy night? To hide the satchel? "Maybe she discovered the stolen money inside."

"But why hide it?"

It was a good question for which she had no answer. Unless. . . Recalling the letter she found in the attic, something occurred to her. "What if she found the money and knew it was stolen. Maybe she wanted to give her brother a chance to turn himself in." It would certainly explain the ultimatum she wrote. If Cotton didn't do what she asked, she would go to the sheriff herself.

Garrett thought a moment. "That sounds like something she might do. She was always trying to get her brother to do the right thing."

Maggie felt a surge of hope. She was on the right track. She felt it in her bones. Of course, this left yet another disturbing question. What did any of this have to do with Katherine's death?

∽

While Rikker fiddled with the jailhouse lock, Maggie poked her head outside. Except for the distant screech of a fiddle, all was quiet.

"What if they come back?" The thought turned her insides to ice. She had a real chance of getting to the truth and possibly saving Garrett, but she needed time.

Rikker gave the lock a sharp tap before answering. "I'll stay here and keep watch till the sheriff arrives in the morning."

She patted him on the back. He was such a dear man, and she thanked God every day for bringing him into her life.

"Let me stay. You have to testify tomorrow, and you need your rest."

"You need your rest, too," he said. "Now quit worrying and go."

She was anxious to run her latest theory by him, but he was already pushing her out the door. "What about tomorrow night and the night after that?"

"Let's get through this night and we'll worry about the rest later."

"Rikker—"

"Go!"

She continued to argue, but he wouldn't take no for an answer. Finally she gave in and returned to the hotel—for all the good it did her.

Instead of using the few hours left till dawn for some much-needed sleep, she practically paced a hole in the carpet. Would Garrett ever forgive her? And what if she couldn't find the proof needed to save him?

Falling to her knees, she prayed. The truth was out there somewhere, and with God's help, she would do everything possible to find it. As for Garrett... *Please, God, help him to forgive me.*

Was she asking the impossible? Probably. Why should he forgive her? When had she ever shown forgiveness? No matter how hard she tried, she still felt bitter toward her father.

But that was the problem, wasn't it? She covered her face with her hands. It's what brought her to this time and place, and look what it got her. Her need to punish her father might well send an innocent man to his death.

Her eyes flew open. *Punish?*

The thought set her back on her heels. Tracking down thieves and murderers was her way of making up to society for her father's crimes. Or at least that's what she had always told herself. But were her reasons really so noble?

The question weighed heavily on her mind as she sat at the desk to write a detailed report to headquarters.

Allen Pinkerton demanded meticulous record-keeping. Reports had to be written in cryptic with indelible ink. She was required to give a full description of a suspect, including every known trait, both good and bad. Every relevant conversation had to be recorded verbatim and the time line accurate to the last minute.

Allan often complained that some of his male operatives didn't put enough details into their reports. Brevity was not Maggie's problem, wordiness was. She never described eyes as merely blue or brown. It was always shades of cobalt (like Garrett's) or nut brown; azure or chocolate.

Tonight she described Cotton's eyes as gunmetal gray. Rikker said he had no prior record but there had to be something, and she hoped that a more detailed description would uncover something in the Pinkerton rogues gallery that had been previously overlooked.

Chapter 34

Maggie rose just as a glimmer of light broke through the darkness. Yawning, she stretched her arms overhead, but her limbs felt heavy. No wonder. Disturbing dreams kept her twisting and turning during the short time spent in bed. It was all she could do to drag herself across the room to the washstand.

Following her morning ablutions, she dressed and left the hotel. The streets were deserted as she hurried to the jailhouse. It promised to be another warm day, but even the glorious pink sunrise couldn't lift her spirits. Much to her relief, the sheriff's horse was hitched out front and all looked peaceful and quiet.

Spotting Rikker as he left the sheriff's office, she picked up her pace and quickly fell in step by his side. "Any problems?"

Despite his whiskered chin and mussed hair, he looked remarkably spry for such an early hour. "None that can't be fixed with cackleberries, bacon, and some strong hot coffee."

"And Garrett? Is he—?"

"He's fine. Though neither one of us got any sleep with all that snoring in the next cell." He regarded her with a slanted look. "You don't look like you got much sleep yourself."

"How could I? I kept worrying about you."

"You were worrying about Thomas."

"I was worried about you both. A man of your age—" Too late she bit her tongue. She could feel his hackles rise as they tended to do whenever the subject of age came up.

"I can do everything I could do as a young man," he said. "I'd just rather not, is all."

She glanced at his profile. It was the first time he'd admitted to not wanting to do anything. He wouldn't admit it for the world, but he was obviously feeling his age. A detective's life was hard, even on the young.

Quickly changing the subject, she said, "I'd feel better if we could put Garrett under twenty-four-hour guard."

"Yeah, well, there're just the two of us," he said. "Let's hope for the best. The trial should soon be over."

If he was trying to make her feel better, he failed miserably. Punishment was swift in the West. Once a guilty verdict was announced, a short walk to the gallows quickly followed.

"Do you think we should wire headquarters for reinforcements?" she asked.

He shook his head. "It'll take too long for anyone to arrive." Rikker sounded as frustrated as she felt. "Besides, the bank has its money. They're not likely to pay Pinkerton to keep investigating a case that appears to be solved. I'm afraid we're on our own."

"We know that two crooks robbed the train. What about the second one?"

He shrugged. "Like I said. The bank got its money back."

She swallowed her frustration. A man died in that robbery, and his family deserved justice. "I have a theory."

"Of course, you do, Duffy." It was a joke between them; he always had a plan and she always had a theory.

"I'm pretty certain that Katherine placed the money in the tree house."

"Are we talking about Katherine, Thomas's wife?"

She nodded. "I think that's why she was out in the storm the night she died. Cotton apparently asked his sister to hold on to something for him. A satchel... If it's the same one I found in the tree house, then there's no question that he's one of the thieves."

"Hmm." He gave her a cockeyed look. "Would you happen to have a theory as to how to prove it?"

"Actually, I was hoping you'd come up with one of your brilliant plans."

"You know me. I can't think on an empty stomach."

"You better get some sleep," she said.

"I will. Just as soon as I catch a bite."

"I'll take tonight's shift."

"No, you won't," he said as if he expected that to be the final word.

She stopped mid-step and whirled about to face him, hands on her waist. "I'm perfectly capable of keeping watch."

He studied her from beneath a crinkled brow. "I don't doubt it for a moment, but I'm not capable of letting you. If you recall, there were five of them, none of whom looked like a choirboy."

She dropped her arms to her side. As much as she hated to admit it, Rikker was right. The only weapon she packed was a derringer—a handy gun for protecting herself at close range, but hardly practical for holding back a mob.

"You can't keep staying up all night." She was pretty certain he was putting on a show for her benefit. Already he had gone above and beyond what friendship required. Staying up all night was one thing when you were in your twenties or thirties, but not at Rikker's age.

"What choice do I have? That lynch mob could come back."

She shuddered at the thought. "I'm still confused about Cotton's motivation. Why try to hang a man who already has his neck in the loop? It makes no sense."

"Revenge seldom does."

"You think that's all there is to it? Revenge?"

He shrugged. "He blames Thomas for keeping that money hidden."

"Maybe," she said. "Or maybe he's afraid Garrett will take the stand. He's the only one who can tie Cotton to that satchel." The more she thought about it, the more sense it made. "When Linc refused to lie on the stand and say that Garrett dropped that hundred-dollar bill,

Cotton must have panicked."

"But why?" Rikker asked. "How would Linc's lie have helped him?"

"It wouldn't unless Garrett testified that the satchel was Cotton's. Linc's testimony would have placed the stolen money in Garrett's hand."

"Ah, so that's what the lynch mob was about. Keeping Garrett from testifying and implicating Cotton."

"What I don't understand is why he doesn't just leave town?" she asked. "Why stay around and take a chance on Garrett implicating him?"

"I think I can answer that question," Rikker said. "Katherine's father cut Cotton out of his will. Apparently he was disgusted that his son hadn't done anything constructive with his life. Katherine got everything, but she placed almost all of her inheritance into a trust for the children. So if something happened to Garrett and his aunt, Cotton would be the only living relative. That would make him the conservator."

The thought made her shudder. "What do you bet the children would never see a penny of that money?"

The implications sent a chill down her spine. It certainly explained why Cotton wanted to see Garrett dead. She didn't even want to think about what that might mean for Aunt Hetty.

They started walking again. The church steeple in the distance gave her an idea. "Go ahead. I'll catch up with you later."

She quickened her step, and he called after her, "Where are you going in such a hurry?"

She waved her hand over her head and kept going. "To solve the guard problem." And maybe even find a miracle.

❦

The morning sun cast a ray of golden light onto the church steeple as she followed the winding footpath to the back of the church. She found Reverend Holly sprinkling flowers with a gray metal watering can. Even at this early hour he wore a bow tie.

He looked up when she approached.

"Ah, the lady detective," he said. "What brings you here on this fine day that God has made?"

"Garrett Thomas," she said.

The reverend shook his head. "I've known Garrett for a long time. Can't believe he did the things they say."

"He didn't."

Holly's eyebrows shot up. "You sound pretty certain."

She nodded. "I am."

"Hmm." Today he was hatless, and his round bald spot shone like a newly minted penny. "I can't tell you how upset I was when he stopped coming to church. I prayed that he would change his mind. When he showed up that Sunday, I thought God had answered my prayers. But he looked none too happy to see me yesterday when I visited him in jail. Said the only reason he came to church was to keep an eye on his son."

The memory of attending church with Garrett and the children felt like another knife to the heart. "Did you know he had a bad experience with the church when he was in Andersonville prison?"

He nodded. "I did know that." He heaved a heavy sigh. "Funny thing about a war. It almost always changes a man's faith. Sometimes for the good, but not always." He tilted the can over a cluster of yellow flowers, and water poured from its spout. "Never met a lady detective before." He looked up. "It seems that you and I are in a similar business."

"How so?"

"The Bible is filled with mystery, and it's up to me to help my flock unravel the clues. I guess that makes me a detective of sorts."

"Never thought about it that way."

He shrugged. "Considering the nature of human beings, the biggest mystery is why God loves us so much."

"I often wonder that myself," she said. The kindly minister at the orphanage had told her that God even loved her father. She didn't believe it then, and she wasn't certain she believed it now. Why would

God love a man so hateful when she, his daughter, could not?

"Why is God so mysterious?" she asked.

"I'll answer that question with another." He moved over to water a scruffy-looking shrub with silvery leaves. "What do you do after you solve a crime and all the questions have been answered to your satisfaction?"

"Do?" She frowned. "I close the file and go on to the next case."

"You see? That's just it. If there were no mysteries in the Bible, we would close the book and go on to something else. Mysteries require answers, and that's what keeps us searching. God loves a seeker, and if we're diligent enough, He sometimes even rewards us with insight and understanding."

Maggie flushed with guilt. She read her Bible faithfully but never really studied it, not like she studied her cases.

He set the watering can on a tree stump. "So tell me, what are you seeking today?"

"Help," she said. "I'm seeking help." She explained the problem as quickly as possible.

Reverend Holly shook his head. "A lynch mob, you say?"

She nodded. "Yes, and we need people willing to stand guard at night. Do you think the church members will help?"

"Miracles have been known to happen around here." His wink told her that he knew more than he'd let on about Toby and the moving cross. "Who knows?" He chuckled. "Maybe we're in store for another."

Chapter 35

The morning routine at the jailhouse never varied. Sheriff Summerhay was a man of habit. He greeted his prisoners each day with a surly "Good mornin'," then sat at his desk, lit his stogie, and settled down to read the newspaper.

Someone from the hotel delivered breakfast, and the coffee was consistently weak, the eggs watery, and the bacon tasted like leather. It didn't matter. Garrett had tasted worse; a lot worse. At least he wasn't required to fight off vermin like he did at Andersonville.

After breakfast the sheriff walked over to the cell as usual and ordered Garrett to sit on the cot with his hands in front of him. The trial didn't begin till nine, but the sheriff always walked him to court early, before the town awoke. An empty street made it easier to secure his prisoner.

The sheriff snapped a pair of handcuffs on Garrett's wrists.

Garrett stared at the manacles, and his mind traveled back in time. All those months he'd been held captive in Andersonville, never once had he given up hope. Not even on the darkest of nights or grimmest of days. The determination to survive had burned in his chest like a torch.

Today, it burned like acid.

Somehow he had to prove his innocence. For Toby's sake; for Elise's. His children had lost their mother, and that had been tough enough. But to lose their father, too? *God, don't let that happen.*

Maggie believed him, and that helped more than words could say. Yes, she'd lied to him. Yes, she'd forced herself into his house under false pretenses and had taken advantage of his trust.

Logically he understood it was her job, but the less rational part of him could never forgive the lies and deception. Still, she had made him the happiest man alive—at least for a short while.

After Katherine died, he never thought he'd smile again, let alone love. Losing a loved one was the worst possible torture. He had never wanted to be that vulnerable again; to feel that much grief. That's why a mail-order bride had sounded like the perfect solution. The idea of picking out a wife based on certain requirements appealed to him.

All he'd wanted was someone to care for his children. That's all. Until meeting Maggie in person, he was willing to consider suggesting a marriage in name only, if that's what the lady wanted. But one look into those big blue eyes of hers and he was hooked.

Not only did she steal her way into his home but also his heart. And there wasn't a blasted thing he could do about it.

He shook his head in disgust. In the name of Sam Hill, what was he doing? Dwelling on his feelings for Maggie was of no help. His testimony. That's what he needed to think about. Somehow he had to convince the jury he really was an innocent man.

God, what a mess! What must be going through Elise's and Toby's heads? He trusted Aunt Hetty to be tactful, but children always knew more than adults gave them credit for.

How could this have happened? Was Katherine involved in the train robbery? Katherine, the mother of his children? It wasn't hard to imagine her brother was involved, but not Katherine. True, she was anxious to leave the Territory; it was the one area they disagreed on, the one flaw in their marriage. But that didn't mean she was guilty of anything other than wanting a better education for her children.

And perhaps even a misguided attempt to help her brother.

The sheriff nudged him, pulling him out of his reverie. "Time to get a move on. Don't want to be late."

∞

Outside, the sun was just rising over the distant mountains, and it took a full moment on the porch for Garrett's eyes to adjust to the light. It was a two-block walk to the courthouse, but today something was different. Instead of the usual deserted street, a dozen or more people were gathered outside the sheriff's office.

He recognized most all of them. Even Wayne Peterson had turned up for his walk of shame. No doubt Peterson was enjoying the sight of him in handcuffs. Just like the rest of them—including those he thought were his friends.

Some, like Peter Fann, had purchased tinware from him. Others had been at church the day he attended with Maggie. A few were at the dance, and one he hadn't seen since Katherine's funeral.

His mind skipped backward to the day he was led to Andersonville as a prisoner of war. The jeering crowd called the prisoners vile names and flung mud and worse at them.

He shook the memory away, but the bitterness remained. "Come to see a condemned man, did they?" he muttered.

The sheriff gave him a look of disgust. "You should be thanking these people."

"Thanking them? For what? Making a spectacle out of me?"

"For trying to save your life."

Garrett frowned. "What are you talking about?"

"These are all members of the church. They stood guard all night to make sure that no one tied a bow around your sorry neck before it's time."

Garrett was stunned. "They. . .they did that?" Even Peterson? He couldn't believe it. All these years he had harbored ill feelings toward the church for its neglect of Andersonville prisoners. And now this?

"You were the enemy," Maggie had said when he tried to explain his aversion to the church.

But he was the enemy here, too. What else would you call a suspected killer and thief? Yet, here they were: the very church people he had accused of lacking Christian values based on experiences of that awful war. Here they were protecting him and probably even praying for him.

Never had he felt more. . .what? Grateful? Humbled? Overwhelmed? He was all those things and so much more.

Moisture filled his eyes. He'd failed as a husband, a Christian, a friend, and even a soldier. Yet with all his shortcomings and flaws, he'd expected perfection from the church. Perfection from others. . .

Odd as it seemed, it felt like someone reached inside him and pulled out all the anger, bitterness, and rage that had resided there for far too long.

He raised his face to the clear blue sky. It had been a long time since he'd felt God's love, but he felt it now, and it burned brighter than the sun.

The sheriff held him by the arm as they walked down the steps. The church people moved back to give them room.

No one said a word as he walked by, and only a few acknowledged his nod of thanks with nods of their own. Peterson showed no response, but it didn't matter. His being there was enough.

Instead of turning away from him as he had turned away from his church, all had put his safety and well-being above any personal feelings. That was more than he deserved, and by God, he intended to make it up to them.

❧

Aunt Hetty lowered her needlework and gazed up at Maggie. "Why all these questions about Charlie Cotton?" She narrowed her eyes. "I thought you didn't want to work on Garrett's case."

"I'm just tying up loose ends." Maggie didn't want to raise Aunt

Hetty's hopes. "We have reason to believe that Cotton knew about the satchel of money." She kept her voice low. It was just the two of them in Aunt Hetty's cramped parlor, but the children were only a short distance away in the kitchen.

Aunt Hetty's eyes widened. "You think *he* put the money in the tree house?"

"Not Cotton. Katherine."

This time Aunt Hetty dropped her needlework altogether. "Are you saying *she* stole the money?"

"No, but I think her brother asked her to keep the satchel for him. She may not have known what was in it at first. When she found out, she hid it."

The lines in Aunt Hetty's face deepened. "But why hide it in the tree house?"

"I don't know. Maybe she didn't want Garrett to find it. Or maybe she was afraid that her brother would search the house."

Aunt Hetty gave her a knowing look. "You really care for him, don't you?"

"What?"

"For Garrett. You care for him."

Maggie opened her mouth in denial but knew it would be no use. The harder she fought her feelings for Garrett, the more they persisted.

"Is it that obvious?"

"I'd have to be blind to miss the way you look at him." After a moment she added, "He cares for you, too. You know that, don't you?"

Maggie shook her head. "He'll never forgive me for deceiving him."

Aunt Hetty scoffed. "You'd be amazed what people can forgive if they put their minds to it. I even forgive that no-good, two-timing husband of mine," she said, sounding anything but forgiving. Belatedly, she added, "May his soul rest in peace."

Maggie bit her lower lip. There it was again, that old bugaboo: forgiveness. *Okay, God, I get it. I get what You're trying to teach me. If only it wasn't so hard.*

Aunt Hetty's shoulders drooped, and she suddenly looked her age. "Garrett's a good man. I don't mean any disrespect to my poor dead sister, but I always thought of him as my son. I never was able to have children of my own. I don't know what I'd do if—"

Maggie reached for Aunt Hetty's hand. "We have to think positive and pray that the truth will come out."

The sound of Elise's voice drew her attention to the kitchen. "I need to talk to the children. It's important. They might know something that will help their father." The chances were slim, but she didn't know where else to turn.

"I hope you're right." Aunt Hetty set her needlework on the table. Placing her hand on her back, she rose slowly from her seat and reached for her cane.

⁂

Elise looked up as they entered the kitchen, and a smile dimpled her cheeks.

"Miss Taylor!" she squealed. She ran over to Maggie and wrapped her arms around her. "Where's Papa?"

"He can't come right now." For the children's sakes she hid her inner torment behind a bright smile

"That's 'cause he's in jail," Toby said without bothering to look up from the contraption he was building.

Aunt Hetty stopped fussing with the kettle on the stove. "He never heard it from me."

Elise looked up with a worried frown. "How come he's in jail?"

Maggie didn't want to overstep her boundaries, but neither did she want to ignore the question. "Some people think that he put that money in your tree house. Maybe you can help me prove they're wrong."

Whitewash must have heard her voice because he started to bark and scratch at the door.

After Elise let him in, Maggie stooped to pet him.

Whitewash greeted her with wagging tail and happy barks. Maggie couldn't help but smile. Crazy as it seemed, she had even grown fond of the fluffy white dog.

"I hope he didn't dig up your yard," she said.

"No, he's been a perfect gentleman," Aunt Hetty said, distracting the dog with a bone.

Maggie led Elise back to the table. Toby was doing something with a pair of wagon springs. Hoping the wagon he'd raided wasn't Aunt Hetty's, she pulled out a chair and sat.

"Whitewash likes it here 'cause there's no boogeyman," Elise whispered.

"Oh, so that's the reason he's been so good," Maggie whispered back.

"Uh-huh."

Anxious to get to the point of her visit, Maggie addressed both children. "All right, now I need you to put on your thinking caps."

Toby stopped what he was doing and reached for his metal helmet. Elise's mouth turned downward. "I don't have a thinking cap."

"Oh dear." Maggie glanced around the kitchen. Spotting a saucepan that looked about the right size, she reached for it. She recognized it at once as Garrett's work, and the pan slipped from her hand. The clamor startled Whitewash, who ran under the table with his bone.

She bent over to retrieve it and quickly placed it upside down on Elise's head. "There. How's that?"

Elise rewarded her with a wide smile.

"All right, now I need you to think carefully." She paused until she had their attention. She planned to ask them if they had seen their uncle recently, and if so, where? But something Elise said stuck in her brain.

"Why do you suppose there's no boogeyman here?" she asked. Didn't children usually take their imaginary friends, foes, and the like with them?

"He doesn't want Aunt Hetty to see him," Elise said. "He doesn't want anyone to see him. That's why he only comes out at night."

Maggie glanced under the table at Whitewash, and something clicked in the back of her mind. No holes. No boogeyman. Could there be a connection? Startled by the thought, she covered her mouth with her hand. What if the boogeyman was real?

"Tell me about him." She rested her hand on her lap and forced herself to breathe. "What does he look like?"

Elise wrinkled her nose. "He looks like a giant and has big feet."

"How do you know he has big feet?" Maggie asked.

"All boogeymen have big feet," Elise assured her.

"Oh, I see."

"And he wears his hair like Aunt Hetty," Toby added.

Maggie puzzled over this. "You mean he wears his hair in a bun like this?" Maggie turned her head so they could see the back of her head.

Elise shook her head. "He wears it like that." She pointed to Aunt Hetty's topknot.

It was hard to know with Elise where reality ended and fantasy took hold. Toby was more realistic—sometimes alarmingly so.

"Can you think of anything to add, Toby?"

"Nope." He was more interested in the wagon springs than in discussing hairstyles.

"What about you, Elise? Anything else you can tell me about the boogeyman?"

Elise shook her head, and the saucepan fell to the floor. She jumped off her chair to retrieve it and placed it back on her head.

Maggie turned the pan so that the handle stuck out in back. Thinking the boogeyman was anything more than the children's imagination was crazy, but the thought persisted.

She directed her next question to Aunt Hetty. "You said you hadn't noticed any holes in the backyard, is that right?"

"Not a one. Why?"

"Just asking."

She always wondered how such a little dog could do so much damage. Now another thought occurred to her: What if Whitewash hadn't dug those holes? What if it was Cotton or his partner looking for the long-lost money? Was that the mysterious boogeyman the children talked about?

Aunt Hetty set a cup and saucer in front of her. "I don't know about you, but all this talk about a boogeyman is making me hungry. How about some tea and cookies?"

She needed to be alone with her thoughts, but rushing off would be rude, and she didn't want to hurt Aunt Hetty's feelings. "Thank you," she said.

She picked up the steaming china cup, but her hand was shaking so much she could hardly hold it steady. Had she inadvertently stumbled upon a clue? Or was she simply grasping at straws?

Chapter 36

No sooner did Maggie leave Aunt Hetty's than she raced to the jailhouse.

Already the gallows were being erected in the empty field behind Main Street. Each pound of the hammer felt like someone was driving a nail into Maggie's heart. What was wrong with these people? Couldn't they have waited until the verdict was read?

The sheriff greeted her with his usual "No visitors."

"I'll only be a moment." She flashed her Pinkerton badge as she walked by his desk. She no longer had time to play his games.

Garrett sat on his cot writing in his notebook. He looked up as she neared his cell and look surprised to see her. "The children—"

"They're fine," she said.

"I was just writing them a letter."

She nodded. "They'll like that." She wished now she'd thought to have the children write to him.

He set the notebook on the cot by his side. "Anything?"

"I don't know. Maybe."

He rose to his feet and grabbed the bars. "That sounds encouraging."

She stepped closer. Casting a look at the sheriff still at his desk glowering, she lowered her voice. "How long have you had your dog?"

He raised his eyebrows. "Whitewash? A couple of years. Why?"

"Was he always a digger?"

"Not so much as a puppy." He rubbed the back of his neck. "Is that important?"

"I don't know much about dogs, but for such a little fellow, he sure does a lot of digging."

He frowned. "So what are you saying? And what does Whitewash have to do with my trial?"

"I don't think he's responsible for all those holes at the back of your house."

"You think it's another animal doing the digging?"

"That's exactly what I'm thinking," she said. "An animal with two legs."

⁂

At long last Garrett was called to testify. It's what he'd been waiting for. Now he could tell his side of the story, and by George, the jury better listen. He took his place on the witness stand, and his eyes immediately sought Maggie's.

Sitting forward in her seat as if to jump to his defense at the slightest provocation, she gave him an encouraging smile. He hated that even now—even after knowing how she'd lied—he still had feelings for her. It didn't seem possible, but it was true.

He pulled his gaze away, but only so he could concentrate on his testimony. His lawyer said it wasn't enough to speak the truth; he also had to sound convincing.

He answered his lawyer Mr. King's questions with a firm, clear voice. He looked at the jury as his lawyer had instructed, but he couldn't keep from glancing at Maggie, who sat so still he wondered if she were even breathing.

"Your witness," Mr. King said, taking his seat.

Mr. Fassbender rose and sauntered over to him. He had the same dogged expression as a certain hateful guard he remembered from Andersonville, and it was all Garrett could do to hide his dislike.

"Mr. Thomas, You testified that you hadn't been in the tree house since your wife died."

"That's correct."

"We heard testimony that you're a conscientious parent," Fass-bender continued.

"I try to be," Garrett replied, not sure where the prosecutor was heading.

"Yet, you never bothered to check your children's tree house. Is that true?"

"Objection," Mr. King said.

"Overruled." The judge turned to Garrett. "You may answer the question."

The implication that he had somehow neglected his children galled him, but he swallowed his anger. "I'm not sure what you mean by *checking* the tree house."

"Most conscientious parents would keep an eye on what their children were doing and make sure their play area was safe."

"It *was* safe," Garrett said. "We made sure of that."

"Yet, you expect us to believe you never set foot in the place for two years. Not even after knowing what your son was capable of?"

"My son?"

"It's well known that your son can't be trusted. Not that long ago, he set his aunt's chicken coop on fire—"

Paternal rage exploded inside Garrett, but before he could respond King had already jumped to his feet. "Objection. Relevance."

Fassbender spun around to face the judge. "Your honor, Mr. Thomas testified that he had no reason to check the children's tree house for safety purposes. I'm simply attempting to understand the logic behind Mr. Thomas's statement. His son set a coop on fire, and yet his father would have us believe that he trusted his son not to do damage to the barn."

The judge banged his gavel. "Overruled."

Fassbender turned back to the witness stand, a smug look on his face. The man had no right to drag his son's name through the mud. No right at all.

"So, Mr. Thomas, would you please explain to the court why you never bothered checking your children's play area?"

Garrett inhaled. "It was my wife's project, and going up there was too painful." He hated having to admit such a thing, especially in open court, but it was the truth.

"We've heard testimony that you are a man of honor." The change of subject surprised Garrett, but his relief was short lived. "Yet you allowed Miss Cartwright to live under your roof without benefit of marriage. Do you think it would be safe to say that you're not quite as honorable as you'd like us to believe?"

"Objection," King said.

"I'll withdraw the question," Fassbender said, but by then the damage had been done. The implication was that a man who had so little regard for a woman's reputation or his own children's safety wouldn't think twice about shooting a man and robbing a safe.

After Fassbender finished his questions, King did his best to repair the damage and restore Garrett's credibility, but it was too late.

The judge banged his gavel. "Court is recessed for the day. Closing arguments will begin tomorrow at nine."

✦

The day following closing arguments, Maggie waited in the lobby of the hotel for Rikker. He'd told her to meet him there, but already he was twenty minutes late. What was taking him so long? The verdict could come in at any minute. They had no time to lose.

Finally he walked through the door and greeted her with a questioning look. "Where is he?"

She slanted her head toward the hotel restaurant where Cotton had been sitting for the last hour. "Let's get to work."

Cotton was at his usual corner table reading a day-old newspaper. He looked up as they approached, coffee cup in hand. "Case you haven't noticed, this table is taken."

"We noticed." Rikker pulled out a chair and sat. Maggie remained standing.

Cotton set his cup down and folded his newspaper. "What do you want?"

"We just want to ask a few friendly questions," Maggie said.

"And maybe a couple not so friendly," Rikker added.

Cotton looked from one to the other. "I don't have to answer your questions, friendly or otherwise."

Rikker drove a fist into the palm of his hand. "If you know what's good for you, you'll not only answer them but sing like a canary."

Cotton's mouth twisted into an ugly smile. "Sorry, the only time this bird sings is for his supper."

Maggie slapped her hands flat on the table and leaned forward. "What were you doing at the jailhouse the other night?"

"How'd you—" He broke off and glanced at Rikker. "What makes you think I was there?" He drew a handkerchief out of his pocket and dabbed his forehead.

Maggie folded her arms across her chest. Well, what do you know? Cotton was sweating bullets. "So you *were* there."

"I never said that."

She glared at him. "And why did you offer to pay Linc to lie on the stand?"

"If the boy told you that, he's a blasted liar."

Elbows on the table, Rikker steepled his hand. "Why are you so anxious to get rid of your former brother-in-law?"

"Like I told her." He tossed a nod Maggie's way. "I blame him for my sister's death."

Maggie looked him straight in the eye. "I think there's another reason. What do you think, partner?"

Rikker shrugged. "I think you're right."

"And what reason is th–that?" Cotton stammered.

"I think you're hoping that once Garrett is out of the picture, you'll find the rest of the money," she said.

Cotton stiffened, and his gaze went back and forth between the two of them. "What money? Whatcha talking about?"

"Oh dear." Maggie drew back and patted the bun at the nape of her head. "I misspoke."

"Don't feel bad," Rikker said. "He'd have found out sooner or later."

Cotton frowned. "Found out what?"

"That only half of the stolen money was recovered," Rikker said.

It was a lie, of course, but one Maggie hoped Cotton would fall for. It had been more than two years since the robbery. Maybe he was desperate enough to believe anything.

Rikker continued. "That means thirty-five thousand dollars is still at large, and we have no idea where it is."

"Do you?" Maggie asked. "Do you know where the money is?"

"I don't know anything about no money," Cotton said, and he sure in blazes didn't look happy about it.

"Just thought we'd ask." Rikker pushed to his feet. "Meanwhile, stay away from the jail."

"And stay away from Linc," Maggie added.

Rikker hammered his palm once again before pivoting.

Maggie and Rikker walked out of the restaurant together. She waited until they had left the hotel before speaking. "Do you think we overplayed our hand?"

"Absolutely."

She gave him a playful punch on the arm. "You always know how to make a girl feel good."

"I aim to please."

"So what's next?" she asked.

"I'll keep my eye on Cotton. If he fell for our ploy, he's got to be thinking about that missing money and where it might be. With a little luck, he'll lead me to his partner in crime. Meanwhile, go to the stables and get yourself a fast horse. I'll meet you at Thomas's house. Unless I miss my guess, that's where Cotton will head."

Maggie felt a surge of hope. *Dear God, please help us to make this work.*

Still, she knew the odds were against them. So much depended on a plan that was a long shot at best. What if they were wrong about Cotton? What if his only interest in Garrett really was revenge for the death of his sister?

"If he shows up at the house," she said, thinking out loud, "that doesn't prove a thing. He'll deny he's looking for the money. We need more. A confession."

Rikker chuckled. "As you know, I've coaxed more confessions out of sinners than a Catholic priest. So quit your worrying and get ready. It could be a very long and interesting day."

Chapter 37

Garrett sat on his cot and prayed long and hard. Things looked bad, real bad. But he refused to give in to despair. Maggie said that hope was the anchor God sent down whenever it was needed. If he ever needed something to hold on to, it was now.

This was worse even than Andersonville. At least then he didn't have two children to worry about. What would become of them? *God, if You can't save me, at least answer my prayers to save them.*

He was so deep in his thoughts it took a moment before a familiar voice penetrated his brain. Not sure that he'd heard right, he looked up.

The last person Garrett expected to walk into the sheriff's office was his former brother-in-law—not after the last angry words they'd exchanged. Maybe he came to apologize. Or simply to wish him well.

The thought left the instant Cotton pulled out a gun and pointed it straight at the sheriff.

"Put your hands up."

Summerhay looked startled but did what he was told.

Stunned, Garrett couldn't believe what he saw. "What are you doing with that gun?"

"Shut up," Cotton hissed.

"But—"

"I said shut up!" Cotton stared at the sheriff. "Put your weapon on the desk," he ordered. "Nice and easy."

Sheriff Summerhay pulled his gun out of the holster and laid it down.

"Unlock that empty cell. Now!"

The sheriff rose from his chair and reached for the key ring on the hook. He hesitated, and Cotton jammed his gun into the lawman's back. "I said unlock it."

Summerhay fiddled with the keys before inserting one into the key-hole.

Cotton took the keys out of his hand. "Step inside, and take it nice and easy." He waited for the sheriff to enter the cell and then slammed the steel door shut with a bang.

Garrett's initial disbelief had faded into uneasiness. Was Cotton trying to help him escape? Was that it? It was hard to believe that his brother-in-law would do anything to help him. They had once been friends, but that was a long time ago.

Cotton's talent for wheeling and dealing had come in handy when the two of them were locked in the stockades. Once, Cotton had even tricked a guard into giving them matches one wintry night for a fire.

Prisoners did everything they could to stay alive. They lied, they cheated, and they stole. Garrett did, too, but he hated it. He hated stealing clothes off dead men just to keep warm. He despised having to hide the bodies of men who died in the night just to claim the extra rations. But while he was often wracked with guilt and disgust, he never stopped asking for God's forgiveness. Far as he knew, Cotton felt no such compulsion.

"You do what you have to do," he'd said. That was his motto, even after the war.

Garrett had given him a job in the shop, but he'd lasted for only a few weeks. During that short time, he stole money from the till, was surly with the customers, and took shortcuts that undermined the quality of the tinware.

He wasn't taking any shortcuts now. He made certain the sheriff was confined in one of the other cells before unlocking Garrett's.

Garrett's mind scrambled. This wasn't the first time Cotton had helped him escape. The last time ended in the Georgia woods after they were chased down by hounds. Garrett had no reason to believe that this time would end any differently. Except perhaps to make him feel like a coward, and that's not how he wanted his children to remember him.

"Don't do this, Charlie."

Cotton lifted the barrel of his gun till it pointed straight at Garrett's head. "Shut your trap."

He looked unbalanced. His eyes were too bright, almost wild looking, and his mouth twisted in an ugly line. Garrett stiffened as a terrifying thought came to the fore. His brother-in-law wasn't there in some misguided way to help him. He was out for one thing and one thing alone—blood.

∞

It took Maggie forever to rent a horse from the stables. No horses were available at first. Finally a gelding was returned, but the animal had thrown a shoe. While the farrier replaced it, Maggie practically paced a hole in the floor.

After leaving the stables, she urged the horse along the dirt road at a fast gallop to Thomas's house. Rikker had told her to meet him in front of the hotel, but he never showed. Nor was he in his room.

If Cotton left town, Rikker would follow him. Maybe she would find them both at Garrett's house.

Her gun was holstered around her waist for easy retrieval. Everyone in town now knew who she was; no need to hide her weapon.

The sun looked like a big orange ball, and a gentle breeze cooled her brow. A sudden unexpected bout of emotion assailed her. This was the same road she'd traveled to take the children back and forth to school. The same road they'd traveled to church. The same road she and Garrett had taken to the barn dance.

The stars had looked particularly bright that night and Garrett especially handsome. And, oh, how he could dance. She could almost feel his hand at her waist and his breath in her hair.

She shook her head and brushed away a tear. *Oh no, you don't. You're not going there.*

Today could mean the difference between life and death for Garrett. It was no time to be distracted by painful memories or even painful regrets. She had a job to do.

She occupied her mind by going over the plan. If Cotton was already at the house, adjustments had to be made. If not, she was to hide her horse behind the barn. Her thoughts were interrupted by a movement ahead.

With a quick tug on the reins, she brought the horse to a halt. She rose from the saddle and craned her neck for a better look.

Dear God, no. Please don't let that be Patches. Unless her eyes were deceiving her, that meant that Toby—

"Gid-up." With a flick of its neck, the gelding took off running, stretching his stride as she urged him on. Reaching the house, she slipped out of the saddle.

It was Patches all right, and the horse looked happy to see her. He swung his tail and nickered as she approached. He nudged her hand with his velvety nose looking for treats.

"Where's Toby, boy?" And what was he doing here? No matter. She had to get him to leave, and there was no time to lose.

Fortunately, there was no sign of Cotton, but that didn't necessarily mean he wasn't there.

She tied the rented horse to the hitching post next to Patches and ran to the porch. The front door was locked. She raised her hand to knock but thought better of it. Never had she known Toby to close the door when entering or leaving the house. She doubted he would start now.

She pulled out her gun. Back pressed against the adobe, she ever so carefully peered through the front window. The house looked empty, but only the parlor and part of the kitchen were visible. She then noticed the scattered chessmen on the floor. The books pulled from the bookshelves. The chair cushions in disarray. Someone had searched the house.

Keeping her head low, she jumped from the porch and ran to the side of the house. She peered into the children's bedroom. The drawers hung open and the mattresses had been pulled off the beds.

The shades were drawn in Garrett's room. That didn't necessarily mean anything, but it worried her.

She quietly tested the back door, but it was locked, too. Maybe Toby was in the barn or even the tree house. She measured the distance from the house. The barn couldn't be reached without being seen from the house, but she had to take the chance.

Now, as always, she considered her options. Should she run in a random zigzag or straight line? The zigzag offered less chance of being shot or seriously shot, but running a straight line was faster. She glanced at the bedroom window. The shades were still drawn. Decision made, she ran a straight line to the barn.

Back against the barn wall, she held her gun in front and swung forward into the open doorway. A local farmer had taken the livestock and chickens to his place, so the two horses in the barn spelled trouble.

One was Cotton's. She didn't recognize the other, but maybe it belonged to his partner.

She hoped Cotton's presence meant Rikker was somewhere nearby, lurking in the shadows. She hoped; she prayed—*Dear God, let it be true.* She strained her ears. Cotton's horse snorted, but it was hard to hear much else over the thud-thud-thudding of her pounding heart. If anything should happen to Toby. . .

And blast it, Rikker! Where are you? If he was on-site, he had to know that she was, too. Rikker was an expert in bird calls. So why hadn't he signaled her?

She strained her ears. Cotton's horse neighed softly, but now there was another sound as well. A soft scraping sound coming from—

She looked up. Someone was in the tree house. Cotton?

Since the loft had been boarded up, the only way to reach it was from outside.

Gun in hand, she peered out the door. Seeing no one, she slipped outside and raced to the ladder at the side of the barn. She glanced around. Still no sign of Rikker, or anyone else, for that matter.

The hay lift had stopped at the top. She stood at the bottom of the ladder and looked up. It could be a trap.

Dreading what she might or might not find in the children's playhouse, she holstered her weapon and grabbed hold of the ladder. Gulping, she lifted her foot onto the bottom rung and started upward.

Chapter 38

The climb up to the hayloft seemed to take forever, though in reality it took only seconds. She paused on the ladder before reaching the top. The air was still and the quiet, almost eerie.

Then she heard it again: a soft scraping sound. The hayloft opening was only about eight inches over her head. At that moment it appeared to be a monstrous mouth waiting to devour her.

She'd burst into her share of outlaw hideouts and other dangerous places through the years, but never on a ladder. She didn't even like heights.

Biting her lower lip, she forced herself to concentrate. Hesitation could be deadly. A detective's best tool was the element of surprise. Holding on to the ladder with one hand, she pulled out her gun.

It was bright outside, and normally she would close her eyes for a full five minutes before entering a darker area. That's how long it took eyes to fully adjust, but today she couldn't afford such luxury. She needed to stay alert to her surroundings.

She closed her eyes for only a few seconds. Okay now, one, two, three...

She pushed up to the last rung in one swift movement and leaned into the window, gun first.

Toby looked up from his "room," his eyes wide with surprise. "Hello, Miss Taylor." He still called her by her assumed name.

Relief flooded through her. Toby was safe and Cotton nowhere in sight. She holstered her gun and climbed through the window. In her haste, she tripped over a bale of hay.

Picking herself up, she brushed off her skirt. "What are you doing here?"

"I came to check on the house and work on my mechanical horse."

"How long have you been here?" Toby's inventions would be the death of him yet.

He shrugged. "Not very long."

"Did you see anyone else?"

"Nope. But someone messed up my things." He indicated the scattered tools on the floor.

"Okay, listen to me, Toby. This is important." She waited until she had the boy's full attention. "Your uncle Charlie is not a very nice man. I'm afraid he might hurt us if we're not careful, so I need you to do exactly what I tell you to do. Understand?"

His eyes widened as she spoke, and he nodded.

"I want you to stay here and not make a sound. Under no circumstances are you to leave until I tell you it's safe to do so."

She moved to the window and gasped. Either her eyes were playing tricks on her or Garrett just stepped out of the house. Cotton was behind him. She couldn't be certain, but it looked like he was holding a gun.

"Pa!"

"Shh." She pulled Toby away from the window.

"You gotta do something," Toby whimpered, "or he'll hurt Pa." He sounded close to tears.

"Okay, now listen to me." She pulled her hands away from his shoulders. "If we're going to save your pa, we have to stay calm." She glimpsed outside again before ducking away from the window.

Confound it, where was Rikker? *Think.* If she could just get close enough to Cotton, perhaps she could disarm or distract him in some way. A dozen different options ran through her mind, but none of them seemed adequate for the task.

If only there was a way of reaching the first floor without using the ladder outside.

She knocked on the wood partition with her fist. It sounded as solid as it looked, but it might be possible to pull a panel away. She just needed a crowbar.

Toby's tool cache revealed a saw and hammer but no crowbar. She stepped on something: Toby's slingshot.

She rushed to the window again, careful not to expose herself. Cotton had a gun all right; no question. But what was Garrett doing with a shovel?

As if reading her mind, Toby said, "Uncle Charlie is making Pa dig a grave."

It was a chilling thought.

She considered the area below, estimating distances and possible covers. Sneaking up on Cotton wouldn't be easy, but neither would it be impossible.

She reached for the slingshot on the floor and shoved it into Toby's hands.

"Don't let your uncle come up that ladder. Do you understand what I'm saying? If he tries, use your slingshot."

Dear God, she was asking a boy to bring down a giant with a slingshot. Not that it hadn't been done before, but still...

Toby stared down at the slingshot in his hands.

She squeezed his shoulder. "I'm counting on you, pumpkin."

If Rikker knew what she was planning, he would have a fit. He never liked a plan with less than a fifty percent chance of success. She preferred closer to seventy-five. She gave this one a ten.

The hardest part would be climbing down the ladder. Even if she reached the ground safely, she would be exposed for a good fifteen or twenty feet before reaching the privy.

Five. She gave her plan a five.

She upgraded her plan to an eight upon reaching the ground unseen. Cotton's back was still turned and Garrett was still digging. Cotton shouted something, but she couldn't hear what he said.

On the count of three, she raced a straight line and dived behind the privy. Peering around the stone facade, she took several deep breaths to calm her nerves. So far, so good.

Had Garrett spotted her? It was hard to know. He was half turned away from her, so it was possible. She glanced back at the barn window. Fortunately the sun slanted off the roof, making it difficult to see the loft window clearly. If she couldn't see Toby, then neither could Cotton.

Was that a bird call? She strained her ears but couldn't be sure. If it was Rikker, where was he? Behind the barn? The house? Where?

She pulled out her gun but decided to give Rikker another minute or two to make his move.

Garrett said something, and Cotton inched closer. Garrett swung his shovel, hitting Cotton on the chest. Cotton's gun flew out of his hands and landed in the newly dug hole.

Surprised by the sudden turn of events, Maggie left her hiding place and ran toward the battling men.

❧

Garrett swung the shovel again, but this time Cotton was ready. He dodged, and the spade hit the ground. Before Garrett could recover, Cotton barreled into him headfirst, and the two fell.

"Stop!" she yelled, gun aimed.

Cotton glanced up, his mouth twisted, and she advanced forward. He rolled away from Garrett, jumped to his feet, and ran. She fired and missed.

Hoping Rikker would take care of Cotton, she advanced toward Garrett, dropping by his side, knees first. "Are you all right?"

He squinted at her. "What are you doing here?"

She grinned. "Looks like I'm the one saving you this time. Can you get up?"

"I think so." He was winded but not seriously injured. Hand on his jaw, he groaned then struggled to sit upright.

"Take it easy." She holstered her gun and pulled a clean handkerchief from her sleeve. "How did you get out of jail?" she asked, dabbing his forehead.

"Cotton. He has some crazy idea that I know where some money is hidden."

A surge of guilt rushed through her. The plan she and Rikker had cooked up put Garrett's and Toby's lives in danger. She had underestimated Cotton, but she wouldn't make that mistake again.

"Thank God you're all right. Can you stand?"

"Hold it right there." It was Cotton again, and this time he had a shotgun. "Drop your gun."

When she didn't move, he repeated the order, this time louder. "I said drop it!"

She laid her weapon on the ground. "You're not going to get away with this, Cotton." She spoke louder than necessary for her partner's benefit. If Rikker was anywhere in the vicinity, now was the time for him to show his face.

"I've done all right so far," Cotton said. "Just tell me where the money is, and we can all get along."

"There isn't any money. We found all of it."

"You said—" His eyes glittered. "You tricked me." He leveled his gun. "I don't like to be tricked."

She had to keep him talking. "It's over, Cotton. We know you and your partner robbed the train."

"My partner?" He narrowed his eyes.

"Yes, the one Detective Greenwood is interviewing as we speak."

His smirk turned into an ugly grin. "Greenwood's dead."

Air rushed from her lungs. Rikker's dead? *God, no. Please don't let it be true.* But it would certainly explain Rikker's absence. Only from years of training and experience was she able to put her emotions aside and focus. Garrett's and Toby's lives—and her own—depended on keeping her wits and thinking clearly.

"You killed him," she said, her steady voice belying the devastation she felt. "Just like you killed your sister."

She felt Garrett stiffen by her side, but it was Cotton who commanded her attention.

Surprise crossed his face. "You think I killed my sister? Why would I do a thing like that?"

"Maybe because she'd hidden the money from you."

He shook his head. "I didn't know that until after her accident. The town was swarming with US marshals, and I didn't want to keep the money at the boardinghouse. I told my sister someone kept going through my room. She agreed to let me store my things at her house until I made other arrangements."

"Other arrangements meaning to leave town," she said.

"Yeah, but I thought it would look suspicious if I left right away."

"What was Katherine doing outside that night?" Garrett demanded, his face marked with loathing.

"How am I supposed to know? All I knew was that she was dead and the money was gone. I thought—"

"What did you think?" Maggie asked. He didn't answer; he didn't have to. "You thought Garrett had killed her and hidden the money."

"It doesn't matter what I thought."

"It matters to me!" Garrett snapped, his voice as hard as his face.

She could feel his tension build, and she didn't want him doing anything foolish. "No one killed Katherine," she said, gently. "It was an accident."

Garrett's head spun toward her. "How do you know that?"

"Yes, how *do* you know that?" Cotton repeated.

"You're the only one who knew she had the money. So unless you came back that night—"

"I didn't."

Somehow Maggie believed him. "I think Katherine discovered what was in the satchel and didn't want it in the house with the children. Or maybe she was afraid you'd come back for it before she had a chance to turn it over to the sheriff."

"She wouldn't do that. I was family. She loved me." His face turned red, and his eyes took on a strange, wild look.

With her peripheral vision, Maggie checked the position of the gun at her feet. She would have preferred Cotton's Colt, but that was at the bottom of the hole. Her derringer would have to do. If only she could find a way to distract him.

"Enough talk," Cotton said. He held the shotgun straight out with his finger on the trigger.

Something whizzed by Maggie's head and hit Cotton square on the chest—a rock. He jerked back and his arm shot upward, followed by a blast.

Maggie dived for the gun, but Garrett's hand got there first. Before either of them could pick it up, they were staring down the muzzle of Cotton's shotgun.

Chapter 39

The rope cut into Maggie's wrists and ankles. Seated on a chair back-to-back with Garrett, she glanced around the parlor looking for something—anything—that could be used to escape.

Wiggling her body in an effort to loosen the cords brought an immediate protest from Garrett.

"Ow! That hurts," he grated over his shoulder. "Can't you keep still? It's like being tied to a bronco. What are you doing?"

Maggie clenched her teeth. "I'm exercising my God-given right to escape."

"You think you're going to break through these ropes?" Garrett asked.

"Did last time."

"Last . . . ? How many times have you been tied up?"

"This is only my third time," she admitted.

"Third!"

"I know it seems like a lot."

"Drat, Maggie! For the average person, once would be a lot."

Cotton made her tie up Garrett first, and that was a blessing. It allowed her to plant her metal Pinkerton badge between her palms before Cotton got around to her. It was just a matter of twisting her hands until she was able to cut through the rope with the badge's sharp edge. Unfortunately, Cotton had tied her in such a way that this was easier said than done.

"Escaping isn't usually so hard." She spoke through gritted teeth.

Talking helped her stay focused. "Providing you remember to expand your muscles while being tied up. It also helps if the rope is old. Even Samson said he would be weakened by a new rope."

"Samson?"

"Yeah, you know, the hairy man in the Bible." In an effort to work her badge in position, she twisted her wrists until tears sprang into her eyes.

"Yeah, well, ole hairy didn't have to contend with a former Andersonville prisoner."

Holding the badge between two fingers she sawed back and forth. She could hardly move her hands, so she didn't expect to see much progress. At least not for a while.

"What does that have to do with anything?"

"We learned a trick or two from our rebel guards about tying people up."

"Rikker was the real expert. I just wish he was here." Just thinking of her partner filled her with such pain she could hardly breathe. "He always knew how to escape."

She felt Garrett jerk and heard his intake of breath. "Maggie, I'm sorry about Greenwood."

She blinked away the tears, and anger ripped through her. This was supposed to be a simple, routine job. Now she'd lost the best partner and friend she'd ever had and ever hoped to have.

She shook her head. Mustn't think about that. There would be time enough later to grieve. Right now she had to concentrate on the task at hand.

"Of all the women I could have chosen as a bride," Garrett said, as if talking to himself.

Her hand stilled. "How many women answered your ad?"

"I don't know. A few dozen."

She moistened her lips. "Why did you pick me?"

"I liked your handwriting," he said, his voice hoarse.

For some reason his answer affected her deeply. The principal had dictated each carefully chosen word, but it was her own hand that caught Garrett's attention.

Gripping the shield until her fingers ached, she continued sawing. "How'd Cotton spring you from jail?"

"With a gun. He kept muttering something about money. I didn't know what he was talking about. But then he saw where the earth had been turned over and was convinced that I had buried it. Where do you suppose he got a cockamamie idea like that?"

She blew out her breath. "I'm afraid he got it from Rikker and me. We were trying to force his hand."

"You forced his hand all right."

"Why don't you just come out and say it? You blame me for everything that happened." She certainly blamed herself.

"I'm just as much to blame," he said quietly.

She stilled. "Why do you say that?"

"When things seem too good to be true, they usually are. And you—"

Her vision blurred with tears, but still she resumed sawing. She'd played her part well—too well. And they both fell into the trap she'd set. *Oh, God, where are You? Why do You feel so far away? Do You blame me, too?*

She paused to rest her sore fingers. "I never meant for any of this to happen," she whispered.

"Yeah, you did. You wanted to prove that I did the things they say. Prove me guilty."

"You're wrong." She tightened her grip on her shield. "From the moment I set eyes on you, I wanted to prove you innocent."

"Why?"

"Because. . ." There were so many reasons why, it was impossible to choose just one. Never had she met a man quite like him. Not only was he the kindest man she'd ever known, her body fairly tingled whenever he walked into the room, and he was the reason she smiled in her dreams.

"Because of the children," she said aloud. Admitting the real reason would only result in more rejection. Forcing herself to breathe beneath the confines of the rope, she suddenly remembered something. *Toby!*

Panicky now, she frantically sawed, but with little progress. At this rate it could take all night.

She felt something snap and, looking over her shoulder, saw Garrett rise out of his chair.

Her mouth fell open. "How'd you do that? How did you get free?"

"You'd be amazed what you can learn in prison if you put your mind to it." He lifted a stocking foot. "Fortunately, Cotton forgot to remove my shoes before he tied me up." Garrett wore the easy slip-off type, an advantage over her high-button boots, and had slipped his feet right out of his shoes and then the ropes.

"Speaking of shoes, would you mind reaching into my boot for my knife?"

He dropped on one knee in front of her and reached into the shaft of her boot. The heat of his fingers reached all the way down to her toes. Knife in hand, his eyes held hers for a moment before cutting her free.

"Now what?" he asked.

She rubbed her sore wrists, but before she could answer, she heard something. Someone was coming. Garrett heard it, too, and he held a finger to his mouth.

Ever so quietly she rose from the chair and grabbed the poker from the fireplace. Thus armed, she flung herself against the wall separating the parlor from the kitchen and held her breath.

Chapter 40

Toby burst out of the kitchen. "Pa!" He cleared the distance in an instant and threw himself in his father's arms.

More footsteps and a voice entered the room first. "You can put the weapon down, Duffy."

She dropped the poker. "Rikker?"

He stepped through the doorway and grinned. "The one and only."

Without thinking, she flung her arms around his grizzly neck.

"Whoa," Rikker said, looking embarrassed. She pulled away, blubbering like a kid whose candy had been stolen.

Rikker handed her a handkerchief. "Sorry to be late for the party," he said. "I would have gotten here sooner, but I was detained."

She wiped her tears away. "Cotton said you were dead."

He raised a bushy eyebrow. "You didn't fall for that old trick, did you?"

"Of course not," she said with a sniffle. She should have known. Telling a hostage a loved one was dead was one way to ensure compliance. "So where were you?"

"Visiting the stars," he said. "Someone hit me over the head, but fortunately your friend Linc found me. I'd have gotten here sooner, but I met Cotton coming the other way."

"You met Cotton?" Garrett asked.

"I did, and I gave him two choices. Either turn himself in like a gentleman or die like a coward. Unfortunately, the man had no sense of pride."

"This generation of criminals never does," she said.

According to Pinkerton files, no crime was more hazardous than holdup robberies; two-thirds of those engaging in such crimes died with their boots on. Too bad Cotton failed to beat the odds. Now they might never learn the name of his partner.

"Looks like he took a bit of you with him," she said. Rikker had a nasty-looking lump on his forehead.

He touched his wound and then wiped the blood off his fingertips with a handkerchief. "I owe this to a certain young man who decided to give David from the Bible a bit of competition."

Garrett stared over his son's head. "Toby did that?"

Toby pulled out of his father's arms. "I heard him coming up the ladder, and I thought he was Uncle Charlie."

"You did good, Toby," Maggie said. "Especially when you tried to save us from your uncle." The rock had barely missed Maggie's head, but it hit Cotton dead center on the chest.

Hand on his son's shoulder, Garrett stared down at him. "We have you to thank for that?"

Toby nodded, and Garrett broke into a grin. "Well, now. What do you know?" He hugged his son again.

"Do you have to go back to jail, Pa?"

"I don't know, son." He leveled a look straight at Maggie. "Do I?"

She glanced at Rikker. "I'm afraid that's up to the judge."

Toby pulled out of his father's arms and grinned at her. "Instead of going to the moon, I'm gonna be a detective just like you and Mr. Greenwood."

Maggie smiled and ruffled his hair. "That sounds like a good plan," she said. A hundred percent plan.

Chapter 41

The next day Maggie took care of a dozen details. A full report had to be sent to Pinkerton headquarters after which she and Rikker met with the sheriff.

Rikker did most of the talking. "I was shadowing Cotton when someone hit me over the head," he explained.

Sheriff Summerhay still wasn't happy about working with Pinkerton detectives, but there wasn't much he could do about it. "Do you know who?" he asked.

"Haven't the foggiest," Rikker said. "All I know for sure is that it wasn't Cotton."

"What I don't understand," Summerhay said as Maggie and Rikker rose to leave, "is why Cotton thought there was still money to be found."

Maggie shot Rikker her best "want to take this?" look.

Rikker slapped his hat onto his head. "Cotton wasn't playing with a full deck. You might even say he was fifty-nine seconds short of a minute."

He grabbed Maggie by the arm. "Let's go and let the sheriff continue his fine and noble work."

"Fine and noble?" she said as they stepped away from the building.

"Would you rather I said what I was really thinking?" He gave her a sideways glance and rolled his eyes upward. "Oh no, don't tell me."

She wrapped her arm around his. "I have a theory."

He sighed. "Of course you do."

"Hear me out."

"Do I have a choice?"

"Let's suppose that Aunt Hetty's friend, Mr. Dinwiddie, was Cotton's partner."

"So we're still stuck on Dinwiddie, are we?"

"I can't get past the timing. He's lived in town for years but only recently decided to cozy up to Garrett's aunt." Aunt Hetty insisted it was the miracle of the moving cross, but then she had no way of knowing that the Holy Spirit got a little help from Toby.

"You're forgetting one important aspect of this case. The witness described the man as being at least six feet tall and having a scar. Dinwiddie barely makes it to five foot five, and the only thing he wears on his face are his sixty-something years."

"Well, he's guilty of something," she said stubbornly. Strange as it might seem, she had grown fond of Aunt Hetty and didn't want to see her get hurt. "I intend to find out what it is."

∞

Linc wasn't home when Maggie stopped at his house to thank him for helping Rikker. Instead, Mrs. Higginbottom opened the door to her knock.

"What are you doing here?" Maggie asked, surprised. "And where's Linc?" He wasn't at his usual corner selling newspapers.

"He's at school."

Maggie couldn't believe her ears. "Really? That's great news, but how?"

His grandmother stepped into the room, and Maggie hardly recognized her. Her hair was combed back into a neat bun and she wore a clean frock. Best of all, her faded blue eyes looked focused and clear.

"I told him that my momma didn't raise no stupid child, and neither would I," Linc's grandmother said.

Maggie couldn't get over the difference in her appearance. "You look wonderful."

Mrs. Higginbottom lowered her voice to a whisper. "The doctor said she was suffering from malnutrition and dehydration. That's why she was acting so crazy." Aloud she addressed her next comments to Linc's grandmother. "I better be going. If you like, I can pick Linc up on Sunday on the way to church. You can come, too, if you like."

The older woman looked pleased, but still she hesitated. "We don't want to be a bother."

"No bother," Mrs. Higginbottom assured her. "I'll be here at nine."

Maggie followed Mrs. Higginbottom outside. "I can't believe the difference in her. She looks and acts like a totally new woman."

"She still has her moments, but don't we all?"

Maggie smiled. "I appreciate your watching over Linc. He's a good boy. He just needs some guidance."

The woman patted her on the arm. "Don't you worry none about Linc. The church's Ladies Auxiliary decided to adopt him. Not officially, of course, but you know what I mean. We'll see that he and his granny are well taken care of." She lowered her voice. "If you ask me, that's what that miracle with the moving cross was all about. Our church had become little more than a social club, and God decided to shake things up."

Maggie smiled. "I guess He did that all right." God had worked through Toby's mischievous ways to change an entire church. Now *that* was a miracle.

"I heard you're leaving," Mrs. Higginbottom said.

"Yes. My job here is done."

"Too bad. Hetty sure did have her mind set on that big wedding. Nothing she'd like better than to see her nephew happily wed."

"Maybe one day she'll get her wish," Maggie said and felt her spirits drop. Some lucky woman was bound to win Garrett's heart. She only wished that woman was her.

Mrs. Higginbottom nodded and started down the walkway. "Maybe so. You just never know what the good Lord has in mind, do you?"

⧫

Aunt Hetty planned a supper party that night to celebrate Garrett's release. Maggie had two reasons for wanting to be there—or at least two that she would admit. One, it would give her an opportunity to observe Dinwiddie up close. Two, it would probably be the last time she would see the children. She wasn't even sure Garrett would allow her to write to them.

Finagling an invitation from Aunt Hetty for her and Rikker was the easy part. Much harder was ignoring the less-than-welcoming look on Garrett's face as he opened the door to their knock.

"Come in, come in," Aunt Hetty said, pushing her nephew out of the way.

She'd gone all out to prepare Garrett's favorite roast beef. The table was set with her best dishes, and a delicious smell wafted from the kitchen.

Elise sat on the floor watching Panhandle draw funny animals. Even in the house he wore his strange cap. "Howdy, Miss Taylor."

"Hello, Panhandle."

Elise looked up and squealed with delight. Jumping to her feet, she ran into Maggie's arms.

"Hello, pumpkin." Aware of Garrett watching, she gave Elise only a quick hug, though she longed to hold the little girl in her arms and tell her how much she was missed.

"My braids are crooked," Elise whispered.

"They're fine," Maggie whispered back, pushing a strand of hair away from her face and retying one of the blue ribbons. "You look so pretty tonight." She wore her favorite floral print dress and black patent shoes.

Toby looked happy to see her, too, but he wasn't about to embarrass himself with a hug. Instead he gave her a quick smile.

"It smells good in here," Maggie said.

Aunt Hetty looked pleased and assured her that cooking the meal had sapped her energy. "Probably took weeks off my life."

Dinwiddie gave her a fond look. "Never has there been a more worthy sacrifice."

Rikker rolled his eyes, and Maggie nudged him with her elbow.

"Dinner's ready," Aunt Hetty said, and everyone streamed into the dining room.

There were eight of them around the table in all. Maggie did her best to ignore Garrett, purposely taking her place between Elise and Dinwiddie, making sure to sit on the side of his good ear. Whether by choice or accident, Garrett sat directly opposite her, which made it hard, if not altogether impossible, to ignore him.

"Garrett, would you be kind enough to give the blessing?" Aunt Hetty said. She looked small, almost demure as she sat at the head of the table, but Maggie didn't doubt for a moment that the woman, with her real and imagined ailments, was very much in charge.

Maggie expected Garrett to turn down the request, but he surprised her by lowering his head and giving thanks to God for the good food and company.

"Amen," he said, and his gaze lit on Maggie for an instant before he reached for the bowl of mashed potatoes.

"So, Mr. Dinwiddie, how long have you worked at the bank?" she asked, keeping her tone casual.

"In July it will be three years," he said.

She spread butter on her roll. The Whistle-Stop bandits obviously knew about the bank shipment, so his answer worked in with her theory.

"Working at the bank is better for the bones but does nothing for my gout," he added, helping himself to a generous serving of gravy.

Toby and Panhandle were discussing outer space. "When is the moon the heaviest?" Toby asked.

"Haven't the foggiest," Panhandle said.

"When it's full," Toby said and laughed.

Maggie laughed, too. Garrett watched her, but his thoughts

remained hidden behind a stoic mask. It wasn't the only time she caught him staring at her. Sometimes he looked away first; sometimes she did, but each visual encounter left her shaken.

He looked especially handsome tonight. The more she had come to know him, the less visible his scar became until she hardly noticed it at all. The only remaining sign of his recent ordeal were the shadows beneath his eyes.

Aunt Hetty was in high spirits, and Maggie tried her best not to put a damper on the party. She smiled at all the right times and even contributed to the light banter.

But her heart ached for Garrett to look at her the way he had the night they'd danced.

At least he looked at her. That's more than he did earlier when she stood with him before the judge waiting for charges against him to be dropped. The easy rapport they once shared had been replaced by the politeness of strangers.

He'd even reverted back to calling her Miss Taylor, though he now knew it was an assumed name. It was as if he didn't want her to forget the lies that stood between them.

The newspaper account declared Toby a hero, and he wore his new status with a wide grin. He even insisted upon being called Detective Toby.

"Mr. Baker is paying me to find out who is absconding with his chickens," he announced with button-bursting pride.

Rikker chuckled. "It looks like my partner and I have some competition."

Her laughter sounded forced even to her own ears, but her feelings for Toby were genuine. He didn't do anything without putting his whole heart and soul into it.

Dinwiddie was the first to bring up the subject that everyone else skirted around. "I still don't understand why Cotton broke you out of jail."

He was looking at Garrett all funny-like, and Maggie exchanged a glance with Rikker. Was it simply curiosity on Dinwiddie's part? Or was he worried about what Cotton might have said?

Garrett stared down at his plate as he cut his meat. "He thought I knew where the rest of the money was." He shrugged. "I had no idea what he was talking about. But I played along. I figured if I didn't, he'd"—he slanted his head toward his young daughter—"well, you know."

"He thought Uncle Charlie would kill him," Toby said in the matter-of-fact way that only an eight-year-old could muster.

Elise looked about to burst into tears. "I don't want anyone to kill Papa."

Maggie squeezed Elise's hand. "It's okay, pumpkin. No one is going to hurt your father. Or anyone else for that matter. Detective Toby will see to that."

Aunt Hetty tapped her drinking glass with a spoon. "Enough of such talk. We need to discuss something more pleasant. Like the wedding."

Garrett looked up from his plate and drew a napkin to his mouth. "There isn't going to be a wedding, Aunt Hetty."

"No wedding?" Aunt Hetty's glance settled on Maggie before returning to her nephew. "But the invitations...the dress...the church..."

"Sorry." Garrett tossed his napkin onto the table and stood. "Miss Taylor and I will not be getting married."

⟋⟍

"That was certainly an ordeal," Rikker grumbled as he and Maggie walked the short distance from Aunt Hetty's house to the hotel.

"What are you talking about?" Maggie asked. "You were having a grand old time."

"I've had a better time sitting in a war zone. I don't know what's worse, watching you and Thomas clash or crossing over enemy lines."

Surprised, she glanced at Rikker. In all the years she'd known him, this was the first time he'd mentioned his wartime experiences. "I don't know what you're talking about. Garrett and I hardly said a word to each other."

"Nevertheless, your message came through loud and clear."

She sighed. "If that's true, then you know he hates me for what I did to him."

"It sure didn't look like that to me. But then, I never was much good at subtleties. At least that's what my first wife used to say."

"Nothing subtle about it," she said miserably.

He stopped her with a hand to her arm. "I don't like seeing you suffer like this, Duffy."

She patted his hand. "I'll be okay."

They started walking again. The orange gas streetlights blurred, and Maggie blinked away the moisture in her eyes. She had no intention of giving in to tears. Nope, wasn't going to happen. After sobbing her heart out at the foot of her father's swinging body, she'd vowed never again to cry over a man. That promise had served her well over the years with only a few lapses, and she saw no reason to change at this late date.

"Maybe you should talk to him," Rikker said.

"I did talk to him, but we didn't get much past his gout," she said.

"Thomas has gout?"

"I'm talking about Dinwiddie."

He gave her an arched look. "Still suspicious of him, are we?"

"He was employed by the bank at the time of the robbery and was an engineer. I can't think of a better suspect."

Rikker laughed out loud. "Ah! Now that's more like the woman I know and admire."

They crossed Main. "You admire me?"

He cupped her elbow as they walked up the steps to the boardwalk. "Yes, but don't tell anyone. It would ruin my reputation." He released her and pulled the hotel door open. "Let's have some hotel pie."

"You just ate."

He shrugged. "I've got to do something while you try to persuade me not to leave town on tomorrow's train."

∞

For once her persuasion skills failed. Rikker was leaving on the morning train, and there wasn't a thing Maggie could do about it. She didn't want to see him go. As she sat in her hotel room later that night, loneliness closed in on her like a shroud.

Rikker was being dispatched to New Orleans, but she had yet to get her next assignment. That's because she had not turned in her final report. She was usually much more efficient, but something held her back. Questions plagued her. Unfinished business kept her twisting and turning at night. One of the Whistle-Stop bandits was still on the loose, and she didn't feel right about leaving town until he was caught.

Was it Dinwiddie? She hated to think that it was, for Aunt Hetty's sake. But who else worked at the bank and knew how to drive a train?

She went over her notes again, searching for that one thing she might have disregarded or thought insignificant. Even the best of detectives missed vital clues on occasion.

She once overlooked a woman's dress hanging in a suspect's closet. That was important because they later learned that after each crime the man had made his escape dressed as a woman. Another time she failed to take note of a spiderweb outside a jeweler's window. Had she done so, she would have known immediately that the theft was an inside job and saved herself weeks of work.

Now she studied her notes line by line. Each time she read through the pages, the word *boogeyman* stopped her. It was a word she never expected to show up in any of her reports.

Was the boogeyman real? Toby and Elise certainly thought so. If they were right, that could explain the overturned soil. She never did believe that Whitewash was responsible for all those holes.

Strangers didn't usually dig uninvited on someone else's property unless burying a body or looking for buried treasure. That would eliminate Cotton as the boogeyman. With all that digging, he would have known the money wasn't there.

She stared at her notes again. Elise described the boogeyman as being tall with big feet and wearing his hair like Aunt Hetty's. Maggie dipped her pen into the inkwell and underlined the hair part.

Finding nothing of any help in her notes, her thoughts soon turned to Garrett.

Dear God, how he must hate her for what she had put him through. The lies and deceit were the least of it. She could still remember the disbelief on his face the day he was arrested. The look of despair at being locked behind bars. . . What terrible memories that must have brought back.

She longed to make it up to him, but how? The emotional distance between them was ocean-wide and sky-high.

Shaking the thought away, she checked her notes again and after a while gave up. Investigations needed a clear head, and hers was too full of painful memories to do her any good.

She gripped the pen tighter and pulled out a piece of paper. Sometimes it helped to write things down, especially her prayers. Her daily reports to heaven were just as precise as her reports to the Pinkerton principal.

Halfway down the page, she blinked. She'd meant to start her report with the familiar words *Dear God*. Instead her pen seemed to have a mind of its own and the salutation read *Dear Garrett* instead.

Chapter 42

Garrett opened the door to Maggie's knock and seemed surprised to see her. Never had she seen him look so tired and disheveled. His hair was mussed and he hadn't shaved.

"Mag. . . ?" He caught himself with a grimace and rubbed his whiskered chin. "Miss Taylor."

"My name is Cartwright," she said. "Maggie Cartwright." It might not be possible to close the chasm between them, but at least they could do away with any pretense. "May I come in?"

He hesitated a moment before stepping aside. He didn't invite her to sit, but she did anyway. She clutched the letters she spent the night writing. The house seemed uncommonly quiet and oh-so familiar. As much as she hated to think it, it felt like home.

"Where are the children?" she asked.

He closed the door. "At Aunt Hetty's."

The thought of never seeing them again brought a lump to her throat. But she couldn't think about that. Not now.

"Is this official business?" he asked.

"Partly." She moistened her lips before continuing. "We still haven't identified Cotton's partner."

His forehead creased. "Any suspects?"

She hesitated. "Maybe."

He arched an eyebrow. "Anyone I know?"

It was hard to think under his intense scrutiny, and she took a moment to gather her thoughts. He wasn't going to like this, but then neither did she. "How well do you know Dinwiddie?"

He looked at her, incredulous. "Don't tell me that you think he—?"

"He doesn't fit the witness description," she hastened to explain. "But there are some things that make him a suspect."

"Like what?" he asked.

She quickly explained.

He shook his head. "You're wrong about Dinwiddie."

"I hope you're right. For your aunt's sake."

"Is that why you came here today?" he asked, his voice cold and distant. "To make more false accusations?"

"I came here because..." Her voice dropped in volume. "I'm leaving town." That morning she had received a telegram with her next assignment. She would be working with Rikker in New Orleans. The news made her partner postpone his journey for a day so they could travel together and work out their new disguises.

She studied him, but the reaction she'd hoped for failed to materialize. He accepted her announcement with the same cold stare.

She wanted to go to him, to throw her arms around him and beg for forgiveness, but something—pride perhaps, maybe even shame—held her in place.

"I understand your anger."

He arched a brow. "Do you?"

"I never wanted to lie to you."

He shook his head. "It wasn't just the lies. You wormed your way into my home. Into my children's affections..."

She waited for him to say that she'd found her way into his affections as well, but the words she longed to hear never came. "It was my job—"

"That's your answer for everything!" He rubbed his forehead and started again, this time in a quieter voice. "No job can justify what you did."

"When I accepted the assignment, I honestly thought you were guilty of the things they said. Had I known the kind of man you were, I never would have—" She broke off and struggled for composure. "Tell me how to make this right."

"No one can make this right." He swept his hand over the chessboard, scattering pieces everywhere like shards of her heart. "No one!"

He sat back but continued staring at the chessboard. Was he remembering the night they played together? The night they danced?

"I fell in love with a woman who doesn't exist."

Love. He said love. For a moment she couldn't move. All she could do was hold on to the word like a gift too precious to unwrap. When at last she was able to rise to her feet, she moved toward him but fell short of touching him. Tears sprang to her eyes. For someone who didn't exist, the wrenching pain sure did feel real.

"I—I'm so sorry," she whispered.

Since there was nothing more to say, she tossed the stack of letters on the floor at his feet.

He stared down at them. "What are those?"

"The letters I would have written had I known the kind of man you are. Read them or not." Holding herself with as much dignity as she could manage, she added, "As you choose."

Turning to the door she stepped on one of the chessmen—a bishop. How easily the name came to her. It was as if her mind scrambled for some level of sanity by zeroing in on meaningless details.

She stooped to pick the piece up and was bombarded with thoughts of the past.

"Did you know that chess was once a game of courtship?"

"I want to get to know you one square at a time."

Shaking away the memory, she set the bishop upright on the chessboard. It was then that Elise's and Toby's words echoed in her head. *"The boogeyman looks like a giant and has big feet. And he wears his hair like Aunt Hetty."*

She picked the bishop off the board. When held a certain way, the bishop's headgear did, indeed, resemble Aunt Hetty's hair.

She gasped for air as a dozen little pieces fell into place, and they all added up to one thing: boogeyman.

Aunt Hetty didn't wait to be invited in. No sooner had Garrett opened the door than she stabbed the doorsill with her cane and barreled past him.

He stared after her. "The children—"

"I just dropped them off at school." Leaning on her cane, his aunt faced him. Her whole body fairly shook with rage. "They're fine. No thanks to their father."

He grimaced. Nothing was worse than seeing Aunt Hetty on the warpath. "What's that supposed to mean?"

"First you call off the wedding—"

"For good reason."

"And then you mope around. Panhandle said you haven't been to work for days."

He slammed the door shut and faced his aunt. "She lied to me."

"For heaven sakes. Do you hear yourself? The girl had a job to do. She also proved you innocent. You should be thanking her."

"Thanking her for what? For accusing me of thievery? Worse? For having me put in jail and standing trial?" *For making me feel things I never hoped to feel again?*

"You can hardly blame her. Most people finding stolen money on your property would have jumped to the same conclusion. Lord knows, if I didn't raise you myself. . ."

He drew back in surprise. "Are you saying that even you—?"

She shrugged but offered no apologies.

He raked his hair with his fingers. It never occurred to him that even his own aunt might have had doubts about his innocence. Given the evidence, he supposed he could hardly blame her. Still. . .

"Why are you taking her side?"

"If you weren't so mule headed, you'd see that it's your side I'm on. It just so happens to be on the same side as hers."

He curled his hands at his side. "I know you're trying to help, but. . ."

Suddenly his aunt's determined demeanor seemed to desert her, and her shoulders slumped. "I hate seeing you make a mistake you'll regret."

"I won't—"

"You already have, and once you make up your mind, there's no changing it."

"I change my mind." Just because he couldn't think of a specific incident to prove his contention meant nothing. "Sometimes."

"Once every fifteen years!"

"That's not true!"

"Isn't it?" She eyed him sharply. "You refused to go to church because of what happened during the war. And you wouldn't listen to no one. You wouldn't even attend your own children's baptisms."

"All right," he conceded. "I made a mistake about the church." God forgive him. "But that doesn't mean I'm wrong about Mag"—he cleared his throat—"about this."

"How would you know if you're right or wrong? You made up your mind without having all the facts."

"I don't need any more facts. Miss Taylor—"

"Her name is Cartwright, and I'll wager the one and only healthy bone in my body that it's the real Maggie you love, not the detective."

He stared at her, dumbfounded. Now she was reading his mind. "I never said I loved her." Okay, maybe he'd mentioned as much to Maggie, but certainly not to his aunt.

She narrowed her eyes. "I may have one foot in the grave, but I'm not dumb. And I'm not blind, either." She started for the door. "And neither are you. So quit acting like you are, and go and make this right before you lose her for good."

❧

Maggie arrived at the train station to find Rikker waiting for her. She was late, and he didn't look happy about it. "Where's your baggage?"

She didn't need any baggage. "I know the name of Cotton's

partner." She'd done some checking around this morning and was certain she was right.

Rikker dropped his valise on the platform with a thud. "See that train? If this is just another one of your theories, I'll be on it in exactly sixty seconds. With or without you." He pulled out his pocket watch.

She didn't need sixty seconds. "One, the witness described the suspect as having a scar."

"Forty seconds."

"Two, when our suspect learned that one of the stolen bills had suddenly shown up, he sent away for Cotton."

"Proof. I need proof."

"I was wrong about the suspect working at the bank. But the suspect knows someone who does."

Rikker's eyebrow quirked upward. "Twenty-nine seconds."

"He's the one who's been digging up Garrett's property. The one the children call boogeyman." She even suspected someone had entered Garrett's house in her absence. Like the day she found chess pieces scattered on the floor and blamed Lila.

"Fifteen seconds."

"Aren't you curious as to who it is?"

"Not till you give me something tangible that the sheriff can hang a warrant on."

Ignoring him, she continued, "It's Panhandle."

He lowered his watch and stared at her. "There's no scar on Panhandle's face."

"What if there was no scar? What if our witness only *thought* he saw a scar."

Rikker didn't appear totally convinced, but neither did he look all that skeptical.

Her hopes lifted until the moment the conductor called, "All aboard," and Rikker picked up his valise.

Chapter 43

Aunt Hetty's visit had put Garrett in an even worse mood. Yes, he had feelings for Maggie. Blast it all; he still had feelings for her. But was it really love? Or merely infatuation?

Something inside answered *love*, but good sense argued for the latter. He'd only known her for a few short weeks. That was hardly enough time to get to know a person, let alone fall in love.

And yet...

He stared at the letters still on the floor where she'd dropped them yesterday. He didn't want to read them. Why would he? After all the lies and deceit...

As far as he was concerned, Maggie was dead to him. Yes, it hurt. It hurt a lot and probably would for a long time. But he'd get over it. Just like he'd gotten over all the other hurts in his life.

He shook his head. Okay, maybe not. The trouble with playing chess is that it sharpened the mind and improved the memory. Thanks to the hours spent at the chessboard, forgetting Maggie would be a monumental chore.

At the moment he was having a hard time forgetting even the little things—like the way the sun brought out the golden highlights of her hair. Or the way her laughter sounded like music.

Forcing the memories away, he gathered up the letters and carried them into the kitchen, intent on throwing them away. The envelopes released a delicate fragrance—her fragrance. It was probably the only thing about her that was real. With the scent came even more memories.

Dancing with her; holding her. The days and nights she sat with him by Elise's sickbed. The gentle way she led him back to God through hope and prayer.

He could almost feel her in his arms as he recalled holding her close. His lips burned with the memory of her sweet kisses.

With a sigh of defeat he tossed the stack of letters onto the kitchen table. He stared at them long and hard before finally pulling out a chair and sitting. He picked up the first envelope and broke the seal. He hesitated before finally pulling out the delicately scented letter inside and unfolding it.

The graceful curved script was all too familiar to him. Out of all the letters he'd received from the ad placed in the mail-order-bride catalog, hers stood out because of the handwriting. Given the nature of her job, it was surprisingly feminine. The letters were rounded, open. Honest.

The last thought almost made him drop the letter, but he didn't. Instead his eyes followed the words across the page as if his eyes had a mind of their own.

Dear Garrett, she wrote.

> *Rikker taught me that when things go haywire and nothing makes sense, it's always best to go back to the beginning and start over. I was born in Georgia, and my father's name was Royce David Cartwright. He's the reason I chose to become a detective.*

She wrote about her father's horrific crime spree, his death, and her determination to make up to society for all the damage he'd done. She wrote about her years in the orphanage and her mother's abandonment. She admitted lying about her family's farm and included the check he'd written with the letter.

The paragraph that contained her misgivings about his guilt and the pain at finding the money stashed in the tree house was so smeared it was hard to read.

Tears had fallen as she'd written those words, just as his own eyes began to mist as he read them.

∝∾

It appeared to be a normal day at the train station. A dozen people, mostly peddlers, were lined up in front of the ticket booth. A black porter whistled to himself as he piled baggage onto a cart. The idling train hissed and snorted like a bull anxious to leave its pen.

Maggie sat on a bench dressed in her traveling suit, her trunk at her foot. On the outside she looked like an average passenger waiting to board the train; inside she was a quivering mass of nerves.

Was it only four weeks ago that she met Garrett at this very station? So much had happened since. Attempting to push the memories away, she clenched her hands tight and tried to focus on the milling crowd around her. It was no use. A vision of Garrett's blue eyes and devastating smile—even the sound of his voice—were now part of her, and nothing she did relieved the pain.

Her chest tightened, and the suffocating sensation in her throat threatened to cut off her breathing. Can't think of that now. Can't think of Garrett. If they had any hope of trapping Panhandle, she had to be sharp and on top of her game. Success depended on it.

After they nabbed Panhandle, she would take the first train out of town. But there would be no leaving, not completely, for part of her would always remain here in Furnace Creek with Garrett and his two adorable children.

An old woman shuffled over to the bench, back bent, and flopped down next to her. She wore a bright floral print dress and a floppy bonnet.

"Ready?" she asked in a high-pitched tone.

"I'm sorry—" Maggie glanced at her and blinked. "Rikker?"

"Shh." She—he—grinned. "What do you think?" This time he spoke in his normal voice.

She looked him up and down and laughed. "You said your days of dressing as a woman were over."

"Yeah, well, anyone tries to get too friendly with me this time will end up full of lead."

"Trust me. You have nothing to worry about. For one thing, your. . . eh. . .bosoms are uneven."

"That's part of my charm."

Now that Rikker was here, she felt considerably better. "I still wish we told Garrett what we were doing. He has the right to know that his employee is under suspicion." If Garrett ever again trusted anyone, it would be a miracle.

"The fewer people who know, the better. It's bad enough I had to tell the sheriff."

"How did he take it?" Summerhay's dislike of Pinkerton detectives had only gotten worse after the Cotton affair. He didn't like strangers coming in and cleaning up his town.

"Like a man about to be hung." He chuckled. "Not to worry. He's up for reelection and wants to look good. He'll do anything for votes, even if it means working with us *bullying* Pinks."

She sighed. "Nothing better go wrong."

"You worry too much, Duffy. You deal with Panhandle, and I'll take care of the rest. With a little luck we'll be on our way to New Orleans in no time."

Their new assignment required him to pose as a rich banker with only a few months to live and in need of someone to handle his daughter's finances when he was gone. She, of course, would pose as his daughter. It sounded relatively easy, and after the emotional highs and lows of these past couple of weeks, she needed something simple—something with no complications.

"I hope that means you'll handle the boss." They were supposed to be in New Orleans by now. When the principal found out they were still in Furnace Creek, he'd have a fit. Nothing he hated more than having his operatives take matters into their own hands.

"Not to worry." Rikker sniffled and pulled out a dainty lace handkerchief. "So how do you feel about playing the part of my daughter?"

Changing the subject was his way of quieting her nerves. It irritated her on some level that she never had to return the favor. He was always calm and confident as the nighttime sky.

"I'll live with it," she said. She'd pretended to be his daughter enough that it seemed almost second nature to her. "I just hope nothing goes wrong today." There were too many people at the station for her peace of mind.

"Relax." Rikker blew his nose in an unladylike way and tucked his handkerchief in his handbag. "You might be interested to know that Panhandle's actual name is James Madison Walker. His family's wagon train was attacked by Apaches. He was only eight years old and the lone survivor. No one knows what happened to him after he was found by the cavalry. Or later, after his arrest. Headquarters checked with the railroads, and no one has a record of anyone by his name working for them."

"That doesn't necessarily mean anything. He could have worked under an assumed name," she said.

"We'll know soon enough," Rikker said. "What we do know is that he has good reason to wear that ridiculous cap."

Maggie cringed. "You don't mean he was—" She couldn't even say it. Nothing seemed more barbaric than scalping, and it was hard not to feel sorry for what Panhandle had gone through at such a tender age. Traumatic childhoods seemed to be the norm for many criminals. It was a pattern she was all too familiar with, not only in her work but in her personal life as well.

Her father had witnessed the brutal murder of his own parents when he was six. It didn't excuse what he did, of course, but it did make her wonder if there was a better way to make up for her father's grisly deeds.

What if there was a way to help children at risk like Linc? Help them follow a godly path like that kindly minister had helped her? Garrett had once likened life to the game of chess, and he was right. Both needed a guiding hand.

Rikker nudged her arm and slanted his head toward the horse and wagon that had just driven up to the station. "There he is now."

"It's about time." She could hardly wait to see Panhandle's face when he realized the jig was up. Earlier she'd noticed the sheriff hidden behind a stack of crates. After delivering the boogeyman to him, her job would be done.

"You better get started, Duffy." As an afterthought, he said, "And good luck." Keeping his head bent, he rose and lumbered toward the ticket booth.

She said a quick prayer before leaving the bench and threading her way through the crowd. No one had been allowed to board the train, and all around her indignant passengers grumbled and complained.

"What's going on?" someone asked.

"The engineer was taken ill," a middle-aged woman answered.

Maggie walked down the platform steps, watching Panhandle from the corner of her eye. It was important not to be caught staring at him.

Rikker had checked to see that Garrett expected the delivery of supplies on today's train. He did. As usual, it was Panhandle's job to pick up any packages that arrived at the station.

She timed herself so that it would look like she had accidently "bumped" into him just before he reached the platform.

"Morning, Miss Taylor," he said. "Heard you were leaving town today."

"I was," she said, feigning a sigh of annoyance.

Right on cue, a woman's scream rose from the knot of passengers waiting to board the train. The sheriff had sounded the alarm as planned, and the platform shook with the pounding of running feet.

Panhandle shaded his eyes against the bright sun. "What's going on? Why is everyone running?"

"I'm afraid there's a problem." She placed her hand on her chest. "The engineer is ill and there's another train heading this way. If they don't clear the tracks—" She shuddered.

He lowered his hand. "Another train, you say? Why don't they just back this train onto the other track?"

"No one else knows how to move it," she said.

He stared at her in disbelief. "That's nonsense. There's always someone else. The brakeman—"

She shook her head. "He's new on the job and says he's not qualified."

"That's...that's just plain dumb." He hesitated. "Maybe I can help."

"Oh, if only you could. That would make you...a hero."

He got all red in the face. "Don't know about that, but if that freight train crashes into this one. . ." He shook his head. "Wish me luck." Without another word he bounded across the street faster than she had ever seen him move and stepped onto the station platform.

"Oh, I do." Maggie held her hands together in a silent prayer. "I do."

By the time Panhandle reached the train, the station was deserted. She watched him board the engine with the ease of a spider climbing a wall. The man knew what he was doing.

Moments later, the train gave a long, low whistle. Smoke spiraled from the stack and steam shot out from the sides. The rods moved and the wheels turned with a clatter. The train slowly slithered backward like a metallic snake and made a gradual turn onto the second track.

Maggie couldn't help but smile. Panhandle knew how to operate a train—no question. Still, that didn't prove he was Cotton's partner, but it was a start.

The crowd gathered on the street across from the station burst into applause. Some people started forward, but the dark-skinned porter held them back.

Panhandle joined her moments later on the still-deserted platform, grinning like a schoolboy.

"Excellent work," Maggie said. "I didn't know you were an experienced engineer."

His grin grew broader and then suddenly died.

"Mr. James Walker," the sheriff called as he advanced toward them, gun drawn. "Put your hands up."

Panhandle's eyes bulged. "What the—"

"We know you're Cotton's partner," Maggie said.

An innocent man would have stood his ground, but Panhandle did exactly what they'd hoped; he panicked.

He took a flying leap off the platform and ran. Shouting for him to stop, the sheriff aimed his gun but didn't fire. Panhandle had disappeared into the crowd.

"Stop that man!" Summerhay shouted.

A collective gasp rose from the crowd, and people quickly backed away. A horse hitched to a wagon whinnied and tried to pull free from its traces.

Only two people remained in the middle of the street: Panhandle and Aunt Hetty. A glint of steel sent a ripple of fear down Maggie's spine.

Panhandle held the muzzle of his gun at Aunt Hetty's neck.

Chapter 44

S tay back," Panhandle yelled. "All of you."

The color drained from Aunt Hetty's face and her lips quivered. "B–be careful of my neck," she pleaded.

"Oh, sorry," Panhandle said. He adjusted his hold, but the gun stayed in place. "Is that better?"

"Yes, thank you."

"Drop your weapon," the sheriff shouted, his gun still aimed.

"Drop yours," Panhandle called back. "Or Aunt Hetty's neck will be the least of her worries."

Aunt Hetty let out a funny sobbing sound, and he apologized again. "Sorry, but it's either you or me."

The sheriff laid his weapon down.

"That's one," Panhandle said, staring at Maggie.

"I'm not armed," Maggie said.

"A detective without a gun, Miss Cartwright? Surely you jest."

Grimacing she slipped her hand into her fake pocket and pulled the derringer from her leg holster. Now that her real identity had been revealed, she was at a disadvantage. She set her gun on the platform.

"You won't get away with this," Summerhay said.

"You're wrong, Sheriff. Thanks to your thoughtfulness, I have an entire train at my disposal." Dragging Aunt Hetty along with him, Panhandle worked his way toward the engine on the second track.

Still dressed as a woman, Rikker emerged from the crowd, hands up, and spoke in a crinkly high-pitched voice. "Leave Aunt Hetty here, and take me instead." He looked and sounded every bit the old woman he purported to be.

"Stay back," Panhandle warned, but Rikker kept advancing.

Rikker persisted. "She could die just like that. Her heart, you know."

While Rikker kept up a litany of Aunt Hetty's known ailments, Maggie inched sideways in an effort to position herself in such a way as to retrieve her gun. Who would have thought that Aunt Hetty's tiresome health issues would one day come in handy?

"If you don't want your hostage to drop dead, you better take me," Rikker continued in his thin, feminine voice.

Panhandle gestured impatiently. "All right, then." He glanced around. "But don't try any funny business."

"Wouldn't think of it," Rikker said. Head bent, he lumbered slowly toward Panhandle, purse swinging from his wrist.

"Hurry up!" Panhandle yelled. "And you!" He glared at Maggie. "Step away from your gun. I said move!"

Maggie did as she was told. She glanced at Summerhay, but he hadn't moved from his spot. A big help he was.

Rikker said something that sounded like, "Hold your horses, big boy."

The moment he reached his destination, Panhandle pushed Aunt Hetty away and pointed a gun at Rikker's temple.

Maggie let out a sigh of relief. At least Aunt Hetty was safe. Now if Rikker could distract Panhandle long enough for her to reach her gun...

No sooner had the thought crossed her mind than she heard something that shook her to the core. "Maggie!"

At the sound of Garrett's voice, she gasped. Oh no! What was he doing here?

The porter tried to hold him back, but Garrett raced past him and jumped onto the platform.

Panhandle aimed his gun at Garrett, and Maggie yelled, "Watch out!"

Rikker tried grabbing his wrist, but Panhandle was too quick for him. He hit Rikker on the side of his head with his revolver, and just that quickly Rikker fell to the ground.

"Hold it, all of you," Panhandle said, his weapon pointed. "Try another trick like that and you'll all be dead."

Maggie, Summerhay, and Garrett stood still as statues.

"You." Panhandle gestured to Maggie with a shake of his head. "You come with me."

She heard Garrett's intake of breath. He looked completely baffled. "I don't know what's going on. Whatever it is I'm asking you not to do this, Panhandle."

"Shut your trap!"

"I thought we were friends—"

Panhandle sneered. "Friends? We were never friends. Cotton was so sure you knew where the money was. That's the only reason I worked for you. I figured eventually you'd get careless and lead me to it. Now you better tell your bride to get over here, or someone's gonna pay."

Garrett raised his hands to show he was unarmed. "Take me instead."

Panhandle shook his head. "We tried that little trick." He gestured with his gun for Maggie to hurry.

She moved forward, senses alert. When a plan went awry it was necessary to improvise. Rikker looked like he was out cold, but a slight movement of his pinkie told her otherwise.

"Make it quick!" Panhandle's voice was thick with impatience.

He was so intent on watching the three of them, he seemingly forgot all about Aunt Hetty. That is, until she lifted her cane and clobbered him soundly on the head.

Just as quickly, Rikker grabbed his leg. Diving forward, Maggie knocked the gun from the dazed man's hand. Before Panhandle could recover, the sheriff had already snapped on the handcuffs.

Maggie rushed to Aunt Hetty's side, reaching her at the same time as Garrett.

"Are you all right?" they asked in unison.

Looking remarkably well following her ordeal, Aunt Hetty nodded. "Except for my neck and hip and. . ."

Maggie smiled. Never had Aunt Hetty's recital of *Gray's Anatomy* sounded more welcome.

"But not to worry. I'll live to see another day." Aunt Hetty leaned on her cane and glared at Panhandle, who was being led away by the sheriff. "No thanks to that awful man." She regarded Rikker. "What you did was very nice. You could have been hurt."

Rikker rubbed his chin. "Not me," he said in his usual rough male voice. Abandoning his old lady walk, he then took off after Summerhay.

Aunt Hetty frowned. "What a strange woman."

"What are you doing here?" Garrett asked.

"I heard Maggie was leaving today, and I came to say good-bye." As she spoke Aunt Hetty afforded her nephew a meaningful look. "Why are *you* here?"

Maggie held her breath and waited for his reply.

"I...uh..." He slid a sideways glance at Maggie and quickly changed the subject. "I'm still confused," he said. "What Panhandle said—"

"I'm afraid it's true," Maggie explained. "He was Cotton's partner and the second Whistle-Stop bandit."

Garrett shook his head in disbelief. "How did you know?"

"Yes, how *did* you know?" Aunt Hetty asked.

"It was the bishop," she said. "The day I came to your house I picked up the chessman, and that's when I knew Panhandle was the boogeyman."

"And you figured this out because of chess?" Aunt Hetty asked, incredulous.

"It sounds crazy, I know, but Toby and Elise described his hair as similar to yours." She pointed to Aunt Hetty's topknot. "I just happened to notice that the bishop's ceremonial hat comes to a point just like Panhandle's cap. The problem was, we had no proof. And we'd already made one mistake." A mistake that could have been disastrous. She moistened her lips and continued.

"One of the thieves backed the train away from the station. Few people know how to operate a locomotive, so Rikker came up with a plan to see if Panhandle could do it."

Garrett rubbed his forehead. "That still doesn't explain why the witness described one of the thieves as having a scar."

"That puzzled me, too." The scar is what made Garrett their prime suspect. "Then I realized what the witness had seen was the rawhide straps from Panhandle's hat. The robbery occurred as the sun was going down. I suspect the leather bands cast shadows on the side of his face that the witness mistook as a scar."

"Well, I'll be," Garrett said, shaking his head. "And to think he's been working with me all this time."

"Like he said, he was keeping an eye on you." It was easier to talk about the case than to give in to the confusing emotions whirling inside. "When those large bills showed up at the school fund-raiser, Panhandle contacted Cotton."

"But how did he know about that?" Garrett asked. "I attended the fund-raiser and even I didn't know."

Maggie glanced at Aunt Hetty. "As you know, Panhandle and your gentleman friend played faro together. What I didn't know until this morning is that Dinwiddie handled the school fund-raiser, and Panhandle helped him count the donations." He must have suspected the hundred-dollar bills came from Garrett and notified Cotton. None of the other parents could afford such a large donation. She shuddered to think what might have happened had the men known the money came from Elise and Toby.

Aunt Hetty's eyes widened in alarm. "You're not saying that Oswald—"

"No," Maggie assured her. "Oswald was visiting his ailing mother in Denver during the robbery."

Aunt Hetty shuddered. "And here I thought all that talk about the boogeyman was only the children's imagination."

Garrett rubbed the back of his neck. "And to think we blamed Whitewash for all the holes."

Rikker joined them, grinning from ear to ear. He was still dressed in his old lady outfit, but his wig was crooked and one bosom had fallen to his waist. "It's over," he announced. "Panhandle confessed to everything."

Maggie grinned back at him. Neither one of them had been happy at the prospect of leaving town with so many unanswered questions.

Aunt Hetty stared at him. "Is that you, Mr. Greenwood?"

Rikker pulled off his gray wig. "It's me, all right."

"I should have known," Aunt Hetty said and laughed. She suddenly looked tired, and Garrett slipped his arm around her waist.

"Come on, I'll take you home."

This time she didn't push him away. Instead, she leaned on him, and relief crossed her face.

"When are you leaving town, Maggie?"

"Not till tomorrow," Maggie said. Sensing Garrett's gaze, her voice deserted her along with her smile. "I just have to tie up some loose ends." She would have to write a full report to headquarters and convince her boss that the end justified both the means and added expense.

Aunt Hetty reached out to squeeze her hand. "Stop by and say good-bye to the children."

Maggie glanced at Garrett, but the eyes boring into hers let nothing in and even less out. "I—I don't know that I'll have time," she stammered. She was always happy to leave town once a job was complete. But not this time; this time she didn't want to go.

"Let's get you home," Garrett said to his aunt.

Aunt Hetty stubbornly held her ground. "What did you want with Maggie?"

Garrett frowned. "What?"

"You came running up here like the cavalry calling her name. It must have been important."

"I . . ." He hesitated. "Just wanted to say good-bye."

Maggie started to say something, but already he had turned away.

"We did it, Duffy," Rikker said cheerfully, slapping her on the back.

She watched Garrett escort his aunt to his wagon through a veil of tears. "Yes, we did."

Chapter 45

Where was he? Maggie paced the station platform with increasing impatience. Rikker should have been here by now.

Earlier, as they'd left the hotel together, he said he had something to do and would catch up with her at the station. It wasn't like him to be that mysterious, but she was too wrapped up in her misery to give the matter much thought until now. What was so important?

Whatever it was, he better hurry. The train was due to arrive in less than ten minutes.

She shaded her eyes against the sun and stared down the tracks. Sun glinted off the rails and the air shimmered with heat, but so far no sign of the train. Maybe it would be late.

People milled around her with an air of expectancy. Mindless chatter filled the air. A baby cried.

Then all at once she saw something that stopped her in her tracks. Crankshaw, the pickpocket, was at it again. As usual he made no effort to hide his dastardly deeds. If she didn't know better, she would think he was purposely trying to get her attention.

She tried to ignore him, but when he stole a doll from a young child, her mouth dropped open. What was the matter with the man? The little girl screamed, and her mother tried calming her to no avail.

"I'll get her doll back," Maggie shouted and took off running.

Gawking over his shoulder Crankshaw jumped off the platform and ran along the tracks, dragging his foot. Maggie chased after him and quickly gained ground. This time she was careful not to trip on the rails.

"Come back, you scoundrel—"

Suddenly, Crankshaw did something totally unexpected. Tossing the doll on the ground, he mounted a handy horse and galloped away.

Maggie stopped running and stared after him. Maybe she was seeing things, but that sure did look like Garrett's horse. It wasn't bad enough that she imagined seeing Garrett in the moon and the stars and everywhere else. Now she even imagined seeing his horse.

She picked up the doll and shook off the dust. She turned and walked back to the station. Something caught her eye. Someone was sitting in the shade of the water tank.

"Garrett?" she whispered. Either her eyes were playing tricks on her again or she was losing her mind. But it sure did look like Garrett sitting in front of a chessboard.

∞

Garrett watched her advance as he arranged the chess pieces on the board, and something stirred inside.

A jaunty feathered hat sat on her head, and she was dressed in the same blue suit she wore the first day he'd set eyes on her. She looked every bit as beautiful today as she had back then. Every bit as intriguing as she'd looked the night they danced. Maybe even more so, now that he'd read the letters—not the mail-order-bride letters but the real ones sprinkled with tears and what had seemed like pieces of her heart.

The letters convinced him that Aunt Hetty was right. It wasn't Maggie the detective he'd fallen for. It was Maggie the woman.

Years of playing chess had taught him that the start of a game makes all the difference in how it ends. The same was often true of life. Thanks to Rikker for hiring the pickpocket, his plan was to go back to the beginning. Go back to when they first met. This time he hoped for a better ending.

He waited until her shadow fell across the chessboard before standing.

"You must be Miss Cartwright." Her true name came easy to him. It was as if part of him always knew the real woman behind the disguise.

The look of disbelief gradually faded from her face. "Yes," she whispered.

"What are you doing here on the railroad tracks?" he asked.

Regarding him with misty eyes, she hesitated for a moment then visibly relaxed. "I was hoping to...convince a thief to return a little girl's doll."

He smiled. She caught on fast. He took his seat again and stood the last of the chessmen on the board. "And how, exactly, did you intend to do that?" He raised an eyebrow. "Convince him, I mean?"

"With a strategically pointed gun."

"You might try a little charm and goodwill," he said.

"Do you think such a thing would work?" she asked. "After...everything that's happened?" They were no longer talking about dolls and pickpockets, and the air between them sizzled with meaningful glances and unspoken words.

"There's only one way to find out." He waved his hand over the chessboard. Wars had been raged and won over a chessboard. But today, much more than kings were at stake.

He gestured toward the empty chair. "Sit." Before this day was over, he intended to know everything there was to know about Miss Maggie Cartwright, one square at a time.

Much to his disappointment, she hesitated. "I should return the little girl's doll."

"Not to worry," he said. "The little girl will soon be clutching a brand-new one."

She smiled, and this time she sat without further ado. "Did Rikker put you up to this?" she asked, holding the doll on her lap.

"No, but he helped me put my plan together."

The corners of her mouth tugged upward. "Why chess?"

"I can think better with a chessboard in front of me. The game brings out my best," he replied.

"That's good because I'm going to need your patience. I'm afraid I've forgotten all the moves."

"Ah. Then you'll be happy about my new rule."

She arched a delicately shaped eyebrow. "Which is?"

"The loser has to grant the winner one wish," he said.

She leveled her clear, observant eyes at him. "Since I'm only a beginner that puts me at a disadvantage."

"Not if we share the same wish."

She studied him. "My wish is that you forgive me."

That wasn't the wish he had in mind, but it would do. For now. "Black or white?"

Chapter 46

Maggie stood perfectly still while Aunt Hetty pinned the garland of flowers on her head and fussed with the veil. Staring at herself in the mirror, Maggie couldn't stop smiling.

So much had happened this past week it was hard to believe any of it real. Incredible as it seemed, she was about to become Mrs. Garrett Thomas. *Please, God, if I'm dreaming, please don't wake me.*

She would miss Rikker, of course, but her work here was cut out for her. Not only did she intend to be the best wife and mother possible, she planned to open a home for orphans and other at-risk children. Reverend Holly and the church agreed to help, and already a "multitude of counselors" as mentioned in the Bible, had volunteered.

She would no longer be chasing down bad guys. That was Rikker's department. Hers was to try and nip potential criminals in the bud. She could never make up for all the pain her father had caused, but maybe, just maybe, she could put a stop to future hurts.

She still didn't forgive him, but she now had a better understanding of how his early trauma had affected him. That, at least, was a start.

Stepping back, Aunt Hetty clasped her hands and sighed. "You look beautiful."

Maggie smiled at her. Aunt Hetty had been so busy with last-minute preparations she'd quite forgotten to complain about her aches and pains.

"Thank you for everything," Maggie said. Aunt Hetty had fussed over her like her own mother never had. For the first time in her life

Maggie felt like she belonged to a real family.

Just then Elise and Toby ran into the room.

Elise looked adorable in her pink ruffled dress. Her hat was decorated with silk rosebuds, and her hair cascaded down her back in long shiny curls.

"You look so pretty," Maggie said, bringing a smile to the child's sweet face. "And you, young man, look mighty handsome and so grown up." Toby's lopsided grin was identical to his father's, and Maggie felt a tug inside.

Aunt Hetty lifted Toby's thinking cap off his head and tackled his cowlick. She then tucked in his shirt and straightened his bow tie—for perhaps the hundredth time that day.

A knock sounded, and Aunt Hetty opened the door an inch. Seeing Rikker, she flung it open the rest of the way.

He strolled into the room and stopped short upon seeing Maggie. "You clean up real nice, Duffy," he said. Despite his casual remark, a suspicious gleam shone in his eyes.

"You're not so bad yourself," Maggie said. He had borrowed a dark formal suit from Mr. Dinwiddie and even got his hair trimmed for the occasion. But it wasn't just his clothes and hair that looked different. He seemed more relaxed, with none of his impatient frowns and constant checking of his watch.

"I'll go see if they're ready for us," Aunt Hetty said. She set her hairbrush down and left the room.

"Did Allan give you a bad time about giving up the New Orlean's job?" Maggie asked.

"No. It was the other way around."

"How do you mean?"

"I told him that I quit."

She stared at him. "What?"

"Allan wasn't happy about losing his two best detectives, but there wasn't anything he could do about it." He grinned. "Meet the new tinker apprentice."

"You? You're working for Garrett?"

He shrugged. "You didn't think I was going to let my adopted *daughter* stay in Furnace Creek without me, did you?"

With a whoop of joy, she flung her arms around his neck.

The door flew open and Aunt Hetty reappeared. Sensing her distress, Maggie pulled out of Rikker's arms.

"What's wrong?" she asked. Did Garrett have a change of heart?

"I don't understand," Aunt Hetty said, wringing her hands. "None of the guests have arrived."

"None?"

"Just Linc and his grandmother." Garrett had asked Linc to be an usher. "It makes no sense. The invitations—"

A horrifying realization struck Maggie, and her hand flew to her mouth. "Oh no! In all the excitement I forgot to mail the invitations." Far as she knew, they were still in the back of the wagon where she'd tossed them.

Aunt Hetty looked aghast. "Oh my! And we have all this cake and—"

"I'll be happy to eat the cake," Rikker said.

"This is no time to joke," Maggie said. She felt awful. Aunt Hetty had gone to so much work. She looked at Rikker, hoping he'd come up with one of his brilliant plans but then suddenly thought of an idea of her own.

She turned to Toby. "Go and fetch Linc," she said. "Tell him we need his help. And hurry!"

⁂

Less than forty minutes later, Aunt Hetty peered through the door. "Our guests have arrived," she said, smiling.

Maggie smiled, too. Linc had raced up and down the street yelling in his loudest newspaper voice for everyone to get to the church posthaste. Amazingly enough, her plan worked.

People dropped whatever they were doing and ran down the street to the church, some dragging young children by the hand. Half-shaven men deserted barber chairs and ran to join the throng. Housewives set their brooms aside and bank tellers left their cages. Farmers abandoned wagons and clerks closed up shop.

All thought another miracle was about to take place—and they were right.

God had worked through a maze of seemingly unrelated events to bring Garrett and Maggie together. That didn't compare to the swinging cross, but it was still a miracle.

Organ music rose from the sanctuary, and Rikker crooked his elbow. "Ready, Duffy?"

She tucked her arm in his and smiled. "Ready, Papa."

He reared back in surprise and then looked pleased. "Well, now."

Epilogue

Reverend Holly closed the Book of Order. "I now pronounce you husband and wife," he said. "You may kiss the bride."

Garrett turned to her, and his eyes brimmed with tenderness. Ever so gently he lifted the veil from her face and took her in his arms. With a whispered *"I love you"* he kissed her, his lips warm and sweet on hers.

"I love you, too," she said between kisses, and her heart swelled with happiness. The truth was she had always loved him, but only now was she able to do it freely and without worry or guilt.

Guests jumped to their feet and applauded. Outside, the bells rang, announcing the happy occasion to the world.

He pulled back with a grin, leaving a delicious tingling sensation on her mouth. "Checkmate," he whispered.

She smiled. This was one time she didn't mind being captured.

Her hand in his, they turned toward their guests.

"Ladies and gentleman," Reverend Holly said, "I present Mr. and Mrs. Garrett Thomas." Hearing her new name said aloud, Maggie's heart leaped with joy.

More applause followed as Garrett and Maggie acknowledge their guests with happy smiles.

Garrett tucked her arm in his, and together they walked down the aisle—their first journey as husband and wife. Maggie felt like she was floating on air.

They'd only made it halfway to the back of the church when Dinwiddie rose from a pew and stopped them.

"Since everyone is already here. I hope you don't mind if I make a couple of announcements," he said.

Maggie glanced at Garrett, but he looked as puzzled as she was.

Without waiting for consent, Dinwiddie continued. "As you're all aware, our new courthouse is almost complete." Applause greeted his announcement, and no one clapped louder than the judge.

Dinwiddie waited for the ovation to die down. "I'm happy to say that pink monstrosity of a courthouse will now be put to better use." He turned to Maggie and handed her an envelope. "I'm a bit embarrassed to admit this, but I'm its legal owner."

She stared at him. "You are?" She always knew Dinwiddie was hiding something. But a former bordello? Even Aunt Hetty looked shocked.

He spread his hand in a shrug. "What can I say? We can't always choose our family members, and I inherited it from my grandfather. It gives me great pleasure to turn the deed over to you as a wedding present."

Maggie fingered the envelope. "I. . .I don't know what to say." Her eyes filled with tears, and Garrett slipped an arm around her waist to steady her.

"What's she going to do with that pink bread box?" someone called out.

Maggie brushed her hand over her damp cheeks. "I know exactly what I'm going to do with it." She glanced at Garrett, and he nodded. "What *we* are going to do with it. We're turning it into a home for troubled youth."

Dinwiddie couldn't have looked more pleased. "That's exactly what I hoped you'd say." He ran a finger across his mustache.

"Of course," Maggie said. She just hoped his next request didn't involve naming the home Dinwiddie. "What is your other announcement?"

"I would like to turn this into a double wedding. I wish to make Hetty my wife."

Garrett glanced at Maggie. "I have no objection."

"Nor do I," Maggie said.

Dinwiddie grinned. "Very well, then. Garrett, if you would do me the favor of being my best man, we'll get started."

"It would be my pleasure."

Dinwiddie held out his hand to help Aunt Hetty to her feet. "Be careful of my back," she moaned.

"Watch my foot," Dinwiddie countered. "My gout's acting up."

"Oh dear, my hip. . ."

Together they hobbled to the front of the church and took their place in front of Reverend Holly.

After exchanging vows and symptoms, Aunt Hetty and Oswald Dinwiddie were joined together in holy wedlock.

As the guests adjourned to the reception hall for cake and lemonade, Garrett held Maggie back with an arm around her waist. "According to the rules of chess, this is called a touch and move law," he whispered in her ear.

She smiled up at him. Never did she think it was possible to be so completely and insanely happy. "Does this mean you're going to move me?"

"Absolutely." And with that he took her by the hand and quickly led her out of the church and into a waiting carriage.

Dear Readers,

You might be interested to know that the Whistle-Stop train robbery was inspired by a robbery that took place at Union City, Tennessee, on October 21, 1871. After the passengers and crew disembarked for a supper break, two men were seen springing aboard the train. When the train began backing up, a porter ran to the station to give the alarm.

The conductor, engineer, and others gave chase on foot, but by the time they reached the train, the safe was empty and the thieves gone. The Pinkerton National Detective Agency was hired, and after many wrong leads, false starts, and some good old-fashioned sleuthing, William Pinkerton finally captured the gang of robbers.

Maggie's way of solving the crime is all her own, though she does use a method or two employed by Pinkerton detectives in those early years.

Crime-solving in the nineteenth century wasn't easy. It's hard to believe, but the Federal Bureau of Investigation didn't get its first forensics crime lab until 1932. It's no wonder that Pinkerton operatives resorted to imaginative tricks (including the mailbox ploy Rikker and Maggie used in the story) to solve crimes. You have to give those early detectives credit. They didn't have fingerprints or DNA back then, but they almost always got their man.

I hope you enjoyed Maggie and Garrett's story. If you haven't read book one in my Undercover Ladies series, *Petticoat Detective* can be ordered from your favorite bookstore or online. Each book stands alone so they can be read out of order.

I love hearing from readers, and you can contact me through my website www.margaret-brownley.com. You can also find me on Facebook, Twitter, and Pinterest.

Until next time,
Margaret

Discussion Questions

1. The Bible states that a multitude of counselors provides safety. Maggie credits a kindly minister and Christian orphanage for helping her stay on a godly path. Name a person or persons in your life who provided you with wise counsel or godly guidance in a time of need.

2. Do you think Maggie's reasons for becoming a Pinkerton detective were valid? Why or why not?

3. Which character, if any, did you most identify with and why?

4. The Furnace Creek church had become lax and failed to reach out to those in need. The congregation got a wake-up call in the form of an unexpected "miracle." In what ways did this impact the town?

5. Why do you think it was so hard for Maggie to forgive her father? Is forgiving a parent more difficult than forgiving others? Why or why not?

6. Her mother's desertion seemed to have less of an impact on Maggie than her father's. Why do you think this was?

7. Chess plays an important role in the story. In what ways does the game of chess resemble real life?

8. Garrett's experiences during the war turned him against the church. Has there ever been a time that you felt alienated from the church, from God, or both?

9. Why do you think Rikker and Maggie's relationship worked so well?

10. In what ways, good and bad, did Garrett's confinement in Andersonville affect him?

11. Name a favorite scene between Maggie and Garrett. How did their relationship change during this scene?

Calico Spy

Coming Soon!

Enjoy this sneak peak. . . .

Chapter 1

Calico, Kansas
1880

Katie Madison tied the black satin ribbon at her neckline and frowned. The lopsided bow wouldn't do. She yanked the ribbon loose and tried again. Today she was all thumbs, and everything that could go wrong did. Already she'd broken a shoelace, snagged a stocking, and tore the hem of her dress.

Just as she finished tying the bow for the third time, the bedroom door flew open, and her roommate's brunette head popped inside. "Katie! Hurry or you'll be late."

"I'm trying, I'm trying."

Mary-Lou's green eyes narrowed, and her southern drawl grew more pronounced. "Pickens is on the rampage. Said if you don't hurry, he'll have your head!"

Katie's stomach knotted. She was already in trouble with the restaurant manager. "I'll be there in a minute."

"A minute might be too late." The door slammed shut, and Mary-Lou's footsteps echoed down the hall as she yelled for the other Harvey girls to hurry.

Katie whirled about for one last look in the mirror and hardly recognized the image staring back. The black dress, with its high collar, starched white apron, and black shoes and stockings, made her look more like a nun than one of Pinkerton's most successful female detectives.

Even her unruly red hair had been forced to conform to Fred Harvey's strict regulations. Parted in the middle, it was pulled back in a knot and fashioned with the mandatory net. The rigid hairdo did nothing for her, appearance-wise. All it did was make her eyes look too big and her freckles stand out like stars in a constellation.

Sighing, she turned away from the mirror. It's a good thing she'd chosen to be a detective as she had neither the looks nor housekeeping skills needed for landing a husband.

Not that she was complaining. Two Harvey girls had been found dead, and it was her job to find the killer. It was the assignment of a lifetime, and it had landed in her lap. Working undercover was never easy, but so far this particular disguise was proving to be the hardest one yet to pull off. It was even harder than last year's job as a circus performer. At least here she didn't have to hobnob with lions, and for that she was grateful.

She paused before leaving the room to check that her leg holster and gun were secured beneath her skirt, and uttered a quick prayer. God knows, she needed all the help she could get.

Leaving the room, she raced along the hall and sped down the stairs. Just as she reached the bottom tread, the heel of her foot caught on the runner. Arms and legs flailing, she hit the floor, and the wind whooshed out of her like juice from a squashed tomato.

Momentarily stunned, she laid facedown. Not till she noticed the black polished shoes planted in front of her was she able to gather her wits. Looking up, she groaned.

The manager, Mr. Pickens, glared down at her, hands on his waist. A large, imposing man, he looked about to pop the buttons on his overworked vest. Judging by his bulbous nose and quivering mustache, his patience was equally tested.

"Miss Madison. You're late!"

Her mouth fell open. Was that all he cared about? No concern for her welfare? No thought that she might be injured?

"Well, are you going to lie there all night?"

"No, sir." She scrambled to her feet and smoothed her apron.

His eyebrows dipped into a V. "Shoulders straight, head back, and for the love of Henry, smile! I want to see some choppers." He spread his thin lips to demonstrate but did a better impersonation of a growling dog than a friendly waitress. "Do you hear me?"

"Yes, sir," she said. "Choppers."

"Tonight you're the drink girl. Do you think you can handle that?"

Plastering a smile on her face, she nodded. How hard could it be to pour tea?

He gave her a dubious look that did nothing for her self-confidence. "We'll soon see. Follow me."

He led her to the formal dining room where tables were already set for the supper crowd. The room was decorated in shades of brown and tan. Floor to ceiling windows overlooked the railroad tracks. Beyond, fields of tall grass and wildflowers spread like a colorful counterpane beneath a copper sky.

The restaurant was shorthanded, and she had been handed a uniform the moment she stepped off the morning train. After that she'd hardly had time to catch her breath. So many rules and regulations to remember. No notepads or pencils were allowed. That meant she was expected to memorize the menu. She was also instructed to radiate good cheer to even the most difficult of patrons.

Her chances of lasting through the night didn't look promising. The investigation into the two Harvey girl murders depended on her keeping her job as a waitress. No one at the restaurant knew her real name or her real purpose for being there. As far as anyone knew, she was simply a farm girl who traveled all the way from Madison, Wisconsin, looking for adventure and a better life.

Pickens quickly pointed out the silver coffee urns and teapots. He stared at her with buttonhole eyes."You do know the cup code, right?"

"Uh."There was a code for cups?

"Cup in the saucer means coffee." He demonstrated as he spoke. "A flipped cup leaning against the saucer is for ice tea. A cup on the table next to the saucer is for milk. Is that clear?"

"Yes, sir, next to the saucer."

"As for tea," he continued, and her heart sank. "The cup will be flipped upon the saucer." He then explained how to tell if the customer wanted black, green, or orange pekoe tea by the direction of the cup handle. "Any questions?"

She had plenty, but he didn't look like he was in any mood to answer them, so she shook her head no.

Satisfied that she had donned the proper attitude, or at least a Harvey-worthy smile, he turned and gave three quick claps and called the others out of the kitchen. "All right, ladies, take your stations!"

"Don't be nervous," her roommate Mary-Lou said as they strode side by side to the back of the room.

Easier said than done. Katie stopped to stare at the cups on the table. She'd come face-to-face with some of cleverest outlaws in the country, and she wasn't about to let a china cup intimidate her. On second thought, maybe just a little. Did the cup handle facing right mean black or pekoe?

Already her cheeks ached from smiling, but that was the least of it. Her collar itched and the stiff starched apron felt like a plate of armor.

As if to guess her rising dismay, Mary-Lou said, "You'll like it once you get used to it. You just have to work fast, be polite, and smile."

"Nothing to it," Katie said. She only hoped she had enough energy left at the end of the workday for sleuthing.

A loud gong announced the imminent arrival of the five-twenty-five. Windows rattled and the crystals on the chandelier did a crazy dance as the Southern Pacific rumbled into the station. With a blare of the whistle it came to a clanging stop in front of the restaurant.

Moments later, the door flew open and travelers filed into the dining room like a trail of weary ants. Only thirty minutes was allowed for meals before the train took off again. The Harvey House restaurants took pride in the fact that no one had ever been late boarding a train because of inept service.

Katie planted a smile on her face and a prayer in her heart. *God, please don't let me be the one to break that record.*

⁂

Sheriff Branch Whitman looked up just as the door to his office flew open. A cultured but no less commanding voice shot inside. "Sheriff! I need a word with you!"

Branch lifted his feet off the desk and planted his well-worn boots squarely on the floor. He recognized his fastidiously dressed visitor at once, though they'd never been formerly introduced.

"What can I do for you, Mr. Harvey?"

The renowned restaurateur stabbed the floor with his gold-tipped cane. He was somewhere in his midthirties, but his meticulous dark suit and Van Dyke beard made him appear older.

"You dare to ask a question like that!" Harvey pushed the door shut and gazed at Branch with sharp, watchful eyes. "You know as well as I that someone is killing off the Harvey girls." His British accent grew more pronounced with each word. Even his bow tie seemed to quiver with emotion. "And what may I ask are you doing about it?"

Branch slanted his head toward the chair in front of his desk. "Have a seat and—"

"I don't want a seat. I want to know what has been done to find the killer!"

Branch indicated the stack of files in front of him with a wave of his hand. "I can assure you that I'm doing everything in my power—"

"Balderdash!"

Harvey's impatience was no worse than his own. The killings had turned into one of the most puzzling crimes he'd ever worked on. Despite weeks of investigation, he still didn't have a single suspect. Given the nature of the town, that was odd.

If a youth took a fancy to a pretty girl or a married man so much as thought about straying, the locals knew about it. Somehow folks even knew that a young one was on the way before the expectant mother. Yet, two young women had been murdered, and no one saw or heard a thing.

"I can assure you that the person or persons responsible will be brought to justice." Before Branch took over as sheriff three years ago, Calico was, by all accounts, the roughest, toughest, and wildest place in all of Kansas, rivaled only by Dodge City. But he'd single-handedly changed all that, and it was now a right decent town. Or was, before the two recent murders.

Harvey's eyes glittered. "It's been six weeks since Priscilla's death." Priscilla was the first woman to die. Less than three weeks later, a girl named Ginger was found dead in an alleyway.

"These things take time."

Harvey straightened a wanted poster on the wall with the tip of his cane. The man was as fastidious with his surroundings as he was in dress and speech. No doubt he took issue with the stack of folders and papers strewn haphazardly across Branch's desk.

"Too much time if you ask me. So what have you got so far?"

"Right now, nothing." Branch's jaw clenched. He suspected the killer was a Harvey employee, but he wasn't ready to reveal that information. Not yet. He couldn't take the chance of word getting out that the crime was an inside job.

"This is no less than what I expected from local authorities." Harvey leaned on his cane and his eyes glittered. "That's why I hired the National Pinkerton Detective Agency. Your services will no longer be needed."

Branch glared at him. Services? Harvey acted like he was firing one of his employees.

"What happens in this town is my responsibility, and any outsiders—"

"Will report to me!" Harvey snapped his mouth shut and leaned over his cane as if to challenge Branch to disagree.

"Now wait just a minute."

Harvey's expression darkened. "No, you wait. We've wasted enough time, and now a second girl is dead."

"And I will find her killer. Both their killers." He didn't know Priscilla all that well, but Ginger was his favorite waitress and had been known to bring his evening meal to the office if she knew he was working late. Since he refused to adhere to Harvey's unreasonable regulations—particularly the *no coat* rule in the main dining room—she did him no small favor.

"I'll have something to report to you soon." He sounded more certain than he felt. Each day that passed made finding the killer that much more difficult. Trails grew cold. Clues were lost. Memories faded. Even more worrisome was the possibility that the killer would strike again.

"Not soon enough." Harvey swung his cane under one arm and pulled his watch out of his vest pocket. "I'm sure the detective has arrived by now. If not on the morning or noon train, then the five-twenty-five," he said, flipping the case open with his thumb. "I trust you'll give him your full cooperation."

Branch stiffened. Over his dead body. "Now see here—" The last thing he needed was some inept detective running loose in his town. Last time the Pinkerton operatives were involved in one of his cases they let the bad guys escape. The Pinkertons were known for their bullying tactics and underhanded methods, none of which he would tolerate.

Harvey tipped his bowler. "Have a good day, Sheriff." He left with less fanfare than when he arrived.

Branch pounded his fist on the desk. "Drat!" The town was his responsibility—no one else's. The very thought of an undercover detective sneaking around like a mole in the ground set his teeth on edge.

Came in on today's train, did he? If the *Pink* was like most other passengers, he'd appreciate a good a meal. Was probably at the Harvey House Restaurant chowing down at that very moment. That was as good a place as any to intercept him. He pulled out his watch. He'd have to hurry if he wanted to reach the restaurant before the train left the station. Decision made, Branch shot to his feet and plucked his Stetson off the wall.

One thing was certain. The man better enjoy his meal, because if Branch had his way, the detective would be back on that train before he could say cock robin.

Margaret Brownley loves hearing from her readers and can be reached through her website. The author of more than thirty novels, she was a former RITA finalist and INSPY nominee. For more love and laughter in the Old West, check out Margaret's latest books at www.margaret-brownley.com.

Available Now!